P9-DHN-531

ALSO BY MARY BALOGH

THE SURVIVORS' CLUB SERIES

The Proposal

The Arrangement

The Escape

THE HUXTABLE SERIES

First Comes Marriage

Then Comes Seduction

At Last Comes Love

Seducing an Angel

A Secret Affair

THE SIMPLY SERIES

Simply Unforgettable

Simply Love

Simply Magic

Simply Perfect

THE BEDWYN SERIES

Slightly Married

Slightly Wicked

Slightly Scandalous

Slightly Tempted

Slightly Sinful

Slightly Dangerous

BEDWYN PREQUELS

One Night for Love

A Summer to Remember

THE MISTRESS SERIES

More Than a Mistress

No Man's Mistress

The Secret Mistress

THE WEB SERIES

The Gilded Web

Web of Love

The Devil's Web

CLASSICS

The Ideal Wife

The Secret Pearl

A Precious Jewel

A Christmas Promise

Dark Angel/
Lord Carew's Bride

The Famous Heroine/
The Plumed Bonnet

A Christmas Bride/
Christmas Beau

The Temporary Wife/
A Promise of Spring

A Counterfeit Betrothal/
The Notorious Rake

Irresistible

Under the Mistletoe

A SURVIVORS' CLUB NOVEL

Mary Balogh

SIGNET
Published by the Penguin Group
Penguin Group (USA) LLC, 375 Hudson Street,
New York, New York 10014

USA | Canada | UK | Ireland | Australia | New Zealand | India | South Africa | China
penguin.com
A Penguin Random House Company

First published by Signet, an imprint of New American Library,
a division of Penguin Group (USA) LLC

First Printing, November 2014

Copyright © Mary Balogh, 2014
Excerpt from *Beyond the Sunrise* copyright © Mary Balogh, 1992
Excerpt from *Longing* copyright © Mary Balogh, 1994
Penguin supports copyright. Copyright fuels creativity, encourages diverse voices, promotes free speech, and creates a vibrant culture. Thank you for buying an authorized edition of this book and for complying with copyright laws by not reproducing, scanning, or distributing any part of it in any form without permission. You are supporting writers and allowing Penguin to continue to publish books for every reader.

REGISTERED TRADEMARK—MARCA REGISTRADA

ISBN 978-0-451-46966-3

Printed in the United States of America
10 9 8 7 6 5 4 3 2 1

PUBLISHER'S NOTE
This is a work of fiction. Names, characters, places, and incidents either are the product of the author's imagination or are used fictitiously, and any resemblance to actual persons, living or dead, business establishments, events, or locales is entirely coincidental.

If you purchased this book without a cover you should be aware that this book is stolen property. It was reported as "unsold and destroyed" to the publisher and neither the author nor the publisher has received any payment for this "stripped book."

I

At the age of twenty-six, Agnes Keeping had never been in love or ever expected to be—or even wished to be. She rather chose to be in control of her own emotions and her own life, such as it was.

At the age of eighteen she had chosen to marry William Keeping, a neighboring gentleman of sober address and steady habits and modest means, after he had very properly called upon her father to make his offer and had then made *her* a very civil marriage proposal in the presence of her father's second wife. Agnes had been fond of her husband and comfortable with him for almost five years before he died of one of his frequent winter chills. She had mourned him with an empty sort of desolation for longer than the requisite year of wearing her black widow's weeds and still sadly missed him.

She had not been in love with him, however, or he with her. The very idea seemed absurd, suggestive as it was of a wild, unbridled sort of passion.

She smiled at her image in the glass as she tried to imagine poor William in an unbridled passion, romantic or otherwise. But then her eyes focused upon herself, and it occurred to her that she had better admire her splendor now while she had the chance, for once she arrived at the ball, it would be instantly apparent that in reality she did not look very magnificent at all.

She was wearing her green silk evening gown, which she loved despite the fact that it was far from new—indeed, she had had it when William was still alive—and had not been in the height of fashion even when it was. It was high waisted with a moderately low neckline and short puffy sleeves and was embroidered with silver thread about the hem and the edges of the sleeves. It was not shabby despite its age. One did not, after all, wear one's best evening gown very often, unless one moved in far more elevated social circles than Agnes did. She had been living for several months now in a modest cottage in the village of Inglebrook in Gloucestershire with her elder sister, Dora.

Agnes had never attended a ball before. She had been to assemblies, of course, and it could be argued that a ball was the same thing by another name. But really there was a world of difference. Assemblies were held in public halls, usually above an inn. Balls were private entertainments hosted by those rich and socially prominent enough to inhabit a house with a ballroom. Such people and such houses did not abound in the English countryside.

There was one close by, however.

Middlebury Park, a mere mile from Inglebrook, was a stately mansion belonging to Viscount Darleigh, husband of Agnes's new and dear friend, Sophia. The long wing east of the massive central block housed the state apartments, which were dazzlingly magnificent—or so they had appeared to Agnes when Sophia had given her a tour one afternoon not long after they first met. They included a spacious ballroom.

The viscount had succeeded to his title when his uncle and cousin died a sudden and violent death together, and it was only now, four years later, that Middlebury Park had again become the social center of the neighborhood. Lord Darleigh had been blinded at the age of seventeen when he was an artillery officer in the Peninsular Wars, two years before the title and property and fortune became his. He had lived a retired life at Middlebury until he met and married Sophia in London in the late spring of this year, just before Agnes herself moved to the neighborhood. His marriage and perhaps a growing maturity had instilled in the viscount a confidence he had apparently lacked before, and Sophia herself had set about the task of assisting him and at the same time making a new life for herself as mistress of a large home and estate.

Hence the ball.

The two of them were reviving the old tradition of a harvest ball, which had always been held early in October. It was being spoken of in the village, however, as more of a wedding dance and reception than a harvest celebration, for the viscount and his wife had married quietly in London a mere week after they met, and there had been no public celebration of their nuptials. Even their families had not been in attendance. Sophia had promised soon after she arrived at Middlebury that a reception would be held at some time in the foreseeable future, and this ball was it, despite the fact that Sophia was already increasing, a condition that could no longer be quite hidden despite the current fashion for dresses with loosely flowing skirts. Everyone in the neighborhood knew, even though no official announcement had been made.

It was no exclusive honor to have been invited to the ball, for almost everyone else from the village and the surrounding countryside had been invited too. And Dora had quite a close connection with the viscount and his wife, since she gave both of them pianoforte lessons as well as instruction in the violin and harp to Lord Darleigh. Agnes had been Sophia's friend ever since they had discovered a mutual passion for art, Agnes as a watercolorist, Sophia as a very clever caricaturist and illustrator of children's stories.

There were to be other, more illustrious guests at the ball than just the people from the neighborhood, however. Lord Darleigh's sisters and their husbands were coming, as well as Viscount Ponsonby, one of the viscount's friends. Sophia had explained that the two men were part of a group of seven persons who had spent several years together in Cornwall recovering from various war wounds. Most of them had been military officers. They called themselves the Survivors' Club and spent a few weeks of each year in company with one another.

Sophia had family members coming too: her uncle Sir Terrence Fry, a senior government diplomat, and another uncle and aunt—Sir Clarence and Lady March—with their daughter.

It all sounded very imposing and had Agnes looking forward to it with something bordering on excitement. She had never thought of herself as a person who coveted social splendor, just as she did not think of herself as someone who would ever fall in love. But she was eagerly anticipating this ball, perhaps because Sophia herself was, and Agnes had grown very fond of her young friend. She earnestly wanted the ball to be a great success for Sophia's sake.

She looked critically at her hair, which she had dressed herself. She had managed to coax some height out of her curls and had left a few tendrils to wave along her neck and over her ears. The style could hardly be called elaborate, nonetheless. And there was nothing remarkable about the hair itself, a nondescript midbrown color, though it did have a healthy shine to it. There was nothing particularly remarkable about the face beneath the hair either, she thought, smiling ruefully at her image. She was not ugly, it was true. Perhaps she was not even quite plain. But she was no ravishing beauty. And, good heavens, had she ever wanted to be? This going-to-a-ball business was turning her head and making her giddy.

She and Dora arrived early, as most of the outside guests did. Being late was fashionable with the *ton* during the Season in London, Dora had commented when they set out ten minutes earlier than the early start they had planned. Or so she had heard. But in the country people tended to have better manners. So they were early.

Agnes was feeling rather breathless by the time they reached the doors of the ballroom. The state apartments looked somehow different and far more magnificent with banks of flowers and hanging baskets everywhere and candles blazing from every wall sconce.

Sophia was standing just inside the double doors, receiving her guests with Lord Darleigh beside her, and Agnes instantly relaxed and smiled with genuine warmth. Although she did not expect to fall in love herself, she could not deny that such a state existed and that it could be beautiful to behold when it did. Lord and Lady Darleigh positively glowed with a romantic affection for each other, though they never openly demonstrated their feelings in public.

Sophia looked gorgeous in a turquoise gown that perfectly complemented her auburn hair. That hair had been boyishly short when she was first married. She had been growing it ever since. It was still not long, but her maid had done something clever with it to make it look sleek and elegant, and for the first time it struck Agnes that her friend was more than just pretty in an elfin kind of way. She beamed at Dora and Agnes and hugged them both, and Lord Darleigh, blind though he was, seemed to look directly at them with his very blue eyes as he smiled and shook them by the hand.

"Mrs. Keeping, Miss Debbins," he said, "how very kind of you to come to make our evening perfect."

As though his guests were the ones doing *him* a favor. He was looking elegant and handsome in black and white.

It was not difficult to pick out the strangers in the ballroom. One result of living in the country, even when one had been here for only a few months, was that one tended to see the same people wherever one went. And the strangers had brought high fashion with them and quite cast Agnes's best green gown into the shade, as she had fully expected. They outshone everyone else too, except one another.

Mrs. Hunt, the viscount's mother, kindly undertook to take Dora and Agnes about to introduce them, first to Sir Clarence and Lady March and Miss March, all of whom were looking very distinguished indeed, even if the height of Lady March's hair plumes was rather startling. They nodded with stiff condescension—the plumes too—and Agnes followed Dora's lead and curtsied. Then there were Sir Terrence Fry and Mr. Sebastian Maycock, his stepson, both of whom were smartly but not ostentatiously clad. The former bowed politely to them and remarked upon the prettiness of the village. The latter, a tall, handsome, personable-looking young gentleman, flashed his teeth at them and pronounced himself to be delighted. He hoped to engage them in some dancing later in the evening, though he did not make any definite appointment with either of them.

A charmer, Agnes decided, but more enamored of his own charms than other people's. And she really ought not to indulge in such unkind snap judgments when she had almost nothing upon which to base them.

And then Mrs. Hunt presented them to Viscount Ponsonby, whose immaculately formal evening clothes, all black except for the pristine white of his linen and intricately tied neck cloth and the silver of his waistcoat, set every other man present into the shade except perhaps Viscount Darleigh himself. He was tall and well formed, a blond god of a man, though his hair was not the white blond or the yellow blond that never looked quite right on a man, in Agnes's opinion. His features were classically perfect, his eyes decidedly green. There was a certain world-weariness to those eyes, and the suggestion of mockery in the set of his lips. One long-fingered hand held a silver-handled quizzing glass.

Agnes felt annoyingly aware of her own ordinariness. And though he did not raise his glass to his eye when Mrs. Hunt introduced them—he was, she sensed, far too well mannered to do any such thing—she felt nevertheless that she had been thoroughly inspected and dismissed, despite the fact that he bowed to both Dora and herself and asked them how they did and even paid attention to their less than scintillating answers.

He was the sort of man who always made Agnes uncomfortable, though she had not met many such, it was true. For such stunningly handsome and attractive men made her feel dull and plodding as well as very ordinary, and she always ended up despising herself. How did she *want* to appear to such men? As an empty-headed eyelid-flutterer? Or as sophisticated and witty, perhaps? What utter nonsense.

She could not get away from him quickly enough in order to feel like herself again as she spoke with Mr. and Mrs. Latchley and commiserated with the former, who had fallen off the roof of his barn only the week before and broken his leg. He could not sufficiently praise Lord and Lady Darleigh, who had paid him a personal visit and insisted upon sending their own carriage to bring him and his wife to the ball and had even coaxed them into staying the night before being conveyed back home on the morrow.

Agnes looked around with great enjoyment as they talked. The wooden floor had been polished to a high gloss. There were large pots of autumn-hued flowers everywhere. Three large chandeliers, all the candles alight, hung from a ceiling painted with scenes from mythology. They glinted off the gilded frieze above the wood paneling of the walls and reflected in the many long mirrors, which made the already spacious room look many times larger and many times fuller of flowers and guests. The members of the orchestra—yes, there was actually an eight-piece orchestra come all the way from Gloucester—had taken their places on the dais at one end of the room and were tuning their instruments.

Everyone, it seemed, had arrived. Lord Darleigh and Sophia had turned into the room, and Sir Terrence Fry was making his way toward them with the obvious intention of leading his niece out for the first set of country dances. Agnes smiled. It was also amusing to watch the Marches maneuver themselves closer to Viscount Ponsonby. It was very clear that they intended him to partner Miss March for the first set. It was doubly amusing to watch him stroll unhurriedly away from them without even glancing in their direction. He was clearly a gentleman accustomed to avoiding unwelcome advances. Oh, she must share this with Sophia when she next saw her after tonight. Sophia was wickedly good at sketching caricatures.

Agnes was so busy observing the look of chagrin on the faces of all three Marches that she did not notice at first that Viscount Ponsonby was moving in the direction of the sofa along which Mr. Latchley's splinted leg was stretched. Except that he was not coming to commiserate or even to nod a greeting to the injured man. Instead he stopped and bowed to *her*.

"Mrs. Keeping," he said, his voice languid, even a trifle bored, "one is expected to d-dance, I believe, at such gatherings. At least, that is what my friend Darleigh informed me this afternoon. And although he is quite b-blind and one might assume he would not see if I did *not* dance, I know him well enough to feel quite c-certain that he *would* see even if no one told him. What is the point of having a blind friend, I sometimes ask myself, if one cannot deceive him in such matters?"

Oh, he stuttered slightly—surely his only outward imperfection. His eyelids partly drooped over his eyes as he spoke to give him his slightly sleepy look, though the eyes themselves did not look sleepy at all.

Agnes laughed. She did not know what else to do. Was he asking her to dance? But he had not said so, had he?

"Ah," he said, raising his quizzing glass almost but not quite to his eye. He had beautifully manicured nails, she saw, on a hand that was nevertheless quite unmistakably male. "Quite so. You s-sympathize with me, I see. But one must dance. Will you do me the honor, ma'am, of hoofing it about the floor with me?"

He *was* asking her to dance, and the opening set at that. She had been hoping quite fervently that *someone* would ask her. She was only twenty-six, after all, and not quite in her dotage. But—Viscount Ponsonby? She was tempted to run for the door and not stop running until she arrived home.

What on earth was the *matter* with her?

"Thank you, my lord," she said, sounding her usual

restrained self, she was relieved to hear. "Though I shall try to dance with some grace."

"I would expect no l-less of you," he said. "*I* shall hoof it." And he offered his wrist for her hand, which she somehow held steady as she set it there, and led her off to join the dancers. He bowed to her as she took her place in the line of ladies before joining the men opposite.

Oh, goodness gracious, she thought, and for a moment that was *all* she could think. But her sense of humor, which she was always quite prepared to turn upon herself, came to her rescue, and she smiled. What enormous fun she would have tomorrow with the memory of this half hour. The grandest triumph of her life. She would live upon it for a week. For a *fortnight*. She almost laughed aloud.

Opposite her, Viscount Ponsonby, ignoring all the bustle of activity around them, raised one satirical eyebrow as he looked directly back at her. Oh, dear. He would wonder why she was smiling quite so merrily. He would imagine that she was delighted to be dancing with him—which she *was,* of course, though it would be gauche to grin with triumph for *that* reason.

The orchestra struck a chord, and the music began.

He had, not surprisingly, completely misrepresented himself as a dancer. He performed the steps and the figures with elegant grace, yet with no sacrifice of masculinity. He drew more than his fair share of glances: envious ones from the men, admiring ones from the women. Even though the intricacies of the dance did not allow for a great deal of conversation, his attention remained focused upon Agnes, so that she felt he danced with *her* and not just for the sake of being socially agreeable.

It was what being a true gentleman was all about, she told herself when the set was over and he led her to Dora's side and bowed politely to both of them before moving away. There was nothing particular in the attention he had paid her. Yet she was left with the unexpected conviction that she had never, ever enjoyed any evening even half as well as she had enjoyed this.

Had enjoyed? As though it were already over.

"I am so pleased," Dora said, "that someone had the good taste to dance with you, Agnes. He is an extremely handsome gentleman, is he not? Though I must confess myself wary of that left eyebrow of his. It has a distinctly mocking quality."

"It does," Agnes agreed, cooling her cheeks with her fan while they both laughed.

But she did not feel mocked by either his eyebrow or his person. Instead she felt smug and delicious. And she knew beyond the shadow of a doubt that she would indeed dream of this ball and the opening set and her dancing partner for days, perhaps weeks, to come. Even years. She would be perfectly happy to return home now, though it was quite impossible to do so this early in the evening. Alas, all was going to seem anticlimactic for the rest of it.

It was not so, however.

Everyone had put aside daily cares in order to enjoy the opulent splendor of a harvest ball at Middlebury Park. And everyone had come to celebrate the happy, soon-to-be-fruitful marriage of the young viscount they had so pitied when he came here three and a half years ago, blind and reclusive, suffocated by the protective care of his mother and grandmother and sisters. Everyone had come to celebrate his marriage to the little slip of an elfin creature whose warm charm and boundless energy had won their hearts more and more completely during the seven months she had been here.

How could Agnes not enjoy herself and celebrate with them? She did just those things, in fact. She danced every set and was delighted that Dora danced a number of times too. She was led in to supper by Mr. Pendleton, one of the viscount's brothers-in-law, an affable gentleman who engaged her in conversation from one side for much of the meal while Mrs. Pearl, the viscount's maternal grandmother, spoke to her from the other side.

There were toasts and speeches and a wedding cake. It was just like a real and lavish wedding reception, in fact.

Oh, no, there was nothing whatsoever anticlimactic about the ball after the first set. And the dancing was to resume after supper—with a waltz. It was the first of the evening and probably the last too, and occasioned a certain interest among the guests, for though it had been danced in London and other, more fashionable centers for a number of years now, it was still considered somewhat risqué in the country and was rarely included in the program at the local assemblies. Agnes knew the steps. She had practiced them with Dora, who taught dancing to some of her music pupils, Sophia among them. It had been planned, Dora had confided to Agnes, that the viscountess would waltz with her uncle.

It was not with her uncle Sophia intended to waltz, however, as Agnes saw when she turned her head to discover the source of a heightened buzz of raised voices mingled with laughter. Someone began to clap slowly, and others were joining in.

"Waltz with her," someone said—it was Mr. Harrison, Lord Darleigh's particular friend.

Sophia was on the dance floor, Agnes could see, her arm stretched out, Viscount Darleigh's hand clasped in hers. There was laughter in her flushed face. Oh, goodness, she was trying to persuade her husband to dance with her. And by now half the guests in the ballroom were clapping rhythmically. Agnes joined them.

And everyone was repeating what Mr. Harrison had said and making a chant out of it.

"Waltz with her. Waltz with her."

The viscount took a few steps out onto the empty floor with Sophia.

"If I make a thorough spectacle of myself," he said as the chant and the clapping died away, "would everyone be kind enough to pretend they have not noticed?"

There was general laughter.

The orchestra did not wait for anyone else to take to the floor with them.

Agnes clasped her hands to her bosom and watched with everyone else, anxious that the viscount *not* make a spectacle of himself. He waltzed clumsily at first, though he did so with laughter in his face and such obvious enjoyment that Agnes found herself blinking back tears. And then somehow he found the rhythm of the dance, and Sophia looked at him with such radiant adoration that even furious blinking would not stop one tear from trickling down Agnes's cheek. She wiped it away with a fingertip and glanced furtively about to assure herself that no one had noticed. No one had, but *she* noticed several other people with unnaturally bright eyes.

After a few minutes there was a break in the music, and other couples joined the viscount and viscountess on the floor. Agnes sighed with contentment and perhaps a bit of longing. Oh, how lovely it would be . . .

She turned to Dora beside her. "You taught Sophia well," she said.

But Dora's eyes were focused beyond her sister's shoulder.

"I do believe," she murmured, "you are about to be singled out for particular attention for the second time this evening. There will be no living with you for the next week."

Agnes had no chance either to reply or to whip her head about to see what—or whom—Dora was looking at.

"Mrs. Keeping," the rather languid voice of Viscount Ponsonby said, "d-do tell me I have no rival for your hand for this particular s-set. I would be devastated. If I am to waltz, it really must be w-with a sensible companion."

Agnes plied her fan and turned toward him.

"Indeed, my lord?" she said. "And what makes you believe I am sensible?" And was that a *compliment* he had paid her? That she was *sensible*?

He moved his head back an inch and let his eyes rove over her face.

"There is a c-certain light in your eye and quirk to your lip," he said, "that proclaims you to be an observer of life as well as a d-doer. A sometimes *amused* observer, if I am not mistaken."

Goodness gracious. She regarded him in some surprise. She hoped no one else had noticed that. She was not even sure it was true.

"But why would you wish for a sensible partner for the waltz more than for any other dance?" she asked him.

What *would* be sensible was to accept his offer without further ado, since she could think of nothing more heavenly than to waltz at a real ball. And surely the music would begin again at any moment now, even though the orchestra appeared to be waiting a little while for other couples to gather on the floor. And she had the chance to dance the waltz with *Viscount Ponsonby*.

"One waltzes face-to-face with one's p-partner until the bitter end," he said. "One must hope at least f-for some interesting conversation."

"Ah," she said. "The weather is an ineligible topic, then?"

"As are one's state of health and that of all one's acquaintances to the third and f-fourth generation," he added. "W-will you waltz with me?"

"I fear it immensely," she said, "for now you have surely tied my tongue in knots. Have you left me with any topic upon which I *may* converse sensibly or, indeed, at all?"

He offered his wrist without replying, and she placed her hand on it and felt her knees threaten to turn to jelly as he smiled at her—a lazy, heavy-lidded smile that seemed to suggest an intimacy quite at variance with the public nature of their surroundings.

She was, she suspected, in the hands of an accomplished flirt.

"Watching Vincent waltz," he said as they took their places facing each other, "was enough to make one *w-weep*. Would you not agree, Mrs. Keeping?"

Oh, dear, had he seen that tear?

"Because he danced clumsily?" She raised her eyebrows.

"Because he is in l-l-love," he said, stumbling badly over the final word.

"You do not approve of romantic love, my lord?"

"In others it is really most affecting," he said. "But perhaps we ought to talk about the weather after all."

They did not do so, however, because the orchestra struck up a decisive chord at that moment. He slipped one hand behind her waist, while she set hers on his shoulder. He clasped her other hand in his and moved her immediately into a sweeping twirl that robbed her of breath and at the same time assured her that she was in the hands not just of a flirt, but of an accomplished dancer too. Even if she had not known the steps, it would not have mattered, she was convinced. It would have been quite impossible not to follow his lead.

Colors and light swirled about her. Music engulfed her, as did the sounds of voices and laughter. There were the myriad scents of flowers and candles and colognes. There was the exhilaration of twirling movement, herself a part of it and at the very heart of it.

And there was the man who twirled her about the floor and made no attempt to conduct any conversation, sensible or otherwise, but held her the correct distance from his body and gazed at her with those sleepy yet keen eyes of his, while she gazed back without ever thinking that perhaps she ought to look away or modestly lower her gaze—or find something to say.

He was gloriously handsome and so overpoweringly attractive that she was unable to muster any defensive wall against his allure. There was character in his face and cynicism and intensity and so much mystery that surely a lifetime of knowing him would not completely unmask him. There was power in him and ruthlessness and wit and charm and pain.

But all the awareness she felt was neither conscious nor verbal. She was caught up in a moment so intense that it felt like an eternity—or like the blink of an eye.

There was no further break in the music. When it ended, the set too was over. And the mocking gleam was back in his eyes, and there was the hint of mockery again too about the curl of his lip.

"Not s-sensible after all, then," he said. "Only enchanting."

Enchanting?

He returned her to Dora's side, bowed gracefully, and moved off without another word.

And Agnes was in love.

Foolishly, deeply, head over heels, gloriously in love.
With a cynical, practiced, possibly dangerous flirt.
With a man she would never see again after tonight.
Which was really just as well.
Oh, yes, undoubtedly.

2

Five months later

It was a pleasant enough day for early March, a bit nippy, perhaps, but it was neither raining nor blowing, both of which it had been doing with great frequency and enthusiasm almost since Christmas, and the sun was shining. Flavian Arnott, Viscount Ponsonby, was happy not to be obliged to proceed over the English landscape in the stuffy confines of his traveling carriage, which was trundling along somewhere behind him with his valet and his baggage while he rode his horse.

It was going to feel odd to have the annual gathering of the Survivors' Club at Middlebury Park, Vincent's home in Gloucestershire, this year instead of at Penderris Hall, George, Duke of Stanbrook's home in Cornwall, as usual. The seven of them had spent three years together at Penderris recovering from their various war wounds. When they left, they had agreed to meet there for a few weeks each year to renew their friendship and to share their progress. They had done just that, and only once, two years ago, had one of them been absent, Hugo's father having died suddenly just as he was about to leave for Cornwall. Hugo had been sorely missed.

And this year they had been in danger of missing Vincent, Viscount Darleigh, who had declared all of five months ago that he would not leave Middlebury Park in March when Lady Darleigh was expecting her first confinement in late February. To be fair, the lady herself had tried to convince him not to miss something she knew meant a great deal to him. Flavian could vouch for that—he had been at Middlebury for the harvest ball at the time. When she had understood, though, that Vincent was quite adamant in his refusal to leave her, she had solved the impasse by suggesting that the Survivors come to them for their gathering instead so that Vincent would not have to miss it *or* leave her.

The remaining five of them had all been consulted, and they had all agreed to the change of venue, though it did feel strange. And there would be wives this year too—three of them, all acquired since their last gathering—to make things even stranger. But nothing in life ever stood still, did it? Sometimes that was regrettable.

He was almost at the end of his journey, Flavian realized as he rode into the village of Inglebrook and nodded to the butcher, who was sweeping the threshold of his shop, clad in a long apron he had obviously been wearing the last time he cut meat. The turn onto the driveway to Middlebury Park was just beyond the far end of the village street. He wondered whether he would be first to arrive at this gathering of the Survivors' Club. For some strange reason, he usually was. It suggested a shocking overeagerness in him that was quite out of character. He was usually fashionably late—or even later—to social events.

On one memorable occasion last spring he had been turned away from the hallowed doors of Almack's in London because he had arrived there for the weekly ball, correctly clad in old-fashioned knee breeches as the rules of the club demanded, at two minutes past eleven. Another of the club's rules was that there would be absolutely no admission after eleven. He had been crushed and heartbroken at the realization that his pocket watch was slow—or so he had assured his aunt the next day. He had promised a dance to his cousin, her daughter. His aunt had looked upon him with reproach and had made an ungracious comment on his poor attempt at an apology. Ginny, though, was made of sterner stuff, and had merely stuck her nose in the air and informed him that her dance card had been so full at Almack's that she would have had to disappoint him if he had deigned to put in an appearance.

Good old Ginny. He wished there were more females like her.

He touched his whip to the brim of his hat as he rode past the vicar's wife—he had a lamentably poor memory for names, though he had been introduced to her—who was chatting with a large woman across the garden gate of the vicarage. He bade both ladies a good afternoon, and they chirruped cheerfully back at him and assured him that it was indeed good and long may it last.

Another lady was proceeding alone along the street toward him, a largish sketching easel tucked under one arm, a bag, presumably of supplies, in her free hand. She had a trim, youngish figure, he noticed appreciatively. She was dressed neatly, though without any nod to high fashion. She lifted her head, having no doubt heard the approach of his horse, and he recognized her.

Mrs. . . . Working? Looking? Darling? Weeding? Drat it, he could not recall her name. He had danced with her at Vince's ball, at the request of the viscountess, whose particular friend she was. He had waltzed with her too—yes, by Jove, he had.

He tipped his hat to her as they drew level.

"Good afternoon, ma'am," he said.

"My lord." She dipped into a slight curtsy and regarded him with wide eyes and raised eyebrows. Then she blushed. It was not just the March chill that rouged her cheeks. One moment they were not rosy, and the next moment they were. And her eyelids went down to hide her eyes.

Well. Interesting.

She was a good-looking woman without being in any way dazzling, though she did have fine eyes, now decently hidden beneath her eyelids, and a mouth that looked designed for humor—or for kissing. There was something about that humor—but, no, though an image pricked at the edges of his memory for a moment, it flitted away without revealing itself. Annoying, but memories tended to be like that for him—little, or perhaps huge, blanks in the past of which he remained unaware until they blinked into existence, sometimes long enough to be grabbed and brought into focus, sometimes winking out again before they could be nailed down. This was one of the *not* times. No matter.

She was past the first blush of youth, though she was probably younger than he was. Undoubtedly younger, in fact. Good Lord, he was thirty, practically a relic.

He did not draw his horse quite to a stop. What the devil was her name? He moved on, and so did she.

Sensible, he thought as he reached the end of the street, saw that the gates into Middlebury stood open, and turned his horse onto the winding, wooded driveway. That had been his impression of the woman after he had dutifully solicited her hand for the first set at the harvest ball. And he had asked her for the waltz after supper with the explanation that he hoped for some sensible conversation from her.

Not very flattering, that, he thought now, five months

too late. It was hardly the sort of word to induce a woman's heart into fluttering with romantic dreams over him. But that had not been the point, had it? There had been no conversation, sensible or otherwise, during that waltz. Only . . . enchantment.

Odd that he should remember that impression now, when the thought had vanished completely from his memory as soon as the ball ended. Odd and a little embarrassing too. What the devil had his mind meant by conjuring that particular word? And—was he remembering correctly? Had he spoken it aloud in her hearing?

Not sensible after all, then. Only enchanting.

What the devil *had* he meant?

She was not enchanting. Trim and neat, vaguely pretty, yes. Nothing more startling than that, though. Fine eyes and a humorous, even perhaps kissable, mouth were not sufficient in themselves to dazzle either the eyes or the mind—or to arouse one's spring fancy. Anyway, it had been October at the time.

Enchantment, indeed. It was not a word that was particularly active in his vocabulary.

He hoped she had not heard. Or, if she had, he hoped she had not remembered.

She had blushed just now, though.

The driveway drew free of the woods, and he was afforded a magnificent view along a neatly clipped topiary garden and then formal flower parterres—colorful even this early in the year—to the wide, impressive front of the house. And it struck him, as it had each time he came here, that his friend had never been able to see any of it. Blindness, Flavian had always thought, must be one of the worst afflictions of all. Even now, knowing Vincent as he did and how cheerful he always was and how he had got on with his life and made something really quite happy and meaningful of it, even now he felt choked up with grief over Vince's blindness.

It was just as well there was still some distance to ride before he had to face anyone at the house. What would people think of Viscount Ponsonby of all men riding up with tears in his eyes? The very idea was enough to give him the shudders.

His approach had indeed been noted, he saw when he turned onto the terrace before the great double doors a few minutes later. They were open, and Vincent was out on the top step, his guide dog on a short leash beside him, his free hand clasped in his viscountess's. Both were beaming down at him.

"I was beginning to think no one was going to come," Vincent said. "But here you are, Flave."

He *was* first to arrive, then.

"How did you know it was me?" Flavian asked, looking fondly up at him. "Confess now. You have been p-peeping."

The two of them came down the steps as Flavian swung from the saddle and abandoned his horse to the care of a groom who was hurrying across the terrace from the direction of the stables. He caught Vincent up in a tight hug and then turned to take the viscountess's hand in his own. But she was having none of such formality. She hugged him too.

"We have been *so* impatient," she said. "Just like a pair of children awaiting a special treat. This is the first time we have entertained guests entirely alone. My mama-in-law stayed with us until after my confinement, but she went home to Barton Coombs last week. She has been simply pining to be back there, and I was finally able to assure her that we could do without her, though we would miss her dreadfully—which we do."

"I trust you have recovered your health, ma'am," Flavian said.

She certainly *looked* as if she was blooming. She had been brought to bed of a boy about a month ago, a couple of weeks earlier than expected.

"I have no idea why people speak of a confinement as though it were some deadly disease," she said, linking her arm through his and proceeding up the steps with him while Vincent, guided by his dog, came up on his other side. "I have never felt better. Oh, I do hope everyone else arrives soon so that we do not burst with excitement or do something equally ill-bred."

"You had better come up to the drawing room for a drink, Flave," Vincent said, "before one of us takes it into our head to suggest that you come to the nursery to worship and adore our son and heir. We are trying to understand that other people may not be as besotted with him as we are."

"Does he have all ten toes and fingers?" Flavian asked.

"He does," Vincent said. "I counted."

"And everything else in its p-place, I trust?" Flavian said. "I am vastly relieved and satisfied. And I *am* p-parched."

Viewing and cooing over infants had never been one of his preferred activities. But here he was swallowing a suspicious soreness in his throat again at the realization that Vincent had never seen his son and never would. He hoped the others would arrive soon. Vince had always been their collective favorite, though none of them had ever said as much. Flavian found it easier to barricade his feelings against a quite inappropriate pity when the others were around too.

Dash it all, Vince would never play cricket with the child.

And here was *he*, Flavian thought, feeling all fragile and on the verge of tears or worse, just because he was here, because he was *home*, though that word had nothing to do with place but only everything to do with the people who would be here with him soon along with Vincent. Then he would be safe again. Then he would be well again, and nothing could harm him. Absurd thoughts!

They had scarcely stepped inside the drawing room when they became aware of the clopping of horses' hooves on the driveway below and the jingling of carriage traces. And it was not his own coach, Flavian saw when he looked through the long windows. It was not George's either, or Ralph's. Hugo's, maybe? Or Ben's? Ben—Sir Benedict Harper—had recently taken up residence in Wales, of all the godforsaken places he might have chosen, and was managing some coal mines and ironworks there for the grandfather of his new wife. It was all rather bizarre and improbable and not a little alarming. Even more astonishing was the fact that all of them except Vincent had traipsed off there in January for the wedding. They might have been marooned there for a month or more. What would one do in Wales for a *month*? In the middle of *winter*? They all needed their heads examined. Of course, his own head had never been quite right since he had been shot through the side of it and then tumbled down onto it from his horse's back during one memorable battle in the Peninsula. Memorable for others, that was. It remained a huge, colossal blank for him, as if it were something he had slept through and merely heard about afterward.

"Oh," Lady Darleigh said, clasping her hands to her bosom, "here comes someone else. I must go back down. Will you stay here, Vincent, and see that Lord Ponsonby has his drink?"

"I shall come with you, Sophie," Vince said. "Flavian is a big boy. He can pour his own drink."

"And without spilling any," Flavian agreed. "But I will c-come down too if I may."

There was that foolish excitement again, the one that always ensured he was first to arrive for the annual gatherings. Soon they would be together again, the seven of them. His favorite people in the world. His friends. His lifeline. He would not have survived those three years without them. Oh, perhaps his body would have, but his sanity most assuredly would not. He would not survive *now* without them.

They were his family.

He had another family of people who shared his bloodlines and his ancestral history. He was even fond of them, almost without exception, and they of him. But these, his six friends—George, Hugo, Ben, Ralph, Imogen, and Vincent—were the family of his heart.

Devil take it, what a phrase—*family of his heart.* It was enough to make any self-respecting male want to vomit. It was a good thing he had not said it aloud.

Keeping, he thought apropos of nothing as he went back downstairs to greet the new arrival. His mind had winked, and there it was—the woman's name. Mrs. Keeping, widow. An odd name, but then, perhaps his own name, Arnott, was odd too. Any name was, when one thought about it long enough.

By the time Agnes had arrived home and removed her bonnet and pelisse, and tidied her hair and washed her hands, her heart had stopped thumping sufficiently that she did not think Dora would hear it when she went downstairs to join her in the sitting room.

It really, *really* was not fair that he looked even more handsome and virile on horseback than in a ballroom.

He had been wearing a long, drab riding coat with goodness knows how many shoulder capes—it had not occurred to her to count them—and a tall hat set at a very slightly jaunty angle on his near-blond head. She had been suffocatingly aware of his supple leather boots and powerful thighs in tight riding breeches, and of his military posture and broad chest and mocking, handsome face.

The very sight of him *just* when she thought she was going to make it home safely had thrown her into such a stupid flutter that she could not remember now how she had behaved. Had she acknowledged him in some civil way? Had she gawked? Had she shaken visibly like a leaf in a hurricane? Had she *blushed*? Oh, dear God, please let her not have blushed. How dreadfully lowering that would be. Good heavens, she was *twenty-six*. And she was a *widow*.

"Oh, there you are, dearest," Dora said, lifting her hands from the keyboard of her ancient but lovingly cared-for and meticulously well-tuned pianoforte. "You are later than you said you would be—but when are you not when you have been painting? You have been missing all the fun."

"I never mean to be late," Agnes said, stooping to kiss her sister's cheek.

"I know." Dora got to her feet and rang the silver bell on top of the instrument as a signal to their housekeeper to bring in the tea tray. "It happens to me when I play. It is a good thing we are both absentminded artists, or we might be forever bickering and accusing each other of neglect. You found something absorbing to paint, then?"

"Daffodils in the grass," Agnes said. "They are always so much lovelier there than they are in flower beds. What is the fun I have missed?"

"The guests for Middlebury Park have begun to arrive," Dora said. "A single horseman rode by a short while ago. He was past the house before I could dash to the window, even though I went at breakneck speed, and I saw only his back, but I believe he might have been the handsome viscount of the mocking eyebrow who was at the October ball."

"Viscount Ponsonby?" Agnes said, and her heart began its heavy thumping again, threatening to deafen her and make her voice breathless. "Yes, you are quite right. I passed him farther along the street, and he actually acknowledged me and bade me a good afternoon. He could not remember my name, however. I could almost hear him searching his mind for it. He called me *ma'am* instead."

Goodness, had she really noticed that much?

"And just a few minutes ago," Dora said, "there were a couple of carriages. There were two people in the first, a lady and gentleman. The second was loaded down with a prodigious pile of baggage and contained a man who looked so superior that he was either a duke or a valet. I suspect the latter. I almost called up to you, but if I had done that, then Mrs. Henry would have heard too and come bustling to one of the front windows, and all three of us would have been seen to be gawking outward and *not* minding our own business as genteel ladies ought."

"Absolutely no one would have paid us any heed," Agnes said. "Everyone else would have been too busy gawking on their own account."

They both laughed and took their seats on either side of the fireplace, while Mrs. Henry carried in the tray and informed them that the guests had begun to arrive at Middlebury Park, but she expected Miss Debbins had been too engrossed in her music to notice.

Agnes and Dora smirked at each other when she had left, and then got to their feet to see who was approaching along the village street this time. It was a young gentleman driving himself in a very smart curricle, with a young tiger in livery up behind him. The driver looked like another lithe and handsome man, except that a wicked scar slashing across the cheek nearest their window was horribly visible despite his hat. It gave him a ferocious, piratical appearance.

"I quite despise myself," Dora said. "But this really is fun."

"It is," Agnes agreed. Though she wished it was not happening. She had really not wanted to see him again. Oh, yes, of course she had. No, she had not. Oh, she *hated* this . . . this juvenile turmoil over a man who had scarcely noticed her five months ago and had forgotten even her name since then.

Sophia had told her about the Survivors' Club and had explained about their annual gatherings in Cornwall, and how she had persuaded them all to come to Middlebury Park instead this year because her husband, the foolish dear—Sophia's words—had refused to leave her so soon after her confinement. There were seven of them, including Viscount Darleigh—six men and one woman. Three of them were married, all within the past year. They were going to be here for three weeks. The whole neighborhood was agog with excitement, even though it was to be a mainly private gathering. Every one of the Survivors was titled: the least illustrious of them a baronet, the most illustrious a duke.

Agnes had decided to keep well out of their way. It should not be difficult, she had thought, although she often went up to the house to see Sophia, especially during the last couple of months before Thomas was born, when it had been increasingly difficult for Sophia to come to see her, and during the month since his birth. She would stop going while there were houseguests. She would have stopped even if *he* was not one of the Survivors, for Sophia would be busy entertaining them all. And though Agnes often went into the park to sketch, at the express invitation of both Sophia and Lord Darleigh, she would avoid the parts of it where the guests were most likely to stroll, and she would be very careful not to be seen coming and going.

She had been careful today—until she had lost track of time. None of the guests would be likely to arrive before the middle of the afternoon, Sophia had told her. Agnes had gone, then, to paint the daffodils, when it was still morning. She could not delay altogether for three weeks, because the daffodils would not delay. She would be home soon after noon, well before anyone could be expected to arrive, she had told Dora before she left. But then she had started to paint and had forgotten the time.

Even then she had taken great care while walking home. She had been painting way over beyond the lake and the trees, close to the summerhouse, not even nearly within sight of the main house. The park about Middlebury was vast, after all. She did not return around the lake and across the bottom of the lawn to the drive. That would have brought her within distant sight of the house for a few minutes, and she would have been exposed along much of the length of the driveway too. No, she had walked down into the woods that grew in a thick band inside the southern wall of the park, and had threaded her way about the ancient trunks, enjoying the green-hued solitude and the lovely smells of the trees. She had emerged far down the driveway, only a few yards from the gates, which stood wide-open, as they usually did during the daytime. Then she had proceeded along the village street toward home. There had been no one in sight except Mrs. Jones, who was standing at the gate outside the vicarage indulging in a gossip with Mrs. Lewis, the apothecary's wife. And Mr. Henchley was brushing sawdust out through the door of his butcher's shop at the far end of the street for someone else to have to deal with. Agnes had put her head down and hurried toward home.

She had thought herself safe until she heard the clopping hooves of an approaching horse. She had not looked up. Horses were not an uncommon sight in the village, after all. But she had had no choice as it drew closer. It would be very ill-mannered of her not to acknowledge a neighbor. So she raised her head and looked straight into the sleepy green eyes of the very guest she had most wanted to avoid. Indeed she had no reason to avoid any of the others, all of whom were strangers to her.

It was wretchedly bad luck.

And she had despised herself anew as she looked at him. She had shaken off the whole nonsense of falling in love only weeks after that infernal ball. Nothing like it had ever happened to her before, and she would make good and sure nothing like it ever happened again. Then Sophia had told her about the Survivors' Club coming here. And Agnes had convinced herself that if she set eyes upon him—which she would take great pains *not* to do—she would be able to look at him quite dispassionately and see him merely as one of Lord Darleigh's aristocratic friends with whom she happened to have a slight acquaintance.

He was quite impossibly handsome. And a whole lot of other things she would prefer not to put into words—or even thoughts, if the wretched things could only be suppressed.

Which they could not.

All the nonsense from last autumn had come rushing back, just as if she did not have a droplet of common sense in her whole body or brain.

"I wonder," Dora said as they returned to their chairs,

"if we will be invited to the house at all, Agnes. I suppose not, but you are a particular friend of the viscountess, and I am her music teacher as well as Lord Darleigh's. Indeed, he remarked to me just last week that since his friends will merely ridicule his efforts on the harp, I had better come and play it for them as it ought to be played, and *then* they would not laugh. But *he* was laughing as he said it. I think his friends tease him a great deal, and that means that they love him, does it not? I believe they must be very close friends. I do not suppose Lord Darleigh *will* invite me to play, will he?"

Agnes shook off her own foolish palpitations and focused her attention upon her sister, who both looked and sounded wistful. Dora was twelve years her senior and had never married. She had lived at home in Lancashire until their father remarried, a year before Agnes's own marriage. Then she had expressed her intention to answer the advertisement she had seen for a resident music teacher in the village of Inglebrook in Gloucestershire. Her application had been accepted, and she had moved here and stayed and prospered in a modest way. She was well liked and respected here, and her talent was recognized. She always had more work than she could accept.

Was she happy, though? She had a whole neighborhood of friendly acquaintances but no particular friend. And no beau. She and Agnes had grown very close since they had lived together here—as they had always been at home. But they were for all intents and purposes of different generations. Dora was contented, Agnes believed. But happy?

"Perhaps you will indeed be invited to play," she said. "All hosts like to entertain their houseguests, and what better way than with a musical evening? And Lord Darleigh is blind and therefore more attached to music than any other form of entertainment. Unless there is a great deal of musical talent among the guests, it would make perfect sense for him to invite you to play for them. You have more talent than anyone else I have known, Dora."

Perhaps it was not wise to raise her sister's hopes. But how insensitive not to have realized until this moment that Dora too had feelings and anxieties related to the arrival of these guests and that she dreamed of playing for an appreciative audience.

"But confess, dear," Dora said, a twinkle in her eye. "You have not known many people, talented or otherwise."

"You are quite right," Agnes admitted. "But if I *had* known everyone in the polite world and had heard them all display their talents at musical evenings galore, I would absolutely have discovered that there is no one to match you."

"What I love about you, Agnes, dear," her sister said, "is your remarkable lack of partiality."

They both laughed and then scrambled to their feet again to watch yet another carriage go by, this one with a distinguished-looking older gentleman and a young lady inside—and a ducal crest emblazoned on the door.

"All I need to be entirely happy," Dora said, "is a discreet and genteel little telescope."

They laughed again.

3

For what remained of that first day, after they had all arrived, and for all of the next day as well as much of the night between and the night following, they stayed together as a group and talked almost without ceasing. It was always thus when there was a year's worth of news to share, and it was still so this year, despite the fact that most of them had met a few times since last spring's gathering at Penderris Hall and when three of them had married.

Flavian had been a bit afraid that those marriages would somehow affect their closeness. He had been a lot afraid, if the truth were told. It was not that he resented his friends' happiness or the three wives they had acquired, all of whom were at Middlebury Park with them. But the seven of them had been through hell together and had come out of it together as a tightly knit group. They knew one another as no one else did or could. There was a bond that would be impossible to describe in words. It was a bond without which they would surely crumble—or explode—into a million pieces. At least, *he* would.

All three wives seemed to know it and respect it, though. Without being in any way overt about it, they gave space to their husbands and the others, though they did not hold themselves entirely aloof either. It was all very well-done of them. Flavian soon had a definite affection for them all, as well as the liking he had felt when he had first met each of them.

One thing he had always valued as much as anything else about the annual gatherings of the Survivors' Club, though, was that the seven of them did not cling together as an inseparable unit for the whole of their three-week gatherings. There was always the company of friends when one wanted or needed it, but there could always be solitude too when one chose to be alone.

Penderris was perfectly suited for both company and solitude, spacious as the house and park were and situated as they were above a private beach and the sea. Middlebury Park was hardly inferior, however, even though it was inland. The park was large and had been designed in such a way that there were public areas—the formal gardens, the wide lawns, the lake—and more secluded ones such as the wilderness walk through the hills behind the house, and the cedar avenue and summerhouse and meadows behind the trees at the far side of the lake. There would even soon be a five-mile-long riding track around the inner edge of the north and east walls and part of the south; the construction of it was almost finished. The track was to allow Vincent the freedom to ride and to run despite his blindness, and had been his viscountess's idea, as had the guide dog and other additions to the house and park.

On the second morning, they all had breakfast together after Ben—Sir Benedict Harper—and Vincent had come up from what Ralph Stockwood, Earl of Berwick, described as the dungeon but was in reality an extension of the wine cellar, which had been turned into an exercise room. It was a sunny day again.

"Gwen and Samantha are going to stroll down to the lake," Lady Darleigh said, indicating Lady Trentham, Hugo's wife, and Lady Harper, Sir Benedict's, "while I spend an hour in the nursery, and then I am going to join them. Anyone else is quite welcome to come too, of course."

"I must spend some time in the music room," Vincent said. "I have to keep my fingers nimble. It is amazing how quickly they develop into ten thumbs when they are not exercised."

"Lord love us," Flavian said. "The v-violin, Vince? The p-pianoforte?"

"Both," Vincent said with a grin, "as well as the harp."

"You have persevered with the harp, then, despite all your frustrations with it, Vincent?" Imogen Hayes, Lady Barclay, said. "You are a marvel of determination."

"You are not planning to favor us with a recital by any chance, Vince?" Ralph asked. "It would be sporting of you to give us all fair warning if you are."

"Consider it duly given." Vincent was still grinning.

George Crabbe, Duke of Stanbrook, and Hugo Emes, Lord Trentham, were going to walk over to see how the riding track was coming along. Ralph and Imogen were going to explore the wilderness walk. Ben, who was still very much in the honeymoon stage of his marriage, having been wed to Lady Harper for less than two months, chose to accompany her and Lady Trentham to the lake.

That left Flavian.

"Come with us out to the track, Flave?" Hugo suggested.

"I am going to stroll over to have a look at the cedar avenue," he said. "I never did get there when I was here last autumn."

No one protested his seemingly odd and antisocial decision. No one suggested coming with him. They understood his unspoken wish to be alone. Of course they did. They must have half expected it after last night.

The late evenings during their gatherings were almost always taken up with the most serious of their talks. They spoke of setbacks they had encountered with their recoveries, problems they faced, nightmares they endured. It had not been planned that way, and even now they never sat down with the express intention of pouring out their woes. But it almost always ended up that way. Not that they were unalloyed grumbling sessions. Far from it. They spoke from their hearts because they knew they would be understood, because they knew there would be support and sympathy and advicc, sometimes even a real solution to a problem.

Last night it had been Flavian's turn, though he had not intended to talk at all. Not yet. Perhaps later in the visit, when he had settled more fully into the comfort of his friends' company. But there had been a lull in the conversation after Ben had told them how his recent decision to use a wheeled chair after he had insisted for so long upon hobbling about on his two twisted legs between sturdy canes had transformed his life and actually been a triumph rather than the defeat he had always thought it would be.

And yet they all felt his sadness too, for taking to a chair had been his admission that he would never again be as he once was. None of them would. There had been a brief silence.

"It is almost a whole year since Leonard B-Burton died," Flavian had blurted out, his voice jerky and unnaturally loud.

They had all turned blank looks upon him.

"Hazeltine," he had added. "After a shockingly brief illness, it s-seems. He was my age. I never did write letters of c-condolence either to his f-family or to V-Velma."

"The *Earl* of Hazeltine?" Ralph said. "I remember now, though, Flave. You told me about his passing when we were in London soon after leaving Penderris last year. He was—"

"Yes." Flavian interrupted him with a flashing smile. "He was my former best f-friend. I knew him and was almost inseparable from him from my f-first day at Eton right up until—"

Well, right up until.

"I remember your talking about him," George said, "though I did not know of his death. He never came near London, did he? You were never reconciled, then, Flavian?"

"He may r-rot in hell," Flavian said.

"I had not heard either," Imogen told him. "What has happened to Lady Hazeltine?"

"Her too. M-m-may sh-she r-r-r-o-o-t-t-t—" He thumped the side of one closed fist several times against his thigh in impotent rage and gasped for air.

"Take your time, Flave," Hugo said, getting to his feet and taking the empty glass from the table beside Flavian in order to fill it again. He squeezed his friend's shoulder as he passed him on the way to the brandy decanter. "We have all night. None of us is going anywhere."

"Take a deep breath," Vincent suggested, "and keep inhaling until the air blows a bubble out of the top of your head, like a balloon. It has never worked for me, but it may for you. Even if it does not, though, waiting to feel a bubble form takes your mind off whatever it was that was getting beyond your endurance."

"I am not really upset," Flavian said after drinking half his brandy in one gulp. His voice was suddenly toneless. "It happened almost a year ago, after all. He was not my friend for more than six years before that, so I have not missed him. And Velma preferred him to me, as was her right, even if she *was* betrothed to me. I never wished them harm. I don't wish her harm now. She means nothing to me."

He had not stammered even once, he realized. Perhaps he really was over it. Over *them*.

"Are you still feeling guilty that you did not write to her, Flavian?" Imogen asked.

He shook his head and spread his hands just above his knees. They were quite steady, he was happy to see, even though they were tingling with pins and needles.

"She would not have wanted to hear from me," he said. "She would have thought I was g-gloating."

But he *had* felt guilty in all the months since he had heard—and resented the feeling.

"You have never been able to close the door on that part of your life, have you?" George asked. "And Hazeltine's dying would seem to make it harder for you ever to do so. It really is too bad, Flavian. I am sorry."

Flavian lifted his head and looked broodingly at him. "It was shut and bolted and locked and the key thrown away s-seven years ago."

He knew—*damn it all!*—that it was not true. They all knew. But no one said so, and no one pursued the topic until he did. They never intruded beyond a certain point upon one another's privacy. But there was a silence to allow him to say more if he wished.

"She is c-coming home," he said. "Her year of mourning over, she is coming b-back."

His mother and her infernal letters! As though he was interested in all the latest gossip from Candlebury Abbey, his ancestral home in Sussex, in which he had not set foot for longer than eight years. Lady Frome had called on his mother with the news, her letter had explained. Sir Winston and Lady Frome lived eight miles from Candlebury, at Farthings Hall. The two families had always been on the best of terms, Sir Winston and Flavian's father having grown up together and attended school and university together. Velma was their only daughter, much adored by her parents.

The letter had reached Flavian in London, just before he came to Gloucestershire. He would surely wish to return home to Candlebury for Easter this year, now that he *would have an incentive*, his mother had written. She had underlined the four key words.

Velma was coming home and bringing her young daughter with her. *Len's* daughter. She had had no son. No heir.

"It does not m-matter that she is returning to Farthings," he added, tossing back what remained in his glass. "I never go near C-Candlebury anyway."

Imogen had patted his knee, and after a brief silence Vincent had started to tell them about the joy the birth of his son had brought into his life—and about the panic attacks he had to fight whenever he was overwhelmed by the realization that he would never see the child or any brothers and sisters he might have.

"But, oh, the joy!" There had been tears swimming in his eyes when Flavian had looked up at him.

No one wondered this morning, then, why Flavian chose to be alone. Some things had to be dealt with on one's own, as they all knew from experience. Which fact led him to wonder about marriage—in particular, the marriages of three of the Survivors—as he stepped out of the house half an hour after breakfast and turned his steps in the direction of the lake. Was there space in marriage? There would have to be, wouldn't there? Or one would feel suffocated. Even if one was wildly in love. Happily-ever-after did not mean being welded together for all eternity—ghastly thought.

What *did* it mean, then?

It meant nothing, of course, because there was no such thing. Even the marriages of his three friends would crumble if they and their wives did not work like the devil to keep them whole for the rest of their natural lives. Was it worth the trouble?

He had believed in romantic love and happily-ever-after once upon a time, silly idiot that he had been. At least—he stopped walking to frown in thought for a moment—he was almost sure he must have believed in it. Sometimes it seemed to him that his mind was a bit like a checkerboard—the dark squares representing conscious memory, the white ones just blank spaces to hold the memories apart. Whether the blanks meant anything more than that, he could not remember. And when he tried too hard to work it out, he either got one of his crashing headaches or else he looked around for something into which he might ram his fist without breaking every bone in his hand.

There was definitely *something* in those white squares. There was violence, if nothing else.

The ladies and Ben—with his canes rather than his wheeled chair—were before him at the lake. Ben had the door of the boathouse open, and the ladies were peering inside. Was he planning to play the gallant and row them across to the island so that they could take a closer look at the temple folly there? Flavian hailed them, and there was a cheerful exchange of pleasantries during which he did *not* suggest helping to row. He kept on walking about the lake and past the band of trees on the other side. It was a lengthy walk.

The uninitiated would assume the park ended with the lake and the trees on its far bank. But it did not. It stretched beyond into a spacious area that was a little less cultivated, more secluded, more designed for solitude or the enjoyment of a tête-à-tête with a chosen companion.

It was solitude he wanted and needed this morning. Where the devil had that outburst come from last night? He had read the notice of Len's death with some surprise about this time last year. It was always a nasty reminder of one's own mortality when a contemporary died, especially when one was only thirty. And more especially when, once upon a time, one had known that particular contemporary almost as well as one knew one's fellow Survivors now. Though he would wager his life that no one of the Survivors would steal away and marry the betrothed of any other who was incapacitated.

He had read the notice with some surprise but with no greater emotion. All that unpleasantness had happened a long time ago, after all, not long after he had been brought home from the Peninsula and just before he had been taken to Penderris Hall for treatment and convalescence. A lifetime ago, it seemed. It had all meant nothing to him last spring. Len had meant nothing. Velma had meant nothing.

A whole alarming lot of nothing.

It still meant nothing now.

Except that she was coming back from the north of England, which had always felt comfortably like the other side of the world. And it did not require any genius to imagine what excitement her return was arousing in the romantic, matchmaking bosoms of his mother and hers. The fact that his mother expected him to go running to Candlebury for Easter just because Velma would be at Farthings told its own eloquent tale. It also told him that they expected he would feel the same about Velma—and she about him—as they had felt before his injuries and Len's betrayal.

He thought back, aghast, to that unexpected outburst last night and that equally unexpected relapse into an almost uncontrollable inability to get his words out. For two pins, if someone had said the wrong thing, he would have lashed out with his fists and done the Lord knew what damage to Vincent's home. He had been alarmingly close to having a complete relapse into the state of animal madness he'd been left in after the war. And he had fought a throbbing headache for most of a largely sleepless night.

He thought of Vince's bubble and chuckled ruefully.

And then he realized that he was not alone back here after all.

It had been unwise to come here today, especially when there was unlimited countryside, all of it teeming with new growth and the wildflowers of early spring, in every direction about the village. It was wildflowers that Agnes loved to paint. But the only daffodils she had seen were in the flower beds of people's gardens—and in the grass of the meadow on the far side of the park at Middlebury. And daffodils did not bloom forever. She could not simply wait for three weeks to pass until Lord Darleigh's houseguests went away.

Daisies and buttercups and clover would bloom in that near meadowland throughout the summer. There had been snowdrops there a few weeks ago, and there still were some primroses. But now was the time of the daffodils and, oh, she could not miss it.

It was a little-used area of the park. There was no direct route to it from the house, and it was a long walk away. One had to skirt about the lake and the band of trees that had been planted along its western bank. It was unlikely the guests would stroll there often, if at all. It was *very* unlikely they would walk there during a morning.

So she had taken the risk of coming back, her easel tucked beneath one arm, paper and paints and brushes and everything else she might need in her large canvas bag. She had tramped through the trees that lined the south wall, and emerged into sunlight and open spaces only when she was well out of sight of the house and the gardens and lawns fronting it.

She had painted a single daffodil two days ago but had been dissatisfied with it. She had made it too large, too bold, too yellow. It had been an object largely divorced from its surroundings. She might just as well have plucked it and carried it home and placed it in a jar and then painted it.

She had come back to paint the daffodils in their meadow. And she was rewarded by the sight of many more of them than there had been just two days ago. They were like a carpet spread out before her, their heads nodding in a breeze she had not particularly noticed. And they had the effect of making the grass in which they grew seem a richer green. Ah, they deserved to be painted just like this, she decided.

But how was she to capture what she saw with her eyes and felt with the welling emotions of her heart? How did one paint not just daffodils nodding in the grass but the eternal light and hope of spring itself? It was her first full spring here with Dora, and she had greeted it with a certain longing for something she could not even put into words. For life to resume, perhaps, as more than just a genteel existence. Or perhaps for life to *begin*, though that was a somewhat absurd notion when she was twenty-six years old and had already been married and widowed.

She did not usually think with her emotions.

She would try to paint. She would always try, for the

road to perfection held an irresistible lure, even if the destination remained always tantalizingly just beyond the farthest horizon.

She set down her easel and bag and just stood and looked for a long time: breathing in the smells of nature, hearing birds singing among the branches of the cedars close by, feeling the cool March air overlaid by the fresh warmth of the sun.

After a few minutes, however, she knew that she was seeing only half the picture and maybe not even that much. For the trumpets of the daffodils were lifted to the sky. The petals about them faced upward. If the flowers could see, as in a sense she supposed they could, then it was the sky, rather than the grass beneath them, upon which they gazed. She, on the other hand, was looking down upon the flowers and the grass. She turned her face upward to see that the sky was pure blue, with not a cloud in sight. But now, of course, she could no longer see the daffodils.

Well, there was a solution to that.

She kneeled down on the grass and then stretched out along it on her back, careful not to crush any of the flowers. The grass sprang up between her spread arms and her body and between her ungloved fingers when she spread them wide. Daffodils bloomed all about her. She could smell them and see the undersides of the petals and trumpets of those closest to her—and the sky beyond them. And now there was a vast blue to add to the yellow and the green.

And she was a part of it all, not a separate being looking upon creation, but creation looking upon itself. Oh, how she loved moments like this, rare as they were, and how she ached with the longing to capture in paint something of the inner experience as well as the outer beauty.

Perhaps this was how truly great painters felt all the time.

Perhaps truly great artists *felt* all the time.

But suddenly there was a sense, sharply intrusive, that she was not alone. And here she was, stretched out in the meadow among the daffodils, defenseless and foolish and trespassing even if she *had* been told by Lord Darleigh as well as by Sophia that she might come whenever she wished.

Perhaps she was wrong. Perhaps there was no one else here after all. She lifted her head cautiously from the ground and looked around.

She was *not* wrong.

He was standing quite still a short distance away, his face in shadow beneath the brim of his tall hat so that she could see neither the direction of his gaze nor the expression on his face. But he could not possibly have missed seeing her. A *blind* man could not have missed her. Even Viscount Darleigh would have sensed her presence. But he was not Viscount Darleigh.

Of all the people he might have been—and there were ten of them at the house—he was the very one she had most wanted *not* to see. Again. What were the chances?

She was the first to speak.

"I do have permission to be here," she said and then wished she had not. She had immediately put herself on the defensive.

"Beauty among the d-daffodils," he said. "How v-very charming."

He sounded utterly bored. If one could speak and sigh at the same time, he did it. He was wearing his drab riding coat. It had six capes—she counted this time. It was long enough to half cover his highly polished boots. It was pure nonsense to feel that he was more male than any other man she had ever encountered—but she *did* feel it.

Instead of leaping to her feet, as she probably ought to have done, she laid her head back down on the grass and closed her eyes. Perhaps he would go away. Was it possible to feel more embarrassed, more humiliated than she did?

He did not go away. A cloud suddenly came between her closed eyes and the sun—except that there were no clouds. She opened her eyes to find him standing beside her and looking down. And now she could see his face, shadowed though it still was. His eyes were green and heavy lidded, as she remembered them from the night of the ball. His left eyebrow was partly elevated. His mouth was curled up at the corners, though whether with amusement or scorn or both, she could not tell. One lock of blond hair lay across his forehead.

"I could offer a h-helping hand," he told her. "I c-could even play the gallant and carry you to the h-house, though I daresay I should expire at your feet of some h-heart condition after arriving there. *Are* you hurt or indisposed?"

"I am not," she assured him. "I am merely viewing the world as the daffodils view it."

She winced—quite visibly, she feared. Was it possible to feel more mortified than mortified? What a ridiculously stupid thing to say! Oh, please let him just go away, and she would gladly agree to forget him for all eternity.

His right hand, clad in the finest, most costly kid, disappeared beneath his coat and came out with a quizzing glass. He raised it to his eye and unhurriedly surveyed the meadow and then, briefly, her. It was a horrible affectation. If there was something wrong with his sight, he ought to wear eyeglasses.

And through it all she lay where she was, just as though she were incapable of rising—or as though she believed she could hide more effectively down here.

"Ah," he said at last. "I g-guessed there must be a perfectly sensible explanation, and now I see there is. I r-remember you as being sensible, Mrs. Keeping."

He had remembered her name, then—or he had asked Sophia. She wished he had not.

"No," he said, removing his hat and tossing it carelessly in the direction of her easel and bag, "that is not strictly c-correct, is it? I expected you to be s-sensible, but you were enchanting instead."

The sun turned his blond hair to a rich gold as he sat down beside her and draped his arms over his raised knees. He was wearing tight buckskin breeches beneath his coat. They hugged powerful-looking thighs. Agnes looked away.

Enchanting.

Oh, dear, he had remembered that waltz.

"And your being here among the d-daffodils now makes full sense," he said.

Why? Because she was not sensible but . . . enchanting? Oh, she wished he spoke as other people did, so that one might understand his meaning without having to wonder and guess.

She was *still* lying full-length in the grass. She ought at least to sit up, but that would bring her closer to him.

"I came here to paint," she told him. "But I will go away. I have no wish to intrude upon your privacy. I did not expect any of the guests to come this far. Not so early in the day, at least."

Finally she would have sat up *and* got to her feet. But as soon as she moved, he set a hand on her shoulder, and she stayed where she was. His hand stayed where it was too, and it scorched through her body right down to her toes—even though he was wearing gloves.

Why, oh, why had she risked coming here? And what unhappy chance had brought him here too?

"You *have* intruded upon my p-privacy," he said, "as I have upon yours. Shall we both turn h-homeward disgruntled as a r-result, or shall we s-stay and be private together for a while?"

Suddenly the daffodil meadow seemed far lonelier and more remote than when she had had it to herself.

"How *do* the daffodils view the world?" he asked, removing his hand and grasping the handle of his quizzing glass again.

"Upward," she said. "Always upward."

One of his eyebrows rose, and he looked mockingly down at her.

"There is a l-life lesson here for all of us, is there, M-Mrs. Keeping?" he asked her. "We should all and always look upward, and all our t-troubles will be at an end?"

She smiled. "If only life were that simple."

"But for daffodils it is," he said.

"We are not daffodils."

"For which f-fact I shall be eternally thankful," he said. "They never see August or D-December or even June. You should s-smile more often."

She stopped smiling.

"Why did you come out here alone," she asked him, "when you are with a group of friends?"

He had the strangest eyes. At a cursory glance, they always looked a bit sleepy. But they were not. And now they gazed at her and into her with apparent mockery—and yet there was something intense behind the mockery. As if there were a wholly unknown person hiding inside.

The thought left her a little breathless.

"And why did you c-come here alone," he asked, "when you have a s-sister and neighbors and f-friends in the village?"

"I asked first."

"So you did." She pressed her head and her hands more firmly into the grass when he smiled. It was a devastating expression. "I c-came here to commune with my soul, Mrs. Keeping, and I found enchantment among the daffodils. I shall go back to the house presently and write a p-poem about the experience. A s-sonnet, perhaps. Undoubtedly a sonnet, in fact. No other verse form would do the incident j-justice."

She smiled slowly and then laughed. "I deserved that. I had no business asking."

"But how are we to discover anything about each other," he said, "if we do not ask? Who was Mr. K-Keeping?"

"My husband," she said and smiled again when his left eyebrow mocked her. "He was our neighbor where I grew up. He offered for me when I was eighteen and he was thirty, and I was married to him for five years before he died almost three years ago."

"He was a gentleman f-farmer, was he?" he asked. "And you were wildly in love with him, I suppose? An older, experienced man?"

"I was *fond* of him, Lord Ponsonby," she said, "and he of me."

"He sounds like a d-dull dog," he said.

She was torn between indignation and amusement.

"You know *nothing* about him," she said. "He was a worthy man."

"If I were m-married to you," he said, "and you described me as w-worthy, I would shoot myself and thus put myself out of my m-misery."

"What utter nonsense!" But she laughed again.

"There was no p-passion, was there?" he asked, sounding bored again.

"You are being offensive."

"That means there was no p-passion," he said. "A p-pity. You look as if you were made for it."

"Oh."

"And most d-definitely enchanting," he said, and he shifted his position, leaned over her, and kissed her.

She was shocked into immobility, even after he had raised his head a few inches to look down at her face. From close up, his green eyes glinted into hers, and his mouth looked slightly cruel as well as mocking. And she felt such a stabbing of lust in her breasts and between her thighs and up into her womb that she was quite incapable of either remonstrating with him or pushing him away.

She wanted him to do it again.

"You ought to have stayed safely locked away inside your v-village this morning, Mrs. K-Keeping," he said. "I came here alone b-because I was feeling somewhat s-savage."

"Savage?" She swallowed and raised her hand to set her fingertips lightly against his cheek. It was warm and smooth. He must have shaved shortly before coming out. And yet she knew that this time he was speaking the truth. She could almost feel leashed danger pulsing outward from the person hidden away inside him.

She had *touched* him. She looked at her hand rather as if it belonged to someone else, and withdrew it.

"I spent three years learning to c-control it," he told her. "My savagery, that is. But it still l-lurks and waits to p-pounce upon some unwary victim. It would have been better if you had not been here."

She was curiously, and perhaps foolishly, unafraid. She could feel his breath warm against her face.

"What brought it so nearly out of lurkdom this morning?" she asked him.

But he merely smiled at her and lowered his head to brush his lips over hers again, and then to taste them with his tongue before reaching inside to the soft flesh behind them and so right on into her mouth.

She lay very still, as though moving might break the spell.

If this was a kiss, it was unlike anything she had ever experienced with William. *Totally* unlike. It was carnal and sinful and lustful and, for the moment at least, quite beyond her power to resist. She could smell the daffodils. And him. And temptation.

And danger.

The hand that had been against his cheek went to the back of his head, her fingers threading their way into his thick, warm hair, while the other hand went to his waist, beneath his riding coat. Even through the remaining layers of his clothing she could feel the hard maleness of his muscles and the heat of the blood pulsing through him.

He was all raw masculinity—something quite outside her experience.

He was dangerous. Terribly dangerous.

But her mind simply refused to answer the call to defend her, and she became all physical sensation—shock and wonder and pleasure and pure lust. And a feeling of fright that enticed her more than it repelled.

His tongue explored her mouth. The tip of it touched the roof and drew a line along the ridge of bone there and sent such a rush of pure desire shivering through her that she reacted at last. She set both hands against his shoulders and pressed him away.

Far more reluctantly than she ought.

He did not fight her or show any other sign of savagery. He lifted his head, smiled slowly, and then sat up before pushing himself to his feet. When she sat up too, he reached out a hand to help her up. It was still gloved.

"One ought to be a perfect g-gentleman even when one encounters enchantment in the grass," he said. "But at the same t-time, one feels the need to p-pay homage to it with a kiss. Life is full of such thorny c-contradictions and conflicts, alas. G-Good day to you, Mrs. Keeping. I have probably frightened away your artistic m-muse for today, have I? Perhaps you will find it here again tomorrow. Or perhaps I will f-find you here before it does. Will I?"

She gazed steadily into his keen, mocking green eyes, over which his eyelids remained half-lowered. What was he saying? Or asking? Was he making an assignation with her?

What type of woman did he think she was? And was he justified, considering the fact that she had not screeched with outrage or smacked his face as soon as it came within one foot of her?

She could still taste him. She could still feel him on her lips. Her mind was still almost numb. That secret, feminine place inside her still throbbed. And she knew that his kiss had been one of the most memorably glorious experiences of her life.

How much more pathetic could she *be*?

"The daffodils will not live forever," he said.

"No," she agreed.

But she would never paint them if she could not be alone with them, her mind placid and composed. Would she come back? And what would be her motive if she did? To paint? To see him again?

He did not wait for any further answer. He stooped to pick up his hat, inclined his head to her before putting it on, and strode away in the direction of the route around the lake.

He was by far the most masculine man she had ever

encountered—or kissed. But then, she had only ever been kissed by William before today, and kisses from William had been more in the nature of affectionate pecks on the cheek or forehead.

Oh, dear, she felt like a novice swimmer suddenly plunged into the very deepest part of a turbulent river.

She touched the fingertips of one hand to her lips. They were trembling—both the fingers and her lips.

4

Vincent was still in the music room when Flavian opened the door quietly and stole inside. He was at the pianoforte, playing something with plodding care. The dog cocked his ears and had a good look without lifting his head and decided the intruder was no threat. The viscountess's cat—Squiggles? Squabble? Squat?—had commandeered one side of the sofa. Flavian lowered himself to the other side, but the cat was not content with simple symmetry. It padded across the cushions, paused to give him an assessing look, made its decision, and took up residence on his lap, a big, curled-up blob of feline warmth. There was nothing to do with one's hands but stroke him between his ears.

Flavian had had pets galore as a boy, none as a man.

The plodding stopped, and Vincent cocked his head to one side.

"Who came in?" he asked.

"Me," Flavian told him vaguely and ungrammatically.

"Flave? Stepping voluntarily into the music room? While I am in it, practicing a Bach fugue at considerably less than half speed so that I can get the notes and the rhythm exact?"

"Squeak? Squawk? S-Squid? What the deuce *is* the name of this cat?" Flavian asked.

"Tab."

"Ah, yes, I knew it was something like that. Tab. He is going to be l-leaving cat hair all over my breeches and coat. And he is quite unapologetic about it."

Vincent turned on the stool and looked almost directly at him in that disconcerting way he had of seeming very *un*blind.

"Blue-deviled, Flave?" he asked.

"Oh, not at all," Flavian assured him, waving a hand airily toward the pianoforte, though Vincent would not see it. "Play on. I thought I might c-creep in here without disturbing you."

Fat chance. Vincent, who for a few months after his near-encounter with a cannonball on the field of battle had been as deaf as he was blind, could now hear a pin drop at a hundred yards—on thick carpet.

"This has something to do with last night?" Vincent asked.

Flavian set his head back and gazed at the ceiling before closing his eyes.

"Play me a lullaby," he said.

And Vincent did and brought him near to tears. Flavian liked to tease Vince about his playing, especially on the violin, but really he was quite good and getting better all the time. There were a few minor accuracy and tempo issues, but the feeling was there. Vince was learning to get inside the music, to play it from the inside out.

Whatever the devil that meant.

And *what* in the name of *thunder* was enchanting about an unfashionably clad, not particularly young, not obviously beautiful woman, who was idiotic enough to stretch out on the grass of a meadow so that she could see the world as daffodils saw it, and then did not have the sense, when interrupted, to hop to her feet and run like the wind for home?

She really was quite *ordinary*. She was tallish and slender with hair of a nondescript brown and unimaginative style. Her face was pleasing but hardly the sort to turn heads on a crowded thoroughfare—or in a half-crowded ballroom. He would surely not have noticed her at that autumn ball if Lady Darleigh had not asked him to dance with her so that she would not be a wallflower. And what had that request said about Mrs. Keeping? He would not have noticed her on the village street the day before yesterday if it had not been nearly deserted. He would not have noticed her this morning if she had not been . . . lying among the daffodils.

Looking all willowy and relaxed and . . . inviting.

Devil take it, she was not ordinary.

He ought *not* to have kissed her. He did not make a habit of kissing respectable females. There were too many dangers involved. And this particular respectable female happened to be the friend of his hostess here at Middlebury Park.

He ought not to have kissed her, especially in his present mood, but he had.

And actually, in retrospect, he knew she had one feature that was definitely out of the ordinary, and that was her mouth. He could have lost himself on it and about it and in it for the rest of the morning and beyond if a bird had not squawked quite unmelodically from a cedar branch and broken his concentration—and if she had not pressed her hands against his shoulders at the same moment.

Dash it all, he should not have kissed her. He would not have noticed her mouth if he had not touched it with his own. And now he craved . . .

Ignore it.

She ought not to have been there at all, trespassing on private property. Though she had told him, had she not, that she had permission, and she *was* the viscountess's friend. He had been speechless with rage when he first spotted her. He had walked all that way because he needed to be alone, and there was a damned woman there before him, taking a nap in the middle of the morning and looking damnably picturesque as she did so. He had almost turned on his heel and stalked away before she saw him.

It was, of course, what he ought to have done.

But he had paused first in order to assure himself that she was not dead, even though it was perfectly obvious that she was not. And then he had just stood there, thinking, like a nincompoop, of fairy tales. Of Sleeping Beauty, to be precise.

Anyone who believed his head had mended while he was at Penderris needed his *own* head examined.

He had told her, in so many words, that he would go back there tomorrow. If she was wise, she would barricade herself inside her house tomorrow and every day thereafter until he was long gone from Gloucestershire.

Would she be foolish enough go back?

Would he?

There had been sunshine and springtime and daffodils all about her. . . .

"Flave." The voice spoke softly.

"Huh?"

"I am sorry to wake you," Vincent said. "I could tell from your breathing that you were sleeping. But it seemed ill-mannered to leave you alone here without a word."

He had been *sleeping*?

"I must have d-dozed off," he said. "R-Rude of me."

"You *did* ask for a lullaby," Vincent reminded him. "I

must have played it better than I thought. I expect Sophie has gone to the lake by now. I should join her and the others there, but I am going to steal half an hour or so in the nursery instead. I don't suppose you would care to come with me?"

Flavian was comfortable where he was. The cat was warm and relaxed on his lap. He could easily nod off again. He had not slept much, if at all, last night. But Vince wanted to show off his infant. He would not say it in so many words, of course. He knew very well that infants bored most men.

"Why ever not?" Flavian said, sitting up while the cat got to his feet, jumped down from the sofa, and went to stand by the door, its back arched, its tail pointing straight at the heavens. "Does he look like you?"

"I have been told he does." Vincent grinned. "But, if memory serves me correctly, babies look simply like babies."

"L-lead on, Macduff," Flavian said, cheerfully misquoting.

And who would have imagined, he thought later, that he would spend a good hour of this particular morning, which he had started in such a . . . savage mood, in the nursery with a baby who looked like a baby and with the child's father, who behaved toward his son for all the world as if he were besotted? And that Flavian would actually feel soothed by the experience? And that he would read through two children's books written by Mr. and Mrs. Hunt—Vincent himself and his wife—and illustrated by the latter? And that he would chuckle over the stories and pictures with genuine delight?

"These books are p-priceless, Vince," he said. "And there are more to come, are there? Whatever gave you the idea of having them published? And how did you go about it?"

"It was Sophie's idea," Vincent told him. "Or, rather, it was Mrs. Keeping's. Have you met her? She is the sister of Miss Debbins, our music teacher. She and Sophie are as thick as thieves. Mrs. Keeping took one look at the first story, which Sophie had written out and illustrated, and remembered that she had a cousin—her late husband's cousin, actually—in London who she thought would like it. She sent it to him, and it turned out that he is a publisher and did indeed like what he saw and wanted more. So we are famous authors, and you really ought to bow down in homage before us, Flave. He wanted to publish the stories under just my name—Mr. Hunt—to protect Sophie's sensibilities. Can you imagine anything more asinine?"

Yes, Flavian thought. Yes, he had met Mrs. Keeping three times. Once at the ball last October, once on the village street two days ago, once in the daffodil meadow beyond the cedars this morning. And he had kissed her, dash it all.

"I have j-just salaamed three times," he lied. "It is a pity you couldn't s-see me, Vince. I looked suitably worshipful."

"You were on your knees when you did it, I hope," Vincent said, his hand stroking over the almost bald fair head of his son.

He would not go back tomorrow, Flavian decided as he turned to the window to watch Ben make his slow, ungainly way up from the lake with the aid of his canes, the viscountess beside him, while Lady Harper walked ahead of them with Hugo's wife. Ben was laughing at something Lady Darleigh was saying, and the ladies were looking back, smiles on their faces, to discover what the joke was.

Everyone at this particular gathering was so damnably *happy*.

Len had been dead for a year, and they had not spoken in more than six years before that. They never would now. Velma had been left with a daughter and was returning home to Farthings.

Mrs. Keeping had laughed when he told her he was going to write a sonnet about meeting her among the daffodils.

She should always laugh.

Sophia came calling during the afternoon, Viscount Darleigh with her, as well as Lord and Lady Trentham and Lady Barclay.

Lord Trentham was a fierce-looking giant of a man, his wife a small, exquisitely pretty lady who smiled a great deal and was warmly charming. It seemed odd, considering the fact that he was one of the Survivors, that it was *she* who walked with a heavy limp. Lady Barclay was the one female member of the club, having been present, Sophia had explained to Agnes, when her husband was tortured and killed in the Peninsula. She was a tall lady of marblelike beauty, though she had kind eyes.

Viscount Ponsonby had not come with them.

"Miss Debbins," Viscount Darleigh said to Dora after they had all drunk tea and conversed on a number of topics, "I have come to beg you to save my guests from the exquisite agony of having to listen to me play on the harp or violin for longer than a few minutes at a time. I must offer them music, but my own leaves something to be desired, despite the fact that I have you for a teacher."

"And mine would please no one but a doting mama if I were eight years old," Sophia said.

"Will you come to the house tomorrow evening as our honored guest?" the viscount asked. "To play for us, that is?"

"And to dine first," Sophia added.

"You would be doing us a singular favor, ma'am," Lord Trentham said with a frown. "Vincent has punished us with his violin during previous years and set cats to howling for miles around."

"The trouble with your teasing, Hugo," Lady Barclay said, "is that those who do not know you may not understand that you *are* teasing. You play remarkably well, Vincent, and are a credit to your teacher. We are all, including Hugo, exceedingly proud of you."

"We will, nevertheless," Lady Trentham said, "be delighted to hear you, Miss Debbins. Both Sophia and Vincent speak highly of your skill and talent on the pianoforte and on the harp."

"They exaggerate," Dora said, but there was a flush of color in her cheeks that told Agnes she was pleased.

"Exaggerate? I?" Lord Darleigh said. "I do not even know the meaning of the word."

"Oh, *will* you come?" Sophia begged. "And you must come too, Agnes, of course. Our numbers of ladies and gentlemen will be equal at the dinner table, for once. What a dream come true that will be as I arrange the seating. Will you come, Miss Debbins? Please?"

"Well, I will," Dora said. "Thank you. But your guests must not expect too much of me, you know. I am merely competent as a musician. At least, I *hope* I am competent."

Dora, Agnes knew as she smiled at her, would be over the moon with excitement for the next day and a half. At the same time, she would probably suffer agonies of dread and self-doubt and have a disturbed night. It would worry her that she must play for a group of such illustrious persons.

"Splendid!" Viscount Darleigh said. "And Mrs. Keeping? You will come too?"

"Oh, she must," Dora said hastily just as Agnes was opening her mouth to make some excuse. "I will need to have *someone* to hold my hand."

"But not while you are playing, it is to be hoped," Lord Trentham said.

"But of course Agnes will come too," Sophia said, clapping her hands. "Oh, I shall *so* look forward to tomorrow evening."

She got to her feet as she spoke, and her fellow guests rose too to take their leave.

No one seemed to notice that Agnes had not given an answer. But it was not necessary to do so, was it? How could she possibly refuse? It was an evening for Dora, and she knew that, though her sister would suffer in the anticipation of it, it could also be one of the happiest evenings of her life.

How could she, Agnes, spoil it?

"Oh, Agnes, dearest," Dora said as soon as they had watched their visitors walk away along the village street, "ought I to have said no? I really cannot—"

"Of course you can," Agnes said, slipping her arm through her sister's. "Imagine, if you will, that they are all just ordinary people, Dora—farmers and butchers and bakers and blacksmiths."

"There is not a single one of them without a title," Dora said with a grimace.

Agnes laughed.

Yes, and one of them was Viscount Ponsonby. Whom she really ought not to want to see again. Her only previous experience with combating churning emotions had come last October, and she'd found it neither easy to deal with nor pleasant. And on that occasion he had not even kissed her.

One would expect to have learned from experience.

* * *

George had been having the old nightmare again, and with increasing frequency. It was the one in which he reached out to grasp his wife's hand but could do no more than brush his fingertips against hers before she jumped to her death over the high cliff close to their home at Penderris. At the same moment he thought of just the words that might have persuaded her to return from the brink and live on.

The Duchess of Stanbrook really had committed suicide in just that way, and George really had seen her do it, though he had not in reality been quite as close. She had seen him running toward her, heard him calling to her, and disappeared over the edge without a sound. It had happened a mere few months after their only son—their only *child*—was killed in Spain during the wars.

"Has the dream been recurring more frequently since the wedding of your nephew?" Ben asked.

George frowned and thought about it.

"Yes, I suppose it has," he said. "There is a connection, do you suppose? But I am genuinely happy for Julian, and Philippa is a delightful girl. They will be a worthy duke and duchess after my time, and it seems there will be issue of the marriage within the next few months. I am content."

"And that very fact makes you feel guilty, does it, George?" Ben asked.

"Guilty? Does it?"

"We should call it the Survivors' guilt," Ralph said with a sigh. "You suffer from it, George. So do Hugo and Imogen. So do I. You feel guilty because the future of your title and property and fortune have been settled to your satisfaction, yet you feel your very contentment with that somehow betrays your wife and your son."

"Do I?" The duke settled an elbow on the arm of his chair and cupped his hand over his face. "And *have* I?"

"Sometimes," Hugo said, "you feel wretched when you realize that a whole day has passed, or maybe even longer, without your thinking even once about those who did not live while you did. And it almost always happens just when you are at your happiest."

"I do not believe a whole day has passed yet," George said.

"A day is a long time," Imogen agreed. "Twenty-four hours. How can one turn off memory for that long? And would one wish to? One thinks one does until it happens for a few hours."

"This is precisely what I mean," Ralph said. "It is guilt pure and simple. Guilt over being alive and *able* to forget—and smile and laugh and feel moments of happiness."

"If I had died, though," Vincent said, "I would have wanted my mother and my sisters to live on and have happy lives and to remember me with smiles and laughter. Not every day, however. I would not have wanted them to be obsessed with remembering me."

"One good way to forget," Flavian said, "is to fall off your h-horse and land on your h-head after someone has shot you through it and then have someone ride over you. Behold the blessing of my poor memory: no g-guilt whatsoever."

Which they all knew to be a lie.

But if he had died, he would have been quite happy at the notion of Velma's marrying Len—his betrothed and his best friend, respectively. At least he *thought* he would have been happy. Except that no one could be happy when he was dead. Or unhappy either, for that matter.

Anyway, he had not died—but it had happened anyway. Velma had come and told him. Len had not. Perhaps he had decided against it when he heard what happened after Velma came. Perhaps he had judged it best to keep his distance.

Now Len was dead, and they had not spoken in more than six years while he still lived. And Flavian felt guilty about it—oh, yes, he did, unfair as it seemed. Why *should* he feel guilt? He was not the one who had done the betraying.

Usually these late-night sessions made them all feel somewhat better, even if they solved nothing. Flavian did not feel better the next morning, however. He had gone to bed feeling as if he had leaden weights in his shoes and in his stomach and in his soul, and he woke up with one of his headaches and deep in one of his depressions.

He hated them more than the headaches—that feeling of dragging self-pity and the fear that nothing was worth anything. It was the one shared mood the Survivors' Club had all fought against most fiercely during those years they had spent together at Penderris. Bodies could be mended and made to work again, at least well enough to enable the person inside them to live on. Minds could be mended to the degree that they worked efficiently again for the one who inhabited them. And souls could be soothed and fed from an inner well of inspiration and from an outer sharing of experience and friendship and love.

But one never quite reached the point at which one could relax and know that one had made it through to the other side of suffering and could now be simply content, even happy, inside a balanced mix of body, mind, and spirit.

Well, of course one did not. He had never been quite naïve enough to expect it, had he? Surely, even when he had been head over ears in love with Velma, and she with him, and they had become betrothed at the end of those brief weeks of his leave and had expected a life of happily-ever-after, surely even then he had not believed it to be literally possible. After all, he had been a military officer, and there had been a war to fight. And his brother, David, had been dying.

Why the devil had they got betrothed and even celebrated the event at a grand ball in London the night before he set off back to the Peninsula, while David was at Candlebury dying, and Flavian had come home for the express purpose of being with him? And why had Flavian gone back to war when the end for his brother had obviously been near and he was about to be landed with the responsibilities of the title and property? He frowned in thought, trying to remember, trying to work it out, but the trying merely made his head thump more painfully.

The sun was shining from a clear blue sky again, he could see, and the daffodils beckoned. Or, rather, the enchantress among the daffodils beckoned. Would she be there? Would he be disappointed if he went and she was not? Would *she* be disappointed if she went there and he did not? And what did he intend if he did go? Conversation? Dalliance? Seduction? On Vince's property? With the viscountess's friend? He had better stay away.

Ben, Ralph, George, and Imogen were going riding. They expected to be gone all morning, since they were going beyond the confines of the park.

"Will you come with us, Flavian?" Imogen asked at the breakfast table.

He hesitated for the merest moment.

"I will," he said. "Vince is taking Hugo and the l-ladies over the wilderness walk, and it sounds alarmingly s-strenuous. I will come with you and l-let my horse do all the exercising."

"What I *am* going to do," Vincent said, "is show everyone what they cannot see because they have eyes."

"The boy has taken to talking in riddles," George said, looking at him fondly. "Yet, strangely, we know just what you mean, Vincent. At least I do."

"I am even going to sacrifice my morning's practice in the music room," Vincent said.

"He p-put me to sleep there yesterday morning," Flavian said.

"With a *lullaby*, Flave," Vincent protested, "for which you asked. I would say I was singularly successful."

Flavian chuckled.

"Oh," Lady Darleigh said, her hands clasped together at her bosom, "I am *so* looking forward to this evening, and I am quite certain you will all be vastly impressed, even though some of you spend time in London and must attend all sorts of concerts with the very best performers."

This evening?

"I do believe," Lady Trentham said, "that Miss Debbins was pleased to be asked, Sophia. What a delightful lady she is. And her sister too."

Miss Debbins? She was the music teacher, was she not? And her sister was . . .

"I am probably as far from being a connoisseur of music as it is possible to be," Lady Darleigh said. "But I do believe that talent in any artistic field is unmistakable when one encounters it. And I believe Miss Debbins is talented. You will all be able to judge for yourselves this evening."

"Miss Debbins is to play here?" Flavian asked.

"I did not *tell* you?" the viscountess asked him. "I am so sorry."

"He was not listening," Hugo said.

"Perhaps he was not present when I announced it."

Lady Darleigh beamed at Flavian. "Miss Debbins is going to play for us this evening, as well as anyone else of our number who can be persuaded to entertain the rest of us. She will be coming for dinner too. For once we will have an even number of ladies and gentlemen at the table."

Even numbers. Flavian did the calculations in his head, but they did not add up. Unless . . .

"Her sister will be coming too," Vincent said. "Mrs. Keeping. We are fond of her, are we not, Sophie, not least because she is the one who made it possible for us to become world-famous authors."

He chuckled, as did everyone else—Flavian included.

The devil, he was thinking. He had just resisted the temptation to stride off in the direction of the meadow and the daffodils. Yet he was to meet her again after all today. Here. She was coming to dinner.

Well, at least tonight she would not be surrounded by little trumpets of sunshine fallen from the sky.

And if he was not very careful, he was going to find himself penning sonnets after all. Shudderingly awful ones.

Little trumpets of sunshine, for the love of God.

But his headache suddenly seemed to have eased.

5

Agnes did not go back to the park, despite the facts that it was a lovely day and the daffodils would not bloom forever or even for much longer. She stayed home instead to wash her hair and dream up excuses for not going out to dinner. She could not do more than dream, however, for Dora looked as though she would snatch at the flimsiest excuse to stay at home with her.

Agnes wondered if *he* had gone back this morning and, if so, how he had felt to discover she was not there. He would probably have shrugged and forgotten her within moments. It must not be difficult for a man like him to find women to kiss whenever he pleased.

A man like him.

She knew nothing about him, apart from the fact that he had once been a military officer and must have been wounded severely enough to have to spend a few years in Cornwall at the home of the Duke of Stanbrook, recuperating. The only sign of any wound now was his slight stammer, and that might have nothing to do with the wars. Perhaps he had always had a speech impediment.

But—*a man like him.* He was extraordinarily handsome. More than that, though, he radiated a magnetic, almost overpowering masculinity. His hooded eyes and mobile eyebrow suggested that he was a rake. And his looks, his physique, his air of assured command would all make him a very successful one and probably a ruthless one.

Not that she could be sure of anything. She did not *know* him.

She donned her pale green silk when it was time to get ready, and remembered that it was what she had worn to the harvest ball. It could not be helped. It was her best evening gown, and nothing less would do for tonight. No one would remember anyway. *He* would not. And apart from Sophia and Dora, no one else among tonight's guests had seen her that night. She dressed her hair a little more severely than she would have liked. She ought not to have washed it today. It was always at its silkiest and least manageable on the first day.

Who would care what she looked like?

Dora looked positively pasty, and her dark hair was even more severe than her sister's.

"Sit down and let me do your hair again," Agnes said. Dealing with her sister's appearance and soothing her jitters helped calm her own discomfort and embarrassment until the carriage arrived from Middlebury, and it was time to go.

There were only ten people gathered in the drawing room when she and Dora were announced, and two of them were Sophia and Viscount Darleigh, with whom they were long familiar. Three of the others had come with them to the cottage yesterday. It really ought not to be an ordeal, then, to meet the others. Yet there seemed to be far more than just ten persons in the room, and it was hard to convince oneself that they were just people like anyone, despite the grandeur of their titles.

Really, of course, Agnes was forced to admit to herself, there was only one of the company she dreaded meeting, and he was no stranger.

The Duke of Stanbrook was a tall, elegant, austere-looking older gentleman with dark hair graying attractively at the temples. Sir Benedict Harper was lean and handsome—and seated in a wheeled chair. His wife, Lady Harper, was tall and shapely, very dark, and stunningly beautiful in a faintly foreign sort of way. The Earl of Berwick was a dark-haired young man who somehow remained good-looking despite the nasty scar that slashed across his face and slightly distorted one eye and one side of his mouth.

Agnes concentrated upon each introduction as well as smiling and nodding to Lady Barclay and Lord and Lady Trentham. It was almost as if she believed that, by doing so, she could avoid looking at the tenth person.

"And you have met Viscount Ponsonby, I believe," Sophia said as she finished the introductions. "Indeed I know that *you* have, Agnes. You danced with him at the harvest ball. Miss Debbins, were you introduced too at that time?"

"I was." Dora curtsied. "Good evening, my lord."

Agnes, beside her, inclined her head.

He smiled and held out his right hand for Dora's. "I understand you are to b-be our savior tonight, Miss Debbins," he said. "If you had not c-come to play for us, we would have been d-doomed to listen to Vincent scrape away at his v-violin all evening."

Dora set her hand in his and smiled back.

"Ah, but you must not forget, my lord," she said, "that his lordship has learned those scrapings from me. And I may wish to quarrel with your description of his playing."

His smile deepened, and Agnes felt an inexplicable indignation. He had set out to charm Dora and was succeeding. She looked far more relaxed than she had when they arrived.

"Ho," Lord Trentham said, "you had better be careful, Flave. There is none so fierce as a mother in defense of her chick or a music teacher in defense of her pupil."

"You coined that one on the spot, Hugo, admit it," the Earl of Berwick said. "It was a good one, though. Mrs. Keeping, you are a painter of some talent, or so Lady Darleigh informs us. In watercolors, is that, or in oils?"

Someone brought them drinks, and conversation flowed with surprising ease for the fifteen minutes or so before the butler came to the door to inform Sophia that dinner was served. But *of course* conversation flowed easily. These people were members of the *haute ton*. They were at ease in company and were adept at dispensing good manners and conversation. It would have taken them no time at all to sum up the visitors as they arrived, frightened and tongue-tied despite the fact that they were gentlewomen themselves, on the threshold of the drawing room.

Sophia had arranged the seating for dinner. Agnes found herself being led into the dining room on the very solid arm of Lord Trentham. She was seated halfway along the table, and he took his place beside her. Dora, she noticed, had been given the place of honor to the right of Viscount Darleigh at the head of the table. She had the Duke of Stanbrook on her other side. Poor Dora! She would appreciate the honor being paid her, yet it would surely terrify her too. Except that the duke had bent his head to say something to her, and she was smiling with genuine warmth.

Viscount Ponsonby took the place at Agnes's other side.

What wretched bad luck, she thought. It would have been bad enough to have had him sitting across from her, but at least then she would not have been expected to converse with him. He had Lady Harper on his other side.

"We are not usually quite so formal," Lord Trentham said, speaking low. "This is all in your honor and that of Miss Debbins."

"Well," she said, "it is good to feel important."

He looked a formidable gentleman. His shoulders were massive, his hair close-cropped, his face severe. As an officer he would have wielded a sword, but he would surely look more at home swinging an ax. But—a smile lurked in his eyes.

"I used to shake with terror," he told her, still speaking for her ears only. "I was born to a London merchant who just happened to have enough money to purchase a pair of colors for me when I insisted that I wanted to be a soldier."

"Oh." She looked at him with interest. "But your title?"

She would swear he almost blushed.

"That was just daft," he told her. "Three hundred dead men deserved it more than I did, but the Prince of Wales waxed sentimental over me. It sounds impressive, though, wouldn't you say? *Lord* Trentham?"

"I do believe," she said, "there is a story lurking behind that . . . daftness, my lord, but you look as if you would be embarrassed to tell it. Is Lady Trentham also of the merchant class?"

"Gwendoline?" he said. "Good God, no—pardon my language. She was Lady Muir, widow of a viscount, when I met her at Penderris last year. And she is the daughter and sister of Earls of Kilbourne. If you prick her finger, she bleeds blue. Yet she chose me. Silly of her, would you not say?"

Oh, goodness, Agnes liked him. And after a few more

minutes she realized what he was up to. He did not, perhaps, have the sort of polished conversation the other gentlemen had to set ladies at their ease, but he had found another way. If *she* was a bit uncomfortable, despite the fact that she was a lady born, he was saying, in so many words, how did she think *he* felt in similar situations, when he was a man of the middle classes?

Wise Lady Gwendoline, to have chosen him, Agnes thought. The lady herself, seated opposite and to their left, was absorbed in something Sir Benedict was telling her.

And then Lady Barclay at his other side touched his sleeve, and he turned his attention to her.

"Agnes," Lord Ponsonby said from her other side.

She turned toward him, startled, but he was not addressing her. He was making an observation.

"A f-formidable name," he said. "I am almost g-glad I was unable to keep our appointment."

She hardly knew where to start.

"Formidable? Agnes?" she said. "And did we *have* an appointment, my lord? If we did, I was unaware of it. I was not there anyway. I had more important things to do this morning."

"This morning? And *where* did you not go this m-morning?" he asked.

What an elementary blunder to have made. She attacked her fish with a vengeance.

"Why formidable?" she asked when she became aware that he was still looking at her, his knife and fork suspended above his plate. "Agnes is a perfectly decent name."

"If you were Laura," he said, "or Sarah, or even M-Mary, I would scheme to kiss you again. They are soft, biddable names. But Agnes suggests firmness of character and a stinging palm across the ch-cheek of any man audacious enough to steal a k-kiss for the second time, when she can be presumed to be on her guard. Yes, I am *almost* glad I was unable to m-meet you. Were you r-really not there? Because I might be? But the daffodils will not bloom forever."

"It had nothing whatsoever to do with you," she said. "I had other things to do."

"More important than your painting?" he asked. "More important than m-me?"

Oh, good heavens, they were at the dinner table. Anyone might overhear snatches of their conversation at any moment, though it was doubtful. And how had she got embroiled in this? She was not his flirt and had no intention of alleviating his boredom for the next two and a half weeks by becoming one.

"More important than me, then," he said with an exaggerated sigh when she did not answer. "Or should that be *I*? More important than *I*. One feels very p-pedantic sometimes when one insists upon using correct g-grammar, would you not agree, Mrs. Keeping? *Who is there? It is I.* It sounds mildly absurd."

She did not look at him. But she did smile at her plate and then laugh.

"Ah," he said, "that is better. Now I know how to coax a l-laugh out of you. I merely have to speak correct grammar."

She picked up her glass of wine and turned toward him.

"Are you feeling less savage this evening?" she asked him.

His eyes went still, and she wished she had not reminded him that he had said that yesterday morning.

"I expect to be soothed by music," he said. "Is your s-sister as talented as Vincent claims?"

"She is," Agnes told him. "But you may judge for yourself later. Do you like music?"

"When it is well performed," he said. "V-Vincent performs well, though I like to tease him to the contrary. We do t-tease one another, you know. It is one of the endearing aspects of true friendship."

Sometimes she felt that he was not as shallow as his almost habitual expression seemed to indicate. She remembered having the same thought during the ball. He was not, she thought with an inward shiver, a man one would be comfortable to know.

"He sometimes p-plays a wrong note," he said, "and he often p-plays more slowly than he ought. But he plays with his eyes wide-open, Mrs. Keeping, and that is what m-matters. That is *all* that really matters, would you not agree?"

And often he spoke in riddles. He would judge her, she sensed, according to how well she was able to interpret them.

"With the eyes of his soul?" she said. "And you are not speaking just about Lord Darleigh or just about the playing of music, are you?"

But his eyes were mocking again.

"You have become too p-profound for me, Mrs. Keeping," he said. "You are turning philosophical. It is an alarming trait in a l-lady."

And he had the effrontery to shudder slightly.

Lord Trentham, she saw, had finished talking with Lady Barclay, at least for the moment. Agnes turned her shoulders and asked him whether he lived in London all year.

Agnes, Flavian thought as they made their way to the music room from the dining room and he watched her talking to Hugo, her arm through his. One could not imagine reciting a sonnet to the delicately arched eyebrow of sweet Agnes, could one? Or weeping over the immortal tragedy of *Romeo and Agnes*. Parents really ought to be more careful when naming their children.

He remained on his feet after seating Lady Harper close to the pianoforte. He clasped his hands behind his back as Vincent played his violin—a lilting folk tune. Vince really had improved—there was more vibrato in his playing than there had been last year—though how he could have learned to play at all when he was blind, who knew? It was a triumph of the human spirit that he had done it. Flavian did not join in the applause that succeeded the piece. Instead he beamed fondly at his friend, forgetting for the moment that Vince could not see him. One *did* tend to forget at times.

The cat purred rather loudly when the applause died down, and there was general laughter.

"I absolutely refrain from commenting," Flavian said.

Lady Harper played the pianoforte for a few minutes, though she protested that she had only recently resumed playing after a lapse of many years. Then she played and sang a Welsh song—in Welsh. She had a fine mezzo-soprano voice, and somehow made one almost yearn for the hills and mists of Wales. Almost.

Now, *there* was a woman, Flavian thought, about whom one might weave romantic and erotic fantasies if she did not happen to be the wife of a dearest friend—and if one felt anything more for her than a purely aesthetic appreciation.

Imogen and Ralph surprised everyone by singing a duet to Lady Trentham's accompaniment. Flavian did not need to tease them afterward—everyone else did it for him. Lady Trentham then played alone and with practiced skill, while Hugo beamed like an idiot and looked fit to burst with pride.

Vincent played on the harp, and Flavian strolled closer to frown in amazement over the fact that he could distinguish so many strings from one another when he could not even see them.

And then it was Miss Debbins's turn to play, and Flavian had no further excuse to prowl, for she would surely play for longer than a few minutes. He really ought to have taken a seat earlier. The choice left to him now was to squeeze between George and Ralph on the sofa, which would have looked a trifle peculiar and might have annoyed the cat, currently curled up on the middle cushion—or to sit beside Mrs. Keeping on a love seat a little farther removed from the pianoforte.

He chose not to annoy the cat.

He wondered whether she had told the truth about not going to the meadow this morning, and then realized how conceited it was of him to imagine that perhaps she had gone there and been so disappointed not to find him that she had pretended she had not gone at all.

He had very possibly given her an eternal disgust of him when he kissed her. She had probably not been kissed by any man other than her husband until then. Undoubtedly she had not, in fact. She had *virtuous woman* written all over her in invisible ink.

"The serious entertainment is to begin, then?" he said as Miss Debbins seated herself at the harp.

"The implication being that the other performances were trivial?" she said.

He grasped the handle of his quizzing glass and half raised it.

"You are in a combative mood, Mrs. Keeping," he said. "But I would g-guess none of those who have already played or sung would care to f-follow Miss Debbins."

"You do have a point there," she conceded.

She was wearing the same gown she had worn to the harvest ball. Now, how the devil had he remembered that? It was hardly an outstanding item of fashion, though it was pretty enough. The light from one of the candles was sparkling off the silver embroidery at the hem, as he remembered its doing on that occasion.

And then he lowered his glass and gaped. At least, that was how he felt inwardly, even if it did not show on his face. For suddenly music poured and rippled and surged about them and did a number of other startling things that words could not begin to describe. And it all came from one harp and the fingers of one woman. After a minute or two Flavian raised his quizzing glass again all the way to his eye and looked through it at the instrument, at the strings, and at the hands of the woman who played them. How was it possible . . .

The applause at the end of the piece was more than polite, and Miss Debbins was begged to play again before moving to the pianoforte. When she did go there, George jumped to his feet just like an underling to position the bench for her.

"And do you p-play, Mrs. Keeping?" Flavian asked while her sister prepared herself at the keyboard.

"Hardly at all."

"But you paint," he said. "Are you talented? Lady Darleigh s-says you are."

"She is kind," Mrs. Keeping told him. "*She* is talented. Have you seen her caricatures? And her story illustrations? I paint well enough for my own pleasure and poorly enough that I always dream of that one perfect painting."

"I s-suppose even Michelangelo and Rembrandt did

that," he said. "Perhaps Michelangelo sculpted the *Pietà* and then stood back and wondered if he would ever sculpt something that was really worth doing. I shall have to s-see your work to judge how w-well you measure up to the masters."

"Indeed?" There was a world of disdain in her voice.

"Do you keep them under lock and key?" he asked.

"No," she said, "but I choose who sees them."

"And I am not to be included in that n-number?"

"I very much doubt it," she said.

An excellent setdown. He looked at her with appreciation.

"Why?"

Her eyes turned his way, and he smiled slowly.

She was spared the need to answer him. Miss Debbins had begun to play something by Handel.

She played for longer than half an hour, though she tried to rise from her place at the end of each piece. No one was willing to let her go. And she did indeed display a quite extraordinary talent. One would not really have expected it. She must be a good ten years older than her sister, perhaps more. She was smaller and plainer. She looked quite unremarkable—until she set her fingers to a musical instrument.

"How easy it is to dismiss the outer packaging without an inkling that one is thereby missing the precious beauty within." His thoughts had acquired sound, and Flavian realized with acute embarrassment that he had spoken aloud.

"Yes." And Mrs. Keeping had heard him.

The recital was at an end, and a number of his friends were clustered about Miss Debbins at the pianoforte. Lady Darleigh excused herself after a minute or two in order to go up to the nursery—Flavian suspected that she was unfashionable enough not to have engaged a wet nurse. Lady Trentham asked if she might accompany her, and the two ladies went off together. Vincent announced that tea would be served in the drawing room if everyone would care to remove there. Ralph was running his fingers silently over the harp strings. George was offering his arm to Miss Debbins and informing her that she must be very ready for her tea. Ben, who had not brought his wheeled chair into the music room, was hoisting himself slowly to his feet between his canes, and Lady Harper was smiling over him and making some remark that was lost in the hubbub of voices.

"Mrs. Keeping." Flavian got to his feet and offered his arm. "Allow me."

He had the feeling she had been sitting very quietly where she was, in the hope that he would wander away and forget about her. Maybe *that* was part of the attraction, was it? That she had never put herself forward to attract his notice? Other women did—except the ones who knew him or knew *of* him, though even some of the latter still pursued him. For some women there was an irresistible fascination about a dangerous man, though his reputation exceeded reality these days. At least he hoped it did.

"Thank you."

She got to her feet and took his arm, the mere tips of her fingers touching the inner side of his sleeve. She really was rather tall. Perhaps that was why he had enjoyed dancing with her. She smelled of soap. Not perfume. Nothing either strong or expensive. Just soap. It occurred to him almost as a surprise that he would very much like to bed her.

He never thought of beds and *ladies* in the same context. And he had better banish the thought now. Which was a pity, for he would not even be able to indulge in a mild flirtation with her if there was any danger that it might lead to bed.

They were very sensible thoughts he was having and in no way explained why, when they entered the great hall from the west wing, he did not turn with her toward the staircase up to the drawing room. Instead he took a candle and its holder from a table, lit the candle from one that was already burning in a wall sconce, nodded to a footman who was on duty there, and was admitted to the east wing of the house.

Most surprising, perhaps, was the fact that Mrs. Keeping went with him without a murmur of protest.

The east wing, equal in size and length to the west wing, consisted almost entirely of the state apartments. They had been ablaze with light and splendor for the harvest ball back in October. They were dark now and echoed hollowly with their footfalls. They were also rather chilly.

And what the devil had brought him here?

"One tends to s-sit for too long in the evenings," he said.

"And it is too early in the year to walk outside much after dinner," she said.

Ah, they were agreed, then, were they, that they were merely seeking a bit of exercise after sitting so long listening to music? How long *had* they sat? An hour? Less for him.

"I must not stroll here for too long, however," she added when he did not leap into the conversational gap. "Dora will believe I have abandoned her."

"I believe M-Miss Debbins is being showered with attention," he told her. "And deservedly s-so. She will not miss a mere s-sister."

"But a mere sister may miss *her*," she said.

"You think I have b-brought you here for d-dalliance?" he asked.

"Have you?" Her voice was soft.

No one admitted to playing a game of dalliance. Well, almost no one.

"I have, Mrs. Keeping," he admitted. "In the ballroom where I first set eyes upon you. I have c-come to w-waltz with you again. To kiss you—again."

She did not haul on his arm and demand to be returned to her sister's side immediately if not sooner.

"I suppose we may see as much of the ballroom as will be visible in the light of a single candle," she said. "We can hardly waltz—there is no music."

"Ah," he said, "we will have to settle for the kiss, then."

"However," she said, speaking deliberately over his last words, "I can hold a tune tolerably well, even if no one in his right mind would think of inviting me to sing a solo before an audience."

He slanted a smile in her direction, but she was gazing straight ahead.

The ballroom was vast and empty, and indeed the light of the single candle did not penetrate very far into its darkness. It was cold. It was about as unromantic a setting as he could possibly have chosen for seduction, if that indeed was what his intention had been in coming here.

He set down the candleholder on an ornate table just inside the tall double doors.

"Ma'am," he said, making her an elegant leg and a flourishing bow, "may I have the pleasure?"

She curtsied with deep grace and placed her fingertips on his wrist.

"The pleasure is all mine, my lord," she told him.

And he clasped her in waltz position, holding her the correct distance from his body, and looked inquiringly at her. She thought a moment, a frown of concentration creasing her brow, and then hummed and finally la-la-

la'd the very waltz tune to which they had danced all those months ago. He twirled her out onto the empty floor, weaving in and out of the shadows cast by the candle. He was aware of its feeble light twinkling off the silver embroidery on the edges of her sleeves.

She was breathless after a couple of minutes. The music faltered and then stopped. But he danced with her a full minute longer, the music and the rhythm inside his body and hers. He could hear their breath, the sound of their shoes on the floor, in rhythm with each other, and the swish of silk about her legs.

In the four years since he had left Penderris, he had had a number of sexual partners, all of whom had given him great satisfaction. He had employed no long-term mistresses. He had occasionally flirted with ladies of the *ton*, always with those old enough to know the game. He had bedded none of them, even those who had indicated a willingness, even an eagerness, to be bedded. He rarely kissed.

Mrs. Agnes Keeping did not fit into any known category, a thought that both rattled and excited him.

When they stopped dancing, he could not think of a blessed thing to say, and it did not occur to him to let her go. He stood with one hand behind her waist, the other clasping one of hers. And he looked down at her until she lowered her head and brushed an invisible speck from the bosom of her gown with the hand that had been resting on his shoulder. She replaced her hand and looked up at him.

He kissed her, holding her for the moment in waltz position, though his hand at her waist gradually tightened and drew her against him.

Her hand squeezed his almost painfully tightly. Her lips were trembling.

Easy, he told himself. Easy. She was a widow of undoubted gentility and virtue. She was Viscountess Darleigh's closest friend. They were in Vincent's house.

But he released her hand in order to wrap both arms about her and deepen the kiss. She twined one arm about his shoulders and spread her other hand over the back of his head.

And the idiot woman kissed him back.

But the thing was that she kissed him with obvious pleasure, even desire, but with no real *passion*. Except that surely, oh, surely, he felt it throbbing below the surface of the enjoyment she allowed herself. There was control in her abandonment—if that was not a contradiction in terms.

What if she lost that control?

He could make it happen.

The desire to do just that smoldered within him as he explored her mouth with his tongue, moved his hands along the curve of her spine, even for a moment cupped her buttocks in his hands and fitted her to his groin.

He could unleash the passion no one had uncovered before in her life—not even her dullard of a husband. The passion she probably did not even know was lurking within.

He could. . . .

He lifted his head and returned his hands to her waist.

"D-did someone say s-something about tea in the drawing room?" he asked her.

"Viscount Darleigh did," she said. "But I believe you took a wrong turn in the hall, my lord."

"Ah, careless of me." He released his hold on her and retrieved the candle from the table. He offered his arm. "Shall we retrace our steps and s-see if there is anything left in the t-teapot?"

"That would be a good idea."

And he wanted her.

The devil!

Forget about dalliance and flirtation. Forget about virtuous widows and genteel respectability.

He wanted her.

Almost, he thought, alarming himself to no inconsiderable degree, he *needed* her.

And if *that* was not a thought to make a man want to run a hundred miles without pausing for breath, he did not know what was.

Especially a man who was savage. And dangerous.

6

Agnes avoided Middlebury, both the house and the park, for three days after the musical evening. It was a decision made easy for two of those days by the fact that it rained.

Middlebury Park came to the cottage, however, in the form of two visits—one from Sophia, Lady Trentham, and Lady Harper the first day, and one from the Duke of Stanbrook and the Earl of Berwick on the third. Sophia brought the baby with her, and he was very much the focus of attention during the visit, as babies almost always were. Both groups came to thank them for coming to dine and to commend Dora on the superiority of her playing. The duke expressed the polite hope that they would hear her again before their visit was at an end.

On the morning of the fourth day, the sun was shining again, though it had to contend with some high clouds, and Dora set off on foot to give the viscount his regular music lesson. Agnes stood in their small front garden to wave her on her way. Often she went with her sister and spent an hour with Sophia while the lesson was in progress, but she would not go this week despite Sophia's assurances just three days ago that she would be very welcome anytime and must not stay away on account of the visitors.

There were horses approaching along the street—four of them. Their riders paused to greet Dora. Agnes would have ducked back into the house, but she feared she had already been seen and it would seem impolite not to wait to bid them a good morning as they passed. And then one of them detached himself from the group and rode ahead and toward her.

Lord Ponsonby.

Agnes clasped her hands at her waist and tried to look cool and unconcerned or at least as though she had not spent far too long during the past four nights—oh, and the days too—reliving that waltz and that kiss. She was like a schoolgirl dizzy with a romantic infatuation, and she could not seem to summon the resolve to shake off the foolishness.

"Ma'am." He touched the brim of his tall hat with his whip and looked down at her with eyes that seemed to burn into her own—foolish fancy. Or perhaps not. Once again she observed that he was very obviously a practiced flirt.

"My lord." She inclined her head to him and clasped her hands more tightly until his eyes dipped to observe them.

"You are not p-painting the daffodils today?" he asked.

"I thought I might later," she told him. It really did bother her that she might miss them at their best and would have to wait a whole year before they bloomed again.

That was the extent of their conversation. He was joined in the roadway by his three fellow riders, all of whom bade her a cheerful good-morning before they rode on. They were going to Gloucester, the duke informed Agnes, to have a look at the cathedral.

It was a fair distance away. Even if they spent no longer than an hour there, they could not possibly be back before late afternoon. Here was her opportunity, then. She would go and paint.

Usually there was joy and serenity in the very thought, for she did most of her painting out of doors, and her subjects were almost always the wildflowers that grew in the hedgerows and meadows beyond the village. While she painted, she could forget her lingering sadness over the end of her all-too-brief marriage, the essential tedium of her days, the loneliness she tried to hide even from herself, the sense that life was passing her by—as it was, of course, for thousands of women like her. She was not unique in that way. She must never give in to the dreadful affliction of self-pity.

There was no particular serenity today, however, as she set off with her easel and her supplies. There was only a determination to quell her whirling emotions and live her life as she normally did, so that in two weeks' time, when the guests had left Middlebury Park, she would not fancy that she had been left behind with a broken heart.

Being in love was not at all a pleasant thing—except perhaps when one relived a certain waltz without music and a certain kiss that had seemed shockingly lascivious at the time but probably had not been by any worldly standards. One could not live forever, though, upon memories and dreams. One could not forever ignore the fact that one was alone and that perhaps one would be alone for the rest of one's life.

She strode off in the direction of the far side of the park.

Flavian did not go all the way to Gloucester. After half an hour or so, he fancied his horse was favoring its right foreleg. Ralph hopped down from his saddle, uninvited, to take a look, making it necessary for Flavian to get down and have a look too. There was nothing obviously wrong, and Imogen, who had been riding a little behind them, remarked that she had not noticed the horse limping. But Flavian declared himself afraid to risk riding farther from home and perhaps laming the horse altogether. He would go back and get Vincent's head groom to examine that leg just to make sure.

He would not hear of everyone else's turning back with him. No, no, they must continue on their way and enjoy Gloucester.

Ralph gave him a hard look before riding on with the others, but he said nothing. Ralph was the only one who had remarked upon his absence with Mrs. Keeping a few evenings ago.

"Got lost between the music room and the drawing room, did you, Flave?" he had asked.

Flavian had raised his quizzing glass.

"Quite so, old chap," he had said. "I shall h-have to ask the viscountess for a ball of yarn to unwind so that I can f-find my way from room to room."

"Or you could ask Vince for a loan of his dog," Ralph had said. "Though it is said three is a crowd."

Flavian had put his glass all the way to his eye to survey his friend through it, but Ralph had just grinned.

He rode slowly back to Middlebury. Last night the conversation had deepened when Ralph had told them about the letter he had received earlier in the day. Damned letters! It was from Miss Courtney, the sister of one of Ralph's three friends who had been killed moments before he himself was severely wounded on the battlefield in Spain. It was not proper for a single young lady to write to a single gentleman, but she had done so periodically ever since her brother's death, claiming the privilege of a sort of honorary sister. Now, at the rather advanced age of twenty-two, she was to marry a prosperous, well-connected clergyman from somewhere near the Scottish border.

"But she still has a *tendre* for you, Ralph?" Ben had asked.

"Probably not," Ralph had said, "else she would not be marrying Reverend Whatshisname, would she?"

But they all knew she had had a *tendre* for Ralph when he was still no more than a lad and she was still in the schoolroom. And that she had worshipped her only brother and turned to Ralph in the desperation of her grief, writing to him at Penderris Hall, seeking him out in London after he had gone back there. He had not answered most of her letters, pleading ill health in the few brief notes he had written, and he had avoided her whenever he could. He had even gone to the extent of excusing himself at one ball to fetch her a glass of lemonade and then leaving her thirsty by walking right out of the house and quitting London the next day.

"You feel guilty," George had said last night, "for not having married her yourself long since."

Guilt again! Nothing but damned guilt. Did life exist without it for some people? Flavian wondered.

"They were inordinately fond of each other," Ralph had explained. "Max and Miss Courtney, that is. There were just the two of them. If I had *really* been Max's friend, as I always professed to be, I would have looked after his sister, would I not? It is what he would have expected of me."

"Even to the extent of marrying her?" Imogen had said. "Surely he would not have wished the sister he loved so dearly to be married for duty alone, Ralph. And that is what it would have been on your part. She would have known it, if not at first, then eventually. And she would have been unhappy. You would have done her no lasting favor."

"I might at least," he had said, "have shown her some compassion, some affection, some . . . *God damn it all to hell,* I used to be able to feel such fine emotions. Sorry for the language, Imogen."

Ralph had been claiming for years that the worst of his many injuries had been the death of his emotions. He was wrong, of course. He felt guilt and sorrow. Clearly, though, there was a great chunk of his emotional life missing that only he could know about.

"One day you will feel love again, Ralph," Hugo had told him. "Have patience with yourself."

"As spoken by the world's g-greatest lover," Flavian had said, raising both an eyebrow and his quizzing glass in Hugo's direction and winning for himself one of Hugo's most ferocious scowls in return.

"Ralph already feels love," Vincent had said. "He loves *us*."

And that had brought tears to Ralph's eyes.

He and three longtime friends had ridden off to war at the age of seventeen with glorious ideals and even more glorious visions of brave deeds of honor to be accomplished in military combat. A short while later, three of them had been blown into a red shower of blood and guts and brains in an ill-conceived cavalry charge that had been met with the great guns of the French army. Ralph had watched in helpless horror before he too was felled.

"It sounds like a decent marriage Miss Courtney is making," George had said. "I daresay she will be happy."

Flavian had not mentioned his own letter from Marianne, his sister. She and her husband and their children were at Candlebury, she had explained, and would remain there over Easter before proceeding to London for the Season. Velma had arrived at Farthings Hall. Had he heard? Marianne was going to call there with their mother. Did Flavian intend coming there after he left Middlebury Park? She sincerely hoped so. The children would be ecstatic to see him, as their uncle had been their favorite person in the world since he took them to the Tower of London last year and then to Gunter's for ices.

Flavian was not fooled by the brief, almost offhand mention of Velma. It was as obvious to him as the nose on his face when he crossed his eyes that his family and hers were hoping to rekindle the grand love story that had ended in tragedy after he had got knocked from his horse in battle and left his mind on the field when he was carried off it, and Velma and Len had consoled themselves by marrying each other. How fortunate for such hopes that Len had died a scant seven years later. It had been very obliging of him.

Velma had married Len because he, Flavian, was incapacitated, dead for all intents and purposes even though he was still alive in body. No one had expected him to recover, even the physician who came at regular intervals to shake his head and cluck his tongue and look grave and learned. They had all said so in his hearing, and whereas he did not understand even half of what people were saying, what he *did* understand was almost invariably the things he would rather not have heard. He was mad, his mind gone forever. Someone was going to have to *do* something about it one of these days instead of clinging to a hope that just was not realistic. Velma and Len had been the first to face up to reality. They had turned to each other in their mutually inconsolable grief and found some comfort in the fact that together they would be able to remember him as he had used to be.

That was the story that was always told within the

family, anyway. His mother, his sister, his aunts and uncles and cousins to the third and fourth remove trotted it out at every family gathering. It made an affecting story and always drew tears to more than one set of eyes. The poignant epilogue to it all, of course, had been the fact that he had more or less recovered his wits after all during his long stay at Penderris. It always reminded one of his aunts—bedamned if he could remember which one—of Juliet awaking from her drugged sleep just after Romeo killed himself, believing her dead.

But now Len was dead. It was no wonder there were stirrings of hope among a certain contingent for a happily-ever-after at long last.

Flavian, however, had never forgiven either one of them.

He had still been unable to speak with any clarity or coherence when Velma had come to tell him less than two months after he had been brought home that the notice of the end of their engagement was to appear in the morning papers the next day, and that three days after that her new engagement announcement was to appear. He had not been able to speak, but he had understood well enough. She had patted his hand gently and wept copiously.

"You will never recover, Flavian," she had told him. "We both know that—at least, no, I do not suppose you do or ever will. Perhaps it is merciful that you know nothing—more merciful than what has happened to me. I love you. I will love you to my dying day. But I cannot remain bound to you. I need more of life, and I will try to find that with Leonard. I am sure if you understood and could speak to me, you would agree wholeheartedly. I am sure you would be happy for me—for us. You would be happy that I will spend my life with Leonard and he with me—two of the people who love you most dearly."

He had tried desperately to speak, but he had not got

beyond a few stuttered and meaningless sounds. Anyway, in those days his mind still had not recovered the concept of sentences. Even a recognizable word or two would not have sufficed if by some miracle he had spilled them out. And chances were they would have been the wrong words, something quite different from what his mind was intending, most probably some horrible blasphemies. His mother had sometimes begged him to stop swearing. But the nature of his injury was such that he lost control of his speech and of the words he used when he could utter a sound.

"I am sure you would give us your blessing," Velma had told him, stroking his hand. "I am certain you would, and so I have assured Leonard. We will always love you. *I* will always love you."

After she had gone, leaving behind the familiar scent of lilies of the valley, he had virtually destroyed the drawing room, where he had been lying on a daybed. It had taken two burly footmen and his valet to subdue him, and they had succeeded only because eventually there was nothing left to destroy.

Len had not come, even if he had intended to, and who could blame him? That had not been Flavian's first violent rage. More and more he found that the frustration caused by the consequences of his injury—his missing memories, his confused mind, his frozen tongue—manifested itself in an urge to physical violence he could not control.

Three days later, the very day the notice of the engagement of Miss Velma Frome to Leonard Burton, Earl of Hazeltine, appeared in all the London papers, George, Duke of Stanbrook, had come to call on Flavian at Arnott House.

Flavian had sworn foully at this new stranger and hurled a water glass at his head, missing by a yard but enjoying the satisfying sound of smashing glass. He had not been in the best of humors, having been locked in his bare room ever since the tirade following Velma's visit. It was amazing, looking back, that there had even been a glass to throw. Someone must have been careless.

But soon he had found himself traveling to Penderris Hall in Cornwall with the duke—without any restraints or hefty guards in the guise of servants. George had conversed quietly and sensibly with him—or, rather, he had delivered monologues, maybe a quarter of the contents of which Flavian had understood—through most of the long, tedious journey, before Flavian discovered that Penderris was not the lunatic asylum he was expecting but a hospital with other patients—other veterans of the war—as badly messed up as he.

And he had loved George with a passionate attachment ever since. A funny thing, love. It was not always, or even mostly, a sexual thing.

He did not go out to the meadow immediately after his return to Middlebury. Indeed, he tried to talk himself out of going at all. Ben and Vincent, the latter's music lesson at an end, were going to ride out to the racetrack with Martin Fisk, Vince's trusty valet. Flavian might have gone with them. But his horse was lame, was it not, though he suspected the groom would be hard put to discover how. Hugo and his wife were going to sit for a while at the highest point of the wilderness walk, from where they could expect the best view. Flavian was invited to go with them, but he agreed with Ralph that three could sometimes be a crowd, and those two had been wed for less than a year and were obviously still delighted with each other. Lady Harper and Lady Darleigh were going to pay a few social calls and would have been happy to have Flavian's escort. He told them that he had a few letters to write and really ought to get on with them before he lost the urge entirely. Then, of course, he felt obliged to write to his sister. He made it very clear that, when he left here, he was going straight to London. He even told her the date he expected to arrive there so that it would be clear that he intended to spend Easter, as he did every year, in London. It did not matter that Parliament would not sit or the Season swing to life until after the holiday. He liked London when it was relatively quiet. Being there was better than being at Candlebury, anyway—especially this year.

He had not been to Candlebury Abbey since four days before David died, two days before his and Velma's grand betrothal ball in London.

What on earth had possessed him to go through with that? At such a time? He frowned, rubbing the feather of the quill pen back and forth across his chin, trying to remember the exact sequence of events during that most eventful and ghastly of weeks. *Ghastly?* But the deeper he thought, the more a headache loomed and the closer he got to the sort of frustration that had once been a prelude to a bout of uncontrolled violence.

He got abruptly to his feet, toppling the desk chair with the backs of his knees, and set out for the far side of the park. She would have left long before now, even if she had gone there rather than somewhere else to paint, he told himself. He tried to convince himself that he hoped she *had* left, though why the deuce he would walk so far just for the exercise he did not try to explain to himself. It *was* a long walk.

He would not be good company.

This morning she had been wearing a simple cotton dress and no bonnet. Her hair had been caught back in a plain knot at her neck. Her posture had been prim and self-contained, her expression placid. He had tried to tell himself that she was quite without sexual appeal, that he must be very bored indeed out here in the country if he was weaving fantasies about a plain, prim, virtuous widow.

Except that he was *not* bored. He had all his closest friends here, and three weeks was never a long enough time to enjoy their company to the fullest. One of those weeks had already gone by while he blinked. This was always his favorite three weeks of the year, and the change of venue had not affected that.

Perhaps he would have convinced himself this morning if he had not noticed the one thing that had betrayed her. Her hands clasped at her waist were white-knuckled, suggesting that she was not as at ease, as unconcerned at seeing him, as she seemed at first glance.

Sometimes sexuality was more compelling when it was not overt.

He had wanted her again at that moment with a quite alarming stab of longing.

And she was not plain. Or prim. And if she was virtuous—and he did not doubt she was—she was also full to the brim of repressed sexuality.

When he arrived at the far side of the park, he found she had not gone elsewhere to paint and she had not left.

She was where she had been five days ago, though she was not flat on her back this time. She was on her knees before her easel, sitting on her heels, painting. He knew why she was so low. She had explained to him that she wanted to see the daffodils as they saw themselves. And though he stopped some distance behind her, one shoulder propped against the trunk of a tree, his arms folded across his chest, he could see that her painting showed mostly sky, with grass below and daffodils reaching up between the two, connecting them. He was not close enough to judge the quality of the painting—not that he was a connoisseur anyway.

She seemed absorbed. Certainly she had neither heard nor sensed his approach, as she had last time.

His eyes moved over the pleasing curve of her spine, over her rounded bottom, over the soles of her shoes, the toes pointing in, the heels out. She was wearing a sun bonnet. He could see nothing of her face.

He should turn and leave, though he knew he would not do so. Not after coming all this way and forfeiting the company of friends and a visit to Gloucester.

He was badly smitten, he thought with some surprise and not a little unease.

And then she dipped her brush in water and paint and slashed it violently across the painting from corner to corner and again from the opposite corner to corner, leaving a large, dark X on the paper. She tore it from the easel, crumpled it, and tossed it to the grass. It was only then that he noticed other similar balls of paper scattered about her.

She was having a bad day.

Surely it was nothing to do with him. Apart from that brief encounter this morning, she had not seen him for four days.

She set her brush in the water and pressed the heels of her hands to her eyes. He heard her sigh.

"Behold the frustrated artist," he said.

She did not whip her head about as he expected. For a moment she stayed as she was. Then she lowered her hands and turned her head slowly.

"Gloucester must have moved closer," she said.

"Gloucester and I were not fated to m-meet today, a-alas," he said. "My horse developed a limp."

"Did it?" She looked skeptical.

"Perhaps not," he said, uncrossing his arms, pushing his shoulder away from the tree, and strolling closer to her. "But it might have if I had gone f-farther."

"It is always best to be cautious," she said.

"Ah." He stopped walking. "Double meanings, Mrs. Keeping?"

"If so," she said, "I do not follow my own advice, do I? I meant to be here for an hour and have probably stayed for three or four. I might have guessed you would find a reason to return early."

She sounded bitter.

"When you told me you would paint later," he said softly, "were you inviting me to d-discover something amiss with my h-horse?"

"I do not know," she said with the ghost of a smile. "Was I? I have no experience with dalliance, Lord Ponsonby. And I have no wish to acquire any."

"Are you quite s-sure," he asked her, "that you are not deceiving yourself, Mrs. Keeping?"

She turned her head to look back across the meadow.

"I cannot paint," she told him. "The daffodils remain out there and I remain in here, and I can find no connection."

"And I am to b-blame?"

"No." She looked up at him. "No, you are not. I might have avoided that kiss here almost a week ago. I might have avoided going into the east wing with you the evening I was there with Dora, and, having gone there, I might have avoided dancing with you and kissing you again. You are a flirt, my lord, and probably a libertine, but I cannot pretend that you have forced anything upon me. No, you are *not* to blame."

He was rather bowled over by her assessment of him.

A flirt? Was he?

A libertine? *Was* he?

And he *was* to blame. He had destroyed her tranquility. He was good at destruction.

He came up beside her, looked at the blank page on

her easel, looked about at the discarded paintings, looked at the daffodils.

"Does your p-painting usually give you this much trouble?" he asked.

"No." She sighed again and got to her feet. "Perhaps because I am usually content to grasp the simple beauty of wildflowers. But there is something about daffodils that demands more. Perhaps because they suggest boldness and sunshine and music, something more than just themselves. Hope, perhaps? I do not pretend to be a great artist with a large vision."

She was looking at her hands, which were spread, palms down. She sounded on the verge of tears.

He took her hands in his. As he suspected, they were like twin blocks of ice. He placed them flat against his chest and spread his palms over the backs of them. She did not make any protest.

"Why did you t-tell me you were coming here?" he asked her.

Her eyebrows rose. "I did not," she protested. "You asked if I was not painting today, and I answered that I might later."

"You were telling me." He dipped his head closer to hers.

"You think I was asking you to join me here?" Her voice was full of indignation. Her cheeks had turned pink.

"Were you?" He murmured the words, almost against her mouth.

She frowned. "I do not *understand* dalliance, Lord Ponsonby."

"But you are d-drawn to it, Mrs. Keeping."

She drew a deep breath, held it, and looked directly into his eyes. He waited for the denial, mockery in his eyes.

"Yes."

The whole trouble seemed to be that she did not play by the rules—for the simple reason that she did not *know* the rules, perhaps. What did one do with a female who admitted to being drawn to dalliance?

Dally with her?

It did not help that he wanted her, that there was a niggling element of need in that wanting.

"If I go away," he asked her, "will you paint any more today?"

She shook her head. "I am distracted. I was distracted even before you came. Even before *I* came."

"Then p-put your things away," he said, "and leave them here. And w-walk with me."

7

She did everything with deliberate care, washing her brushes, drying them with a threadbare towel, covering her paints, emptying the water onto the grass, stuffing the balled-up sheets of paper into her bag, folding her easel, laying it flat, setting the bag on top of it. Then she stood and looked at him again.

He offered his arm, and she took it. He led her toward the cedar avenue, passing between the trunks of two trees and coming out halfway along the grassy walk. Cedars of Lebanon had none of the erect tidiness of limes or elms. The branches grew in all directions, some close to the ground, some almost meeting overhead. The avenue made one think of Gothic novels—not that he had read many of them. There was a summerhouse positioned centrally at the end of it.

He could smell soap again. Someone should bottle the scent of soap on her skin and make a fortune off it.

"Of what does dalliance consist?" she asked him.

He looked down at the poke of her bonnet and almost laughed. *Of this,* he almost said. *Of precisely this.*

"Risqué repartee, s-smoldering glances, kisses, touches," he said.

"No more than that?"

"Only if the two p-people concerned wish for more," he said.

"And do we?"

"I c-cannot answer for you, Mrs. Keeping."

"Do *you*?"

He laughed softly.

"I suppose that means yes," she said. "I do not know any risqué repartee. And I believe I would consider it silly if I did."

He felt almost suffocated with wanting her. No courtesan could ever be half so clever. Except that this was not deliberate on her part.

They moved in and out of sunlight in the avenue. His eyes were slightly dazzled. So was the rest of him. He felt strangely out of his element.

"There are no r-rules, actually," he said. "Or, if there are, I have not s-seen them."

"What do you want of me, Lord Ponsonby?" she asked.

"What do you want of *me,* Mrs. Keeping?"

"No," she said, "I asked first."

So she had.

"Your company," he said. He could not have come up with a lamer answer if he had had an hour to think of it.

"And that is all? You have the company of your friends, do you not?" she asked.

"I do."

"Then what do you want of me that they cannot give?"

"Does there have to be an answer?" he asked. "Can we not just w-walk here and enjoy the afternoon?"

"Yes." She sighed. "But I seem to be the last sort of woman a man like you would seek out for company."

"A flirt?" he said. "A l-libertine?"

"Well." There was a short silence. "Yes." And then she laughed. "*Are* you?"

"I think, Mrs. K-Keeping," he said, "you had better tell me what you mean by saying you are the last sort of woman I might seek out. And I think we had b-better sit inside the summerhouse while you do it. The air is rather chilly out here. Unless, that is, you are afraid I w-will p-pounce upon you in there and have my wicked way with you."

"I daresay," she said, "that if you intended to pounce, the outdoors would not deter you."

"Quite so," he agreed, opening the door so that she could precede him inside.

It was a pretty little structure, its walls almost entirely of glass. A leather-cushioned seat ran around the inside perimeter. Trees around the outside would offer shade from the hottest rays of the sun in summer but did not keep out the heat at any other season. It was pleasantly warm today.

"Tell m-me how you come to be living with your sister," he said after they had seated themselves on opposite sides of the bench, though even so their knees were not far from touching.

"My husband's entailed property passed to his younger brother," she told him. "And while he was kind enough to assure me I might continue living there, I did not think it fair since he is unmarried himself and would have felt constrained to live elsewhere. My father remarried the year before I wed, and his wife's mother and unmarried sister moved in after I left. I did not wish to return there. I went to stay with my brother in Shropshire for a while—he is a clergyman, but he has a family too, and I did not wish to stay forever. When Dora came to visit and suggested that I move here with her, I accepted gladly. She was in need of companionship, and I was in need of a home in which I did not feel I was intruding. And we have always been particularly fond of each other. The arrangement has worked well."

He was very glad he was not a woman. There were so few options.

"Does your stammer result from your war wounds?" she asked him.

He looked at her and half smiled. She sat with a straight back and her hands arranged neatly in her lap. Her feet were side by side together on the floor between them. Prim virtue could sometimes look inexplicably enticing.

"I am sorry," she said. "That was a very personal question. Please do not feel obliged to answer."

"It was a h-head wound," he told her. "Doubly so. I got shot through it and then f-fell off my horse on it before being r-ridden over. I should have been dead thrice over. For a long while I d-did not know where I was or who I was or w-what had happened. And when I did, I could not c-communicate with anyone outside my h-head. Sometimes everyone's words were a j-jumble, or it t-took overlong to work out what they m-meant. And then the w-words to r-reply to them would not come out, and when they did, they were not always the w-words I was thinking. And I had forgotten about s-sentences."

He did not mention the crashing headaches or the great memory gaps.

"Oh." She frowned in concern.

"Sometimes when the w-words would not come out," he said, "other things came out of me instead."

She raised her eyebrows.

"I was d-dangerous, Mrs. Keeping," he told her. "I did with my fists what I could not d-do with my mind or my voice. I was soon p-packed off to Cornwall and k-kept there for three years. Sometimes I still have what my family call t-tantrums."

She opened her mouth to speak, thought better of it, and closed it again.

"You would be well advised to stay away from me." He mocked her with his eyes, with his smile.

"Your friends do not fear you," she said.

"But I do not w-wish to bed any of my friends," he said. "Even Imogen."

Her cheeks turned a deeper pink.

"Someone cannot be both a friend and a lover?" she asked.

"Only in a m-marital relationship where there is love," he said.

"Is this why you warn me away from you, Lord Ponsonby?" she asked. "Not because you may turn violent but because you do not have either love or marriage in mind?"

"I w-will never have either of those to offer any woman," he told her.

"Never?"

"Happy endings can t-turn without warning to v-very b-bad endings," he said.

She paused at his words and looked steadily into his eyes, as if she saw something there. "Did you once believe in happy endings?" Her voice was very soft.

He felt suddenly as though he were looking at her down a long tunnel. *Had* he? It was strange that he could not remember. He must have believed in them, though, on that glittering night of the betrothal ball in London. He had abandoned his dying brother for it. For Velma.

His hands curled into tight fists on either side of him on the seat, and he saw her glance down at them.

"There is no such thing, Mrs. Keeping," he said,

spreading his fingers to curl lightly over the edge of the seat. "You know that as w-well as I."

"I ought not to have married William, then," she said, "because he would die? But we had five years of companionship. I do not regret marrying him."

"Companionship." He mocked her again. "But no p-passion."

"I believe passion is much overrated," she told him. "And perhaps companionship and contentment are much underrated by people who have not known them."

"People l-like me?"

"I think," she said, "you have known much unhappiness, Lord Ponsonby, and that it has made you cynical. *Personal* unhappiness unconnected with your injuries. And now you have persuaded yourself that passion is of greater importance than quiet contentment and committed love, because passion requires no real commitment but makes you feel alive when much has died in you since your life changed irrevocably."

Good Lord! He sucked in air that did not seem to be there in any abundance and forced his hands to remain relaxed. But his temper was suddenly close to snapping.

"And I think, m-ma'am," he retorted, "you are indulging in s-speculation upon s-something you know n-nothing of."

"I have made you angry," she said. "I am sorry. And you are quite right. I do not know you at all."

It would *not* snap. It took a great deal to make him lose control these days. He did not enjoy watching that madman who was himself destroy his outer world because he could not sort out his inner world. It was strange how there was always an inner watcher when the madman burst into action. Who was that man?

"Well, Mrs. Keeping," he said, looking lazily at her

and lowering his voice, "we might set *that* r-right anytime you w-want."

"By . . . *being* together?" she asked.

He folded his arms. "You have only to say the w-word."

She looked down at the hands in her lap and took her time about answering. She laughed softly.

"I keep expecting to wake up," she said, "to find this is all a bizarre dream. I do not have conversations like this. I do not spend time alone with gentlemen. I do not listen to propositions so improper that I really ought to crumple to the floor in a dead swoon."

"But it is all happening."

"I am twenty-six years old," she said, "and almost three years a widow. Perhaps at some time in the future, if too much time does not pass in the meanwhile, someone else will offer for me, though I do not know who in this neighborhood. Perhaps there is marriage, even motherhood, in my future. Or perhaps not. Perhaps my life will remain as it is now until I die. Perhaps I will never know . . . *passion*, as you call it. And perhaps I will regret that when I am older. Or perhaps, if I give in to temptation, I will regret *that*. We can never know, can we? We can never benefit today from the wisdom we will have gained tomorrow."

What he ought to do was get to his feet and hurry off back to the house and never return. If he had imagined a pleasant, mindless sort of dalliance with her, even perhaps a brief affair, he was beginning to realize that nothing would be simple and straightforward with Mrs. Agnes Keeping. He did not want to be her one chance at passion, her one experiment at breaking free of the dull mold of her life. Heaven help him. He did not want to leave her with regret that she had given in to the temptation to explore passion. He did not want to break her heart—*if* he had the power to do that.

This . . . tryst was not developing at all as he had imagined when he devised a way of coming here to find her.

Suddenly, and quite unfairly, he resented her. And this place and the change of venue this year. Nothing like this ever happened at Penderris.

He got abruptly to his feet and stood by the door, gazing along the length of the cedar avenue.

"You will paint tomorrow?" he asked her.

"I do not know."

And he did just what he had told himself he ought to do. He opened the door and stepped outside, stood undecided for a few moments, and then strode off down the avenue without her.

If he had turned back, he might have made love to her. And she would not have stopped him, idiot woman. At least he did not think she would.

Perhaps tomorrow . . .

And perhaps not.

He needed time to think.

Agnes worked at home for the next week. She painted the daffodils from memory, even though she really was almost sick of them, and she was pleased with her very first effort. Indeed she was quite sure it was the best work she had ever done. Surprisingly, she found herself painting them from above, as though she were the sun looking down on them. There was no sky in the painting, only grass and flowers.

Time crawled by when she was not painting, and sometimes even when she was. She could not see the Middlebury Park visitors leaving quickly enough. Perhaps her peace would be restored when they had gone away.

When *he* had gone away.

She was *never* again going to make the mistake of falling in love. It was an emotional state that was supposed to bring great happiness, even euphoria. She had felt almost none of either. Of course, poetry and literature in general were full of stories of tragic love lost or spurned. She ought to have taken more notice when she was reading. Except that caution would not have helped her. She had had no intention whatsoever of falling in love with Viscount Ponsonby, who was unsuitable and ineligible in almost every imaginable way. She missed William with a dull ache of longing for the plodding contentment of their life together.

Would Lord Ponsonby's leaving bring her peace?

Once in, when did one fall out of love? It had taken several weeks back in October—though it seemed the feeling had merely lain dormant instead of going away altogether. How long would it take this time? And when would it be gone forever?

And why had he let a whole week—no, eight days—go by without seeking her out? Every time she heard a horse on the street or a knock on the door, she held her breath and waited, hoping it was not him. Hoping it was.

And then, on the morning of the eighth day, Sophia sent Agnes a note apologizing abjectly for so neglecting her friend and begging both Agnes and Miss Debbins to come and take tea with her and the other two wives.

I have a new story with new illustrations to show you, she had written. *We told it to Thomas, and he gurgled. I showed him the pictures and he almost smiled.*

Agnes did smile as she folded the note. Thomas was not even two months old.

"We are invited to Middlebury for tea with Sophia and two of the lady guests," she told Dora when her sister had finished giving a music lesson to a twelve-year-old who had had the misfortune to be born with ten thumbs and an incurably prosaic soul—or so said Dora with growing exasperation almost every week. And with doting parents who were tone-deaf and determined to believe that their daughter was a prodigy.

"Oh, that will be delightful," Dora said, brightening. "And it will be good for you. You have been in the mopes lately."

"Oh, I have not," Agnes protested. She had been making a determined effort to appear cheerful.

Tea in the drawing room at Middlebury Park really was just for the three married ladies and their two guests. Lady Barclay had gone off somewhere with the other six members of the club, Sophia reported.

"I was afraid," she said, "that coming here this year instead of going to Penderris Hall as usual, and having three wives here too this time, would spoil things for them, but I do not believe it has."

"Ben told me last night when he finally came to bed," Lady Harper said with her slight trace of a Welsh accent, "that this gathering with his friends has been the very best part of his honeymoon so far. And then he had the grace to do some smart verbal scrambling to assure me that it is *entirely* because I am with him this year."

They all laughed.

Sophia read the new story aloud at the request of Lady Trentham, and the illustrations were passed from hand to hand so that they could all admire and chuckle over them.

"Bertha and Dan," Agnes said, "are my very favorite literary characters."

Sophia laughed gleefully. "You have very unsophisticated tastes, Agnes. Have you painted the daffodils yet? You said you were going to."

"I have," Agnes told her. "But they were very resistant to being captured in paint."

"Agnes has been in the dismals for that very reason, I think," Dora said. "But I have seen the finished painting and it is remarkably lovely."

Agnes smiled fondly at her. "You say that about all my paintings, Dora. You are quite indiscriminately biased."

"As all sisters ought to be," Lady Harper said. "I always wanted a sister."

And then, just when it was almost time to get up and take their leave, the others arrived home and came into the drawing room in a noisy body, bringing the outside world in with them, or so it seemed.

Tab, Sophia's cat, who had been curled at Dora's side, rose to his feet, arched his back, hissed at Lord Darleigh's dog, and settled back to dozing; Lord Darleigh smiled about him, just as though he could see them all; Sir Benedict Harper commented on the fact that he would not have believed the new racetrack was five miles long if he had not just propelled himself along almost a third of the length of it in his chair; the Duke of Stanbrook bowed to the newcomers and bade them a good afternoon; Lady Barclay accepted a cup of tea from Sophia's hands and sat down to converse with Dora; Lord Trentham set an arm briefly about his wife's waist and pecked her on the lips before frowning ferociously as if he hoped no one had noticed; the Earl of Berwick helped himself to an iced cake from the tea tray and made sounds of appreciation as he bit into it; and Viscount Ponsonby stood just inside the door, looking sleepy.

And Agnes hated him. No, she hated *herself*. For she was aware of no one else even half as much as she was of him.

"I believe we have all walked our feet down to stumps," the earl remarked. "We tried to bribe Ben out of his chair, but he was selfish and obstinate as always and would not budge." He winked at Lady Harper.

"Is that your newest book, Lady Darleigh?" the duke asked. "May we be permitted to see it?"

"It is brilliant," Lord Darleigh said as he felt the seat of his chair by the fireplace before lowering himself into it. "See for yourselves."

"Author, violinist, harpist, pianist," Lord Trentham said. "There will soon be no living with the lad."

"But only Sophie is called upon to do it," Lord Darleigh said, smiling sweetly.

"The illustrations are so very clever, Lady Darleigh," Lady Barclay said as she looked at them over the duke's shoulder. "I wonder who had the silly notion that children's books are not also for adults."

"There is a child in all of us, is there not, Imogen?" the earl asked.

"Yes, precisely, Ralph," she said, glancing up at him with a look of such raw longing in her eyes that Agnes felt jolted.

Viscount Ponsonby was the only one of them who had said nothing.

After a few minutes Dora got to her feet, and Agnes followed her lead.

"We must take our leave, Lady Darleigh," Dora said. "Thank you for inviting us. It has been delightful."

"It has," Agnes agreed. "Thank you, Sophia."

Lord Ponsonby was still standing squarely in the doorway, she noticed.

"I will give myself the pleasure of escorting you home, if I may," the Duke of Stanbrook said.

Dora looked at him in some surprise. "After your long walk, Your Grace?"

"It will be like dessert to a banquet," he assured her. "And the dessert is always the best part."

But he spoke with a twinkle in his eye and no suggestion of flirtatiousness. Dora, who was terrified of his titled magnificence, actually laughed.

"I'll come with you, George," Viscount Ponsonby announced in that languid way he had, almost as if he spoke on a sigh.

Inevitably, when they set off, they divided into two couples, and since the duke had offered Dora his arm even before they left the house, Agnes had little choice but to take Lord Ponsonby's.

"This was unnecessary," she said after a minute or so of silence. Dora and the duke, striding along and deep in conversation, had already outdistanced them.

"You are being ungracious, Mrs. K-Keeping," he said.

She was. Though she would have been happy not to have to endure this.

"Have you been b-back?" he asked her.

She did not need to ask what he meant or, rather, *where* he meant.

"No," she said. "I have painted at home. The weather has been chilly."

Had *he*? Gone back, that was. But she would not ask him.

They proceeded on their way in silence. She would not break it, and neither, it seemed, would he—until, that was, they came within sight of the gates. The duke and Dora had already turned onto the village street.

Viscount Ponsonby came to a sudden halt, and Agnes of necessity stopped beside him. He stared broodingly at the ground a little way ahead of them before turning his head and looking at her.

"I think, Mrs. Keeping," he said abruptly, "you had better marry me."

She was so shocked that her mind stopped functioning. She stared back at him, and thought began to return only as she watched the unusual openness of his countenance revert to the heavy-lidded, mocking-mouthed expression with which she was more familiar. Almost as if he had pulled a mask back into place.

"That was p-poorly done of me, by Jove," he said. "I ought at least to have g-gone down on one knee. And I ought to have l-looked s-soulful. *Did* I look soulful?"

"Lord Ponsonby," she asked foolishly, "did you just make me a marriage proposal?"

"It *was* poorly done," he said, wincing theatrically. "I did not even m-make myself clear. F-Forgive me. Yes, I asked you to m-marry me. Or, rather, I told you, which w-was not at all the thing. A man of my age ought to know better than to b-behave with such g-gaucherie. *Will* you m-marry me, Mrs. Keeping?"

He was stammering rather more than usual.

She slid her hand free of his arm and noticed for the first time the pallor of his face, the dark shadows beneath his eyes as though he had had a sleepless night or two.

"But why?" she asked.

"Why would you m-marry me?" He lifted one eyebrow. "Because I am h-handsome and charming and titled and w-wealthy and you have conceived a *t-tendre* for me, perhaps?"

She tutted. "Why do *you* wish to marry *me*?"

He pursed his lips, and his eyes mocked her.

"Because you are a virtuous woman, Mrs. Keeping," he said, "and marrying you may be the only w-way I can b-bed you."

She felt her cheeks grow hot.

"How absolutely absurd," she said.

"That you are virtuous?" he asked. "Or that I want to t-take you to bed?"

She clasped her hands, raised them to her mouth, and stared at the ground before her feet.

"What is this all about?" She looked up at him then and kept her eyes steady on him. "And, no, you will not get away with looking at me like that. Or with making a foolish reply, like saying you wish to . . . to *bed* me. Or with making me a marriage offer as though it were some sort of jest and then scurrying away to hide behind your mask of mockery and cynicism. That is *insulting*. Did you intend to insult me? *Do* you intend it?"

He had grown paler.

"I did not mean to offer you an insult," he said stiffly. "I b-beg your p-pardon, m-ma'am, if it is insulting to b-be offered the p-position of V-Viscountess P-Ponsonby. I b-beg your p-p-pardon."

"Oh," she cried, "you are impossible. You have deliberately misunderstood me."

But he was standing as straight as the military officer he had once been, his booted feet slightly apart, his hands clasped behind his back, his eyes hooded, his mouth in a straight line. He looked like a stranger.

"I am not insulted that you wish to marry me," she said, "only that you will not tell me why. Why *should* you wish to marry me? I am a twenty-six-year-old widow with neither noble birth nor fortune to recommend me and no extraordinary beauty either. You scarcely know me or I you. The last time we met, you assured me that you would never offer marriage to any woman. Yet today, suddenly, after making no attempt to see me for a week, you blurt out a proposal, or what I take to be a proposal—*I think you had better marry me.*"

His posture relaxed slightly.

"I ought to have written a s-speech and m-memorized it," he said and smiled at her with such dazzling charm that she almost took a step back. "Though my m-memory has been lamentable since I was knocked on the h-head.

I might have forgotten it. I m-might even have forgotten that I meant to propose."

She stood her ground.

"What you will surely remember tonight, Lord Ponsonby," she said, "is that you escaped a nasty fate this afternoon."

He tipped his head slightly to one side.

"*You* would be a n-nasty fate, Mrs. Keeping?"

Oh, she would not succumb to his charm.

"My sister and His Grace will be wondering where on earth we are," she said.

Lord Ponsonby offered his arm and, after a small hesitation, she took it.

"I am curious," she said as they turned onto the street. "When exactly did you conceive the idea of marrying me?"

All the mockery was firmly back in his face.

"Perhaps when I was born," he said. "P-Perhaps the idea of you, the p-possibility of you, was there with my v-very first intake of breath."

Despite herself, she laughed.

"You think I exaggerate," he said.

"I do."

"I shall go back to M-Middlebury," he said, "and write that s-speech—if I remember. I may even compose it in blank verse. You will p-permit me, if you will, to call on you in the m-morning. *If* I remember."

Dora and the Duke of Stanbrook were standing outside the garden gate, looking their way. Although the street was deserted, Agnes guessed that more than one neighbor lurked behind more than one window curtain, watching. And she could not feel any indignation against them, for that was exactly what she and her sister had done on the day the guests arrived at Middlebury Park.

"Very well," she said, and there really was no time to say more.

The gentlemen bowed and took their leave, and Dora preceded Agnes into the cottage.

"How very kind it was of them to escort us home," Dora said as she removed her bonnet and handed it with a smile to the housekeeper, who offered to bring them tea. "No, thank you, Mrs. Henry. We have just had some. Unless Agnes wants more, that is."

Agnes shook her head and led the way into the sitting room.

"His Grace talked to me all the way home," Dora said, "just as if I were a person worth conversing with."

"You have recovered from your terror of him, then?" Agnes asked.

"Well, I suppose I have," Dora said, "though I am still in awe. I feel as dazzled as if I had met the king himself. I hope the viscount was as polite with you. I never quite trust that young man. I believe him to be a rogue—a handsome, charming rogue."

"The secret is not to take him at all seriously," Agnes said lightly, "and to let him know that one does not."

"Are not all the ladies delightful?" Dora said. "I *did* enjoy myself, Agnes. Did you?"

"I did," Agnes assured her. "And I think Sophia's illustrations get better and better."

"And the stories funnier," Dora agreed.

They chattered on aimlessly about their visit, while Agnes held a cushion to her bosom and wished she could escape to her room without her having done so being remarked upon by her sister.

What *on earth* had that been all about? He could not possibly want to marry her. Why had he asked her, then? And she could not possibly want to marry him. Not *really,* not beyond the realm of fantasy.

But how could she live on now, after he was gone, knowing that she might have married him even though it had been perfectly obvious that he had blurted out his proposal without any forethought whatsoever?

What had possessed him?

Would he come tomorrow, as he had said he would—*if* he remembered? What would he say? What would *she* say?

Oh, how was she to stop her heart from breaking?

8

They did not talk while they were still on the village street. After they had passed between the gates, George turned off the driveway without hesitation to thread his way among the trees. Flavian followed, but under protest.

"Have we not w-walked far enough this afternoon but m-must now take a long way home?" he complained.

George did not answer until the trees thinned out slightly and they could walk side by side.

"Do you want to talk about it?" he asked.

"About what?"

"Ah," George said. "You must remember to whom you are speaking, Flavian."

To George Crabbe, Duke of Stanbrook, who had once traveled all the way from Cornwall to London in order to fetch a raving, violent lunatic who had bumped his head in Spain and knocked everything out of it except the compulsion to hurt and destroy. Who had somehow, over the next three years, given each of his six main patients the impression that he spent all his time and care upon that one. Who had assured Flavian soon after his arrival at Penderris that there was no hurry, that there was all the time in the world, that when he was ready to share what was in his mind, there would be a listener, but that in the meanwhile violence was unnecessary as well as pointless—he was loved anyway just as he was. Who found a doctor patient and skilled enough to coax words out of Flavian at last, to provide strategies for relaxing and stringing words together into whole sentences, to help him deal with his headaches and his memory blanks as an alternative to simply panicking and lashing out.

George was the one who knew the six of them perhaps better than they knew themselves. Sometimes it was a disconcerting realization. It was also endlessly consoling.

But who knew George? Who offered *him* comfort and consolation for an only son killed in battle and a wife dead by her own hand? Were his recurring nightmares *all* that he suffered?

"L-letters," Flavian said abruptly as they came out of the trees close to the lake. "I w-wish they had not been invented."

"From your family?" George asked.

"Another one from Marianne," Flavian said. "It was not enough to write to t-tell me that she was going to Farthings to call on V-Velma. She then had to write again to inform me that she *had* called. And my m-mother had to write to give me her version of the s-same visit."

"They were all pleased to see one another, were they?" George asked.

"They were always t-terribly f-fond of her, you know," Flavian said. "She was always sweetness itself. And they thought I t-treated her badly, though they do concede I knew no better. I did treat her badly too. I threw the contents of a g-glass in her face once, just as I threw a whole glass at you. It was w-wine. And in her case I did not miss."

"You were very ill," George said.

"They s-supported her decision to b-break off with me and marry Len instead," Flavian said. "They seemed to think it was a f-fine thing for the two of them to do because he had always been so close to me—a man doing something n-noble for his best friend and all that. They thought it was all some sort of romantic t-tragedy. It is a pity Shakespeare was not still alive to wr-write about it. They wept oceans apiece over her at the time, and then they s-sent for you by s-special messenger when I behaved badly and reduced the drawing room to k-kindling."

"You were very ill," George said again. "And they did not know what to do for you or with you, Flavian. They had not stopped loving you. They heard I took in the most desperate cases, and they sent for me. They prayed I could perform a miracle. They did not stop loving you. But we have spoken of this many times before."

They had, and Flavian had come to believe it was true—to a certain degree.

"They want me to b-believe," he said, "that V-Velma loved me—all the time, without ceasing, even while she was m-married to Len. And that Len knew it and encouraged it and l-loved me too. It is all a b-bit distasteful, is it not? N-Nauseating, even? And s-surely not true? I h-hope it is not true."

"Is that what Lady Hazeltine told your mother and sister?" George asked. "Perhaps they thought it would comfort you to know that those two always remembered you with tenderness."

They were walking past the boathouse. Flavian alarmed himself and even made George jump when he slammed the edge of his fist against a sidewall, making it boom like a great gun and causing splinters of wood to shower off it.

"God damn it," he cried. "Does *no one* know *anything*?"

"Do you still love her?" George asked quietly into the

silence that ensued. Always quietly. He never rose to passionate outbursts.

Flavian picked a splinter out of the side of his hand and pressed his handkerchief to the little bubble of blood that appeared there.

"I just asked Mrs. Keeping to marry me," he said.

George did not exclaim in disbelief. It was virtually impossible to shock him.

"Because of your letters?" he asked.

"Because I w-want to marry her."

"And did she accept?"

"She w-will," Flavian said. "I f-forgot the roses and the bended knee this time. And I forgot to c-compose an affecting speech."

They strolled along beside the lake.

"I danced with her at Vince's h-harvest ball last autumn," Flavian explained. "And I have met her a few times back there." He jutted his chin in the direction of the trees on the other side of the lake. "There is a meadow, and it is full of d-daffodils at the moment. She was trying to paint them. I met her there."

"And the attraction is that she is very different from Lady Hazeltine, is it?" George asked.

Flavian stopped walking and looked out over the lake before closing his eyes.

"I can find peace with her," he said.

He had not planned the words. He did not *know* why he was drawn to Agnes Keeping. He had not thought beyond the obvious—that he wanted to bed her, though he could not really understand that either. She was very different from the females with whom he usually slaked his sexual appetites. Sexuality was not the first thing one noticed about her.

But why did he say he could find peace with her? He did not believe peace could be found in any woman. Or at all, in fact. Peace was not for this life, and he was not sure he believed in any other.

It had been stupid of him to ask her to marry him.

George stood beside him, a short distance away, silent. He always knew when to speak, when not to. What made him as he was? Had he always been thus? Or did it have something to do with his own sufferings?

Flavian laughed and listened to the harsh sound.

"P-Peace is the v-very *last* thing she would find with me," he said. "You had better w-warn her to refuse me, George."

"Has she not already done that?"

"When I ask again, I mean," Flavian explained. "With the roses and the b-bended knee and the flowery speech. Tomorrow."

"I like her," George said, "and Miss Debbins. They are unaffected ladies, living blameless lives."

"It is a terrible fate," Flavian said, "being a woman."

"It can be," George agreed. "But women tend to settle to something and somewhere better than we do. They are more inclined to accept their lot and make the best of it. They are less inclined than we are to flounder around wondering where we should go and what we should do next."

We, he had said. Not *you*. But George did not *flounder*, did he? And who would not be happy to accept the fate of being the Duke of Stanbrook? Or Viscount Ponsonby, for that matter.

"Do you love her?" George asked—the same question he had just asked about Velma.

"Love." Flavian laughed shortly. "What is love, George? No, don't answer. I am not so j-jaded that I don't know what love is. But what is r-romantic love? This being-in-love b-business? I was head over heels in love once, but f-fortunately I grew out of the feeling. Does that mean I did not love at all? *Love is not love which alters w-when it alteration finds.* Where the d-devil did I hear that? Is it from a poem? Did I quote it right? Who wrote it? When all guesses fail, choose Shakespeare. Am I right?"

"One of his sonnets," George said. "I did not ask if you were *in* love with Mrs. Keeping."

"You asked if I l-love her." Flavian turned his back on the lake and made for the path up to the house. The viscountess had had it constructed last year with a sturdy rail alongside it so that Vincent could walk to the lake alone whenever he chose. "I love Lady Darleigh."

George chuckled softly. "It would be hard not to," he said, "when one sees all she has done to make life easier for our beloved Vincent—and when one sees how very happy she has made him."

Flavian stopped, his hand on the rail.

"Do I love Mrs. Keeping enough to m-make life easier for her? Enough to make her happy? If I do, I suppose I m-must show it by never p-proposing to her again."

"Flavian." George's hand came to his shoulder and squeezed. "You do not destroy everything and everyone you love, you know. You love *us*—Ben and Hugo, Ralph and Vincent, Imogen and me. You have not destroyed any of us and never will. You have enriched our lives and caused *us* to love *you*."

Flavian blinked rapidly while his head was still turned away.

"I don't want to m-marry any of you, though," he said.

George squeezed his shoulder again before removing his hand.

"I would say no even if you asked," he said.

When people spoke of crying themselves to sleep, Agnes thought at some time around two o' clock the next morning, they surely lied. Her nose was so blocked that she had to breathe through her mouth. Her eyes were red and puffy. Her lips were swollen and dry and chapped. She was a mess. The last thing she could do was sleep.

And she was sick of herself.

Either say yes to that horrid man, she thought as she gazed at her image in the dressing table mirror by the flickering light of a single candle—she looked like something hovering above a graveyard on All Hallows' Eve. Either say yes—*if*, that was, he came tomorrow and asked again, which was far from certain—or say no.

It sounded like a simple choice.

What *on earth* was she doing, weeping her heart out for such a muddle-headed *rake*? But rakes did not blurt out marriage proposals to faded widows—well, fad*ing*, anyway. And rakes did not walk around in the afternoon with pale complexions and shadowed eyes from lack of sleep. Oh! Oh, yes, perhaps they did. But *that* was not the reason for his pallor today—yesterday. Neither was anxiety over a marriage proposal about to be made, its outcome uncertain.

He had no more intended to propose to her than she had thought to climb the nearest tree.

Why was she crying? And why could she not sleep? She sniffed without any satisfactory result. There was only one remedy—for both her sleeplessness and her blocked nose. A cup of tea would soothe her stomach and clear her nasal passages. It would comfort her. It would restore her to herself.

She would be *very* surprised if *he* was lying awake, shedding tears over *her*.

What had kept him awake last night, then, and perhaps the night before? Not her, certainly. She felt a twinge of jealousy for whatever or *whoever* it was, and then gazed at her image with self-loathing.

It was not easy to get the fire going again in the

kitchen. It was even harder to do it and fill the kettle and get down a cup and saucer noiselessly. She had shut the door firmly behind her, but inevitably it opened just when she had accomplished all the tasks that would create the most sound.

Dora, a warm shawl wrapped about her shoulders over her nightgown, stepped inside and closed the door. Of course it was Dora. An earthquake would not wake Mrs. Henry once she was asleep.

"I could not sleep," Agnes explained as she busied herself over the fire, as though the kettle needed skilled coaxing in order to boil. "I tried not to wake you."

"It is not frustration over your painting that has put you out of sorts lately, is it?" Dora asked, reaching up into the cupboard for another cup and saucer and checking the teapot to see whether Agnes had put in the tea leaves yet.

Agnes sniffed and discovered that she could breathe again through one nostril—just.

"He asked me to marry him," she said. "Or, rather, he informed me that I had better."

Dora did not ask *who*.

"I have always thought," she said instead, sounding almost wistful, "that if anyone ever asked *me* to marry him, I would weep tears of joy. But yours are not joyful, are they?"

"He did not mean it, Dora."

"Then he is a very foolish young man," Dora said, "for you might have said yes. I assume you did not?"

"How could I," Agnes asked, "when I knew he did not mean it?"

The kettle was starting to boil. Dora made the tea and left it to steep in the pot.

"But you would have accepted if he had?" she asked. "Do you *know* him, Agnes, beyond dancing with him at the harvest ball and going off with him for twenty minutes or so on the evening of the concert and walking home with him today?"

Dora had noticed her absence, then, on that evening when she had played? Who else had? Everyone, she supposed.

"He came upon me one morning when I went into the park to paint the daffodils," Agnes explained. "That was before the concert. And he found me there again one other day."

She poured the tea. She did not add that he had kissed her. Dora would be shocked. Besides . . .

"A romantic setting," Dora said. "Have you conceived a *tendre* for him, Agnes? But of course you have, or you would not be down here at this ungodly hour with your face looking the way it does."

Agnes sniffed again and then blew her nose. She could almost breathe again.

"I miss William," she said.

Dora reached over and patted her hand.

"William was a rock of stability," she said. "But—forgive me—he was hardly a romantic figure, Agnes. I was a little troubled when you married him, for I always thought you could do better. Oh, that word was very poorly chosen. *Better*, indeed. No one could have been better than William, God rest his soul. But I always thought you were made for sunshine and laughter and . . . oh, and *romance*. You were my dear little sister, and I expected to live vicariously through you as I dwindled into old age. I am talking nonsense. Viscount Ponsonby is titled and handsome and . . . what is the word? Attractive. And mysterious. One wonders what lies behind that mobile eyebrow of his. And . . . dangerous. Or perhaps it is just my spinster's sensibilities that cause me to see him that way."

"No," Agnes said, stirring sugar into her tea. "He *is*

dangerous. To the peace of mind of anyone foolish enough to fall in love with him, anyway."

"And you have fallen," Dora said.

"Yes," Agnes admitted. "But I will not marry him. I would be foolish."

Dora sighed.

"I am hardly in a position to advise you, Agnes," she said. "I have no experience. None whatsoever. I want you to be happy. I love you, you know, more than I love anyone else in the world."

"Don't set me off again," Agnes said, lifting her cup to her lips and inhaling the steam. The fact that Dora had no experience, that she was a spinster at the age of thirty-eight, was at least partly Agnes's fault. Or, if not exactly her fault, then at least it was on her account. But she could not dwell upon that now, or she would be a watering pot again. Besides, she never willingly thought about their mother and what she had done all those years ago, and Agnes and Dora never talked about it.

"Come." Dora drank her tea, scalding as it still was, and set down her empty cup. She led the way into the sitting room and went immediately to the pianoforte. "Let me play for you."

She had used to do it when the infant Agnes had refused to take her afternoon nap and had then been cross and droopy. Dora had always been able to put her to sleep with music.

Agnes sat and put her head back against the sofa cushion.

What was it that had given him sleepless nights?

Why had he suddenly thought the solution to whatever troubled him was to marry her?

She knew only the mask of bored, mocking ennui he presented to the world—with a few brief glimpses behind it. She suspected there were layers upon layers to be uncovered before one approached anywhere near his soul. Could anyone do it? Would he ever allow it, even with the woman he would eventually marry?

And would anyone rash enough to explore beyond the mask lose herself in the process?

She felt herself drifting toward sleep and opened her eyes to listen to the end of the piece Dora was playing. It was time they were both in bed. What on earth was she going to look like in the morning?

There was less than a week of their annual gathering left—a melancholy thought. Vincent was going to take everyone on a tour of his farms after breakfast. Lady Harper was going along to see the lambs and other newborns. Lady Darleigh was going to stay behind for a pianoforte lesson from Miss Debbins and to tend her baby. Lady Trentham was in bed, despite the fact that last night she had expressed enthusiasm for the farm visit. She was sleeping off a bout of nausea.

Hugo announced that last fact at the breakfast table with a look that was half-sheepish, half-triumphant.

"She is apt to be like this some mornings for a while," he said, "though she has been able to fight it off until today. Not that she is ill or anything like that. Far from it. But . . . well."

He rubbed his hands together, looked over the breakfast fare on the sideboard, and then proved that *his* appetite was not impaired, even if his wife's was.

"Congratulations are in order, then, are they, Hugo?" George asked.

"You did not hear it from me," Hugo said with some alarm. "Gwendoline does not want anyone to know. She does not want any fuss. Or embarrassment."

"I have not heard a thing," Ben said. "This silverware is clattery stuff, Vince. It drowns out conversation at table and leaves one horribly uninformed. *What* did you say, Hugo? Or what did you *almost* say?"

"I had noticed that about the cutlery too," Imogen said. "But I daresay we did not miss anything of great importance."

Flavian did not go out with everyone else. He had letters to write, he informed them before remembering that he had used that excuse once before. Good Lord, they would be thinking he was becoming the world's champion correspondent.

He lurked alone at the drawing room window so that he would have a clear view down the driveway, and he watched Miss Debbins make what seemed to be her snail-like way up to the house, though no doubt she was walking at a perfectly respectable pace. As soon as she had disappeared up the steps below the window and he had allowed a moment or two for her to move from the hall toward the music room, he went downstairs, took up his coat and hat and gloves, which he had left there earlier, nodded genially to the footman on duty, and strode off down the steps and through the formal parterres.

It was one of those not-a-cloud-in-the-sky days again. They had been fortunate enough to have had several of them during their stay. The wind was almost nonexistent too. Tulips were blooming in a riot of color. They were surely earlier than usual this year. They would not suit Agnes Keeping's soul, however. They were regimented and organized.

Organized.

He had not written a speech. He had not even planned one in his head. Every time he had decided to do it, his thoughts had scattered in fright to the four corners of the earth and stayed away, no doubt searching for corners that were not even there.

He had no roses either. It was the wrong time of year.

Tulips did not seem quite right. And, Vince's gardeners might have looked askance at him if he had sallied forth into the beds, scissors or shears in hand. And daffodils, she would no doubt inform him, were better left to bloom in the grass.

So he arrived outside the cottage empty-handed and empty-headed.

He knocked on the door and then wondered whether it was too late to bolt. It was. A woman with a little boy in tow and a large basket over her free arm was passing on the other side of the street. She was watching him curiously and bobbed an awkward curtsy when she saw him looking.

Anyway, he had said he would come.

The door opened, and he prepared a polite smile for the housekeeper. But it was Mrs. Keeping herself who stood there in the doorway.

"Oh," she said, the color deepening in her cheeks.

"May I hope," he asked her, removing his hat and making her a bow, "that the mere s-sight of me robs you of coherent s-speech, Mrs. Keeping?"

"Dora has gone up to the house," she said, "and Mrs. Henry has gone to the butcher's shop."

"The coast is c-clear for the big, bad wolf, then, is it?" he asked.

She looked at him in apparent exasperation. But, really, did the woman have no more sense of self-preservation than to inform a man at the door that she was alone in the house?

"I c-cannot come in, then," he said. "Your n-neighbors would fall into a collective s-swoon before recovering and r-rushing off to share the scandalous news with their more d-distant neighbors. Fetch your cloak and b-bonnet and come walking with me. It is too fine a day, anyway, to s-spend indoors."

"Do you ever ask rather than state?" she asked him, frowning. But her shoulders lost their tension when he merely raised one eyebrow, and she sighed. "I suppose you knew Dora was at Middlebury."

"I did," he admitted. "I did not know your h-housekeeper was at the butcher's, however. Would she have informed me that you w-were not at home?"

Mrs. Keeping gave him a speaking glance and shook her head slightly, as though she were dealing with a troublesome child.

"I will fetch my outdoor things."

It did not appear that she had been waiting on pins and needles and with bated breath for him to come and renew his addresses, then. Had he expected that she would?

9

He made light conversation as they walked back down the street and turned through the gates to Middlebury. And she was ready enough to contribute her mite. It was better than silence, she had probably decided.

They fell silent, though, after he had drawn her off the drive to walk among the trees. He took a diagonal path, though there was no walking a straight line in the woods, of course. They came out close to the lake, as he and George had done yesterday. She looked inquiringly at him. No doubt she had expected they would walk out to the cedar avenue and beyond again.

"Have you been across to the island?" He nodded in its direction.

"No, I never have."

He led her toward the boathouse.

Seated in the boat a few minutes later while he rowed, she looked out across the water and then directly at him. She looked rather pale, he thought. Her cheeks looked slightly hollow, as though she had been ill or had not slept well—as she very probably had not. For someone who was supposed to be worldly-wise, he had bungled yesterday's proposal abominably. It would have helped, he supposed, if he had known he was about to make it.

He wanted to say something. She looked as if *she* wanted to say something. But neither of them spoke. They were like a pair of bashful schoolchildren just discovering that the opposite sex meant more than just people dressed differently from oneself. She shifted her gaze to the island, and he looked over his shoulder to make sure he did not crash against the little jetty there. He busied himself tying up the boat and helping her out, and he took her to look inside the little temple folly as though this were a mere sightseeing outing.

It was a pretty shrine, complete with finely carved chair and altar and rosary and stained glass.

"I believe it was built for a former viscountess," Mrs. Keeping told him. "She was Catholic. I can just picture her sitting alone here in quiet meditation."

"With her beads clicking piously between her fingers, I suppose," he said. "Rowed herself across, d-did she? I have my doubts. She probably b-brought a hefty, lusty footman with her."

"A lover, I suppose." But she laughed softly as she moved past him back to the outdoors. "How you would destroy the romance of the place, Lord Ponsonby."

"That depends," he said, "upon your d-definition of r-romance."

"Yes, I suppose it does." She looked back at him. "Where is everyone else?"

"Tramping and riding about the f-farms," he said. "Lady Darleigh and Lady Trentham are at the h-house."

"Why did you not go too?" she asked. "I suppose you have an estate and farms of your own. You are surely interested. And they are your friends, and this is a special gathering. Why did you not go with them?"

"I w-wanted to see you instead," he said. "And I had t-told you I would come."

She walked back behind the folly, and he followed.

There was a stretch of grass there, sloping down toward the water. It was completely secluded. The temple would hide it from the house side of the lake. Trees growing down to the banks of the lake and overhanging them hid it from prying eyes on the other three sides.

She stopped halfway down the slope.

"Why?" she asked.

He stood with his back against the folly and crossed his arms over his chest.

"I m-made you what was probably the most inept m-marriage proposal in h-history yesterday," he said. "I c-came to make amends."

She turned her head to look back at him.

"Why?"

Did all women ask why when a man proposed marriage to them? But he had trapped himself now, idiot that he was, by his failure to speak up sooner. He could hardly sink in picturesque elegance onto one knee before her now and draw some flowery speech out of the empty recesses of his mind. He would get grass stains on one knee of his pantaloons, anyway.

And why the devil *did* he want to marry her? He had had all night to work it out, but his thoughts had flitted among any and every subject on earth except that one. He had even slept. Had he been so incapable of focusing before his injuries? It was hard to remember. And had it always been hard to remember?

He stared at her from beneath half-closed lids, and she waited for his answer, her eyebrows raised, her hands clasped at her waist. She looked picturesque and wholesome and . . . safe.

Good Lord! He had better not tell her either of those last two things.

What she looked like was the end of the rainbow. No—ghastly image. She bore no resemblance whatsoever to a pot of gold—crass stuff. Ridiculous image. She was like that dream everyone dreams of something that is always just out of reach but perhaps attainable if only . . .

He swore under his breath, tossed his hat down onto the grass, sent his gloves in pursuit of it, and strode toward her. His hands closed about her upper arms and yanked her against him.

"Why else would I want to m-marry you but to be able to d-do this and more whenever I want, night or day?" he said between his teeth before kissing her hard and openmouthed.

He expected her to push him away, and he would have allowed her to do it. He had no right. . . . She *ought* to push him away. Instead she somehow slid her gloved hands up between them and cupped his face with them and gentled the kiss.

He drew his head back a little, closed his eyes, and rested his forehead against hers beneath the brim of her bonnet. He could not have made a worse ass of himself or insulted her more if he had tried. He had just told her he wanted to marry her for sex and nothing else. He had grabbed her and kissed her like a randy schoolboy who had never even heard the word *finesse*.

"Let's sit down," she said with a sigh, and she released him and sat on the grass before removing her gloves and setting them beside her.

He sat next to her, draped his arms over his knees, and stared out over the water to the trees at the other side.

"Lord Ponsonby," she said, "you do not even know me."

"Then tell me," he said.

"Oh, you know the bare facts," she said, "and there is nothing much to add. I have not lived a life of high adventure. I am gently born on both my mother's and my father's sides, but there is no whisper of aristocracy in our bloodlines. We are ordinary people. I was married to William Keeping for five years."

"The dull dog," he said.

She rounded on him.

"You did not *know* him," she cried. "And I would not tolerate disrespect of him even if you had. I miss him. I miss him dreadfully. There is gaping emptiness *here*." She patted a hand to her bosom.

"I beg your pardon," he said. Maybe there *had* been some passion after all.

"My father's second wife was one of our neighbors too," she said, "the widow of his particular friend. I was and am happy for them, though I was eager enough to marry and move away after they wed. Dora had left, and our home just did not seem the same any longer. Since I came to live here, I have involved myself in community and church activities whenever I feel I can be useful. I read and I paint and I darn and embroider. I have a modest competence from my late husband on which to live. It is quite sufficient for my needs. Sophia—Lady Darleigh—is my closest friend, not because of her grand title but because of *who* she is. I have never been ambitious. I am not now. The idea that I might marry a viscount does not make my heart palpitate with delirious hope. I am perfectly happy with my life as it is."

He was glad of that last sentence.

"I think y-you lie, Mrs. Keeping," he said.

She looked cross.

"You asked," she said, "and I have told you. There is very little to tell. But you do not *know* me for all that. Facts tell only a small part of the whole story of who a person is."

"You are *not* p-perfectly happy," he said. "No one is except m-maybe for brief moments. And you admitted once before that you are n-not fully contented. P-Perhaps there is marriage and motherhood in your f-future, you told me, and your voice was w-wistful when you said it. But you d-did not know who in this neighborhood was likely to offer. *I* am offering."

"Why?" She frowned at him. "You could have any woman you wanted. Any lady of rank and fortune. And beauty."

"*You* are beautiful," he said.

"Yes, I am," she surprised him by saying, and her chin came up and her cheeks warmed with color. "But not in any way that might attract a man like you, Lord Ponsonby."

She was determined to see him as a libertine.

He smiled and regarded her lazily.

"Is there a c-correct answer to your *why*?" he asked her. "If I give it, will I w-win the prize?"

She shook her head slowly. "I would be mad to marry you," she said.

"Why?" Now it was his turn. "Is it over m-me you have been losing sleep?"

"I have not been—" she began, but he had set a hand behind her neck and moved purposefully toward her.

"Liar."

He kissed her and then raised his head. She gazed back into his eyes and did not complete her interrupted sentence. He untied the ribbon bow beneath her chin and tossed her bonnet to the grass on top of her gloves.

And he kissed her again before unbuttoning his coat and then her cloak at the neck. He slid his hands into the warmth beneath it and drew her to him inside his coat.

Sometimes, he thought, there was something more erotic than naked flesh.

He reached his tongue into her mouth, held her head steady with one hand, and circled one of her breasts with the other. It was small, firm, uptilted above her stays. Not voluptuous. Just . . . perfect.

When one of her hands cupped his cheek, he withdrew a few inches. Her eyes were bright with tears.

"Do you w-want me to— " he began.

"No," she said, her mouth slanting, open, over his.

She was on the grass then, on her back, and he was half over her, bracing himself above her with his elbows, his hands on her breasts, one of his legs nestled between hers, his mouth moving over her cheeks, her temples, her eyes, her ears, and back to her own. His erection was pressed to her hip.

He moved himself more fully over her, his hands moving down her sides and beneath her to cup her buttocks. He nestled and rocked against her between her thighs, the layers of their clothing separating them. He wanted nakedness then. He wanted to explore her heat with his hand, and he wanted to put himself there and press inside her. He wanted to claim her body for his own.

And he would be safe.

Strange thought—and it was not the first time it had popped into his head like an alien thing.

Safe.

Safe for whom?

And from what?

He set his face in the hollow between her shoulder and neck and willed his heartbeat to a more normal rate.

"W-Would you stop me?" he asked, raising his head at last and looking down at her. "Would you h-have stopped me?"

It was probably an unfair question. But he did not think she would have.

He moved off her and lay beside her, the back of one hand draped over his eyes. He breathed as deeply and as silently as he was able, bringing his body under control.

"I lost my v-virginity when I was sixteen," he told her. "I have not been celibate since then, except for the three years I spent at P-Penderris Hall. But I do not b-believe I am a rake. And I *do* believe that any solemn vow f-freely given ought to be binding in honor, including marriage vows."

She sat up and clasped her arms about her knees. One lock of her hair had come loose from the knot at her neck and lay along the back of her cloak, shiny and slightly wavy. He raised one hand and ran the backs of his fingers along it. It was smooth and silky. She hunched her shoulders but did not move away from him.

"I just accused you of not knowing me," she said. "But I do not know you either, do I? I have made assumptions, but they are not necessarily true. But I *do* know that you hide behind a mask of careless mockery."

"Ah, but the question is, Mrs. Keeping," he said, "do you *w-want* to know me? Or do you wish to c-continue undisturbed with your placid, blameless, not quite happy but not entirely *un*happy existence here? I may be d-dangerous to know."

Agnes got to her feet and moved to the water's edge. But it was not far enough. She walked along the shore until it bent away to her right. She stood still and gazed sightlessly across at the west bank and the trees that overhung it. He did not follow her, and she was thankful for that.

He had been lying right on top of her. For a minute or two all his weight had borne her down into the grass. He had been between her thighs. She had felt him. . . .

Only their clothes had stopped them.

And she had wanted him. Not just the being-in-love sort of wanting. Not just the desire for kisses. She had *wanted* him.

She had never wanted William—which was just as well, she supposed, since she had not had him very often. Once a week, as a regular routine, for the first year or so, then at less frequent intervals, and finally, for the last two years, not at all. She had never denied him his rights when he had claimed them, and she had never shrunk from their encounters or found them particularly unpleasant. But there had been a certain relief, a certain feeling of freedom, when he had stopped coming to her—except that she would have liked to have had a child. The friendship and affection between them had endured, though, and the comfortable sense of belonging. He had often told her how fond he was of her, and she had believed him. She had been fond of him too, though, if she was honest with herself, she would have to admit that she had married him only because home had no longer felt quite like home with Dora gone and her father's new wife in her place, with the strong likelihood that her mother and sister would come to live with them soon—as they had.

She had wanted Viscount Ponsonby as she had never wanted her husband. She could still feel the tenderness of physical longing in her breasts and along her inner thighs. And it frightened her—or at least it disturbed her, if *fright* was too extreme a word. But it was *not* too extreme. She was terrified of passion, of wanton abandon.

Her thoughts touched upon her mother, but she pushed them firmly away, as she always did when they threatened to intrude.

She continued along the shore until she could see the house across the water. He was sitting on the jetty close to the boat a short distance away, one knee raised, an arm draped over it, the picture of relaxation and well-being—or so it seemed. He was watching her approach.

I do believe that any solemn vow freely given ought to be binding in honor, including marriage vows.

Considering the fact that she had fallen in love with him last autumn and again this spring, she should be over the moon with happiness that he wished to marry her, especially in light of those words. Why was she not? Why did she hesitate?

I may be dangerous to know.

Yes, she felt that it was so. Not that she feared him physically, despite the violent rages he had admitted to and the leashed energy she sensed lurking beneath the often sleepy-seeming exterior. Those rages had happened at a time when he had been all locked up inside his head as a result of his war injuries. He was past that stage now. A slight stammer, sometimes a little worse than at other times, was not enough to frustrate him to the point of violence. But—she feared the danger that was him.

He represented *passion*, and she feared that almost more than anything else in life. Violence came from passion. Passion killed. Not the body, perhaps, but certainly the spirit, and all that had most value in life. Passion killed love. They were mutually exclusive things—a strange irony. It would be impossible to separate the two with Viscount Ponsonby, though. She would not be able simply to love him and keep herself intact. She would have to give all and . . .

No!

He got to his feet as she came closer. He had her bonnet in one hand. He looked lazily into her eyes as he fitted it carefully over her hair, and she stood like a child, her arms at her sides, while he tied the ribbon in a bow beneath her left ear. She looked back into his eyes the whole time.

Would you stop me? Would you have stopped me?

He had not insisted that she answer, and she had not done so—which had been cowardly of her. *Would* she have stopped him? She was not at all sure she would. Indeed she was almost certain she would not have. Her heart had sunk with disappointment when he had stopped. And *why* had he stopped? A rake would surely not have done so.

Her gloves, drawn from a coat pocket, materialized in one of his hands. He held one out and then fitted it onto her fingers. He did the same with the other glove, and she half smiled.

"You would make an excellent lady's maid," she said.

His eyes gazed keenly into hers from beneath heavy eyelids.

"I would indeed," he said. "This is a mere foretaste of the services I would provide."

"I could never afford you." She laughed softly.

"Ah," he said, "but I would not exact payment in coin. You *can* afford the payment I would demand, in abundance. In superabundance. Ma'am."

Her knees almost buckled. And there was surely not as much air on this side of the island as there was on the other.

The corners of his mouth lifted in that wicked half smile of his, and he offered one hand to help her into the boat.

They were on the other shore and he was handing her out of the boat when she became aware that Sophia and Lady Trentham were strolling toward the lake from the direction of the house. Sophia was carrying the baby, bundled up warmly in a blanket.

Whatever would she *think*?

But whatever she thought, she was smiling as she called out to them.

"You have been to the island," she said. "It is the perfect morning to be outdoors, is it not?"

She looked more searchingly at Agnes as she came closer with Lady Trentham. The viscount was putting the boat away in the boathouse.

If only one were able to control one's blushes!

"I have never been there before," Agnes said. "The little temple is more beautiful than one expects, is it not? The stained glass makes the light inside quite magical. Or perhaps *mystical* would be a more appropriate word."

"Sir Benedict rowed Samantha and me over there a couple of weeks ago," Lady Trentham said. "I agree with you, Mrs. Keeping. And that stained glass window gives me ideas for *our* park."

"Dora has gone home?" Agnes asked.

"She praised me and scolded me in equal measure." Sophia laughed. "By some miracle I played all the notes of last week's piece correctly, but I played with wooden fingers. It is the very worst censure your sister can possibly deal out to one of her pupils, Agnes, and it is quite devastating when she does it. And thoroughly deserved on this occasion. I have not been practicing as conscientiously as I ought."

She lifted a corner of the blanket and smiled at her son's sleeping face.

"She would not stay for a cup of coffee," she continued, "and Gwen and I decided to come out without stopping for one either. The sunshine was too inviting."

Viscount Ponsonby came out of the boathouse, and all eyes turned his way.

They had not exchanged a word in the boat on the way across. Agnes did not know whether he was finished with her now or whether he would renew his addresses. There was less than a week remaining. . . .

She had a sudden premonition of how she was going to feel on the day all the guests left Middlebury Park.

Her stomach seemed to sink like a leaden weight all the way to the soles of her shoes, leaving nausea and near panic behind in its place.

He smiled.

"I was not in the m-mood for writing letters after all," he said. "It was too late to g-go with everyone else, and there was no one in sight in the house except for a few f-footmen, who did not look as if they would enjoy being engaged in c-conversation. I took myself off to the v-village to see if Mrs. Keeping would take p-pity on me, and she did."

"Come up to the house and have coffee with us," Sophia said, smiling at Agnes.

"But you have just come outside," Agnes protested.

"Not so," Lady Trentham told them. "We walked through the formal gardens before coming down here."

"Come," Sophia said.

Being sociable was the last thing Agnes felt like doing, but none of the alternatives appealed to her either. Dora would be back home and would expect to know where her sister had been. And even if she could get away from Dora after a brief explanation and retreat to her room, she would have her thoughts to contend with again, and they would not be happy company for a while.

"Thank you," she said.

"And now I face a dilemma," Viscount Ponsonby said. "Three l-ladies and only two arms to offer."

Sophia laughed.

"How a child who is not yet two months old can weigh a ton, I do not know," she said, "but that is precisely what Thomas *does* weigh. Here, my lord, you may carry him to the house, and we three will find our way unassisted."

He looked almost comically alarmed. He took the blanket-wrapped bundle—Sophia gave him no choice—and held it as though terrified he would drop it.

Lady Trentham linked her arm through Agnes's, and Viscount Ponsonby looked down into the baby's face.

"Well, my l-lad," he said, "when the l-ladies do not want us, we men band together and talk about horses and races and boxing mills and . . . well, the interesting stuff. Yes, you may well open your eyes—b-blue like your papa's, I see. We are about to indulge in a heart-to-heart chat, just the t-two of us, and it would be ill-mannered of you to nod off in the m-middle of it."

Sophia laughed again, and Agnes could have wept. There was surely *nothing* more affecting than seeing a man holding a baby and actually talking to it. Even if it was *not* his own, and he had not chosen to hold it and probably wished himself anywhere else on earth than just here, holding his friend's infant.

He tucked the child into the crook of his arm and made off across the grass, leaving the path to the three of them.

"Agnes," Sophia said, her voice low, "does he have a *tendre* for you? What a sensible man he is, if he does."

"I have a soft spot for him, I must confess," Lady Trentham said. "But then, I do for *all* of them. Hugo is so very fond of them, and they have all suffered dreadfully."

Agnes wondered about Lady Trentham's limp, which did not seem to be a temporary thing. Wondering kept her mind off the events of the morning so far. Well, almost, anyway.

He still wanted to marry her—perhaps.

He had kissed her again. And more than just kissed her.

But he had not once expressed any fondness for her. Only a desire to *bed* her, to use his own language.

"I still have not seen any of your paintings, Mrs. Keeping," Lady Trentham was saying, "even though we have been here longer than two weeks. *May* I see some of them if I walk into the village one day before we leave? Sophia says you are very talented."

He had reached the house ahead of them and was sitting on one of the steps outside the front doors, the baby on his lap, head outward, one of his hands spread beneath it. He was still talking.

Agnes swallowed and hoped she had muffled the gurgle of unshed tears in her throat.

10

Agnes sat in the morning room for half an hour with the ladies, enjoying her coffee and the conversation. Viscount Ponsonby had taken the baby up to the nursery, having assured Sophia that he did indeed know the way and that he would not abandon young Tom until he had placed him safely in his nurse's care.

Agnes thought he was not going to join them, but he did so just as she was getting to her feet to take her leave.

"Ah, well-timed," he said. "I shall escort you home, Mrs. Keeping."

"There is really no need," she assured him. "I come back and forth to Middlebury all the time to call upon Sophia, and it never occurs to me to bring a maid or other escort."

She needed to be alone to think.

"But if a w-wolf should happen to leap out at you from the woods," he said, "there really ought to be someone there to f-fight it off with his bare hands. Me, in fact."

Lady Trentham laughed. "A hero after my own heart," she said, clapping a hand theatrically to her bosom.

"And the woods are full of them," Sophia added. "Not to mention the wild boars."

Agnes looked reproachfully from one to the other of

the ladies, and Sophia tipped her head slightly to one side and looked searchingly at her again.

Viscount Ponsonby escorted her home. She clasped her hands determinedly behind her back as soon as they left the house, and he walked a little distance to one side of her and talked agreeably almost the whole way on a series of inconsequential topics.

"No wolves," he said when they were close to the gates, "or wild b-boars, alas. How is a man expected to impress his l-lady in this civilized age when he may not perform some g-grand deed of heroism in order to pluck her from d-deadly danger and s-sweep her swooning form into his strong, sheltering arms?"

His lady?

He had stopped walking—in almost the exact spot as he had chosen yesterday to inform her that she had better marry him.

She smiled at him.

"You would like to be a knight in shining armor?" she asked him. "You would like to be that cliché of worthy manhood?"

And it struck her that he must have looked quite irresistibly gorgeous clad in his officer's uniform with his scarlet coat and white pantaloons and red sash and cavalry sword swinging at his side.

"You do not f-fancy being a damsel in distress?" He raised one mocking eyebrow. "What a p-poor sport you are, Mrs. Keeping."

"A man does not have to slay dragons to be a hero," she told him.

"Or wolves? Or boars? What must he do, then?"

She had no answer to that. What *did* make a man a hero?

"Go away?" he offered softly as an answer to his own question. "Is that what he must do?"

She frowned briefly but said nothing.

Silence hung between them for a few moments until he took her upper arm in a firm grip and moved her off the driveway and into the trees for a few paces, before turning her back against a broad tree trunk and setting his hands flat against the bark on either side of her head. His face was a mere few inches from her own.

"I saw something enchanting," he said. "In a ballroom and in a daffodil meadow. And I became obsessed—with b-bedding you, I assumed. It is what one *does* assume when one finds a woman enchanting. But I have not bedded you, though the desire is there on both our parts and the opportunity has presented itself on m-more than one occasion. I am on unfamiliar territory, Agnes Keeping, and you must help me. Or not. I cannot command your help. I want you in my life, and there is only one way I c-can have you there since you are not the sort of woman to whom one offers c-carte blanche, and I would not offer that to you even if you w-were. I offer m-marriage instead with a title, a large ancestral home and estate p-plus a house in London, wealth, p-position in society, security for a lifetime. But these m-material things mean n-nothing to you, I know. I do not know what else to offer except passion. I can give you that. I can bring you alive as you have never been alive before. I can g-give you children, or I suppose I can. And yet . . . and yet you would be well-advised to r-refuse me. I am d-dangerously unstable. I must be. I told you just recently that I would never offer m-marriage to anyone, yet now I offer it to you, and I do not even know how I could have m-meant what I said then, yet mean what I say n-now. You would not have an easy life with me, Agnes."

"Or you with me," she said through lips that felt too tight to obey her will. "I cannot give you what you want, my lord. And you cannot give me what *I* want. You want someone you can sweep away on a grand tide of passion so that you can forget, so that you can ignore all that still needs to be settled in your life, whatever that might be. I need someone quiet and steady and dependable."

"So that *you* can ignore all that needs to be s-settled in *your* life?" he asked her. "Whatever that might be?"

She licked lips turned suddenly dry.

He gazed at her, his eyes very green in the double shade of the tree and the brim of his hat.

"You are wrong about me," he said, "and you are wrong about yourself. Don't say n-no. If you cannot say yes, at least do not say no. It is such a final word. Once it is said, it cannot be argued against without the appearance of harassment. After I have left here, I will not come b-back. You will be free of me f-forever. But I have not left yet. Say no when I am leaving if you must, but not before then. P-Promise me?"

She did not want to say no. She desperately did not want to. But she could not say yes either. How could the answer to a simple question be neither yes nor no?

After I have left here, I will not come back. You will be free of me forever.

Forever suddenly seemed like an awfully long time. Panic coiled inside her.

"I promise," she whispered.

He lowered his hands to his sides, turned away from her for a moment, and then turned back to offer her his arm. He led her onto the driveway again, and they walked in silence to the cottage.

Dora was pulling weeds from one of the flower beds.

Viscount Ponsonby was immediately at his most charming. He complimented her on the garden, and he thanked her profusely for making Lord Darleigh tolerable to listen to on the violin and harp.

"I am a lover of animals, Miss Debbins," he explained.

"It would break my h-heart to hear Tab and all the neighborhood cats howl in pain."

He had Dora laughing in no time at all. And when he took his leave, he bowed elegantly to them both and sauntered away as if he had never in his life entertained a serious thought.

Dora was looking at Agnes with raised eyebrows.

"He let everyone else go off with Viscount Darleigh to look at the farms this morning," she explained, "while he wrote some letters. But then he got bored and came down here to persuade me to go walking with him."

"And?" Dora said.

"He rowed me over to the island," Agnes told her. "The temple is beautiful inside, Dora. I had no idea. There is a stained glass window facing south, and it catches all the light and disperses it in a kaleidoscope of colors. And then, when we were coming back across the lake, Sophia was walking down from the house with Lady Trentham and invited me for coffee. She said you would not stay."

"The weeds awaited," Dora said. "Did he ask again, Agnes?"

"They will be here for less than a week longer," Agnes said. "He says that once he has gone, he will not return. Ever. But forever is a long time, and Viscount Darleigh *is* his friend."

"He asked again," Dora said quietly, answering her own question. She turned to gather up her gardening tools. "Why do you hesitate, Agnes? You are in love with him, and it would be a hugely advantageous match for you. And for him."

"I would have to leave *you*," Agnes said.

Dora looked over her shoulder at her.

"I am a big girl," she said. "And I was alone here for a number of years before you came. *Why* do you hesitate? Does it have anything to do with Mother?"

Agnes's knees almost gave way beneath her—for the second time in one day. They *never* spoke of their mother.

"Of course not," she said. "Why should it?"

Dora continued to look at her without turning fully to face her.

"You must not consider me, Agnes," she said. "I chose my course in life. It is *my* life. I have done with it what I have wanted to do, and I am happy with it. I was happy before you came, I have been happy since you came, and I will be happy if you should ever choose to leave. You have *your* life to live. You cannot live mine too—and you do not need to live Mother's. If you love him . . ."

But she stopped without completing the thought, shook her head, and turned back to what she had been doing. Agnes suspected there might be tears in her eyes.

"I should have come back here instead of going for coffee," Agnes said. "You have not left any weeds for me."

"Oh, look again tomorrow," Dora said, "or even later this afternoon. One thing this world is never short of is weeds."

It was Imogen's turn that night. It did not happen often. She was always very well in control of her thoughts and emotions. Almost always, anyway. People who did not know her as well as her fellow Survivors did might assume that her marble exterior went right through to her heart. And even to them she did not reveal much of herself these days except an undying affection for the six of them and an unwavering readiness to support them in any way she could. It would have been easy to assume she was healed, except that none of them ever made that mistake. Of all of their wounds, hers went deepest and were the least likely to heal. Ever.

"I hope," she said, "I did not make an utter idiot of myself this morning."

"Everyone assumed you had tramped about and stood about for too long, Imogen," Hugo assured her. "Everyone loves a frail lady."

"What a ghastly image," she said, but she looked relieved nevertheless.

Apparently, when they had stopped outside the gamekeeper's hut this morning to listen to the estate manager's account of something or other, Imogen had collapsed to the ground in an insensible heap, and various persons had gone running for a chair and water while Hugo scooped her up in his arms and Ralph fanned her face with a large handkerchief.

"The door of the hut was propped open," she explained. "Anyone might have got inside. Children . . ."

"But the gamekeeper was right there," Ben pointed out.

"And he always keeps the door locked when he is not," Vincent added. "One lock is at the very top of the door, well out of the reach of any child. I have a firm policy on safety. Everyone knows it."

"I know, Vincent," Imogen said. "I am so sorry. I *know* your employees are not careless. I really do not know what came over me. I see guns all the time. I have made myself see them. I have even been out shooting. George has taken me three times now, and one of those times I actually fired my gun."

She shuddered and covered her face with her hands.

"I looked at those guns this morning," she continued, "and I suddenly saw them pointing at my face with no one behind them. They were just waiting for me to reach around and take hold and fire."

She was gasping for breath, and Flavian walked up behind her and set a hand against the back of her neck while Vincent, seated beside her, fumbled for her knee and patted it.

"Will I *never* forget?" she asked. "Will *none* of us ever forget?"

"No, we will not," George said, his voice quite cool and matter-of-fact. "But neither will you ever forget that he loved you, Imogen."

"Dicky?" she said. "Yes, he did."

"Or that you loved him."

"Did I?" She tipped her head downward, and Flavian massaged her shoulders lightly with both hands while Vincent patted her knee. "I had a strange way of showing it."

"No," Vincent said. "It was the *best* way anyone could possibly show love, Imogen."

She made a choking sound but then pulled herself together and lowered her hands and looked as calm as ever.

No, none of them would ever forget.

He never would, Flavian thought—which was a strange thought, when he suspected there were still all sorts of things he did not even remember. But he would never forget *one* thing. One thing, two persons.

Would he ever forgive?

"I am going away at first light tomorrow," he said abruptly. "I'll be gone for a few days, but I'll be b-back."

They all looked at him in surprise. He had been thinking about it all afternoon but had made no definite decision until this precise moment. His whole life these days seemed to be governed by sudden impulses.

"Going away for a *few days*, Flave?" Vincent asked. "When this is our final week together?"

"I have some urgent business to attend to," he said. "I'll be back."

They all continued to look at him—even Vincent, whose sightless gaze missed his face by only a few inches. But none of them asked the obvious question. None of them would, of course. They would not intrude. And he did not volunteer the answer.

"If you are going far, Flave," Ralph said, "take my curricle. Just be sure to leave my team at a decent posting inn. You can pick them up on your way back."

"It's London," Flavian said. "And thank you, Ralph. I will."

"If you are leaving at cockcrow," George said, "we had better get to bed. It is already well after midnight."

But I have not left yet. Say no when I am leaving if you must, but not before then. Promise me?

And Agnes had promised. It had been a remarkably easy promise to keep. How could one say no—or yes, for that matter—when one was not given the chance? For four whole days she had not set eyes upon Viscount Ponsonby even once, and the visit was almost at an end. After he had gone from here, he had told her, he would not return. Ever.

Well, he might as well be gone now, and she might as well start getting over him now.

If she had not been a lady long practiced in quiet self-control, Agnes thought as the days crawled by, she would surely start throwing things—preferably things that would smash.

She was on the rotating church sick visiting list with Dora, and it was their turn this week. Not that they ignored ailing or aged neighbors at other times, but this week attending to them was their official responsibility. Dora took along her little harp wherever they went so that she could provide some soothing music—and occasionally a lively tune to entertain the children or to set aged toes to tapping. Agnes took along small watercolor sketches of wildflowers she had painted especially for such occasions and propped them on mantels or tables close to the sick person and left them there.

She was glad of the distraction. The visits helped pass

the days and stopped her from expecting a knock on the door every waking moment. She looked forward fervently to the time when she could stop counting days and pick up the threads of her life again and be at peace once more.

Though she suspected that peace would not come easily once hope was gone. And she shuddered at the idea that it was *hope* she still felt.

On the fifth day Lady Harper called with Lady Trentham just after Agnes and Dora had arrived home. Lady Trentham had come to beg the favor of a viewing of Agnes's paintings. Both ladies looked at them all with flattering attention and much appreciation, though they would not stay to take tea. They had come on an errand from Sophia and had one more call to make, upon Mr. and Mrs. Harrison. They had already been to the vicarage. Sophia hoped some of her friends and Viscount Darleigh's would come up to the house this evening for cards and conversation and refreshments.

"Do say you will both come," Lady Trentham said, looking from Dora to Agnes. "We will be at Middlebury Park for only one more day after today. How the time has flown. It has been lovely, though, has it not, Samantha?"

"It has been a pure joy," Lady Harper said, "to observe such a very close-knit friendship as that of our husbands and the other five. I do wish, though, that Viscount Ponsonby had not gone away."

Agnes's heart and stomach plummeted in the direction of her slippers, and it felt as though they collided on the way down.

"He has left?" Dora asked.

"Oh, he assured the others he would return," Lady Harper said, "but they do miss him. And he gave no explanation, the wretched man."

Lady Trentham's eyes were resting upon Agnes. "I am

sure he *will* return if he said he would," she said. "Besides, he took the Earl of Berwick's curricle and horses, and will feel obliged to return them. Will you come this evening? Miss Debbins? Mrs. Keeping? We were to tell you that no would not be an acceptable answer and that the carriage will be sent for you at seven."

"In that case, we must be gracious about it and say yes," Dora said, laughing. "There is no need to send the carriage, though. We will be happy to walk."

Lady Harper laughed. "We were told you would say just that, and we were given an answer from Lord Darleigh himself. We were to inform you that the carriage will be here whether you choose to walk beside it or ride inside."

"Well, then. We would look silly walking beside it, I suppose." Dora laughed again.

He was gone. Without a word.

He had said he would return, and it seemed he *must* return, since he had a borrowed conveyance with him. But there was only one day of the visit left.

Agnes turned and half ran up the stairs to her room after she and Dora had waved the ladies on their way. She did not want to talk about it. She did not want to talk at all. Ever. She wanted to climb beneath the bedcovers, pull them up over her head, curl into a ball, and stay there for the rest of her life.

And *this*, she thought, catching a glimpse of her image in the dressing table mirror and pausing to nod at herself in some disgust, was a fine way to be behaving when one was twenty-six years old, a staid, refined widow, and wise enough to have turned down an advantageous marriage offer because it could lead only to lasting unhappiness.

This was not unhappiness?

Besides, she had not turned it down, had she? She had promised not to until he left.

He *had* left. But he had also said this time that he would return. It all seemed *so typical* of Viscount Ponsonby. She would be a fool. . . .

But at least she could prepare for this evening without a palpitating heart. He was not at the house. She could occupy her mind with nothing more disturbing than the enormously important question of which of her three evening gowns she would wear. Certainly not the green. The blue or the lavender, then. But which?

She grimaced at her image and turned away.

II

There was a degree of tiredness at which one was bone weary yet beyond feeling sleepy.

It was a point Flavian had reached by the time he drove himself through the village of Inglebrook in the middle of the evening. There was no light in the cottage. They must be in bed already. He could not remember when he had last slept, though he had taken a room at the same inn both going and coming and had certainly lain down on the bed on both occasions. He remembered hauling off his boots and wishing for his valet.

He should drive straight to the stables, abandon his rig—or rather Ralph's—to the care of Vince's grooms, go up to his room, and collapse on the bed without summoning his valet, who was probably still sulking anyway over the unexpected five-day holiday he had been given.

There were lights blazing in the drawing room windows, he saw as he was approaching the house. That was not surprising, of course. It was not *that* late, even though it was dark outside already.

There were two unfamiliar gigs outside the stable block. Ah, visitors. Another reason why he should go straight to bed. He would have to change and wash and shave even to appear before his friends and their ladies, of course, but he would have to make a more special effort for visitors. And he would have to smile and be sociable. He was not sure he *could* smile. It sounded like too much of an effort.

He would not sleep either, though, he suspected. He felt wound up like a child's spinning top. And the closer he had come to Middlebury, the madder his whole errand seemed. What the devil had possessed him? It was too late to ponder that question now, however. He had gone and he had returned, and if he had wasted his time, then there was nothing he could do about it now.

He nodded to the footman on duty in the hall and directed the man to send his valet up to him. Perhaps a wash and a shave and a bit of sociability would make him properly tired and enable him to sleep tonight.

Who *were* the visitors? he wondered.

He found out half an hour later when he sauntered into the drawing room, quizzing glass in hand. Vincent was sitting by the fire with Imogen and Harrison, his neighbor and particular friend. George was standing beside the fireplace, one elbow propped on the mantel. Harrison's wife was seated at one card table, as was the vicar. The vicar's wife and Miss Debbins were at another. Ben, his wife, Ralph, and Lady Trentham made up the two tables. Lady Darleigh was carrying two drinks to the vicar's table. Hugo was standing behind his wife's chair but was conversing with Mrs. Keeping, who stood beside him.

She was wearing a very modest, almost prim blue gown, which had surely never, ever been even remotely fashionable. He suspected its color was slightly faded too. Her hair was ruthlessly tamed, with not a single strand fallen loose by accident or design to tease the imagination.

She looked utterly delicious.

Short as he had been of time in London, he had nevertheless looked about him quite deliberately at the ladies. There had been some real beauties among them, and others who had made themselves *seem* beautiful or at least alluring by what they wore and how they wore it. He had been quite unenchanted by every single one of them.

It had been most alarming.

He met her eyes for a heartbeat before Lady Darleigh spotted him at the same moment George and Imogen did.

"Flavian!"

"Lord Ponsonby!"

"You are back, Flavian," Imogen said, coming toward him, both her hands extended. She turned her cheek for his kiss as he dropped his quizzing glass on its ribbon and clasped her hands.

"I h-had to return Ralph's curricle and horses," he said, "or he would have borne a g-grudge for the next ten years or so. He is t-touchy that way."

"I would have taken your carriage instead, Flave," Ralph said, looking up from his cards. "No carriage seats have any right to be so plush and cozy."

"Do let me fetch you a drink and something to eat," Lady Darleigh said after everyone else had greeted him—with one or two exceptions. "Are you cold? Do move closer to the fire."

He went to squeeze Vincent's shoulder and tell him how good it felt to be back among all his friends again. He exchanged a few words with George and Harrison, he spoke with Hugo for a minute or two, and then he went to stand beside Mrs. Keeping, who had moved to look intently over her sister's shoulder as though it was *she* who was playing the hand.

She pretended not to notice him. It might have been

a convincing performance if every muscle in her body had not visibly tensed as he approached.

"Far from being cold in here," he observed to no one in particular, though all except one person close by was involved in the card game, "it is actually overwarm. Quite b-boiling with heat, in fact."

No one either agreed or disagreed.

"And although d-darkness has fallen," he persisted, "and it is still only M-March, it is not a cold night, and there is not a breath of w-wind. It is perfect for a stroll on the terrace, in fact, p-provided one wears a warm cloak."

It was Miss Debbins who answered. She looked over her shoulder, first at him and then at her sister.

"Take mine, Agnes," she said. "It is warmer than yours."

And she returned her attention to her cards.

Mrs. Keeping did not react at all for a moment. Then she turned to look at him.

"Very well," she said. "For a few minutes. It *is* warm in here."

And she turned to precede him from the room. He had to move smartly in order to open the door for her.

And here he went again. Acting from sheer impulse before he had prepared himself properly or composed any pretty speech or gathered any rosebuds or their March equivalent. And with a mind befuddled from lack of sleep. Would he never learn?

He suspected that the answer was no.

She asked the footman in the hall for her sister's cloak, and she and Flavian stood side by side, not touching, not looking at each other, while it was fetched. He took it from the footman's hand and draped it about her shoulders, but before he could touch the fastenings, she very firmly buttoned the cloak herself.

The footman had moved ahead of them and was holding open the door.

Flavian hoped the Survivors, their wives, and all the guests were not lined up at the drawing room windows, looking down at them. It might as well be daylight. The moon was more or less at the full, and every star ever invented was beaming and twinkling down from a clear sky.

But, no, not a single one of them would even peep from a window. They were far too well-bred. But he would wager there was not a one of them who had not noticed and drawn his own conclusion. Or *her* own conclusion.

Mrs. Keeping kept her hands very firmly inside her cloak as he indicated the terrace that ran along the east wing of the house.

All Agnes had been able to think of when he had walked into the drawing room, looking immaculate and immaculately gorgeous, was that she ought to have worn her lavender. On balance she preferred the blue, but it was primmer than the lavender.

How stupidly random and trivial one's thoughts could sometimes be. As if his coming into the room had not turned her world on its head.

"Did you m-miss me?" he asked.

"Miss you?" she said, her voice surprised and brittle—she would surely be booed off any stage and perhaps even helped off with a rotten tomato. "I did not even realize you were gone until someone mentioned it today. Why *should* I miss you?"

"Quite so," he said agreeably. "It was mere v-vanity that made me hope you had."

"I would imagine," she said, "it is your *friends* who have missed you, Lord Ponsonby. I thought this annual gathering of the Survivors' Club meant more to any of the seven of you than any fleeting pleasure that might draw you off for a few days to enjoy yourself elsewhere."

"You are angry," he said.

"On their behalf," she told him. "And yet, even now that you have returned, you are not spending time with them. You have stepped out here with me instead."

"Perhaps you are one of those f-fleeting pleasures," he said with a sigh.

"Much of a pleasure I am to you," she said tartly, "when you can go away for five whole days without a word in order to indulge some other whim."

"You are a whim, Agnes?" he asked her.

"*I* am not what took you away," she told him. "And I am Mrs. Keeping to you."

"But you are," he protested. "You are Mrs. K-Keeping to me. As well as Agnes. And you *are* what took me away."

Her nostrils flared. And her steps slowed. She had been setting a cracking pace. With a few more steps they would be beyond the terrace and beyond the end of the east wing, and setting off across the lawn leading to the eastern end of the wilderness walk. She had no intention of walking in any wildernesses with Viscount Ponsonby.

"I am scarcely hard to avoid, my lord," she said. "It is not as though I put myself deliberately in your path every hour of every day. Or ever, in fact. You did not need to go away for five whole days in order not to see me."

"Counting, were you?" It was his lazy, slightly bored voice.

"Lord Ponsonby." She stopped walking altogether and turned toward him. She hoped he could see the indignation in her face. "You flatter yourself. I have a *life*. I have been too busy—too *happily* busy—to spare you a thought. Or even to notice that you had gone."

His back was to the moon. Even so, she could see the sudden grin on his face—before she took a sharp step backward and then another until the wall was behind her and there was no farther to retreat. He advanced on her.

"I did not know you could be p-provoked to anger," he said softly. "I like you angry."

He lowered his head toward hers, and she expected to be kissed. She even half closed her eyes in expectation.

"But I did need to go away," he said, his voice no more than a whisper of sound and breath, "so that I could come back."

"On the assumption that absence makes the heart grow fonder?" She raised her eyebrows.

"*Does* it?" he asked her. "Are you fonder of me now than you were f-five days ago, Agnes Keeping?"

It was hard to speak with the proper indignation when one had a man standing so close that one could feel his body heat and when, if one moved one's head forward even an inch, one's mouth would collide with his.

"*Fonder* implies that I was fond to start with," she said.

"*Were* you?"

He was a rake and a libertine and a seducer, and she had always known it. How dare Dora aid and abet him by offering her own cloak because it was warmer than Agnes's? Dora ought to have leapt to her feet and forbidden him to take her sister one step beyond the door of the room.

Agnes took her hands away from the wall behind her and braced them against his chest instead.

"Why did you go?" she asked him. "And, having gone, why did you come back?"

"I went so that I *could* come back," he said, and he covered the backs of her hands with his palms. "What sort of wedding would you prefer, Agnes? Something g-grand with b-banns and all sorts of time to summon everyone who has ever known you and all your relatives s-stretching back to your g-great-grandparents? Or something quieter and more intimate?"

That weak thing happened with her knees again, and she licked dry lips.

"If it is the f-former," he said, moving his head back just a little so that he could look down into her face, his eyelids lazy, his eyes keen beneath them, "then there is all the t-trouble of deciding upon a venue. St. George's on Hanover Square in London would p-probably be the most sensible choice because one can invite half the world, and a g-good half of that number already has a town house there or knows someone who does, and the other half will have no bother in f-finding a good hotel. If it is elsewhere—your f-father's home, mine, here—one has all the h-headache of deciding where everyone will stay. If it is the l-latter—"

"Oh, do stop," she cried, snatching her hands away. "There is to be no wedding, so it does not matter which type I would prefer."

He ran the backs of his fingers lightly along her jaw to her chin and up the other side to cup her cheek.

"In five d-days with nothing much to do but drive a curricle," he said, "I did not compose an affecting marriage proposal. Or even an *un*affecting one, for that matter. But I do know that I w-want you. In bed, yes, but not just there. I want you in my life. And p-please do not ask your usual question. *Why* is the h-hardest question in the world to answer. Marry me. Say you will."

And suddenly it seemed ridiculous to say no when she ached to say yes.

"I am afraid," she said.

"Of me?" he asked her. "Even at my worst, I n-never

physically hurt anyone. The w-worst I did was fling a glass of wine in someone's face. I lose my t-temper at times, more than I did before, but it does not last. It is all just sound and fury—am I quoting s-someone again? If I ever yell at you, you may f-feel free to yell b-back. I would never hurt you. I can safely promise that."

"Of myself," she said, fixing her eyes on the top button of his coat and leaning her cheek a little into his palm despite herself. "I am afraid of *me*."

He gazed deeply into her eyes. It was strange how she could see that in the darkness.

"Even tonight," she said, "I was angry. I *am* angry. I had no idea I was going to be, but it has happened. You play with my emotions, though perhaps not deliberately. You find me and talk with me and kiss me and then—*nothing* for days, and then it all starts again. You made me promise five days ago that I would not say no, and then you left and gave me no chance to say either yes or no. You did not tell me you were going away. You did not need to, of course. I had no right to expect it. And now I have a premonition that this is what marriage with you would be like, but on a grander scale. Life as I have known it for years, including the five years of my marriage, would be turned on its head, and I would not know *where* I was. I could not stand the uncertainty."

"You fear passion?" he asked her.

"Because it is *uncontrolled*," she cried. "Because it is selfish. Because it hurts—other people if not oneself. I do not want passion. I do not want uncertainty. I do not want you yelling at me. Worse than that, I do not want me yelling back. I cannot stand it. I cannot stand *this*."

His face was closer again.

"What has happened in your life to hurt you?" he asked her.

Her eyes widened. "*Nothing* has happened. That is the point."

But it was not. It was not the point at all.

"You w-want me," he said, "as much as I want you."

And his eyes blazed with a new light.

"I am afraid," she said again, but even to her own ears her protest sounded lame.

His mouth, hot in the chill of the late evening, covered hers, and her arms went about his neck, and his about her waist, and she leaned into him, or he drew her against him—it did not matter which. And she knew—ah, she knew that she could not let him go, even though she *was* afraid. It was going to be like stepping off the edge of a precipice blindfolded.

He had said *nothing* about love. But neither had William. What was love, after all? She had never believed in it or wanted it.

He raised his head.

"We could marry tomorrow," he said. "I was thinking of the d-day after, but that was when I did not expect to s-see you until the morning. And the vicar is here at the house. I could have a word with him tonight. We could marry tomorrow morning, Agnes. Or would you rather that g-grand wedding in St. George's? With all your family and mine in attendance."

She braced her hands on his shoulders and laughed, though not with amusement. She was more afraid than ever before in her life. She was afraid she was about to do something she would forever regret.

"There is the small matter of banns," she said.

He flashed a grin at her.

"Special license," he said. "I h-have one on the table beside my bed upstairs. It is why I went to L-London, though it struck me when I was on the way there that I c-could probably have got one somewhere closer, maybe even Gloucester. I am not v-very knowledgeable on such things. No matter. I managed to avoid everyone I know except an uncle, who was not to be avoided by the time I s-spotted him. He is a g-good fellow, though. I informed him that he had not seen me, and he raised his glass and asked who the devil I was anyway."

Agnes was not listening.

"You went to London to get a *special license*?" she asked, though he had been perfectly clear on the matter. "So that you could marry me here without the benefit of banns? *Tomorrow?*"

"If it were done," he said, *"then 'twere well it were done quickly."*

She stared at him, speechless for a moment.

"Macbeth was talking about *murder*," she said. "And you missed *when 'tis done* in the middle—*If it were done when 'tis done* . . . Those words make all the difference to the meaning."

"You have this disturbing effect upon me, Agnes," he said. "I s-start spouting p-poetry. Badly. But—*'twere well it were done quickly*. I stand by that."

"Before you can change your mind?" she asked him. "Or before I can?"

"Because I want to be s-safe with you," he said.

She looked at him in astonishment.

"Because I w-want to make l-love to you," he added, "and I cannot do it before we are m-married, because you are a v-virtuous woman, and I have a rule about not seducing v-virtuous women."

But he had said, *Because I want to be safe with you.*

Yet she was afraid of *not* being safe with him.

"Lord Ponsonby—" she said.

"Flavian," he interrupted her. "It is one of the m-most

ridiculous names any parents could possibly inflict upon a son, but it is what my parents d-did to me, and I am stuck with it. I am Flavian."

She swallowed.

"Flavian," she said.

"It does not sound so b-bad spoken in your voice," he said. "Say it again."

"Flavian." And, surprisingly, she laughed. "It suits you."

He grimaced.

"Say the rest of it," he said. "You spoke my name, and there was m-more to come. Say the rest."

She had forgotten. It had something to do with whether they would be safe together or not. But—*safe*? What did it mean?

Tomorrow. She could be married *tomorrow*.

"I think my father and my brother would find it an inconvenience to travel all the way to London," she said. "Especially for a second marriage. Do you have a large family?"

"Enormous," he said. "We could fill two St. George's and still allow for s-standing room only."

It was her turn to grimace.

"But what will they all *say*?" she asked him.

He threw back his head, his arms still about her, and—bayed at the moon. There was no other way of describing the sound of triumph that burst from him.

"*Will* say?" he said. "Not *would* say? They will be as cross as b-blazes, all s-seven thousand and sixty of them, at being denied the fuss and anguish of having a say in my w-wedding. Tomorrow, Agnes, if it can be arranged? Or the day after tomorrow at the latest? Say yes. Say *yes*."

She still could not understand. Why her? And why the complete turnaround from the time, not long distant, when he had told her he would never have marriage to offer anyone? What sort of attraction did she hold for a man like Viscount Ponsonby?

Because I want to be safe with you.

What could those words possibly mean?

She slid her hands behind his neck again and raised her face to his.

"Yes, then," she said in exasperation. "You will not take no for an answer anyway, will you? Yes, then. Yes, Flavian."

And his mouth came down on hers again.

12

Flavian was feeling as fresh as a daisy—or some such idiotic thing. He had gone to bed at midnight and had awoken at eight o'clock only because his valet was bumping around in his dressing room with deliberate intent.

And then he had remembered that it was his wedding day.

And that he had slept all night without a hint of a dream or any other disturbance.

Good Lord, it was his wedding day.

He had gone back up to the drawing room with Agnes Keeping last night, and no one would have shown they had noticed the two of them had gone or returned—until he cleared his throat. That had got an instant silence. And he had told them that Mrs. Keeping had just done him the honor of accepting his hand in marriage. Yes, he believed he really had used pompous words like those. But they had got the message across.

And, looking back, it seemed to him that everyone had collectively smirked, though that smug reaction had soon been followed by noise and backslapping and hand shaking and hugs and even tears. Miss Debbins had shed tears over her sister, and so had Lady Darleigh. And even

George. Not that he had shed tears exactly, and certainly not over Agnes, but his eyes had looked suspiciously bright as he squeezed Flavian's shoulder fit to dislocate it.

Flavian had followed up with the announcement that the nuptials were going to be in the morning, provided Reverend Jones was willing to perform the ceremony on so little notice.

"*Tomorrow* morning?" Miss Debbins and Hugo had chorused in unison.

The vicar had merely nodded congenially and reminded Lord Ponsonby that there was the small matter of banns to be considered.

"Not if there is a s-special license," Flavian had said. "And there *is* one. I have just c-come from London with it."

"Why, you old rogue, Flave," Ralph had said. "*This* is the use to which you put my curricle?"

And there had been more noise and backslapping, and Lady Darleigh had rushed off to find her cook and housekeeper, and rushed back a while later with the news that the state bedchamber in the east wing was to be prepared for tomorrow night so that the bride and groom could spend their wedding night in luxury and privacy. George had offered to give Agnes away, but, after thanking him, she had said she would rather have her sister do that for her if there was no church law against a woman performing the office. And Flavian had asked Vincent to be his best man, which would be, Vince had replied, beaming with pleasure, a bit like the blind leading the blind.

And then, some time later, the outside guests had left, including Agnes Keeping, and it was close to midnight, and Flavian had felt drunk without the benefit of liquor and so exhausted that he could scarcely persuade his legs to carry him to his room, and might not have made it there if George and Ralph had not accompanied him to his door. He might not have got undressed either if his valet had not been waiting for him and insisted that he was *not* going to be allowed to sleep in his evening clothes.

But here he was, almost eleven hours later, as fresh as a daisy and waiting at the front of the village church for his bride to arrive. His friends and their wives were sitting in the pews behind him, and the vicar's wife and the Harrisons were in the pews across the aisle.

Vincent was afraid he would drop the ring—Flavian had remembered to buy one, though he had had to guess the size—and then not be able to find it.

"But I would," Flavian said, patting his friend's hand. "I would like nothing better than to g-grovel about on the stone floor of a country church on my w-wedding day in my white knee breeches and s-stockings."

"That is supposed to *comfort* me?" Vincent asked. "And wait a minute—it is supposed to be the best man soothing the bridegroom's nerves, not the other way around."

"A bridegroom is s-supposed to have n-nerves?" Flavian asked. "Better not warn me about it, old chap, or I m-might discover I have some."

But he did not—unless it was a sign of nerves that he half expected his mother to appear in the doorway behind him, twice her usual size, forefinger twice its usual length as it pointed full at him while she ordered him to cease and desist.

He was feeling . . . happy? He did not know what happy felt like and was not sure he wanted to, for where there was happiness, there was also unhappiness. Every positive had its corresponding negative, one of the more annoying laws of existence.

He just wanted her to come. Agnes. He wanted to

marry her. He wanted to *be married* to her. He still could not free his mind of the notion that he would be safe once he was. And he had still not worked out what his mind meant by that.

Some things were best not analyzed.

His valet was a wonder and a marvel, he thought. What on earth had possessed him to pack knee breeches, and white ones at that, for a three-week stay in the country with the Survivors' Club?

Fortunately, perhaps, for the quality of his thoughts, there was a minor stir at the back of the church, and the vicar came striding down the aisle, resplendent in his clerical robes, to signal that the bride had arrived and the marriage service was about to begin.

Agnes donned her moss green morning dress and pelisse with the straw bonnet she had bought new just last year. There was no time, of course, to purchase new clothes for her wedding. It did not matter. It was just as well, in fact. If she had had time to shop or to sew, then she would also have had time to think.

Thought, she suspected, was her worst enemy at the moment. Or perhaps it was the *lack* of thought that was the long-term enemy. She had *no idea* what she was getting herself into.

What on earth had possessed her?

But, no, she would not think. She had said yes last night because she had found it impossible to say no, and it was too late to change her mind now.

Besides, if she had said no, he would be going away tomorrow with everyone else, never to return, and she could not have borne that. Her heart would have broken. Surely it would have, extravagant and silly as the idea seemed.

The state bedchamber . . .

No, she would not think.

There was a tap on her door, and Dora stepped into her room.

"I keep expecting to wake up, as from a dream," she said. "But I am glad it is no dream, Agnes. I am happy for you. I believe *you* will be happy. I *like* that young man, though I would still not trust that eyebrow of his any farther than I could throw it. And *that* image does not bear scrutiny, does it?"

"Dora." Agnes clasped her hands very tightly to her bosom. "I feel dreadful. About leaving you."

"You absolutely must not," Dora said. "It was inevitable that you would remarry one day. I never expected that you would be here with me forever. All I ask is that you be happy. I have always loved you more than anyone else in my life, you know, which is a shocking thing to say when I have a father and a brother and nieces and a nephew. But you have always felt almost as much like a daughter to me as a sister. You were five when I was seventeen."

When they had been left alone except for their father, who had retired into himself after their mother left, and been an almost invisible presence in their lives. Oliver, their brother, had already been at Cambridge.

"Dora." Agnes hesitated. She had never asked, had thought she never would. It was certainly not a question for today. But it came out anyway. "*Are* we sisters?"

Dora stared back at her, eyes like empty caves, mouth half-open.

"I mean," Agnes said, "are we *full* sisters?"

Their father, Oliver, and Dora all had dark coloring and brown eyes. So had their mother. But not Agnes, born so many years after the other two. It was a small thing. There were explanations other than the one she had tried half her life not to consider. Traits of appearance sometimes skipped a generation.

"If we are not," Dora said, "I have never known it—I was only twelve when you were born, remember. And I have never wanted to know."

So she had wondered too.

"I *do* not want to know," Dora said with emphasis. "You are my *sister*, Agnes. My beloved sister. Nothing—*nothing*—could ever change that."

"You gave up so much for me," Agnes said.

Dora had been planning and dreaming about the come-out Season she was to have in London when she was eighteen. The five-year-old Agnes had shared her hopes and her excitement and had thought her grown-up sister vibrantly pretty and certain to get herself a handsome husband. But when their mother was gone suddenly, everything came to an end for Dora, and she had stayed to care for Agnes, to raise her, to love her, to keep house for their father. And she had never been vibrantly pretty since.

"What I gave up," Dora told her, "*I* gave up, Agnes. It was *my* choice. Aunt Millicent would have had me. She would have brought me to Harrogate and found a husband for me there. I *chose* to stay, just as I *chose* to come here when Father remarried. This is *my* life, Agnes. I have done with it and am doing with it what I have chosen to do. You owe me nothing. Do you hear me? *Nothing.* If you feel you owe me something anyway, then do this for me, something you could not really do with William, good and worthy though he was. Be *happy*, Agnes. It is all I ask. And even that is a request, not a demand. I have made no sacrifices for you. I have always done only what I have wanted to do."

Agnes swallowed awkwardly.

"And I absolutely *forbid* you," Dora said, her voice

wobbling strangely, "to shed tears, Agnes. It is time to leave for church, and you do not want Lord Ponsonby to take one look at you and imagine that I have had to drag you there."

Agnes laughed and then bit her upper lip.

"I love you," she said.

"That," Dora said, wagging a finger at her, "is enough. It is unlike you to be sentimental, Agnes. But it is your wedding day, and I will make allowances and forgive you. Come along, now. You do not want to be late."

They were not late. It was right on eleven o'clock when they stepped inside the church. There were three carriages outside, one of them festively decorated with flowers. And there were people there too. Word must have spread, though who could have spread it, Agnes could not imagine. News in a village seemed to travel on the very air. People nodded and smiled at her and looked as though they planned to stay awhile.

And then they were inside, and Agnes could see that the church had been decorated too. The familiar smells of ancient stone and incense and candles and old prayer books mingled with the perfumes of spring flowers. And it struck her, as if for the first time, that this was her wedding day. Her second. She was leaving behind her first forever, even relinquishing William's name today, and entering upon her second.

To Viscount Ponsonby.

Flavian.

She almost panicked for a moment then. Flavian *what*? She did not even know his last name. It was going to be hers within the next few minutes, yet she did not know what it was.

Dora took her hand in a firm clasp and smiled at her, and they proceeded along the aisle together, hand in hand.

He was standing waiting for her, dressed with old-fashioned and magnificent formality in white knee breeches and linen with a dull gold waistcoat and a form-fitting dark brown tailed coat. His hair gleamed golden in a shaft of light from one of the high windows. He looked as handsome as a prince in any fairy tale.

Foolish, foolish thought.

Last night Flavian had tried to convince Lady Darleigh that they would have the wedding breakfast at the village inn, at his expense, and that he and his bride would be happy to stay for the night somewhere on the road to London. The viscountess was a small lady, a little slip of a thing, in fact, and she looked scarcely older than a girl. But when she made up her mind about something, there was no moving her. And last night, even before he was able to speak up on the matter, she had made up her mind.

They would eat together at Middlebury, she had told him, and she would have the guest suite in the state apartments prepared. It had been furnished a hundred years or so ago, apparently, for a royal prince and his princess who had been expected to grace Middlebury Park with their company. Whether they had come or not was a detail lost to history, but the apartments were still there in all their opulent splendor.

And so it was to Middlebury Park they went after the marriage ceremony was over and the register signed. The church bell was ringing its single note as they stepped outside, and the sun was just breaking free of a cloud, and a small crowd of villagers exclaimed and applauded and set up a self-conscious cheer. And Ralph and Hugo, damn their eyes, were waiting with grins they could have hooked over their ears, and fistfuls of flower petals, which were soon raining about Agnes's head and his. Flavian would be willing to wager half his fortune that his carriage was now bedecked with more than *just* a ton and a half of flowers.

He turned his head to look at Agnes, so familiar though he had known her for only three weeks and for two dances five or six months ago, and so . . . safe. He could still think of no more appropriate word. She was flushed and bright eyed and familiar, and he felt a welling of contentment. It sounded almost like a contradiction in terms.

"This is unbelievable," she said, laughing.

The others were coming out behind them, and there was all that noise and backslapping and hand shaking and hugging and kissing business going on again. And the villagers beamed from out on the street.

"Well, Agnes," Flavian said at last, taking her by the hand, "sh-shall we lead the way?"

He handed her into the carriage, while George held the door open like a footman, and then shut it upon them and gave the signal to the coachman. Flavian bent his head to kiss his bride so that all the spectators would not be disappointed.

They jumped apart a moment later—the same moment as the carriage moved ahead, dragging behind it what sounded like a veritable arsenal of old pots and pans. At least Flavian hoped they were old.

"Goodness gracious," she said, looking considerably alarmed.

He grinned. "I have done it to three of my friends in the l-last year," he said. "It is only fair that they do it to m-me."

And he gazed into her eyes amidst all the din, and she gazed back.

"Lady Ponsonby," he said.

It seemed unreal. He still could not quite believe that

he had done it, that she had agreed to it, that they were *married*.

What was his mother going to say? And Marianne?

"Any regrets?" he asked as the carriage turned off the street and onto the drive through the woods.

"It is too late for regrets," she said. "Gracious, that is an unholy din. We are going to be deaf."

Yes, it was too late for regrets. Or for more considered deliberation and planning. Lord, he scarcely knew her or she him. Had he always been so impulsive? He could not remember.

He held one of her hands in both his own and looked her over with lazy eyes. She was neat and trim and pretty. She was dressed in what was obviously her best daytime outfit. It was decent, and the color suited her. It was also prim and unfashionable and clearly not new. She sat with a straight back and her knees pressed together and her feet side by side—a familiar pose. She looked quiet and demure.

If he had been asked a month ago to describe the sort of lady who least appealed to him, he might have described Agnes Keeping with uncanny accuracy, not even remembering that he had once met and danced with just such a woman. Yet even back then, five or six months ago, he had gone back for a second dance—a waltz, no less—when there had been no need. And he had found her enchanting.

Agnes Keeping—no, Agnes *Arnott*—and enchantment ought to seem poles apart. Why were they not?

What *was* it about her?

He raised her hand to his lips and kissed her gloved fingers.

His wife.

* * *

Agnes might have been feeling guilty for all the trouble she was causing if Sophia had not been looking so very pleased with herself and if Lord Darleigh had not been beaming with pleasure too.

Though Sophia had pointed out last evening that luncheon would have to have been served for all their guests, even if no one had thought of getting married on the final day of their visit, and that a few more guests at table really made very little difference, it was obvious that the meal that awaited them on their return from church was very far from being an ordinary luncheon.

It was a wedding breakfast in a dining room festooned with flowers and ribbons and candles. There was even a cake—*iced*. How the cook could possibly have baked and decorated it along with everything else since just last night, Agnes could not imagine. Certainly no one could have slept. She would have asked Sophia whether she might go down to the kitchen to compliment the cook in person, but it struck her that doing so might merely add chaos to what must be a dizzyingly busy place indeed. She sent her compliments with Sophia instead.

There was a sumptuous meal, and there were speeches and toasts with a great deal of applause and laughter.

There was a ceremonial cake cutting.

They all lingered at the table while conversation became general, and Agnes remembered that this was the last day of the gathering for the Survivors' Club, that they would have been clinging to one another's company and turning a bit sentimental even without the added distraction of the wedding of one of their number. Not that they were in any way exclusive in their conversation, those seven. They were far too well-bred for that. The Harrisons were drawn into the conversation, as were Reverend and Mrs. Jones. Dora was quiet and smiling, but she was being made much of by Lord Trentham on her right.

And then, when it was already late afternoon, the vicar and his wife rose to take their leave, and the Harrisons followed suit and offered Dora a ride home.

Suddenly, it seemed, they were all in the great hall. Mrs. Harrison and Mrs. Jones were hugging Agnes and telling her, with a laugh, that she was a mite beyond their touch now that she was *Viscountess* Ponsonby.

Dora, having offered Flavian her hand, was drawn into a hug instead. And then she was standing in front of Agnes and setting both hands on her elbows.

"Be happy," she said softly, so that no one else would hear. "Remember, it is all I ask. It is all I have ever wanted for you." And she kissed Agnes on the cheek before stepping back, the smile she had worn all day firmly in place. "I will see you in the morning as you are leaving," she said.

"Yes." Agnes could not trust her voice to say more. But she grabbed Dora and hugged her tightly. It was strange that she had not felt this way when she married William. Was it because she had not expected happiness then? Did that mean she expected it now? And what did she *mean*—she had not expected happiness with William? She had certainly expected contentment, and she had found it. And that was better than happiness, was it not? It was more lasting, a surer foundation upon which to base one's life. "You must come and stay with us. You *will* come?"

"Even if I am not invited," Dora promised, pulling back. "You will wake up one morning to find me camped on your doorstep, and you will take me in out of pity. And then I will refuse to go away again."

She was laughing.

But *where* would she invite Dora? Agnes almost panicked again. She did not even know where her home was going to be. She knew *nothing*—except that her last name was Arnott. She was Agnes Arnott, Viscountess Ponsonby. She sounded like a stranger to herself.

And then everyone was gone. The vicar's gig was already clopping along the terrace and turning to skirt about the formal parterres. The Duke of Stanbrook was handing Dora into Mr. Harrison's carriage, and it too moved off as soon as Mr. Harrison had climbed in after her and shut the door.

Dora was gone home to a cottage that was no longer Agnes's. Her trunk and bags were already packed—she had spent a few hours of last night getting them ready, as well as a bag of things she would need tonight and tomorrow morning. Her possessions would be picked up tomorrow, and then she would no longer belong in Inglebrook. She did not know when she would see Dora again.

Flavian had drawn her arm through his and was peering into her face, a large white handkerchief in his free hand.

"I will see to it that you are never s-sorry," he said, his voice low. "I p-promise, Agnes."

The tears that had been brimming in her eyes spilled over then, and she took the handkerchief from him to mop them up.

"I am not sorry," she said. "I am only sad about saying good-bye to Dora. It is not easy to leave one's home, even though it has been my home for less than a year. And I do not even know where my new home is to be. I did not even know what my *name* was to be when I arrived at the church this morning."

"Arnott?" he said. "I kept it from you. I thought it m-might tip the scale against me last night. I thought you might not like the s-sound of Agnes Arnott."

She folded the handkerchief and allowed him to take it from her.

"You are sometimes quite absurd," she said.

He smiled. It was a new expression, one she had not seen before. It crinkled his eyes at the corners and contained not a discernible trace of mockery. She thought he was going to say something else, but he appeared to change his mind. He merely patted her hand on his arm and turned back into the house with her.

Oh, dear heavens, he was her *husband*.

13

The guest suite was above the state drawing rooms—both of them. It was large, to say the least. Two people could, Flavian concluded, hide quite effectively from each other if they wished. There were two bedchambers, with two side-by-side dressing rooms between, each large enough to hold a prince or princess with all their attendant ladies- or gentlemen-in-waiting, with space to spare for them to breathe. And there was a grand sitting room, spacious enough to accommodate all the aforementioned court of persons, plus a generous allotment of guests.

The whole of the apartment had been cleaned to a shine. The top of one sideboard was more than half-covered with wines and liquors and glasses. There were silver and crystal dishes of fruit and nuts and bonbons on various tabletops. There were covered plates of cakes and sweet biscuits on another sideboard, with a tray of both tea and coffee, which had been delivered only moments after the bride and groom had arrived. And supper would be brought at nine o'clock, the liveried servant informed them with a bow—in two hours' time, in other words.

"But you surely wish to be with your friends tonight," Agnes informed Flavian after she had finished sinking into one of four cushioned seats on a magnificent and obviously extremely comfortable sofa with gilded feet and arms and back. "It is your last night together."

"And by coincidence," he said, taking up his stand before her, his hands clasped at his back, his feet slightly apart, "it is my *first* night with my b-bride. Those friends might well beat me about the h-head with one of Ben's c-canes if I were to choose them over you."

She was still wearing her green dress. She was still looking like a prim and pretty governess. He had almost told her so out on the terrace when she had said he was sometimes quite absurd. But she might have been offended to be called prim, and not even have noticed the *pretty*. Women could be like that.

"And *y-you* might well beat me about the head with your b-bare hand if I chose them," he added. "You would all have to draw lots."

"I would n—" she began.

"And *I* would beat *myself* about the head if I was t-tempted for even a moment to be such a d-dolt as to leave you here and d-dash off to them," he said. "We would *all* have to draw lots. I believe I and my head will be safe, however. Conversation with one's f-friends on the one hand and sex with one's new w-wife on the other is not even a fair competition."

As he had expected, her cheeks, and even her neck and the small amount of bosom that had been allowed to show above the neckline of her dress, were suddenly suffused with color. Her lips did something that made her look even more like a governess. But she held his eyes.

"I wish you would not loom over me like that," she said, "trying to look sleepy when I know very well you are not."

He smiled slowly at her. "I am *definitely* not s-sleepy," he said. "Not yet, anyway."

He sat on the cushion beside hers and found himself at least two feet away from her. Where the deuce had a former Viscount Darleigh found such a monstrous piece of furniture? It probably weighed a ton and a half, and it would surely accommodate twenty persons seated side by side, provided they were slender and did not mind cozying up to one another. Yet it did not come even close to dwarfing the room.

He took her hand in one of his and curled his fingers about it.

"What shall we do between now and nine o'clock?" he asked her. "Sit here and c-converse like polite s-strangers, or go to bed?"

She drew a breath through her nose and released it through her mouth. "It is not even quite dark."

Which remark spoke volumes. Sex in her first marriage had been conducted under cover of decent darkness, then, had it? But he did *not* want to think about the dull William.

"Where is home?" she asked him.

She had opted for the conversation between strangers, it seemed.

"Candlebury Abbey in Sussex," he said. "The old part r-really was an abbey once, though you will not be expected to move from room to room along d-draughty cloisters or sleep in a b-bare stone cell. I do not spend much time in the country—or any at all, in fact. There is also Arnott House in L-London."

"Why?" The inevitable question. "Why do you never go to Candlebury Abbey?"

He shrugged and opened his mouth to tell her it was too large a place for one man to rattle around in alone. But she was his wife. She probably ought to know a few simple facts about the man she had married.

"I still think of it as David's," he said. "My elder

brother's. He loved every inch of it, and he knew the history of it. He had r-read and reread everything about it he could get his hands on. He knew every b-brushstroke on every p-painting. He knew every stone and flagstone in the old abbey. He knew the p-peace of it all, the h-holiness. He always wished he could conjure spirits or ghosts, but the only spirit there is h-his. Or so I imagine. He died there at the age of twenty-five. There were four years between us. He was the viscount before I was, though it was becoming increasingly clear even before our father died when David was eighteen that he was not going to live a full lifespan. He had always been of delicate health—I was more than half a f-foot taller than he by the time I was thirteen, and a good deal heavier even though I was a g-gangly youth and all elbows and knees. We all understood he had c-consumption, though it was never spoken aloud in my hearing. I *was*, though, being f-firmly prepared to take over the position of v-viscount myself by the two of our six hundred uncles who had been named our guardians. No b-bones were made about it either. No attempt was made to be t-tactful or subtle. David was aware of it—how could he not have been? But he allowed it to h-happen without comment. I was his heir, after all. Even if he had been robust and healthy, I would have been his heir until he m-married and fathered a son. Finally I could s-stand no more of it. I r-refused to go to university when I was eighteen, as they had planned for me. I insisted on a m-military career instead, and David purchased my commission. He was of age by that time and my official guardian."

There. That was a few simple facts, slightly distorted. He had not given the real reason he had wanted that commission and David's real reason for obliging him.

But she had asked him why he never went to Candlebury. He had not really answered her.

"He lingered longer than anyone expected," he continued. "But three years after I left, he was clearly dying, and I came home on leave from the Peninsula. Everyone assumed I was home to stay. I even assumed it myself. I was facing new responsibilities. But meanwhile he was d-dying, and nothing else mattered. He was my b-brother."

He paused to swallow. She made no attempt to say anything.

"And then I left him," he said. "I was d-due to return to the Peninsula, and I decided to go even though he was close to death. Indeed, I left home four days before I needed to and went to London to enjoy myself at a g-grand ball. He died the day after I sailed. I got the news two weeks later, but I did not go back home. What would have b-been the point? He was gone, and I had not been with him when it m-mattered, and I did not w-want the title that had been his or everything else that was now mine. I d-did not w-want Candlebury. So I stayed until a bullet through the head and a fall from my horse did what his death had not accomplished. I came home, or, rather, I was b-brought home—to London, though, not Candlebury, thank God."

He waited for the recriminations. Why had he left his brother? Just to go to a *ball*? Why had he returned to the Peninsula? Why had he not sold out and come home after the news reached him? He would be able to reply, though the answers made little sense to him. Even allowing his mind to touch upon the questions brought the threat of a crashing headache and of blind panic. It brought the danger of clenched fists and a lashing-out at inanimate objects, as if reducing them to firewood would clear all the fog from his mind and make sense of his past and excuse every dastardly deed he had ever committed.

But she did not ask any of the questions. She did not

even ask her usual why. Instead she was holding both his hands in hers.

"I *am* sorry," she said. "Oh, poor Flavian. How wretched for you. I can only imagine having to face such a thing with Dora. No, I do not *want* to imagine. But I think I too might have run away and tried to forget it all by enjoying myself at a crowded and glittering party. I do not suppose it helped, but I can understand why you did it. And why you could not stay. But you have not been able to let him go, have you, because you were not there. And you have not forgiven yourself either."

She drew her hands free of his and got to her feet.

"Let me pour you some tea or coffee while they are probably still hot. Or would you prefer something from the sideboard?"

"Tea," he said. "Please."

He watched her as she engaged in the quiet domestic task of pouring his tea and placing a couple of biscuits on the saucer. This was destined to become a familiar scene to him, he thought, just such a simple activity as this—taking tea with his wife. Perhaps there was peace to be had after all.

And absolution. She did not have the power to give it, but she had comforted him anyway. He had left out whole chunks of information, though. It was all much worse even than he had made it sound.

"Tell me about the rest of your family," she said as she seated herself beside him, her own cup and saucer in hand. She smiled. "Six *hundred* uncles?"

"There is my mother," he said, "and one sister, Marianne, Lady Shields. Oswald, Lord Shields, her husband. Two nephews and a niece. Six *thousand* aunts, uncles, and c-cousins at the last count—did I say six hundred? We will go to L-London first when we leave here, and you can meet some of them. There are other things to be done there too. Maybe we will go to C-Candlebury for Easter. My mother is there and my s-sister and her family. I will write to my mother and w-warn her to expect us."

He ought to take Agnes straight to Candlebury, he supposed. She needed to do a mountain of shopping, but it could possibly be delayed until after Easter, when they moved to London for the Season with the rest of the fashionable world. And she *ought* to be there for the Season, perish the thought. As his viscountess she would need to be introduced to the *ton*, perhaps even presented at court. Sometimes one could wish that reality in the form of the proprieties did not have to intrude quite so soon or so often upon one's life.

He had ignored reality when he had dashed off for the license and dashed back again to marry her.

She lifted her teacup to her lips. There was a very slight tremor in her hand, he thought.

"Your mother and sister will be upset with you," she said. "And with me. I am not a very eligible bride for Viscount Ponsonby."

They would be more upset than she realized. They would be predisposed to dislike her no matter who she was, simply because she was not Velma. He ought to have been more forthcoming with her, but it was too late now—too late for her to change her mind about marrying him, anyway. He must explain a few things before they went to Candlebury, though. It would not be fair to allow her to walk blind into that potentially explosive situation.

But he would do that later. Enough about him.

"Nonsense," he said. "And what about your father? Will he be upset that I did not apply to him for your hand but rushed you into m-marriage even before he knew about me? I must write to him too."

"He would appreciate it, I am sure," she said. "Though

I did write to him this morning, and to my brother. I am sure they will both be pleased as well as surprised. They will see that I have done very well for myself."

"Even without s-setting eyes upon me?"

"When they *do*, they may change their minds." Her eyes twinkled at her own joke.

"When did your mother die?" he asked.

"When I was—" But she stopped to set her cup very carefully in the saucer, and she leaned forward to set them rattling down on the tray. "She did not. As far as I know, she is still alive."

He stared at her as she came to sit beside him again and spread her fingers over her lap to examine the backs of them with careful attention.

Hang on a minute. Her father had remarried, had he not?

"She left when I was five," she told him. "My father petitioned Parliament soon after and divorced her. It took a great deal of time and trouble and money, though I knew nothing about any of it as a child. All I did know was that she was gone and was not coming back and that I missed her and cried for her night after night and often in the daytime too. But Dora was still there, and was staying after all instead of going to London for her come-out Season and the husband she had dreamed of finding there. I was very happy about that. She had always been my favorite person in the world—apart from our mother, that is—and she assured me over and over again until I believed her that she would far rather stay with me than go anywhere else. How innocent children are. She stayed until our father remarried, and then the year after that *I* married William. It was only then that I understood that we had once had very decent dowries set aside for us, Dora and I, but that most of the money had gone on the divorce, and almost all of the little that remained had been used to set Dora up at Inglebrook before she started to earn her own way. Not many men would have taken me when I was virtually portionless. William always assured me that it was *me* he had wanted to marry, not money."

Good God! Did *everyone* have a story to tell when one took the time to listen to it—or when the person concerned could be persuaded to tell it?

"*And* he was willing to take me despite the disgrace," she added, still addressing the backs of her hands. "He knew about it, of course. He had always been our neighbor. I did not give you the choice, did I?"

"What happened to her?" he asked. "To your mother, I mean."

She shrugged her shoulders and kept them up close to her ears for a few moments. "She was never spoken of," she said, "especially around me, I suppose. I heard snatches of things anyway, of course, from servants, from the children of neighbors. I believe she married her lover. I do not know who he was. I believe, though I do not know for certain, that he had been her lover for some time before she left with him. I have a few memories of her. She was dark and beautiful and vibrant with life. She laughed and she danced and she lifted me high and tossed me upward until I shrieked with fright and begged for more. At least I *think* she was beautiful. Perhaps a mother always looks beautiful to her infant child. And she cannot have been really young. Oliver was fourteen when I was born."

"Are you c-curious about her?" he asked.

She raised her eyes to his at last.

"No," she said. "Not even to the smallest degree. I do not know who he was or is, and I do not want to know. I do not know who *she* is or even for sure *whether* she is. I would not recognize her name or her face, I daresay. I would not wish to recognize either. I do not want to know *her*. She abandoned Dora as well as me, and the consequences for Dora were far more dreadful than they were for me. No, I am not curious. But there is something else you ought to know—something you ought to have known before this morning."

He had set down his own cup and saucer and taken one of her hands in his again. It was cold, as he had expected it to be. He sensed what was coming.

"I am not even sure," she said, "that my father *is* my father."

Her eyes were flat, her voice toneless, and he simply did not believe that she was not curious. Ah, his calm, quiet, disciplined, *safe* Agnes, who had carried inside a universe of pain since she was little more than a baby.

"Has anyone ever said he is not?" he asked her.

"No."

"Has he ever treated you differently from your brother and sister?"

"No. But I do not look like him or Dora or Oliver. Or *her*."

"Perhaps you resemble an aunt or uncle or grandparent," he said. "Your father *is* your f-father regardless, Agnes. Birth and b-breeding do not always depend upon small matters like who provided the seed."

She looked away from him.

"You may have married a bastard," she said.

He might have laughed if she had not looked so serious.

"There will be those who will tell you that it is y-you who have married the b-bastard," he told her, and then he did smile as he raised her hand to his lips. "I have something in common with your W-William after all, it seems, Agnes. I married you this morning because, even though I s-scarcely know you, I wanted you for my wife.

I still w-want you, even if you are a bastard ten times over. Is it p-possible to be ten times a bastard? It s-sounds rather dire, does it not?"

He had moved his head closer to hers, despite the infernally giant size of the sofa cushions, until she was forced to gaze into his eyes. And she . . . laughed.

"You are *so* absurd," she said.

And he kissed her while her hand clung to his and her lips trembled against his and then pushed back, and he wound one arm about her shoulders.

She was, he thought, as horribly damaged as he was.

They managed to keep a conversation going for the hour that remained before their supper was brought and during the meal itself—and one that was far lighter in tone. The two footmen who came with their food set up a table in the middle of the sitting room with a crisp white cloth and the finest china and silverware and crystal and wine Lord Darleigh had to offer. They lit two tapers set in silver holders. It was a gloriously romantic setting.

He told her more about his mother and his sister and the latter's husband and children. He recounted a few anecdotes involving his brother and himself in their younger years, and it was clearer than ever that he had adored his smaller, less robust older sibling. He told her about his years in school at Eton—his brother had been educated at home—and a little about his years with his cavalry regiment, though nothing touching upon the battles in which he had fought. She told him about her brother and his wife and their children. She told him about her father's wife, whom she had always liked and still did, though she would find it a severe trial to have to live with her in the same house. She recounted some incidents from her childhood that included Dora.

It was only toward the end of the meal, when Flavian was sitting back at his ease, wineglass in hand, that something shocking struck Agnes.

"Oh, goodness me," she said, "I did not change for dinner."

"Neither did I," he said, his eyes roaming lazily over the part of her dress he could see above the table.

"Oh, but you are dressed splendidly," she pointed out, "while I am wearing just a day dress."

"This was not dinner, Agnes," he said. "It was s-supper."

"But I ought to have changed, nevertheless," she said. "I do beg your pardon."

Into the blue or the lavender or the green. No, not the green. It was a little too festive, though this *was* her wedding evening. Oh, he would grow mortally sick of seeing the green—and the blue and the lavender.

He regarded her thoughtfully for a few moments before setting down his glass and getting to his feet. He came around the table and held out a hand for hers. And she was conscious of the fact that it was after ten o'clock and that she was nervous, just as if she were still a virgin.

She might as well be. It had been so long. . . .

She set her napkin on the table, put her hand in his, and rose to her feet. He brought her hand to his lips.

"Go and change now, then," he said, "into your nightgown. I will ring for the dishes to be removed and for my valet to come. You do not have a maid?"

"Oh, no," she said. "It is quite unnecessary."

"You nevertheless will h-have one," he told her, "as soon as we reach London. As well as new clothes."

"Oh, that will be quite un—" she began.

"They will be of the *first* necessity when we arrive in L-London," he told her. "The maid and the clothes. You are no l-longer Mrs. Keeping from the village of Inglebrook. You are Viscountess Ponsonby of Candlebury A-Abbey. I will see you clothed accordingly."

It was strange that she had not thought of that—of the fact that she no longer had to support herself on the small legacy William had left her, of the fact that she was now the wife of a wealthy aristocrat who would be shamed by a shabby wife. Not that her clothes were *shabby*, only not very new or plentiful, and never fashionable.

"Are you very wealthy?" she asked him.

Oh, it was shocking indeed to have married him without knowing the full extent of his fortune.

"You ought to have r-remembered to ask me that last night instead of this," he said, using his sighing voice and drooping his eyelids over his eyes. "For all you know, you may have m-married a pauper or a man with a p-pile of debts as high as Mount Olympus. But you can be comforted. My m-man of business in London has never yet resigned or had a f-fit of the vapors when he has met me, nor has he scolded me for extravagance or warned me that d-debtors' prison looms large in my near future. And my s-steward's accounts always show a healthy balance on the p-plus side. A few pretty frocks will not b-beggar me, though we may have to drink water for a month instead of tea if we add bonnets to the pile." He smiled, then added, "I do not have expensive vices, you will be r-relieved to know. When I do gamble, which is not often, I break out in a c-cold sweat as soon as my losses creep up near one hundred pounds, and I arouse the derisive annoyance of all my fellow players by throwing in my h-hand. And horses are fickle creatures, except in battle. I never b-bet on them."

"Was that a yes?" she asked.

"It was," he said. "I will never be able to accuse you of m-marrying me for my money, will I? You have d-deprived me of one weapon to use when we quarrel."

"I married you for your title," she said.

He smiled lazily at her.

"Did you s-sleep well last night?" he asked.

"We were late getting home." She looked warily at him. "Then I had to pack my things. I slept well enough after I finally lay down."

Apart from the wakeful spells. And the vivid dreams.

"You will not s-sleep much tonight," he told her. "And I would rather the night be no shorter than it need be. Go and get undressed."

What? It was not long after ten. Surely they would be able to get a good night's sleep after . . . Well, *after*. If she could sleep, that was. She might still be wound up by the strangeness of the day's events, including the one soon to be enacted.

They were leaving in the morning. For London.

She made her way to her dressing room, feeling his eyes on her back as she went.

It was a prim nightgown, as he had fully expected. It was not inexpensive—none of her clothes were. Neither was it new—none of her clothes were. And it had certainly not been made to excite a man's imagination or lust.

It did both anyway. It covered her to the ankles and the wrists and the neck. What was left to do *but* imagine and lust after what was hidden from sight?

Her hair was in a single neat braid down her back and drawn smoothly over her head and ears. She was standing by the window of her bedchamber, though he did not believe there was much of a view beyond it. It faced the hill and the wilderness walk, and there was not much moonlight tonight. She was looking back over her shoulder at him, her face wiped of all expression. Like a martyr headed to the bonfire. Or was it witches who were destined for that particular fate? She looked bewitching enough to be one. She could give the most experienced courtesan a few hints.

He had tapped on the door and waited for her summons. He advanced into the room now after closing the door behind him.

"Have you ever seen such an opulent bedchamber?" he asked her. "It is a good thing the w-window does not face east. We might be blinded by sunlight on all the g-gilding in the morning."

"I wonder if the prince and his princess *did* stay here," she said. "It must have seemed like a horrid waste if they did not."

"We will have to make good use of it t-tonight," he said. "And then every farthing spent on it will have been worthwhile."

It was a good thing his valet had dug up a nightshirt from somewhere in his baggage, he thought—perhaps from the same remote corner his knee breeches had occupied. She might have been disconcerted to discover nakedness beneath his dressing gown.

"How l-long did it take you to braid your hair?" he asked her.

"Two minutes?" she said as though she was not sure. "Three?"

"Let me see if I can unbraid it in one," he said.

It took him longer because he stood in front of her to do it instead of behind, and he was distracted by her eyes, which were on the grayish side of blue and looked slightly smoky in the candlelight, fringed as they were by lashes that curled slightly at the ends and were a darker shade than her hair. Then he was distracted by her mouth, which no one would never compare to a rosebud, for which fact he was thankful. Wider mouths were far more kissable. And he was distracted by the smell of her hair or her skin or *her*. It was a scent beyond description and certainly came from no bottle or even entirely from any bar of soap. It was a scent that would be worth a fortune if he *could* bottle it, but he was far too selfish to share it, and why have it in a bottle when he had her?

He was distracted by the tip of her tongue, which took its time about moistening her lips, though it was perfectly obvious she did it with no intention whatsoever of causing a tightening in his groin.

She caused it anyway.

She had never had a come-out, because her father had used the money set aside for it to secure his divorce. Would she have learned feminine wiles if she had? He was glad she had not learned any. He liked the ones that came naturally and were not real wiles at all, for the very word suggested something deliberate.

It was like being married to a nun. Though he had not discovered yet what bed skills she had acquired during her previous marriage. He would be willing to wager, though. . . . No, he would not. A wager had to be made with another person.

He hoped she had no skills.

Strange thought. He had on occasion paid exorbitant prices for skills, as well as mere access to a female body.

She did not *look* like a nun after he had unraveled her plait and spread her hair over her shoulders. It was almost waist length—unfashionably long.

"It is neither dark nor blond," she said. "Just a nondescript brown."

"I would not l-like you with dark or blond hair," he said. "I like you with *this* color hair."

"Well, that is very gallant of you," she said.

She looked at least five years younger with her hair unconfined. Though he did not at all mind her the age she was.

He kissed her, threading the fingers of one hand

through all that heavy, silky hair and drawing her whole slim length to him with the other while he plundered her mouth. It was wet and scorching hot. She clutched his shoulders, and there was a tension in her that had not been there during previous embraces. Perhaps because she knew this time there would be no stopping.

"It has been a long time," she said a little breathlessly, a little apologetically, when he raised his head.

She did not mean since he last kissed her.

"*How* long?" he asked.

"Oh, five or six years."

And then she flushed and bit her lip, and he knew that if she could recall the words, she would do so in a heartbeat. For she had told him on another occasion that she had been a widow for three years. What sort of a marriage had she been in? What sort of a man had William Keeping been? Had he been sick for the last two or three years of their five-year marriage?

But he was not remotely interested in either William Keeping himself or the man's sex life. He was not even interested in William Keeping's widow.

He was on fire for his own wife.

"Time for bed," he said.

14

They did sleep, but only for an hour or so at a time when a sort of languorous exhaustion overcame them. They made love over and over again when they were awake.

In her mind Agnes called it making love, though she was aware that what happened between them was far more raw and carnal than that romantic term suggested.

He unclothed her and himself even before they lay down, and he did not extinguish the candles, though she drew his attention to the fact that they were still burning—four in a candelabrum on the dressing table, with the mirror multiplying them to eight, and one on the tables on either side of the bed.

"But I must s-see you, Agnes," he protested, "and what I do to you, and what you do to me."

The bed itself was enormous. It was surely wide enough to allow six adults to sleep side by side in roomy comfort. They used every inch of it in the course of the night but very few bedcovers, despite the fact that it was still only March and was probably chilly outside.

Neither of them noticed the chill. They had each other for bedcovers and for a mutual source of heat.

It was an inextinguishable source.

Agnes was shocked by their nakedness and by the lit candles and the lack of bedcovers. She was shocked by the way his eyes burned a hot trail over her whole body, including her most intimate parts, and by his hands, his fingers, his fingernails, his mouth, his tongue, his teeth as they moved all over her, stroking, tickling pinching, scratching, licking, blowing, biting—and doing myriad things to her body that aroused her to a fever pitch of wanting. But she was no virgin despite the very limited nature of her sexual experience. And she was no girl. She had repressed yearnings of which she had been almost entirely unaware since she really was a girl and a virgin, and she saw no reason to repress them any longer when he so obviously wanted her to share his pleasure. She did not lie a passive recipient of his lovemaking for long. Being able to do to and with a man all those things she had not even known of as well as those she had dreamed of but never known personally was invigorating and glorious beyond belief.

Lovemaking, she discovered, was not a brief, almost clandestine groping and joining of the lower halves of bodies under cover of blankets and darkness, and a hurried withdrawal as soon as the act was over, and a murmured, almost furtive good night and a subsequent sleeping in separate rooms. Oh, no, it was something else entirely. They played the first time with hot, vigorous sensuality, she and Flavian, for what seemed like long ages and might have been half an hour before he came inside her body with one long, hard thrust, robbing her of breath, almost of sanity. And even then he was in no hurry. He worked with slow thoroughness and deep, firm strokes until her hips and inner muscles fell into rhythm with him and they worked together, arms and legs twined about each other, both of them hot and slick with sweat and panting from their exertions.

And when, finally, he sighed against the side of her head and held deep inside her and she felt the hot gush of his seed, it was not relief she felt that duty was over for another week. It was an earth-shattering cresting of a wave and a wild, free-fall descent down the other side to the tranquil ocean beyond. It was the end of the world and the beginning of eternity—or so it felt for the first few minutes after it happened, until her breathing returned to normal and her heart ceased its thudding and she was aware of his warm weight pressing her into the mattress and of the fact that they were still joined and that they were man and wife indeed.

She should feel ashamed, embarrassed, exposed. She felt none of those things, even when he moved off her and lay beside her, gazing at her in the flickering candlelight with green, half-closed eyes. She felt only a certain sadness that it was over and that now he would go to his own bedchamber and that perhaps she would not experience this again for a while, even maybe a week.

But he did not leave. He slid one arm beneath her neck and the other about her waist and rolled her into him instead, and she slid into a doze, lulled by the steady beat of his heart and warmed by his damp heat and comforted by the sweaty, musky smell of him, which seemed to her to be masculinity in its very essence.

Flavian in *his* very essence.

She was deeply, irrevocably in love with him.

They made love an incredible six times before she awoke in daylight to find him standing beside the bed and looking down at her while slipping his arms into the sleeves of his dressing gown. He still looked glorious in his near-nakedness, though his body was not unmarred by war, as she had both seen and felt during the night. There were numerous hard-ridged seams of old saber wounds and one puckered scar of an old bullet wound near his right shoulder. A number of the injuries must have been near-fatal when they were incurred.

The scars did not mar his beauty. And he was incredibly beautiful, all golden and handsome and strong and virile.

"I have woken Sleeping B-Beauty," he said. "My apologies, Lady Ponsonby. But I will be mocked for the rest of m-my natural life if I do not p-put in an appearance before my friends leave. And *we* must leave sometime this morning."

He bent over her, kissed her with lingering, open-mouthed thoroughness, cocked one eyebrow at her when she sighed against his mouth, told her she would quite have cast Eve into the shade if she had happened to wander into the Garden of Eden at the beginning of time, and disappeared into one of the dressing rooms. He shut the door behind him.

They had made love both slowly and with fierce swiftness, with her on her back and on top of him—and once very, very slowly, when they were side by side, her leg drawn up over his hip while he watched her face and she watched his. Each time he had seen to it that she achieved as much physical completion as he. He was marvelously skilled at that, as if he took pride in being a good lover.

It was half past six, Agnes saw when she looked at the ornate clock on the mantel.

And she realized something as she felt the coolness of the morning air on her naked body and swung her legs over the side of the bed and sat up. Two things, actually. One was that she felt thoroughly . . . married. Every part of her ached, and she was sore and tender inside. Her legs felt unsteady. She felt marvelous.

She also realized that for him the night had had nothing to do with love or even being in love. It had had nothing to do with the duty a husband owed his wife and his marriage. It had not even had anything to do with the consummation of yesterday's rituals. For him it had been all about the giving and taking of pleasure.

It felt good to know that she had pleased him. And she *had* pleased him. There was no doubt about that. Just as he had pleased her—which was surely the understatement of her life. It also chilled her a little to know that it had been *only* pleasure for him, that it probably always would be. Oh, she believed he liked her, even perhaps felt some fondness for her. She believed, despite the raw masculinity he always exuded, that he would be faithful to her, at least for a while.

But she must always remember that for him the sexual side of their marriage would be purely pleasure. She must never assume that it was love. And she must never look for love in other aspects of their relationship. She must never risk having her heart broken.

Oh, but it was pleasure for her too. She had had *no* idea. . . .

But she must get dressed and ready to leave.

To leave.

To leave home and Dora and all that had grown familiar and comfortable in just a year. She must have been *mad* to marry a man about whom she still knew very little. Except that she was not sorry. She had been cautious for too long. All her life.

She got to her feet and felt all the delicious unsteadiness of her legs and tenderness of her breasts and inner parts, and dared to hope that she would never be sorry. And that perhaps at last—oh, *at last*—she would conceive and have a child. Maybe even children. Plural. Dared she dream that big?

But she was only twenty-six. Why must she always believe dreams were for other people but not for her?

* * *

They were in the dining room in the west wing of the house before half past seven. Even so, they were the last to arrive for breakfast.

"What?" Ralph said when he saw them. "Couldn't sleep, could you, Flave?"

"Quite so, old chap," Flavian said on a sigh as he raised his quizzing glass all the way to his eye and regarded with some distaste the kidneys piled upon Ralph's plate. "I assume you *did*?"

"I arranged to have breakfast sent to your suite at half past eight," Lady Darleigh said. "But how lovely that you have joined us here instead. Agnes, do come and sit beside me. I hate good-byes, and there are a lot of them to be said this morning. But not for a while. Come and talk to me. I am going to miss you dreadfully."

Agnes was looking pink cheeked, Flavian saw—probably from morning-after embarrassment. And perhaps she had good reason to feel self-conscious, he thought with unabashed male satisfaction. Tidy as her appearance was, she still somehow looked well and truly tumbled.

He had never, *ever* enjoyed a night of sex as he had enjoyed last night. As he had suspected, and *more* than he had expected, she had been a powder keg of passionate sexuality just waiting to be ignited. And he had spent a glorious night doing the igniting and riding the waves of the ensuing fireworks.

And she was his for the taking tonight and tomorrow night and every night—and every day too if they wished—for the rest of their lives. Perhaps it was just that he had not had enough sex since his injuries. Perhaps he was just as starved as she obviously was. But he did not have to consider that possibility. They would feast after the famine until they were sated—and then work out what lay ahead.

Perhaps the banquet would last a lifetime. Who knew?

He sat between George and Imogen, and felt all the wretchedness of the fact that their three weeks were over, and he had more or less squandered the final week with his mad dash to London and back and then his wedding and wedding night.

"You are going to be in London during the Season, George?" he asked.

"Duty in the form of the House of Lords calls," George said. "Yes, I will be there, at least for a while."

"And you, Imogen?" Flavian asked.

She had made a rare appearance there last year for Hugo's wedding and then Vincent's fast on its heels.

"Not me," she said. "I will be at home in Cornwall." She covered his hand with her own, curled her fingers into his palm, and squeezed. "I am so glad you have found happiness, Flavian. And Hugo and Ben and Vincent too, and all within a year. It is quite dizzying. Now if Ralph can only find someone."

"And you, Imogen," he said. "And G-George."

"I am rather too old a dog to be learning new tricks," George said with a smile. "I will revel in my friends' happiness instead. And in my nephew's. I have grown closer to Julian since his marriage. He has turned out far better than anyone could have expected during the days of his wild youth."

"How old *are* you?" Flavian asked. "I had not realized you were d-doddering."

"Forty-seven," George said. "I was a child bridegroom and still a child when my son was born. A long time ago."

Good Lord, yes, that must be true. Flavian had never worked it out before. George must have been only seventeen or eighteen when he wed. Appallingly young.

Imogen's attention was on her empty plate.

"Do not look for romance from me, Flavian," she said. "It will not happen. Ever again. By my own choice."

She had removed her hand, but he took it again in his own and raised it to his lips.

"Life will be k-kind to you yet, Imogen," he said.

"It already is." She looked into his eyes and favored him with one of her rare smiles. "I have six of the most wonderful friends in the world—and all of them handsome men. What more could any woman ask—even if they *are* showing an annoying tendency to fall in love with and marry other ladies?"

He smiled back and caught Agnes's eye across the table. She was still looking flushed and tumbled. He closed one eyelid in a slow wink, and she flushed brighter and half smiled before returning her attention to Lady Darleigh and Lady Trentham.

He wanted her again and found himself wondering what sex in a closed carriage bumping and swaying over English roads would feel like. Cramped and uncomfortable and dangerous and very, very good, he suspected. Perhaps he would put his theory to the test later.

But now everyone was rising from the table. It was time to leave Middlebury Park and one another. It was that most dreary day of the whole year. Except that this year he would not be leaving alone. This year he had a wife to take with him.

And his mother to face in Candlebury, when he got up the courage to go there. And Marianne.

And Velma.

He was glad he had not eaten any of the kidneys. He felt slightly sick to his stomach as it was.

Everyone was leaving at the same time in a flurry of carriages and horses and grooms and voices and laughter—and tears. Everyone hugged everyone else and held the hug for several long moments. And Agnes was included in it.

They were different from yesterday's hugs. Yesterday she had been a bride, and people always hugged brides. It was almost an impersonal thing.

Today she was hugged, and today she hugged back because in a way she was one of the group—the Survivors' Club and their spouses.

She had never been an emotional sort of person, not since her early childhood, anyway. She was not the sort who went about touching others, beyond the occasional social handshake. She rarely hugged anyone, and people rarely hugged her. Normally she shrank from such contact. Just as she had shrunk somewhat from the physical contacts of her first marriage—though only ever inwardly, never outwardly—and had been relieved when they dwindled in frequency and finally came to an end.

Last night she had been consumed by an intense physical passion, and this morning she gave hug for hug to people she scarcely knew, except for Sophia. And she felt a bond, a warmth about the heart, a fondness that defied reason and common sense.

She felt fully alive for perhaps the first time ever. Oh, and deliriously in love, of course, though she would not let her mind dwell upon that, or her heart. She was Flavian's wife, and for now that would suffice.

She touched her fingers to the back of his hand as they drove away from the house and circled about the formal flower parterres to join the driveway between the topiary gardens and on toward the trees and the gates. And he took hers in his own and held it warmly, though he did not look at her or say anything. She knew that it was impossible for her to understand fully the ties that bound that group of seven. They went deeper than the bonds of family, though, she knew.

But the good-byes had not all been said.

Dora was standing in the garden outside the cottage,

watching the carriages go by, smiling and raising her hand as each slowed and farewells were exchanged through opened windows. She was still smiling when Flavian's carriage stopped and his coachman descended from the box to open the door and set down the steps. Flavian got out and handed Agnes down, and she was enveloped in Dora's arms, the gate between them. For a few moments neither of them spoke.

"You look beautiful, Agnes," Dora said when they broke apart. Which was a strange thing to say when her sister was wearing a traveling dress and bonnet she had worn a thousand times before. But she repeated the words with more emphasis. "You look *beautiful.*"

"And do I look b-beautiful too, Miss Debbins?" Flavian asked in his languid, sighing voice.

Dora looked him over critically.

"Well, yes," she said. "But you always do. I would not trust you an inch farther than I could throw you, though. And you had better call me Dora, since I am your sister-in-law. Flavian."

He grinned at her and opened the gate to catch her up in a tight hug.

"I will t-take c-care of her, Dora," he said. "I p-promise."

"I will hold you to it," she said.

And then Agnes hugged her again, and she was being handed back into the carriage, and the door was being shut with a decisive click, and the coachman was throwing her trunk and other bags into the boot, and a few moments later the carriage rocked slightly on its luxurious springs and moved forward. Agnes leaned close to the window and raised a hand. She watched her smiling, straight-backed sister until she could not see her any longer, and even then she kept her hand raised.

"I lived there for scarcely a year," she said, "yet I feel as if my heart were being ripped out." Which was perhaps not a very complimentary thing to say to one's new husband.

"It is your s-sister you are leaving behind, Agnes," he said, "not a village. And she was once more your m-mother than your sister. You will see plenty of her, though. When we go to Candlebury Abbey to live, we will have her come to s-stay with us—for as long as she l-likes. She can stay with us f-forever if she w-wants, though my guess is that she would p-prefer her independence. But you will see l-lots of her."

Agnes sat back in her seat, her face averted, but he set an arm about her shoulders and drew her against him until her head had nowhere to go but onto his shoulder. He pulled free the bow beneath her chin and tossed her bonnet onto the seat opposite with his hat.

"Good-byes are the most wretched things in this w-world," he said. "Never say good-bye to me, Agnes."

Almost, she thought, *almost* he was telling her that he really cared. But he quickly ruined that impression.

"I have been w-wondering," he said on a familiar-sounding sigh, "how possible or impossible and how s-satisfactory or unsatisfactory it would be to have sex in the carriage."

Was she expected to *reply*? Apparently not.

"We would not wish to be s-seen, of course," he said, "though there is something mildly t-titillating about imagining the expressions on the faces of stagecoach passengers as they p-passed by. There are perfectly serviceable curtains to cover the w-windows, however. As to s-swayings and bouncings, my coachman will scarcely notice them if we are on a n-normal stretch of road. We will try it sometime this afternoon. I b-believe the experience will rival for pleasure that of r-rolling around on a bed large enough for ten."

"Is pleasure all you think about?" she asked him.

"Hmm." He gave the question some thought. "I sometimes think about hard l-labor too, the kind that has one damp from one's exertions and panting for air. And I sometimes think of the near pain of holding b-back from going off like a firecracker that will not wait for the main show or like a schoolboy who has never h-heard of self-control. And sometimes I think about the p-propriety of waiting until evening before having marital r-relations with my wife, who might consider it improper to have them in the daytime. Except at half past five o'clock in the morning, that is, when she shows no r-reluctance at all or spares not a single thought to p-propriety."

Agnes's shoulders shook. She would not laugh. Oh, she *would* not. He ought not to be encouraged. But he was holding her shoulder and must know she was either laughing or suffering from the ague. She gave up the struggle to stay silent.

"You are *so* absurd," she said, laughing out loud.

"No!" He shrugged his shoulder so that he could look into her face. His eyelids, as she had expected, were half-lowered over his eyes. "I thought I was m-maybe one of the world's great lovers."

"Well, I would not know, would I?" she said. "Though I daresay you come pretty close."

His eyes opened wide suddenly and his face was filled with laughter, and her stomach performed a complete cartwheel inside her.

"You would not dare," she said. "Do *that* in *here* in broad daylight, I mean."

He leaned back in the seat again and tipped his head sideways to rest his cheek against the top of her head. And she realized that he had prattled on about absurdities in order to take her mind off the parting with Dora, and perhaps to take *his* mind off the parting with his friends.

"Agnes," he said a few minutes later, when she was feeling a bit drowsy and thought he might have dozed off, "*never* issue dares to your husband if you even suspect for a moment that you may be a poor loser."

Oh, he was *serious*. It was scandalous and horrifying and undignified and . . .

She smiled against his shoulder but did not answer.

Flavian had written to Marianne a week or so ago. In the letter he had informed her when he expected to arrive in London. But he had said nothing about going down to Candlebury for Easter, and he had said nothing about bringing a wife with him. How could he? He had not even known at the time that there was going to be a wife.

He wrote to his mother from the inn where they spent the first night of their journey. It was only fair to warn her. He informed her that he had married by special license, his bride being Mrs. Agnes Keeping, widow of William Keeping and daughter of Mr. Walter Debbins of Lancashire. He made a special note that she was a particular friend of Viscountess Darleigh of Middlebury Park. He was taking her to London for a short while but would bring her to Candlebury for Easter.

His mother would not be pleased, and that was surely a gigantic understatement. But there was nothing she could do about it now that the deed was done, and she would understand that, given a day or two of reflection. And practicality and good manners would of course prevail. By the time she was presented with Agnes, she would be gracious and impeccably good mannered at the very least. How could she not be? Agnes was the new mistress of Candlebury Abbey.

It gave even Flavian a jolt to realize the truth of that fact. Time had moved on. David had been pushed back a little further into history. So had his mother. She was now the *Dowager* Lady Ponsonby.

The carriage drew to a halt outside Arnott House on Grosvenor Square late in the afternoon of the third day of their journey, only an hour or so later than he had predicted.

He did not move for a few moments after the coachman had opened the door and set down the steps. He would have been quite happy to extend the journey by a few days. He was in no hurry to move on to the next phase of his life after this brief, mindlessly delightful honeymoon.

He had not for a moment regretted his impulsive marriage. The sex was the best of his life, both what had happened each night in decent beds and what had happened three separate times in the carriage—*especially* what had happened there, in fact. As he had expected, it had been extremely difficult and horribly cramped and uncomfortable and earth-shatteringly satisfying.

Agnes would not admit it. She had remonstrated with him each time, both before and after. But each time she had been unable to hide the passionate pleasure she got from copulating inside a carriage on the king's highway.

That was one thing about Agnes. She was the very proper lady in public. She could have passed for a prim governess any day of the week. But in private, with him, she could be transformed into hot, uninhibited passion. Steam rose around them when they coupled.

He could not get enough of her and wondered whether he ever would.

But the honeymoon—if a three-day journey could be called that—had to end, and here they were outside his London home, and the door of the house stood open, and there was nothing to do but get out and proceed with the future. At least he had brought her here first. At least he would have her to himself for a few days longer. And there was novelty and appeal in the thought of his familiar home with the unfamiliarity of a wife to share it with.

His butler bowed stiffly, welcomed him home, and glanced warily at Agnes.

"My wife, Viscountess Ponsonby, Biggs," Flavian said.

Biggs bowed again, even more stiffly and warily, and Agnes inclined her head.

"Mr. Biggs," she said.

"My lady."

And then the great cannon boomed, and the shell dropped at Flavian's feet and exploded in his face. Or so it seemed.

"Her ladyship, your mother, is upstairs in the drawing room, my lord," Biggs informed him, "awaiting your arrival." He looked as though he might say more, thought better of it, and shut his mouth with an almost audible clacking of teeth.

His mother? *Here?* Waiting for him? And if she was here, then so, almost certainly, was Marianne. They had not stayed at Candlebury after all. But was it possible for them to have come in response to his letter? He had written it only two nights ago. Or . . . did they *not know*?

Almost certainly it was the latter, he realized. Biggs had clearly not known, and servants always knew what their employers knew, and often they knew it first.

Good God! He closed his eyes for a moment, appalled. And for that same moment he considered turning and doing an ignominious bolt, dragging Agnes with him. He turned to her instead and offered his arm. She was looking as pasty of complexion as he felt.

"Come up and m-meet my m-mother," he said with what he hoped looked like a reassuring smile. "Come and g-get it over with."

He drew her hand through his arm, and they followed Biggs's stiff, impassive back up the stairs. This, he thought, was massively unfair to both Agnes and his mother. But what was he to do? He flatly refused to feel like a naughty little boy caught out in some childish mischief. Deuce take it, he was thirty years old. He was the head of his family. He was free to marry whomever he pleased whenever and however he pleased.

He had not expected his mother to be alone in the drawing room. He had steeled himself to find Marianne there too and possibly her husband, Shields, as well. And he was quite right—all three of them were there.

So were Sir Winston and Lady Frome.

And so was their daughter, Velma.

15

The sudden realization that Flavian's mother was actually in London and in this very house almost completely unnerved Agnes, who was already feeling weary after another day of travel and a little overwhelmed at the discovery that Arnott House was a massive, imposing edifice on one side of a large and stately square. When her foot was on the bottom stair, she almost drew her hand free of his arm and urged him to go up to the drawing room alone, while she went . . . where?

She did not have a room yet, and she did not know where his was. She could not simply turn and flee. Besides . . . well, besides, she was going to have to go through the ordeal of meeting her mother-in-law sooner or later. She had just not expected it to be *now*. She had hoped for a few days, perhaps even a week, and some exchange of letters first. It seemed highly unlikely that Flavian's letter had reached his mother before she came to town. Which meant *she did not know*.

It really did not bear thinking of.

And then they were upstairs, and the butler was opening the high double doors of what Agnes assumed was the drawing room, and she was stepping inside on Flavian's arm—and realizing in some horror that there were people in the room. *Six* of them, to be exact.

She slid her hand free and came to a stop just inside the doors, which Mr. Biggs was closing behind her, while Flavian proceeded a few steps farther.

There were four ladies, three of them seated, one standing to one side of the fire that was crackling in the hearth. Of the two gentlemen, the elder stood on the other side of the fireplace, while the younger stood behind the chair of one of the ladies.

All of them looked fashionable and formidable and . . . But there was no time for any further details to impress themselves upon Agnes's mind. The lady in the chair closest to the door had risen to her feet, her face lighting up with gladness and . . . relief?

"Flavian, my dear," she said. "At last."

She set her cheek to his and lightly kissed the air beside his ear. His mother, no doubt. She seemed the right age, and he looked a bit like her.

"We were beginning to think you must have delayed your journey by a day or two, Flavian," a younger lady said, also getting to her feet and hurrying forward to kiss his cheek, "without a word to anyone, which would have been *just* like you, but most provoking today of all days."

There was a family resemblance with this lady too. She must be his sister.

One of the other two ladies, the one standing by the fire, took a few hurried steps toward him before stopping, her eyes shining with some barely repressed emotion, her hands clasped to her bosom. She was probably Agnes's age, perhaps a little older, but she was quite breathtakingly lovely. She was on the small side of medium height, slender and shapely, with a delicately featured, beautiful face, wide blue eyes, and very blond hair.

"Flavian," she murmured in a soft, sweet voice. "You are home."

And he spoke for the first time.

"Velma."

It all happened within moments. Agnes could not go long unnoticed, of course. Unfortunately she was not invisible. And everyone seemed to notice her at the same moment. Flavian's mother and sister both turned their heads toward her and looked blank. The blond lady—*Velma*—stopped advancing. The gentleman on the other side of the fireplace raised a quizzing glass to his eye.

And Flavian turned and held out a hand for hers, looking noticeably paler than he had in the carriage a couple of minutes or so ago.

"I have the great pleasure of presenting Agnes, my wife," he said, gazing unsmiling into her eyes before turning toward back to the others. "My mother, the D-Dowager Viscountess Ponsonby, and my sister, Marianne, Lady Shields." He indicated the others in turn as he introduced them. "Oswald, Lord Shields, Lady Frome, Sir Winston Frome, and the Countess of Hazeltine, his d-daughter."

Sir Winston had taken a step closer to his daughter. Lady Frome had got to her feet and also moved closer as if to protect the younger lady. From what? She was the Countess of Hazeltine.

There was a moment—an eternity—of silence.

Lady Shields reacted first.

"Your wife, Flavian?" she said, looking at Agnes with mingled shock and revulsion. "Your *wife*?"

His mother clutched one hand about the pearls at her throat. "What have you done, Flavian?" she asked faintly, her eyes fixed upon her son's face. "You have married. And you have done it quite deliberately, have you not? Oh, I might have expected it. You have always been an unnatural son. Always, even before your brother died. And even before you went off to war when it was irresponsible to do so and were wounded and took leave of your senses and turned violent. You ought never to have been let loose from that place we sent you. But this . . . *this* . . . Oh, this is the *outside* of enough."

"Mother," Lord Shields said sharply, striding around the chair on which his wife had been sitting and catching his mother-in-law by the upper arm as she stumbled back to her own chair. He leaned over her, frowning.

Flavian's fingers had closed so tightly about Agnes's hand that he was actually grinding her fingers together and hurting her. But she was unsurprised to see when she glanced up at him that he was regarding the scene about him with lazy eyes and a mocking mouth.

And you have done it quite deliberately, have you not?

"This is a sudden thing, Ponsonby," Sir Winston Frome said, his voice cold and haughty. He completely ignored Agnes. "You might have given more consideration to your mother's sensibilities."

"You are married, Flavian?" Lady Hazeltine said with a smile that looked ghastly in a face turned almost as pale as her hair. "But what a delightful surprise. My congratulations. And to you too, Lady Ponsonby. I hope you will be very happy."

She came the rest of the way across the room, her eyes upon Agnes, her right hand extended. It was as cold as ice, Agnes discovered when it rested limply for a moment in her own.

"Thank you." Agnes smiled back.

"I have just completed a year of mourning for my husband," the countess said. "Mama and Papa insisted upon bringing me to town before the Season begins so that I may shop at some leisure for new clothes, though it has been very much against my inclinations to put off my blacks. Lady Ponsonby came up early too—pardon me, the *Dowager* Lady Ponsonby—with Marianne and Lord Shields. We were invited to tea this afternoon. I came because your husband was expected, and it is years since we last saw each other. We grew up as neighbors, you know, and were always the dearest of friends."

She was all pale, smiling dignity.

"I was s-sorry to hear of your b-bereavement, Lady Hazeltine," Flavian said. "I o-ought to have written."

"But you were never much of a letter writer, were you?" she said, flashing him a smile.

"Lady Ponsonby," Lady Frome said, addressing Flavian's mother, "we will take our leave and allow you some privacy in which to rejoice with your son over his delightful news and acquaint yourself with your new daughter-in-law. The tea and conversation have been most pleasant. Lord Ponsonby, it is to be hoped you will be happy."

She smiled uncertainly at Agnes as she left. Her husband ignored her completely. Their daughter expressed the wish that she would make Agnes's better acquaintance soon.

The door closed behind them, but their presence still seemed to loom large in the room. There was something, Agnes thought. There was most definitely *something*. *Flavian,* the countess had said with a look of bright welcome on her face. *Velma,* he had said in response.

Velma.

But they had grown up as neighbors. As friends. Childhood friends called one another by their first names.

There was no time to ponder the matter, however. Her mother-in-law and her sister- and brother-in-law were still in the room. And Flavian's news had shocked them deeply.

You have always been an unnatural son. Always, even

before your brother died. And even before you went to war when it was irresponsible to do so and were wounded and took leave of your senses and turned violent. You ought never to have been let loose from that place we sent you. But this . . . this . . . *Oh, this is the* outside *of enough.*

That place was presumably Penderris Hall in Cornwall, the Duke of Stanbrook's home.

. . . *You have done it quite deliberately, have you not?*

His mother was recovering some of her poise. She was sitting very upright in her chair.

"You have married, then, Flavian," his sister said. "And Mama was quite right. Of course it was deliberate and just the sort of thing you *would* do. Well, you are the one who must live with the consequences. Agnes, you will pardon us, if you please. We have had a severe shock and have quite forgotten our manners. But, really, where on earth did the two of you meet? And how long have you known each other? And who exactly *are* you? I am quite certain I have never set eyes upon you in my life before today."

And that was hardly surprising, her expression seemed to say as her eyes swept over her new sister-in-law from head to toe.

"We met at Middlebury Park last autumn," Agnes explained, "and again this past month. We were married by special license there four days ago."

She was given no chance to answer her sister-in-law's last question. Flavian had released Agnes's hand in order to set his own firmly against the small of her back.

"C-come and sit down, Agnes," he said. "Sit by the f-fire. Pull the b-bell rope, if you will, Oswald, and order up a f-fresh tray of tea in case Biggs has not thought of it himself. I thought you were all remaining at Candlebury for Easter. I s-sent a letter there."

"In punishing us so cleverly, Flavian," his mother said

as if he had not spoken, "you have, of course, punished yourself too. It is so typical of you. But, as Marianne observed, it is you who must suffer most as a result, just as you did when you refused to sell out after your brother's death. How very different your life might have been if you had done your duty then. *Agnes.* Who are you? Who *were* you before my son elevated you to a viscountess's title?"

It was all worse than Agnes's worst nightmare. But she tried to make allowances for shock. She suspected this first meeting would not have been quite as bad if events had been allowed to unfold according to plan. If his family had remained in the country and had read his letter with a few days to spare before meeting her, and if *she* had had a chance to write before going, then they would have had at least a little time to prepare themselves and to hide the rawest of their horror behind good manners.

"I was born Agnes Debbins in Lancashire, ma'am," she explained. "My father is a gentleman. I married William Keeping, a gentleman farmer and our neighbor, when I was eighteen, but I was widowed three years ago. I stayed for a short while in Shropshire with my brother, a clergyman, and then moved to the village of Inglebrook, close to Middlebury Park in Gloucestershire, to live with my unmarried sister."

"Debbins? Keeping? I have never heard either name," the dowager complained, looking at her daughter-in-law with obvious irritation.

"Neither my father nor my late husband moved in tonnish circles, ma'am," Agnes said, "or had any interest in spending time in London or at any of the fashionable spas."

Though Papa would have come to London the year Dora turned eighteen if his wife had not left him for a lover. Even then, though, they would not have mingled with the very highest echelons of society.

"They were not prosperous gentlemen, I suppose." The dowager's eyes swept over Agnes as her daughter's had done a few moments before.

"I have never coveted riches, ma'am," Agnes said.

Her mother-in-law's eyes snapped to hers. "And yet you have married my son. You surely knew that you were making a brilliant match."

"Agnes has m-married a m-madman, Mama, as you can a-attest, and deserves some s-sort of m-medal of h-honor," Flavian said in his bored voice, though he was having a harder time than usual getting his words out. "I am the one who has m-made a b-brilliant m-match. I have f-found someone w-willing to t-take me on. I am s-sorry you had no chance to r-read my letter before we w-walked in upon you, b-but you did not inform me you were c-coming to my London home—of which Agnes is now m-mistress. Ah, the tea t-tray at last."

"We have been heaping blame upon Flavian's head for springing such unexpected news upon us," Lord Shields said, smiling at Agnes, "when it is we who are at fault for coming up to town so impulsively and even inviting visitors here the very day we were expecting my brother-in-law home. Agnes, you have had a sorry welcome to your husband's family, and I apologize most profusely. I can only hope that Flavian would be having just such a welcome if you had sprung him upon your papa without any warning. Shall I set the tray before you?"

It had been set down before the dowager, and she had already reached out a hand to the teapot.

"Oh, no, please," Agnes said, holding up a staying hand. "I will be very happy to be waited upon."

"You must indeed be weary, Agnes," Lady Shields

said as she brought Agnes a cup of tea. "Traveling is a tedious and uncomfortable business at the best of times."

Agnes thought back on the journey with some longing. She had known even at the time that it was in a sense a bridge between her old life and the new, and she had clung to it as a sort of time out of time. Her mind touched for a moment upon what they had done three separate times to alleviate the boredom of a lengthy journey. That was the excuse Flavian had given, anyway.

She had been right to cling to that bridge.

Of course it was deliberate and just the sort of thing you would *do. Well, you are the one who must live with the consequences.*

In punishing us so cleverly, Flavian, you have, of course, punished yourself too. It is so typical of you. But, as Marianne observed, it is you who must suffer most as a result. . . .

And somehow it all had something to do with the very sweet and beautiful Velma, Countess of Hazeltine, who was at the end of her year of mourning for her husband. And to whom Flavian had never written with any regularity. Was there some reason he ought to have done so?

"Thank you, ma'am," Agnes said in acknowledgment of the tea.

"Oh, that must be Marianne, if you please," Lady Shields said. "We are sisters. And how very strange *that* sounds. I have been deprived of involving myself in your wedding, which is perhaps just as well, for Flavian would doubtless have called it *interference*. Do tell us all about the wedding. Every detail. And you may save your breath to drink your tea, Flavian. Men are utterly hopeless at describing such events at any length that exceeds one sentence."

He had taken the chair on the other side of the fireplace and sat there looking across at Agnes, his sleepy, slightly mocking expression firmly in place. She wondered whether his mother and sister realized that it was a mask that covered all sorts of uncertainties and vulnerability.

She described her wedding and the wedding breakfast at Middlebury Park. And she wondered what they had meant by saying that he had married her *quite deliberately*.

The trouble was, Flavian thought some time later as he led his wife upstairs, that he had never taken charge. Never. It had been quite deliberate when he was still a boy and David had inherited the title after their father's death, and everyone had tried to prepare *him* for the day in the not-so-distant future when the title would be his. There had been plans, of course, for David to marry, and the faint hope that he would beget an heir of his own, but that faint hope had come to an end when Flavian was eighteen and old enough for everyone to try arranging a marriage for *him*.

He had flatly refused to have anything to do with any of it.

The bedchamber next to his own had already been prepared, he was relieved to discover when he entered it with Agnes. No one had given the order, least of all himself, though he *ought* to have done so, but servants could almost always be relied upon to act on their own initiative. A young maid was visible through the open door to the dressing room on the far side of the bedchamber. She was unpacking his wife's bags. She bobbed a curtsy and explained that she had been "assigned to my lady until my lady's own maid" arrived.

"Thank you," Agnes said, and Flavian nodded at the girl before shutting the door.

He turned then to Agnes. "I am s-sorry," he said,

breaking the silence that had held since they left the drawing room.

"Oh, and so am I," she said on a rush. "It was horrible, and it was a ghastly shock for your mother and sister. But you were hardly to blame, Flavian."

Her brushes had already been set out on the dressing table. She moved closer to rearrange them.

"The thing is," he said, "that I have n-never asserted myself. I have been Ponsonby for longer than eight years, and I have n-never established my authority. They would not have behaved as they did today if I had. I am s-sorry."

She positioned two candleholders more to her liking on either side of the dressing table and then moved them together on the same side.

"You were ill for several of those years," she said.

It was a pretty room, furnished mostly in mossy greens and cream, very different from the rich wine brocades and velvets in his own room. It was here he would most enjoy making love to her, he suspected.

Good God, Velma! It had felt like walking through some warp in time. Seven years had fallen away just as if they had never happened, and there she was again, but moving toward him rather than away, smiling joyfully instead of weeping in grief and agony. And looking every bit as lovely as ever.

He rubbed the edge of a closed fist across his forehead. There was a headache trying to move in.

"Who is Velma?" Agnes asked him, just as if she could read the direction of his thoughts. She was looking at him over her shoulder.

"The Countess of Hazeltine?" He frowned.

"You called her Velma at first," she said. "And she called you Flavian."

He sighed.

"We were n-neighbors," he said. "She told you that.

Farthings Hall is eight miles from Candlebury. Our families were always quite close."

She sat on the padded bench before the dressing table, facing him, her hands clasped in her lap.

"Velma was intended for D-David," he said. "They were to be betrothed when she t-turned eighteen. He was b-besotted with her. But when the time came, he w-would not do it. It was already obvious he had c-consumption and was not getting any better. He r-refused even though everyone tried to insist that he could still father an heir and m-maybe even a spare. He w-would not do it. And his heart b-broke."

"Oh," she said softly. "Did she love him?"

"She w-would have done her d-duty," he said.

"But she did not love him?"

"No."

"Poor David," she said, looking at him. "And your heart broke for him?"

He wandered restlessly to the window and drummed his fingers on the sill. Her window, like his in the adjoining room, looked down on the square and the immaculately kept garden in the center of it. The headache niggled. Something snatched at the edge of his mind and made it worse.

"I had him purchase a commission for me," he said, "and I went off to join my regiment."

It seemed like a non sequitur. It was not. He had refused to be betrothed to her himself when David would not. He had had to get away. It had been the only way he could save himself—by running away.

The headache started to pound like a heavy pulse.

"And Velma?" she asked.

"She married the Earl of Hazeltine a few years l-later," he said. "He died last year. There is a daughter, or so I h-have heard. No son, though. She must have been d-disappointed about that."

He wondered whether Len had been too. But of course he must have been. Why had he even wondered? Drat this wretched headache.

"Did David die before she married?" Agnes asked.

"Yes." He kept his back to her.

"You must have been glad about that for his sake," she said.

"Yes." She did not know the half of it, and he did not have the energy or the will to tell her.

She had come to stand beside him, he realized. He wrapped one arm about her shoulders and turned to draw her against him. He touched his forehead to the top of her head. She had not yet changed or cleaned up after a day of travel. Neither of them had. But he breathed in that familiar soap smell of her and folded her even more tightly into himself.

"We are right by the window," she said.

He reached up a hand and jerked the curtains closed. And he kissed her with openmouthed urgency, reaching for the safety she represented.

"This c-conversation needs to be continued on that b-bed," he said against her mouth.

"In broad daylight?"

"It w-worked well enough in the carriage," he pointed out.

"The maid." She glanced at the dressing room door.

"Servants will not enter an occupied room uninvited," he told her.

He did not wait to unclothe either her or himself. He tumbled her to the bed, hiked her skirts to the waist, unbuttoned the fall of his pantaloons, positioned himself on top of her and between her thighs, and plunged into her as though his life depended upon finding some sort of salvation in her hot depths. He pounded into her, the blood thundering in his ears, and exploded into release a good few seconds before he heard the breath sobbing out of him and in again.

He rolled off her and flung an arm over his eyes. His headache was still hovering.

"I am s-so s-sorry," he said.

"Why?" She turned onto her side and spread a hand over his chest.

"Did I h-hurt you?"

"No," she said. "Flavian, you must forgive yourself for being alive when your brother is not."

She did not know the *half* of it. But he withdrew his arm and turned his head to look at her. He smiled lazily. "It was good s-sex?" he asked. "Even though there was not much f-finesse?"

"And there was in the carriage?" she asked, her cheeks turning pink.

He raised one eyebrow. "You have no idea of the skill involved in such maneuverings, ma'am," he said.

"I believe I do," she told him. "I was *there*."

"Ah," he said, narrowing his eyes and gazing at her lips, "that was *you*, was it?"

And he turned over to kiss her again, more slowly this time, more skillfully, with more of a thought to pleasing her. He wondered how Velma was feeling. Her heart had surely been in her eyes when he first stepped into the drawing room.

And how was *he* feeling?

He was feeling safe with the wife of his own choosing. His headache had done an about-turn and was marching away into the distance without him.

"Agnes," he whispered, and sighed with contentment.

16

Life then changed more radically than Agnes could possibly have expected it would.

Her mother-in-law recovered by dinnertime on that first day from the worst of her shock and dominated the conversation. It was not difficult to do, for Marianne and Lord Shields had returned to their own town house, Flavian chose to be sleepy, and Agnes could not seem to marshal her thoughts well enough to initiate any social talk.

It was a very good thing Easter was late this year, the dowager commented, and it would be a couple of weeks yet before the *ton* descended upon London in any great numbers and the Season began in earnest. They would have those weeks in which to assemble a wardrobe at the very least. She had taken one look at Agnes's lavender evening gown earlier, and her expression had become pained.

Agnes must be made to appear more like a viscountess, the dowager said quite bluntly. She would summon her own modiste to the house tomorrow and her hairdresser within the next few days. That way there would be no chance of Agnes's being seen by the wrong people before she was ready to meet anyone at all.

Flavian exerted himself at that point.

"The *wrong* p-people may go hang if they do not like Agnes as she is, Mother," he said. "And I will take Agnes to Bond Street m-myself tomorrow. The best dressmakers are to be found there."

"And *you* know exactly who they are, I suppose?" his mother said. "And you know all the latest fashions and the newest fabrics and trims, I suppose? Really, Flavian, you must leave such things to me. You cannot want your viscountess to look a frump."

"I do not believe that would be p-possible," he said, leaning to one side so that a footman could refill his wineglass.

"And now you are being quite deliberately foolish, Flavian."

It was time to intervene. Agnes was beginning to feel like an inanimate object over which mother and son were wrangling.

"I would be very *happy*," she said, "to go to Bond Street or anywhere else reputable dressmakers may be found. Perhaps you will *both* accompany me there tomorrow. I would appreciate your escort, Flavian, and I am sure your mother would too. And I will certainly appreciate your advice and expertise, ma'am."

Flavian pursed his lips and raised his glass in a silent toast to her. His mother sighed.

"You had better call me *Mother*, Agnes, since I am your mama-in-law," she said. "Tomorrow morning, then. We will go to Madame Martin's. She dresses at least one duchess that I know of."

Flavian's eyes—what could be seen of them beneath his eyelids—gleamed, but he refrained from commenting. He must have recognized a compromise when he heard one.

"I shall look forward to it, Mother," Agnes said.

She was going to have to be presented at court, the dowager went on to say, and to society, of course, since she was an unknown. They were going to have to put on a grand ball at Arnott House early in the Season, but before that she must take her daughter-in-law to call upon all the best families. And after the ball there must be frequent appearances at all the most fashionable parties and soirees and breakfasts and concerts, as well as visits to the theater and the opera house and Vauxhall. There must be walks and drives in the parks, most notably Hyde Park during the fashionable hour in the afternoon.

"You will certainly not wish anyone to suspect you are hiding your viscountess away because she is not up to the position," she said to Flavian.

He considered, crossing his knife and fork over his roast beef and picking up his wineglass by the stem. "I am not sure, Mother," he finally said, "that I would wish to c-control anyone's suspicions. People m-may believe what they wish with my blessing, even an asinine thing like that."

She tutted.

"The trouble with you, Flavian," she said sharply, "is that you have never cared. You do not care about either your responsibilities or the pain you cause others. But you can no longer honorably avoid caring about either. You have made an impulsive marriage to Agnes, who is a gentlewoman by birth but without any connection to the beau monde or any experience whatsoever of the sort of society into which she has married. You *must* care, for her sake even if not for mine or Marianne's. Or your own."

His expression was mocking as he cut into his beef again.

"Ah, but I do care, Mother," he said. "I always have."

"We came to London immediately after our nuptials, Mother," Agnes said, "so that I might learn something of what my new status will demand of me. New clothes, I understand, are the mere beginning. And though I was upset earlier to discover that you had come here too before having a chance to learn of our marriage and accustom yourself to the knowledge, now I am glad you are here. For in many ways my mother-in-law and, I hope, my sister-in-law can do far more to help me fit into my new life than Flavian alone can do. I am perfectly willing to do all that is proper and necessary."

She hoped she did not sound obsequious. She was actually perfectly sincere. She really had not given enough thought before her marriage to the fact that, as well as being Flavian's wife, she was also going to be his *viscountess*. Though in truth, of course, she had not given enough thought to *anything*.

Flavian smiled at her with sleepy eyes. The dowager gave her a hard look, in which there were perhaps the stirrings of approval.

And life became a whirlwind, something so far beyond Agnes's experiences that she might as well have been snatched away into a different universe.

She spent much of her first morning and all the afternoon at the Bond Street salon of Madame Martin—pronounced the French way, though Agnes suspected the petite modiste, with her eloquently waving hands and heavy accent, had been born and bred no more than a few miles from her shop. There Agnes was fitted for a dizzying array of garments for every occasion under the sun. And there she was shown book after book of fashion plates, bolt after bolt of cloth, and so many different trims and buttons and ribbons and sashes that she ended up feeling rather like a sponge long since saturated with water.

Flavian escorted her there, but it was his mother who stayed the whole time while he wandered off after ten minutes or so to destinations unknown and did not reappear for more than five hours. *Five.* And even then they were not quite ready to go with him. It was his mother who suggested and advised and had her own way more and more as the hours ticked by, even though it was soon obvious that her tastes differed in some significant ways from her daughter-in-law's. But how could Agnes fight against the combined expertise of a lady who had moved all her life in the world of the *ton* and of one of London's leading modistes, who was not shy about proclaiming the fact that she dressed *two* duchesses?

It was all very bewildering and rather depressing when perhaps it ought to have been exciting. Or perhaps it was merely exhausting.

Agnes gave up thinking of the money that was being lavished upon her, especially when, on the second day, she and her mother-in-law and Marianne began a round of other shops on Bond Street and Oxford Street in search of bonnets and fans, reticules and parasols, stockings and undergarments, perfumes and colognes and vinaigrettes, slippers and boots, and goodness knew what else, all of them deemed the very barest of necessities for a lady of quality.

For that was what she now, was by the simple fact that Flavian had married her. But if she was a lady *of quality* now, she asked herself ruefully, what had she been before her second marriage? Did *of quality* have an opposite? It would be very lowering if it did.

On that second day, after she had returned home exhausted and dispirited, the butler informed her that three candidates for the position of her personal maid were in the housekeeper's parlor awaiting her pleasure. For once in her life Agnes understood that she was going to need a maid, and she had also quickly learned that Pamela, the chambermaid who had been assigned to her temporarily, had neither the aptitude nor the ambition for the promotion. But must she see the candidates *now*? She probably must, if she did not want someone else choosing for her.

"Let them come to me one at a time in the morning room, Mr. Biggs," she said, handing him her bonnet and gloves, and feeling thankful that her mother-in-law had stopped off at Marianne's house to see her grandchildren. Agnes had professed herself too weary to accompany her.

She decided against the first candidate. The woman came highly recommended by Lady Somebody-or-other, a friend of the dowager's, but she addressed Agnes as *madam* in tones of such superior condescension that Agnes felt diminished to half her size. And she rejected the second, who sniffed wetly throughout her interview and spoke in a nasal monotone, but denied having a cold when asked—she even looked rather surprised at the question.

The third candidate, a thin, rather scrawny-looking girl sent by an agency, told Agnes her name was Madeline.

"Though Maddy will do nicely, my lady, if you prefer, since Madeline sounds a bit uppity for a maid, doesn't it?" she said. "My dad give us all big names. If there couldn't be nothing else grand in our lives, he always said, God rest his soul, at least we had our names."

"What a lovely thought, Madeline," Agnes said.

The girl did not wait to be interviewed. She launched into speech.

"They said you was going to have your hair cut tomorrow," she said. *They*, Agnes guessed, was the housekeeper. "I can see it must be very long, my lady, and it would be a good idea to have it neatened up if you haven't done so for a while. But don't let them chop off too much. Some ladies look fine enough all crimped and curled, but you can do better than that, if you'll pardon me for telling you so when you haven't asked. You can look *elegant* and turn heads wherever you go."

"And you can style it elegantly, can you, Madeline?" Agnes asked, beginning to relax despite her sore feet.

"Oh, I can, my lady," the girl assured her, "even though I don't look as hoity-toity as *her* down below, who thinks herself good enough to dress a duchess." Ah, Finchley, her mother-in-law's dresser, must have shown herself in the housekeeper's room too, Agnes thought. "I got six sisters as well as my mum, and I love nothing in the world more than doing their hair. And they are all different. That's the whole secret, really, isn't it? To do someone's hair to suit their faces and figures and ages and hair type, not just to make them look like everyone else, whether they ought to or not."

"If I were to employ you, Madeline," Agnes said, "there would be more for you to do than just style my hair."

"You were out at the dressmaker's all of yesterday," Madeline said, "and other places today for all the things to go with the dresses. They told us so when we got here."

"Oh, dear," Agnes said. "Were you kept waiting long, Madeline? I am so sorry."

The girl looked shocked and then laughed merrily.

"You are a right one," she said. "I can see that. No wonder they was sniffing downstairs—well, *her,* anyway—and saying as how you come from the country and don't know nothing about nothing. I hope you didn't let no one talk you into having lots of frills and flounces."

Agnes feared she had probably done just that, though in truth she could scarcely recall what she had ended up agreeing to.

"I ought to avoid them?" she asked. "I must confess, Madeline, that I have never thought of myself as a frilly sort of person."

"Nor you aren't," the girl said.

"But dullness is not permitted by the *ton*, it would seem." Agnes smiled ruefully.

Madeline looked shocked again.

"Dull?" she said. "You? You could knock them all into a tall hat, my lady, with the right clothes and the right hair. But not by outcrimping and outfrilling them. You ought to look *elegant*. Not in an old-lady sort of way, I don't mean. How old *are* you?"

Agnes was hard put not to laugh out loud.

"Twenty-six," she said.

"Just what I thought," Madeline said. "Ten years older than me. But not *old* even so. Not a girl either, though, and I bet they have all been trying to get you to look like all those young things that will be flocking here soon to look for rich nobs to marry. If I had the dressing of you, my lady, I would tell you what to wear, and I wouldn't let you wear the wrong things. Not that I ought to speak so freely when everyone tells me I'm wasting my time coming here and ought to think myself lucky if I can get a scullery maid's job. I'm talking too much, aren't I? I do that when I want something terrible bad."

"And you want to dress me terribly badly," Agnes said, smiling at her, "and my hair."

"Yes, my lady, I do," Madeline said, suddenly looking all big eyed and anxious. "Especially after seeing you. You are lovely. Oh, not in that pretty-pretty way of some, but you got *potential*. Don't you love that word? I learned it new a few weeks ago, and I been looking for a suitable chance to use it."

"I think, Madeline," Agnes said, "you had better move your things here tomorrow and get yourself properly outfitted for the position of personal dresser to Viscountess Ponsonby. No scullery maid's job for you. Your talents would be wasted on a scrubbed floor, I suspect. I will give instructions. And the day after tomorrow you will accompany me to Madame Martin's shop on Bond Street. I will need to make some minor changes to the instructions I left for the clothes she is making for me. There is no point in having them made and delivered if you will not allow me to wear them, is there?"

"I got the job?" Madeline looked afraid to believe the evidence of her own ears.

"You have the job," Agnes said and smiled. "I hope I will not disappoint you."

Madeline jumped to her feet, and for one startled moment Agnes thought the girl was going to hug her. Instead she clasped her hands very tightly to her bosom and bobbed a curtsy.

"You won't be sorry, my lady," she said. "Oh, you won't, honest. You'll see. I'll make you all the rage. Oh, *wait* till I tell Mum and the girls. They won't *believe* me."

Agnes had two inches taken off her hair the following day, just enough to tidy the ends. Mr. Johnston, the hairdresser to whom she was taken, was not happy with her. Neither was her mother-in-law. But Flavian approved and said so when he came to her that night and saw her hair down.

"I expected to f-find a shorn lamb at the d-dinner table earlier," he told her. "But instead I found Agnes with shining, elegant t-tresses. Is that what the hairdresser d-did for you?"

"He merely trimmed it," she told him. "Madeline dressed it—my new maid."

"That little s-slip of a thing in her new uniform that looks s-stiff enough to stand up without her in it?" he asked. "The one who f-frowned at me when she passed me outside your d-door, as though she did not think me worthy to kiss as much as your little toenail?"

"Oh, dear," she said, "she seems to like me. She persuaded me to leave my hair long and to aim for elegance instead of youthful prettiness in my appearance. I have *potential*, it seems, and I am not *old*, though I am ten years her senior and therefore tottering on the brink. I really ought not to try competing with all the young girls who will be making their come-out this year, though."

"She is someone to be f-feared despite appearances, then, is she?" he said. "Especially by a m-mere husband? I shall look h-humble the next time I see her. Perhaps she will stop frowning at me and allow me to keep c-coming to your room."

Agnes laughed, and he twined his fingers in her hair and drew her to him by the nape of her neck.

"Thank heaven for M-Madeline," he said against her mouth. "I hope I am paying her a decent wage. I like your hair l-long, Agnes. And you already are elegant. All those young g-girls would be well advised not to try c-competing with you."

"Absurd." She laughed again.

And then she abandoned herself to passion.

She could believe in impossible dreams when he made love to her—and when she made love to him. It was always mutual. Who would have expected that a wife could make love to her husband?

And why should dreams be impossible just because they *were* dreams? Didn't dreams sometimes come true?

Agnes did indeed return to Madame Martin's the next morning. After three days of unrelenting shopping, her mother-in-law had announced her intention of lying abed until a decent hour of the morning or early afternoon, and it was easy to slip out of the house alone with just Madeline walking decently—and proudly—beside her. Flavian had gone off after breakfast to indulge in some masculine pursuits that included various clubs, and a boxing and fencing saloon, and Tattersall's.

Adjustments—most of them minor, a few rather more major—were made to the massive order Agnes had left with the modiste two days before. Two of the designs—one for a ball gown, the other for a walking dress—were tossed out altogether and replaced with simpler, more classic designs. Flounces were sacrificed quite ruthlessly and replaced with delicate embroideries and laces and scallops. Madame Martin, who had looked askance at Madeline at the start and suggested tactfully that perhaps "my lady" ought to bring the dowager viscountess back with her to discuss any proposed changes, ended up regarding the maid with something like respect.

"My sister-in-law mentioned yesterday," Agnes said as they were leaving the salon, "that I really ought to take out a subscription at Hookham's Library. I have taken a look in the book room at home, but the volumes there all seem very ancient and dry of topic. They lean heavily toward sermons and moral treatises."

They had surely been purchased by a former viscount.

"Well, I ask you, my lady," Madeline commented in some disgust. "Why bother learning your letters if you can't find something more cheerful to read than sermons? It's bad enough that you have to sit on them hard pews at church and listen to them once a week. And don't some vicars go on and on and on?"

They found the library without any trouble, and Agnes paid her subscription and spent some time happily browsing among the shelves. There were books of poetry here, and novels and plays, and the main problem was going to be choosing just one or two to take with her. Though she could come back anytime, of course, to exchange them for other books. What a wonderful invention a library was. There was a positive wealth of knowledge and entertainment here.

"Lady Ponsonby?" a light, sweet voice asked. "Yes, it *is* you."

Agnes turned her head in surprise. No one knew her, and she knew no one.

Ah, but yes, of course she did.

"Lady Hazeltine," she said, taking the gloved hand that was being offered.

The countess was dressed in varying light shades of blue and in what Agnes already recognized as the first stare of fashion. Shining waves of her blond hair curled on her forehead, and trailed over her ears and along her neck beneath her fetching poke bonnet. Her blue eyes smiled, her cheeks were pink tinged, her teeth were pearly white, and her chin was ever so slightly dimpled. She was the very picture of beauty and warm amiability.

"I am so glad you spoke to me," Agnes said. "I was absorbed in the books and did not see you; I am sorry. How do you do?"

"I am very well, I thank you," Lady Hazeltine said. "And all the better for seeing you again. I was disappointed that you did not come with Flavian when he called yesterday."

Agnes clasped her two chosen books to her bosom and somehow held her smile.

"I am sorry to have missed the visit too," she said. "I was out shopping with my mother-in-law and Lady Shields for the third day in a row. I had no idea I needed so much, but they have both insisted that this is just the start."

The countess's eyes flicked down her person, and her eyes danced with merriment.

"I have only recently left off my widow's weeds," she said. "I know all about feeling dowdy."

Flavian had called upon the countess yesterday—and presumably upon Sir Winston and Lady Frome too—without *her*. And without even mentioning it to her when she had asked about his day last night.

"I am sorry for your loss," she said, "even if it was more than a year ago. I know that grieving does not end as soon as the mourning clothes are put off."

"Thank you." Lady Hazeltine's smile was tinged with melancholy. "You need not be sorry for me, however. Hazeltine and I lived virtually apart for the last two years of our marriage. We entered into it with unconsidered haste, in order to comfort each other for a mutual grief, and we lived to regret it. I ought to have waited longer to see what would happen with—well, with my first and only true love. But I did not, alas, and it is forever too late now."

Agnes was feeling decidedly uncomfortable. How did one respond to such a confidence from a near stranger?

"I am so sorry," she said again. "Did you love him very much after all, then? Viscount Ponsonby, I mean?"

The countess's blue eyes widened, and she looked suddenly stricken. She set a gloved hand on Agnes's sleeve.

"Oh, has he *told* you, then?" she asked. "How very naughty and *cruel* of him. But impetuous behavior rarely brings lasting happiness, as I might have informed him from personal experience if he had waited to ask. Especially when it leaves one with no choice but to live with the consequences. But maybe they will not be as dreadful in this particular case as they were in mine. Maybe . . . Well, I hope all will turn out well. I *most* sincerely do."

She rested a hand on Agnes's arm again and squeezed, smiling with warm, melancholy sympathy.

Agnes was not sure she understood just what was being said. Yet she had the strange feeling that Lady Hazeltine was choosing every word with great and deliberate care.

"I told Mama I would be in here for the merest moment," she said, dropping her hand to her side, "while I picked up the latest novel from the Minerva Press. Do you read them? I swear I am addicted, silly as they are. Mama will be awaiting me in the carriage, and the drivers of other conveyances will be very cross if it stands there half blocking the road for much longer. I do hope I will see you again soon, Lady Ponsonby. We are to be neighbors and . . . friends, I trust."

"Yes." Agnes clutched her books even more tightly. "Yes, I hope so too."

She watched the countess weave her way to the front of the library and stop for a moment at the desk to present her book. Madeline was still standing patiently just inside the door, looking about herself with interest.

What had that been about?

Oh, has he told *you, then? How very naughty and* cruel *of him.*

What had been said before that? Agnes frowned as she tried to remember.

I ought to have waited to see what would happen with—well, with my first and only true love. But I did not, alas, and it is forever too late now.

Agnes had assumed she was talking about Flavian's older brother, for whom she had been intended. But she could not have waited longer to see what happened to him. He had already been dead when she married the earl. Flavian's elder brother had been Viscount Ponsonby. But so was Flavian now. He must have had the title before the marriage of the Earl and Countess of Hazeltine.

I ought to have waited to see what would happen with—well, with my first and only true love.

. . . It is forever too late now.

And Flavian had called upon the countess yesterday without a word to *her*.

There was nothing so strange about his calling on the Fromes, though, or upon their daughter, was there? They were his neighbors in the country, after all, and perhaps he had felt he ought to offer some apology for the awkwardness of their meeting at Arnott House a few days ago.

But without Agnes?

And without even telling her about it?

But impetuous behavior rarely brings lasting happiness, as I might have informed him from personal experience if he had waited to ask. Especially when it leaves one with no choice but to live with the consequences.

Whose impetuous behavior? And *what* impetuous behavior? What consequences?

"Pardon me, ma'am," a gentleman said politely enough but with a hint of impatience in his voice.

"Oh," she said, realizing that she had been standing in front of the same shelf for far too long. "I do beg your pardon."

And she made her way to the desk, hardly remembering which books she had selected.

17

Flavian had called at Sir Winston Frome's town house at Portman Place the afternoon before. The Fromes were his neighbors in Sussex, after all, and if he intended to spend time at his country home in future, as he surely must now that he was married, then he would inevitably meet them socially there. It would be as well to dispel any awkwardness caused by their last meeting.

If it *could* be dispelled.

And if Velma was going to be living with them again, as it appeared she was, then he would have to meet her again too—in the country as well as here in London. There could be no avoiding her forever. Len's home had been in Northumberland, and he and she had stayed in the north of England after their marriage, where Flavian was unlikely to run into either of them ever again.

It was too bad Len had died.

Good God, it *was* too bad he had died.

They had met as young boys at Eton. Each had blackened an eye of the other when they came to fisticuffs the very first day. They had both had their backsides caned as a result, and they had been firm, almost inseparable friends thereafter. Len had even spent most of his school holidays at Candlebury, Northumberland being too far away for short visits. They had purchased their commissions at the same time and in the same regiment. Len had sold out six months before Flavian was wounded and sent home. Len had returned home on the death of his uncle and the acquisition of his title, as Flavian had *not* done on the acquisition of his. In retrospect, their differing reactions to the new responsibilities their titles brought was perhaps the first small herald of the rift that came between them.

They would never see each other again now, never talk things through, never. . . . Well, there was no point in dwelling upon such thoughts. They were stranded on the opposite sides of death, at least for now, and that was all there was to it.

Flavian went to call upon the Fromes, well aware that perhaps his real purpose in going so soon and in going alone was to see Velma again, to try to sort something out in his mind, to try to put a tangled multitude of baggage behind him.

For a headache threatened whenever his mind touched upon that baggage. And that sense of panic he could never quite account for.

What there was to be sorted he did not quite know. She had broken off their engagement and married Len, and now, when she was free again, *he* had married. He was safe from any renewed matchmaking schemes of their combined families. And they would have been renewed. Why else had Velma and her parents been awaiting his arrival at Arnott House a few days ago? Just as if the marriage of his betrothed and his best friend had been a minor irritant of a delay in their nuptials.

He was still not sure exactly how he had he felt when he walked into his own drawing room to find her coming toward him, a look of glad welcome on her face. It did not *matter* how he had felt. He was married to Agnes.

But what if he really had married her, as his mother and sister had accused him of doing, to punish Velma? And himself. What sort of a blackguard would that make him in regard to Agnes?

He needed to work out some answers. And so he went calling—alone.

There were only ladies present when he was shown into the drawing room—Lady Frome and Velma, two sisters, Mrs. Kress and Miss Hawkins, and a young child clad in her frilly best to be shown off to the visitors. She was dainty and blond and pretty, with a strong resemblance to Velma at that age, and also a disturbing resemblance to Len.

The other two visitors took their leave almost immediately, and the little girl was instructed to make her curtsy to Lord Ponsonby before her nurse took her away. Then Frome himself wandered into the room and inclined his head frostily to Flavian.

There was a sudden sag in the conversation, which had centered about the child for a few minutes.

"I a-am sorry," Flavian said, addressing himself to Velma, "about L-Len, I mean. I really o-ought to have written. It was b-bad of me not to."

Had he already said this a few days ago?

She smiled at him, her eyes filling with tears. "Almost his last thoughts were of you, Flavian," she said. "He never forgave himself, you know. It seemed the right thing to do at the time. We both thought it was something you would like us to do, and Mama and Papa and even *your* mother agreed. We did not believe . . . Well, your physician held out no hope for your recovery. But Leonard felt wretched from the first moment of our marriage until he drew his last breath. He believed he had betrayed you. We *were* a comfort to each other, but when we heard that you were recovering after all . . . Well, it was dreadful—for us. And wonderful for you. Leonard was so very happy for you. We both were. But . . . we had made a tragic mistake."

Flavian had forgotten how soft and sweet her voice was. It wrapped about his senses, as it always had.

Len had never written to him. Perhaps he had found it as difficult to put pen to paper as Flavian had after Len's death. He wondered how much his friend had been to blame for that marriage, and his mind blinked, as it had an annoying habit of doing from time to time, and then shut down again. There was the faint stabbing of pain above one eyebrow.

"You must not upset yourself, Velma," Lady Frome said as her daughter raised a lace-edged handkerchief to her eyes and blotted away tears.

"It was Leonard's dearest wish as he lay on his deathbed," Velma said, lowering the handkerchief again, "that you would forgive *me,* Flavian, and that you and I would . . ."

She bit her soft lower lip.

"There is n-nothing to f-forgive," Flavian said.

"Ah," she said with a sigh, "but obviously there is, or you would not have punished me so cruelly. It *is* cruel, you know, and perhaps to more than just me. Poor Lady Ponsonby. She does not *know*, I suppose? Who *is* she?"

"She is the daughter of a Mr. D-Debbins from Lancashire," he said, "and the widow of a Mr. Keeping of the same county. And she is my wife."

"Yes." Velma smiled again and put her handkerchief away. "And I wish her well, Flavian. And you. I ought to bear a grudge, perhaps, but that would be unfair of me. I hurt you badly once, though that was *never* my intention."

Frome stood at the window, his back to the room, his hands clasped behind him, his stance rigid.

"And I expect you will have a happy future, Lord Ponsonby," Lady Frome said, "now that you are well again and now that you are settling down."

Flavian had always liked her. She was a comfortable, amiable lady whom Sir Winston had married, or so it was rumored, because her father's fortune had rescued him from the considerable financial embarrassment his love of the card tables was forever bringing upon him.

"Thank you, ma'am," he said.

Sir Winston turned from the window and looked steadily at him but said nothing. He was less forgiving of the slight against his family and his daughter, his expression seemed to say.

Flavian took his leave, not sure whether his visit had cleared the air or made matters worse. But it had gone better than he had feared. Although Velma had all but admitted being disappointed, she had behaved with dignity and some generosity of spirit toward Agnes. Perhaps there would be peace after all between Candlebury and Farthings.

What he ought to do now, he thought, was go home in the hope that Agnes was back from her day of shopping, and tell her everything. Get it all off his chest and convince her once and for all that he had married her because he had *wished* to do so. She would probably not be back yet, though, not if he knew his mother and Marianne, and he could not bear the thought of being at home and pacing the floor, waiting for them to return.

He headed off for White's instead to fill in an hour or two in congenial male company.

By the time he arrived home later, just in time to dress for dinner, he had changed his mind. Telling Agnes everything would surely be quite the *wrong* thing to do. How would he ever convince her that his hasty marriage proposal to her and his impulsive dash off to London to procure a special license had had nothing to do with any need to punish Velma? He did not even know himself what his motive had been.

The last thing in the world he wanted to do was hurt Agnes.

The *very* last thing.

He ended up not telling her anything about his afternoon—not even that he had called upon his neighbors, the Fromes.

By the time Agnes arrived home from the library, two of the dresses she had purchased from Madame Martin had been delivered. They had been ready-made items, both of them evening gowns, and had needed only minor alterations. They were also, fortunately, up to Madeline's exacting standards.

Agnes was ready to face the world, then, her mother-in-law declared, even if only in a minor way. They would have Flavian escort them to the theater that very evening after dinner. It would not be packed with many of the people who really mattered, of course, the *ton* not having returned to town in any great numbers yet, but it would be a start. And perhaps a *wise* start. Agnes would be able to ease her way gradually into society instead of being overwhelmed by it at her presentation ball.

Agnes felt more like crawling into her bed and drawing the curtains tight about it. But since that was impossible, an outing seemed preferable to an evening spent at home with only her husband and her mother-in-law for company.

She could not get Lady Hazeltine's lovely face out of her mind—or her sweet, light voice telling Agnes that she ought to have waited for her only true love.

Agnes did not say much at dinner, but allowed Flavian and her mother-in-law to carry the conversation.

She did not say much in the carriage or at the theater either. Fortunately there was a play to be watched—with great attention, though she would not have been able to say afterward what it was about. And during the intermission there were people to be met and greeted and conversed with—Marianne and Lord Shields and a few acquaintances of the dowager's and Flavian's.

It was a pity her mind was so preoccupied, she thought a few times in the course of the evening. She should have been overwhelmed by her first visit to a theater, by the splendor of her surroundings and by the excellence of the acting, as well as by the pleasure of wearing a new and flattering evening gown and of knowing that her hair looked elegant and becoming.

It was one of the worst evenings she could remember.

She waited for Flavian when the evening was over, standing at the window of her bedchamber and staring down on the square. There were still lights in several of the other houses. A carriage was drawn up outside the house next door. She could hear the distant sound of voices and laughter.

And then the voices were silent, and the carriage was gone, and most of the lights had been extinguished, and she realized she had been standing there for a long time. She shivered and realized that the air was chilly. She had not put a dressing gown on over her nightgown.

She went to fetch one from her dressing room. She looked at the bed on her return. Was he asleep in his own room? Were they to sleep apart for the first time since their wedding? And was that only a week ago?

Had he even come up to bed? She had not heard him.

She picked up the single candle that still burned on her dressing table and went back downstairs. He was not in the drawing room. She found him in the book room, which was lit only by the fire that burned low in the hearth.

He looked up when she came in, and smiled his hooded smile.

"Sleeping Beauty s-sleepwalking?" he asked.

She set her candlestick on the mantel and stared down into the fire for a few moments. She had not realized just how chilled she was.

"Tell me about the Countess of Hazeltine," she said.

"Ah," he said softly. "I w-wondered if that was it."

She turned to look at him. He was sprawled in his chair, his neck cloth and cravat discarded, his shirt open at the neck. His golden hair looked as if he had passed his fingers through it one too many times. There was an empty glass on the table beside him, though he did not look drunk.

"I met her at Hookham's Library this afternoon," she said.

"Ah."

"You called upon her yesterday."

"Her and Sir Winston and Lady Frome."

She waited for more, but more did not come.

"She had an unhappy marriage," Agnes said. "She told me she ought to have waited to see what would happen with her first and only true love—her words. I thought she meant your brother. I thought perhaps she had loved him after all."

"Ah," he said again.

"Is that *all* you can say?" she asked him.

He heaved an audible breath, held it for a long moment, and exhaled it on a sigh. "She was sowing m-mischief," he said. "I wondered if she would."

Agnes wrapped her dressing gown more closely about her and sat down on a chair some distance from his. In the flickering light of the candle and the dying fire, he looked almost satanic. His head was against the chair back.

"We grew up together," he said. "When we were both fifteen, we f-fell h-head over ears in l-love with each other. I was home from school for the summer. We saw ourselves as t-tragic figures, though, for she had always been intended for D-David and still was. He was nineteen by that time and p-painfully in love with her. Painful because he was thin and a b-bit undergrown and not at all robust, while she was already b-beautiful. She knew her duty, though, and I loved my brother. We renounced each other, V-Velma and I, thinking our love the stuff of legend. After that, we tried to stay away from each other. But David guessed. When she turned eighteen and they were to be officially b-betrothed at last, he surprised everyone and r-refused to do it. He set her free. It broke his heart."

Flavian's eyes were closed, and he was frowning and rubbing the side of a tight fist back and forth across his forehead as though to erase the memories.

Agnes stared at him, her heart turned to stone. Though stone did not ache unbearably, did it?

"Then they all w-wanted *me* to marry her," he said, "because it was obvious I was going to be Ponsonby sooner rather than later. They were overjoyed about it, actually. They d-did not even try to get David to change his m-mind. And they did not even want to w-wait for him to d-die first. I was eighteen too. I was old enough at least to be betrothed, even if not married. I wouldn't do it. I w-wouldn't. I m-made David purchase me a commission instead and went off to war. I suppose I thought myself one d-devil of a noble fellow."

He opened his eyes and looked at her then. He laughed softly and closed them again when she said nothing.

"Every time my mother wrote, it was to say David was w-weakening," he said. "Finally, when it was clear he was d-d-dying, I took leave and c-came home to see him. I spent most of my time with him at Candlebury. I was going to stay home until he died. I r-remember that. Velma was in London—it was the Season. And then she was back home. I think she must have come because of David. But I saw her again, and I—"

He was frowning and rubbing his forehead again. Then he used the same fist to pound on the arm of his chair over and over again until he stopped and spread his hand over it, palm down.

"I can't remember. *I can't bloody remember.* Oh, dash it all, Agnes, forgive me. But I *can't remember*. David was *d-dying*, and I thought I would die too, and yet suddenly I was in love with Velma again, and our engagement was being announced, and a big betrothal ball had been planned in London for the day before I was scheduled to return to the P-Peninsula. My mother and sister were ecstatic. So were the Fromes. I think—yes, I think they w-wanted it to happen before David died, so that the mourning period would not delay it. I suppose I wanted it too. I w-wasn't going to leave David at all, but I ended up going to London and dancing at my b-betrothal ball, and setting off back to the Peninsula the very next day. The n-night I sailed, David d-died."

Agnes had one hand over her mouth. Surely, oh, surely there was more to the story than that. It made no real sense. But he could not remember. She had come down here to accuse him, to force the sordid truth out of him. It was sordid indeed if it had happened as he remembered it.

"I did not even come back to England after I heard," he said. "I stayed where I was. I did not come home until I was c-carried home. I was c-conscious, but I could not speak or f-fully understand what was happening around me or what p-people were saying. I c-could not even think c-clearly. I was d-dangerous. V-Violent. George came and g-got me eventually and took me off to C-Cornwall, where he f-found some g-good treatment for me. But j-just before I went, Velma came to t-tell me there was to be an announcement of the end of our b-betrothal in the morning papers next day, and that a few d-days later there was to be an announcement of her b-betrothal to Hazeltine. My b-best f-friend since school days. She said she was heartbroken, that they both were, but that they would f-find comfort together and w-would always love me."

Oh.

"I understood what she s-said," he said, "but I could not t-talk. Not even with a s-stammer. Only gibberish came out of my mouth when I tried. I was d-desperate to stop them. After she had g-gone, I destroyed the drawing room. I was d-desperate to talk to L-Len, but he did not c-come."

"Your best friend," Agnes said.

"They m-married each other," he said. "She told you they were unhappy?"

"She said they lived virtually apart for the last two years of his life," Agnes told him.

His mouth twisted with mockery, and he laughed without humor.

"I should be gloating," he said softly. "But poor Len."

"You knew she was back with her parents?" Agnes asked.

"My sister wrote while I was at Middlebury Park," he said, "and then my mother. They could not call on her at Farthings fast enough."

"Both families hoped to revive the old plan for the two of you to marry?" she said.

"Oh, yes," he said. "The whole l-lot of them."

"Lady Hazeltine too, I suppose," she said. "And so you married me."

For a moment there was a buzzing in her head, but she shook off the impulse to just faint away and so avoid facing the truth. It must be faced sooner or later.

He did not rush into denial—or confirmation. He turned his head her way and stared at her with hooded eyes, though not with his usual lazy mask of mockery.

"I married you," he said at last, "because I w-wanted to."

She stared back at him for a while and laughed softly.

"What a very heartwarming declaration," she said. "*Because you wanted to.* You married me, Flavian, to avenge yourself upon Lady Hazeltine and upon your families, who did not stop her from marrying your best friend. And your choice of a plain, uninteresting nobody was inspired. I can see that now. No one could fail to get the point. Least of all me."

"You are neither plain nor uninteresting nor a nobody, Agnes," he said.

"You are right." She got to her feet, hugging her dressing gown about her. "I am not—except in the eyes of your mother and sister and the *woman you love* and her family, and that is all that really matters, is it not?"

"Agnes—" he began, but she held up a staying hand.

"I am not putting *all* the blame upon you," she said. "I am to blame too. Marrying you was utter madness. I did not even know you, or you me. I *knew* it was madness, but I married you anyway. I allowed myself to be swept away by passion. I wanted you, and finally I persuaded myself that the wanting was enough. And then, after we were married, I convinced myself that what happened between us really *was* enough, when in reality it was nothing but base physical gratification, divorced from either mind or reason. I have been no better than a—a *courtesan*."

"Courtesans feel no passion, Agnes," he said. "They are too busy arousing it. Their living d-depends upon it."

"Then I am no better than my *mother*," she spat out.

She turned toward the embers of the fire again so that she would not have to look at him.

"Unlike her, you have not left me for someone else yet," he said.

"Passion is a *destroyer*," she told him. "It is the ultimate selfishness. It kills everything but itself. She left me when I was little more than a baby. Worse, she left Dora with all her hopes and dreams forever destroyed. Dora was seventeen, and she was pretty and eager and vivacious and looking forward to courtship and marriage and motherhood. Instead she was left with me. It was the lesson of a lifetime for a young child—or ought to have been. Passion was to be avoided at all costs. I chose wisely the first time I married. But at the first advent of passion into my life with *you*, I grabbed it without having any thought to anyone or anything else. Because I *desired* you in the basest physical way. And for *that* I do not blame you. Only for your dishonesty."

"Agnes—" he said.

"I am going back to Inglebrook," she said. "It will not make any difference to you. You are stuck with me for life anyway, and that will be enough to feed your revenge. You cannot also marry her unless I die. I am going back to Dora. I ought never to have left her. She deserved better of me."

"Agnes—"

"No!" She swept around to look down at him. "No, you will not talk me out of it. When you think about it—if you ever do stop to *think*, that is—you will find yourself glad to have me out of your life. I have served my purpose, and I am going. Tomorrow. And you need not concern yourself. I will go on the stage. I have enough of my own money to pay for a ticket."

Suddenly his mask was firmly in place—hooded, lazy eyes, slightly twisted mouth.

"Agnes," he said, "you are a p-passionate woman whether you wish to be or not. And you are m-married to me whether you wish to be or not."

"Passion," she said, "can and ought to be controlled. And when I go home, I can forget that we are married."

He raised one mocking eyebrow, and she wanted nothing more than to sink to her knees before the hearth and curl into a ball and sob her heart out. Or stride toward him and smack him hard across the cheek.

She had been married for revenge against the woman who had once hurt him beyond bearing.

But what about the woman who *loved* him?

What about *her*?

18

His wife's bed had been slept in, Flavian could see—or lain upon at least. The dressing table had been swept bare of everything that had adorned it the last time he been had been in her bedchamber, however, except for the two candlesticks with their burned-down candles. Nothing littered the room.

Flavian might have feared she had gone already, if the sound of muffled sobs had not been coming through the partially open door to her dressing room.

He had not been to bed. He had spent the night in the book room, sprawled in the chair where she had found him sometime after midnight. He had not slept either. He had not got up to rekindle the fire or to pull his coat back on, though he had been aware that the room was chilly. He had not got up to refill his glass. Experience had taught him that drunkenness would only deepen his gloom, not lighten it or obliterate it. He had never had much success with liquor. He sometimes envied happy drunks.

He was aware that his evening shirt was horribly wrinkled, that his hair was hopelessly disheveled, that he was badly in need of a shave, that his eyes were undoubtedly bloodshot, and that he probably did not smell all that pleasant. He could not be bothered to go and change and get cleaned up. Besides, she would probably be gone before he had made himself presentable.

It was still dashed early, but then, daylight was all she had waited for, he guessed.

His life could not possibly be more messed up if he had tried.

He went to the doorway of the dressing room and set his shoulder against the frame after pushing the door a little wider. She was dressed for travel. All but one of her bags were packed and closed up. The remaining one was ready to be closed. It was not she who was sobbing, though, he discovered. It was the skinny little maid.

"Madeline," he said when she looked up and spotted him. "W-Will you leave us, please?"

She had probably just been dismissed, her services no longer needed, poor girl.

"It just isn't right, it isn't," she said, glaring at him with watery accusation.

"Madeline." Agnes, her voice quiet but firm, cut the maid off from explaining exactly what it was that was not right. "Leave us, please. I will talk to you before I go."

Still glaring from reddened eyes that did nothing to improve her looks, the girl passed him in the doorway.

Agnes set her brush on top of the still-open bag and closed it. She straightened up and looked at him—with a pale, composed face and empty eyes.

"Do you realize," he said to her, "that yesterday was our f-first anniversary? Our one-week anniversary?"

"Would that I could go back and obliterate that week and take a different road," she said. "But it is not possible. One can only move forward."

"Are you not trying to go back anyway?" he asked her. "In time as well as in place?"

She seemed to consider her answer.

"No," she said. "A short while ago I held a faint hope that I might marry again someday and perhaps even have a child or two, and that I would be as contented with my new marriage as I was with the old. Now that hope has been wiped out forever. Apart from that, though, my life will return to what it was until I made such an impulsive and disastrous decision. I will be with Dora. I believe she draws as much comfort from my company as I do from hers."

"I think you will s-sadden her," he said.

She laughed, though she did not sound remotely amused.

"She always said she did not trust your mobile left eyebrow," she said. "I daresay she will not be altogether surprised to be proved that she was right."

"I b-believe she likes me," he said.

Agnes looked him over and laughed again. He wished he had at least buttoned his shirt to the neck. He must look the wreck he felt, not to mention disreputable.

"Don't g-go," he said.

She raised her eyebrows—both of them.

"It has been only a w-week, Agnes," he said. "Since we are m-married anyway and nothing can change that, ought we not at l-least to g-give m-marriage a ch-chance?"

He thought suddenly of Ben once saying that he often wished he could just drop his canes and walk away from them without even thinking—or stumbling or falling. Flavian wished *he* could just open his mouth and say what his mind was thinking, without tripping and stumbling over his words—especially when he was most agitated.

"But it never was a marriage, was it?" she said. "Except, of course, that there was a ceremony binding us for life, and there was the consummation. Those things do not make a *marriage*, however, except in law. You married me so that you could hurt Lady Hazeltine and your family and hers as they hurt you years ago. And I married you because I—well, because I *lusted* after you. Now you have had your revenge and I have sated my lust, and it is time for me to go home. You are not going to try to stop me, are you? You are not going to try asserting your authority and order me to stay?"

She lifted her chin, and her jaw hardened.

"I w-want to be m-married to you," he said. "I c-cannot explain why, and I am not going to s-spout reasons you would recognize as f-fabrications. But it was not revenge, Agnes. Or at least not . . . That w-word never entered my head. I w-wanted to be s-safe. I do not even know what I m-mean by that, but I felt it when you said yes, you would m-marry me, and I felt it when we m-married and walked out of the church. I felt s-safe. That may not s-seem very flattering, but it *is* the truth. And it was *you* I w-wanted to marry, not just any woman. And it was not just lust on your part. You would not have m-married me just to be bedded. You b-belittle yourself when you say that. You wanted *me*, not just my body. You wanted *me*, Agnes."

"I do not even know who you are," she said.

"But you knew I was *s-somebody*," he said. "Somebody you w-wanted to know. Somebody you wanted to spend a l-lifetime getting to know. It was not just lust."

"More fool me, then," she said. "There was nobody worth knowing inside that beautiful body after all, was there?"

He flinched and swallowed.

"Don't go," he said. "You may r-regret it. And I know *I* would."

"Your *pride* would regret it," she said.

"Probably," he admitted. "And all the rest of me too."

She stared at him, her face stony, her eyes blank.

"W-wait another week," he pleaded. "Give me that much time. Stay for s-seven more days, and then I will t-take you to Candlebury if you s-still want to leave me. We can say we are going d-down there for Easter, and you can r-remain there afterward, and anyone who s-says you ought to be presented to the *ton* as my v-viscountess may go hang. You may have your s-sister come to live with you if you wish and if she wishes. She will find music pupils enough if she w-wants them, and you will find enough wildflowers to p-paint to last a lifetime. But g-give me a week first."

She had not moved and did not now.

"Or if you must leave t-today," he said, "then l-let me take you to Candlebury now. I'll not s-stay if you do not want. I'll never go near the place again unless you invite me. Agnes?"

"Do you still love her?" she asked.

He expelled his breath audibly, tipped his head back against the doorframe, crossed his arms, and gazed upward.

"The f-funny thing is," he said, "and I think it *must* be funny because it makes no sense whatsoever—the funny thing is that I am not s-sure I ever did. I mean, I want to be honest with you because I think it is my only chance. I must have loved her, mustn't I? But I c-can't remember how it was or how it felt. And when I saw her again the day you and I arrived here, I d-didn't know if I loved her or hated her. I still didn't know when I called on her yesterday. I was afraid I loved her. But I did not want to. I *do* not want to. I w-want to . . . I want to be married to *you*. I want to be safe with you. And I could not sound more selfish if I tried, could I? I want, I want, I want . . . I would like to try to m-make you h-happy, Agnes. I think it would be good to make someone h-happy. I think it would be the best feeling in the world. Especially if it were you. Don't go. Give me a chance. Give *us* a chance."

There was a longish silence while he closed his eyes and waited for her decision. He was *not* going to impose his authority on her, though he could do it as her husband, he supposed. If she must leave, then he would let her go. Even by the stage, if that was what she chose.

And, good God, he could not even assure her that he did not still love Velma—or that he ever had. Why the devil had the physician at Penderris ever released him upon an unsuspecting world? He was a walking lunatic.

"There is a terrible pain," she said softly, "about being abandoned by someone who loves someone else more than you. A pain and an emptiness and a determination never again to give anyone that power."

He was bewildered for a moment before he realized she was talking about her mother, who had left her own children in order to be with her lover.

"Marriage with William brought peace and tranquility," she said.

"I am not William."

She looked back at him, her eyes still blank, until suddenly they crinkled unexpectedly at the corners, and she laughed with what sounded like real amusement.

"That must be the understatement of the decade," she said.

"Stay," he urged her. "You may decide to leave me later, Agnes, and I will not s-stop you, but I will never abandon you. Never. I swear it."

It was not literal abandonment she feared, though, he knew, but emotional abandonment—his loving Velma instead of her. Good God, he had never thought of Agnes in terms of *love*. Love—romantic love, that was—always made him feel slightly sick, though he had no idea why. Hugo loved Lady Trentham, and there was nothing at all nauseating about what they obviously felt for each other. The same was true of Vincent and his wife, and Ben and his. Why could it not be true of him?

She was looking steadily back at him, her smile gone.

"For one week," she said at last.

He rested his head against the doorframe again and closed his eyes briefly. "Thank you," he whispered.

"Go and get some sleep, Flavian," she said. "You are exhausted."

"There is n-nothing like having your w-wife of one week s-saying she is going to l-leave you for keeping you awake," he said.

"Well, she is not *going* to leave you," she said. "Not for another week, anyway. But if I am to stay, Flavian, then I am going to call upon Lady Hazeltine and Lady Frome, preferably this afternoon, if by chance they are at home."

He frowned. "You will take my m-mother with you? Or m-me?"

"Neither," she said.

He continued to frown, and had mental images of Daniel walking into the lions' den. Which was a strange way of thinking of Frome's house.

"I shall take Madeline for respectability," Agnes said, "since this is not the country. Will it be very bad *ton* anyway to go essentially alone?"

"Very," he said.

"I hope they *are* at home," she told him, "and I hope they are alone. There needs to be some plain speaking."

He had married a brave woman, he realized, quiet and unassuming as she always seemed. Such a visit would surely be incredibly difficult for her.

"Go and get some sleep," she said.

"Yes, ma'am." He pushed his shoulder away from the

doorframe and turned back in to her bedchamber en route to his own.

He rang for his valet when he got there.

As Agnes, with a newly happy Madeline trotting along quietly at her side, strode in the direction of Portman Place and looked for the right house number, she hoped fervently that the ladies *were* at home and unencumbered by other visitors. At the same time, and quite irrationally, she hoped fervently that they were out.

The butler did not know but would go and see. Ordinarily it would amuse Agnes that the butler of a house should profess himself ignorant of who was in the house and who was not, but on this occasion she merely crossed her fingers on both hands and made a muddled wish. *Let them be home. Let them not.*

"He might have asked you to sit down while you wait," Madeline said. "Rude, I call it, for all his uppity ways."

Agnes did not reply.

The ladies were at home, though Agnes could see as soon as she was shown into the drawing room that they were dressed for the outdoors. Curiosity must have caused them to decide to admit her when the butler informed them of her arrival.

Both were dressed with fashionable elegance. Agnes was not. A few more of her new clothes had arrived from Madame Martin's during the morning, and Madeline had laid out one of the walking outfits when she knew that her mistress was going to make an afternoon call. But she had not argued when Agnes had told her she would prefer to look like herself. The girl had merely given her a shrewd look, nodded briskly, and pulled out something old, which had nevertheless been freshly brushed and ironed so that it looked at least two years younger than it was.

"Lady Ponsonby, how delightful," Lady Frome said, smiling as she indicated with one hand that Agnes should take a seat. "But your mama-in-law has not come with you?"

The countess meanwhile had come hurrying across the room, a smile of warm welcome on her face, both hands outstretched.

"How kind of you to call," she said. "I said to Mama yesterday after I had met you at Hookham's Library that I hoped we would become close and dear friends as well as just neighbors. Did I not, Mama? And here you are the very next day. But without Flavian?"

Agnes offered just her right hand, and the countess shook it before they all seated themselves.

"I came alone from choice," she said.

Both ladies looked expectantly at her.

"I wished to make it clear," Agnes said, addressing herself to the older lady, "that I regret the embarrassment my unexpected appearance in town as Flavian's wife caused you. It was never my intention to hurt anyone."

Lady Frome looked embarrassed anyway.

"We were certainly taken by surprise," she said. "And so, of course, were Lady Ponsonby and Marianne. We cut short our visit because our continued presence in your drawing room would have been an intrusion upon what was clearly a private family matter. I hope we did not give offense by leaving so abruptly. I would not have any hard feeling between our families for worlds. We are neighbors, you know. But of course you know. Our two families have always been on the best of terms."

It was a gracious response, and Agnes instinctively liked the lady. For a moment she was tempted simply to smile and change the subject and remain for a decent time before taking her leave. Perhaps it would be best to say no more. But she abandoned the idea with some reluctance. She had come to do some plain speaking, and if she did not do it now, she never would, and something, some mutual wound, would fester beneath the surface of all their future dealings.

Enough had been suppressed in her own family life for her to want to avoid its happening again within her marriage.

"I hope our families will remain on as good terms as they always have been, ma'am," Agnes said. "We must speak first, though, about what threatens to be an embarrassment. I think it must have been extremely sad for you all, and for you in particular, Lady Hazeltine, when the late Lord Ponsonby—*David*, I mean—judged himself too ill to continue with the marriage plans both your families had encouraged. That is to say, it must have been very sad for you when he set you free."

The countess turned rather pale.

"I was dearly fond of him all my life," she said, "and I yearned to marry him and give him some happiness, even though it was perfectly clear he would not live long. But he was so foolishly *noble* and would not let me do it. I begged and I wept, but it was all to no avail. He would not have me. He insisted that I be free to marry someone who had a life ahead of him, someone I loved. Though I loved *him*."

She sounded sincere enough.

"He was the dearest, sweetest young man," Lady Frome said. "I am sure he loved Velma very much, but once he had decided that it would be selfish to tie her to a dying man, there was no shifting him."

"It must have seemed like double punishment," Agnes continued, addressing herself now to the countess, "when Flavian was so badly wounded in the Peninsula after you had transferred your love to him and had celebrated your betrothal to him with such joyful festivities."

Lady Hazeltine bit her lip and looked stricken.

"He has *told* you," she said. "But I suppose it was inevitable *someone* would have done so sooner or later. We *were* in love, Lady Ponsonby. I will not deny it even if Flavian does. I will even go farther. I was dearly fond of David and wished more than anything to marry him and make him happy. But it was Flavian I *loved*. Just as he adored me. We had loved each other quite hopelessly for years before David set us free. Yes, and he did it *because* he knew we loved each other and he loved us both. He was the dearest of men."

"My love." Lady Frome sounded reproachful. "This is hardly—"

"No, Mama," her daughter said, two spots of color blossoming in her cheeks, her eyes flashing, "she *ought* to know the truth, since she is the one who broached the subject. I would not have said a word if she had not. Flavian was out of his mind when he was brought home, Lady Ponsonby. He did not know anyone or anything. And he was *violent*. He was little more than a wild animal. His physician informed us all he would never be any better, that sooner or later he would have to be confined to an asylum, where he could harm no one but himself. What was I to do? It was worse than if he had died. And Leonard was dreadfully upset too. He was Flavian's dearest friend in the world, and kept blaming himself for selling his own commission a few months before Flavian was wounded, and leaving Flavian alone—as if his staying could somehow have averted disaster. He was distraught. We both were. And we turned to each other for comfort. We married. But I never loved him or he me. Indeed, I think we came to hate each other."

"Velma, my love," her mother pleaded, "you must not say these things. Not to Lady Ponsonby. It is not kind."

"Perhaps we would have made something of our marriage if Flavian had not started to recover," Lady Hazeltine continued, just as if her mother had not spoken. "But Leonard never forgave himself, and I . . . Well, I ought to have waited longer."

Agnes felt a bit sick. Perhaps she had been mistaken at the library yesterday. She had thought then there was some calculation, even a hint of spite, in the countess's words.

"And now," Lady Hazeltine said, "just when I might have made amends, I have been treated as if I had been merely faithless and heartless all those long years ago. And I have become the object of a cruel revenge. Was it justified, Lady Ponsonby?"

No, Agnes thought. Oh, no, she had not been wrong.

"My love." Lady Frome was clearly distressed. "Lady Ponsonby is in no way to blame."

"Your bitterness is understandable, Lady Hazeltine," Agnes said. "At this point, however, it will accomplish nothing. You and Flavian loved each other years ago, but people change. He has changed, and I daresay you have too, and will recover from your disappointment and even be thankful that you are no longer tied to the past. Flavian married me last week because he wished to do so, and I married him for the same reason. It is an accomplished fact."

"It is clear that you have never loved," the countess said with a sad, sweet smile. "True love does not die, Lady Ponsonby, or recover from *disappointment*. It is not affected by the passage of time."

Agnes sighed.

"I wish you well," she said. "I wish you future happiness with all my heart. And I wish for peace and amicable relations between our families. But I will not be made to feel like someone whom my husband married only because he wished to punish a former love of his. I will not tolerate being seen as the other woman in a tragic love story. He married *me*, Lady Hazeltine. More important, as far as I am concerned, I married *him*, and I *count*. I am a person, too."

She had got to her feet while she was speaking, and picked up her reticule in preparation for leaving. Her legs were not feeling any too steady, though at least her voice had not shaken.

The other ladies had stood too.

"I do assure you, Lady Ponsonby, that I wish you every happiness," Lady Frome said with apparent sincerity. "And I do thank you for calling. It was a brave thing to do, and all alone too. I shall look forward to our being neighbors."

"I wish you well too," the countess said. "Though I believe, Lady Ponsonby, you will need all the good wishes you can get."

Agnes nodded and took her leave.

At first she walked briskly homeward, Madeline at her heels, but after a few minutes she calmed and slowed her steps to a more ladylike pace. She was not sure the visit had accomplished a great deal beyond upsetting her horribly. But she was not sorry she had gone. She hated situations in which people did not talk out their differences. At least if there must be malice and enmity between her and the Countess of Hazeltine—and she suspected there must—then it was as well that its existence and causes be out in the open.

Nothing had ever been said after her mother left. Nothing. Ever. One day a five-year-old child had had her beautiful, vibrant, laughter-filled mother there with her, and the next day her mother was gone, never to reappear. No explanation had ever been given. Agnes had

had to piece together the little she knew from snatches of conversation she had heard down the years, none of it ever spoken directly to her.

And so the hurt, the sense of abandonment, had festered. Perhaps it would have anyway, but the pain would have been different. Or so she had always believed. Perhaps not. Perhaps pain was simply pain.

She had planned to be on a stagecoach by now, on her way home to Dora. After just one week of marriage. What a dreadful humiliation that would have been. Instead she had agreed to stay for one more week, and then, perhaps, to go to Candlebury Abbey instead of to Inglebrook.

One more week. To piece together a marriage. Or to bring it to an end in a lifelong separation. But the sense of defeat in that last thought filled her with sudden anger.

She would be . . . Oh, what was the very worst word she could think of? She would be *damned* before she would give up her marriage after two weeks just because Flavian had once loved a beautiful woman who had chosen spite over stoical dignity when he had married *her*. She would be . . . Well, she would be *double* damned.

So there!

He wanted to give their marriage a chance.

Well, then. So did she. More than a chance. She was going to make a *marriage* of what they had. See if she didn't.

19

Flavian did not sleep or even try to. He had one week. Seven days. He was not about to waste even an hour of one of them catching up on his beauty sleep. The trouble was, though, that he did not know what he could do to convince Agnes to stay with him, beyond making love to her night and day. He was good at that, at least. Or, rather, *they* were good at it.

He did not think sex alone would persuade her to stay, however. And he was not even sure she was going to allow him near her bed in the next seven days or nights. Besides, good sex might actually convince her *not* to stay. She had that alarming belief that passion must be obliterated from her life if she was to maintain any sort of control over it. All because of her mother.

He had his valet prepare a bath for him. He felt a bit better once he was clean and in fresh clothes, and once he was shaved. He had also done some thinking. He had not come up with any short-term solutions, and they were what he really needed, but at least he could do *something*. He went back to the book room, seated himself at the desk, and wrote two letters—*not* his favorite activity at the best of times. But they were necessary and overdue. He could hardly call in person on his father-in-law, since to do so he would have to leave London and squander his precious week. The same applied to his brother-in-law. It was a courtesy to write to them both. More than that, though, he had a few questions to ask them, and he hoped at least one of them would be more forthcoming with him than they had ever been with Agnes.

Having written the letters more or less to his satisfaction, and sealed and franked them and handed them into the care of his butler, Flavian sallied forth to White's Club, partly because he could not think of anywhere else to go, since Agnes had other plans for the day and he was not involved in them. But partly he went in the hope that he might find someone to whom he might address a few discreet questions. Maybe there *was* something he could do.

Any number of gentlemen greeted him there. He might have attached himself to congenial company for the rest of the day and most of the night if he had wanted to, despite the fact that at least half the *ton* was still waiting for Easter to come and go before descending upon London. Most of the company was roughly his own age, however, and of no use to him today. And he was not well enough acquainted with any of the older men, he realized as he sat down in the reading room and gave the morning papers only a small amount of his attention.

And then two of his uncles and one of his cousins arrived together and greeted him with hearty good humor, slapping his back and pumping his hand, talking and laughing. Not surprisingly, they drew the frowning attention of other occupants of the room, who had been quietly reading their papers until now.

Uncle Quentin and Uncle James had just arrived in town, Flavian understood, with the aunts and all the cousins for whose existence they claimed responsibility. One of the latter, Cousin Desmond, Uncle James's eldest son and heir, beamed his pleasure at seeing someone roughly his own age. Two of the other cousins, one for each uncle, were female and eighteen years old and ripe for the marriage mart, so there had been all the necessity of descending upon the capital early enough to do a mountain and a half of shopping, all of which was absolutely necessary, according to the aunts, and all of which would beggar them for the next half century or so, according to the uncles.

Flavian shepherded his relatives into the coffee room, where they could talk without drawing upon their heads the censure of the newspaper readers.

They had just heard about Flavian's marriage, and both uncles professed themselves delighted that he was showing some sense at last, though rumor had it that he had married an unknown, a matter that could be easily remedied, of course, by making her *known* without further ado, an endeavor in which the aunts would be only too happy to have a hand. The uncles were positively bursting with curiosity. Who was the lucky lady, eh? Eh? Or was it the groom who was the lucky one?

The uncles were twins. They spoke in tandem, the one often beginning a sentence, the other completing it, so that one's head tended to swivel rhythmically between the two of them.

Hearty guffaws ended their latest series of questions.

Flavian relaxed into the pleasure of seeing some family members again. He explained that Agnes had been a widow living with her unmarried sister in the village close to Middlebury Park, where he had just spent three weeks with friends. He was careful to add that he had met her six months ago, so his courtship and marriage were not quite the whirlwind affair people were undoubtedly thinking.

"I say, though, Flave," Desmond said, "there may be a

spot of trouble brewing around Lady Ponsonby. I suppose you have heard?"

"Eh?" Uncle James said.

"What's that, Des?" Uncle Quentin asked.

Flavian merely looked his inquiry.

"There was a bit of a party at Lady Merton's last night," Desmond said. "Bidulph and Griffin dragged me along there with them. It was a crashing bore, actually. But your wedding seemed to be big news, and a bit of a surprise to some just when the Countess of Hazeltine had come back to town. She was there too last night, though all the gossips were careful not to talk in her hearing. She is looking as fetching as ever, by the way. Have you seen her, Flave?"

"What was the s-spot of trouble?" Flavian asked.

"It seems Lady Ponsonby's mother was not all she ought to be," Desmond said. "Ran off with a lover, you know, and her husband—*Debbins*, was it?—divorced her. You need to be careful, Flave, if it is true, or even if it is not, for that matter. It is awkward enough that your wife is unknown, but if she is also seen to be not quite respectable . . ."

He did not complete the thought, perhaps because he saw the expression on his cousin's face.

Who knew? Flavian scoured his mind. *Who knew?* They had told his mother who she was, and Marianne and Oswald too. They had named her father and her late husband. But they had not made any mention of the old scandal. He had told *no one*, and he was sure Agnes had not either. No one else had even been told who her father was.

Except the Fromes. And Velma.

He could almost hear Velma asking him who Agnes was, and himself answering.

She is the daughter of a Mr. Debbins from Lancashire.

His main purpose in coming here this morning suddenly seemed of the greatest urgency. And it struck him that both uncles were of the approximate age to help with answers. Both spent as much time in London or at one of the fashionable spas as they did in their own country homes, and were always a mine of information and news and gossip. And what the uncles did not know, the aunts very well might.

"If anyone w-wishes to know if my w-wife is respectable," he said, "he m-may address the question to m-me."

Desmond recoiled and held up both hands, palms out.

"I am merely saying what was being whispered last night, Flave," he said. "It was nothing much, but you know how gossip can fan the flames of the smallest fire."

And Velma had been at last night's party.

"Does either of you remember that divorce?" he asked his uncles. "A Debbins from Lancashire. Twenty years or so ago."

"Divorce," Uncle James said. "By act of Parliament, do you mean? A bit drastic, that, on the part of your father-in-law, Flavian. It would have cost a king's ransom and been horridly public. Nasty for his children too. And she was your *mother-in-law*? That's the devil's own luck for you, boy. I don't recall it. Do you, Quent?"

Uncle Quentin had planted one elbow on the table and was drumming his fingernails against his teeth.

"I remember old Sainsley divorcing his wife for adultery when everyone knew it was a trumped-up charge," he said. "She was starting to cut up nasty about his three mistresses and all the natural children he was supporting. That must have been, oh, ten, fifteen years ago. Remember, James?"

"Was it that long ago?" James asked. "Yes, I suppose it was. I remember. . . ."

Desmond exchanged a long-faced stare with Flavian. The uncles could never be rushed.

"Havell," Uncle Quentin said suddenly, slapping a hand flat on the table and causing some of Uncle James's coffee to slosh into his saucer. "Sir Everard Havell, the one everyone called the beautiful boy on account of his smile. He had a mouthful of perfect white teeth."

"I remember," Uncle James said. "The ladies used to swoon at one smile from him."

"He was forced to rusticate when he ran low on funds," Uncle Quentin continued. "Went to stay with some doddering uncle or other who might or might not leave him everything. Went to butter up the old boy, I suppose. And it was *Lancashire*. I am sure of that. I thought, poor fellow, having to be incarcerated somewhere in Lancashire, of all the godforsaken places."

"He was not to be envied," Uncle James agreed.

"He ran off with someone's wife, and her husband divorced her, and Havell got cut off without a penny." Uncle Quentin looked triumphantly across the table at Flavian. "That was it. Must be. I can't remember the husband's name, but it was about twenty years ago, and it was Lancashire. It would be too much of a coincidence if there had been two such elopements and two such divorces."

"But does Lady Ponsonby not *know*, Flave?" Desmond asked.

"She chooses not to talk of it," Flavian said, sitting back in his chair. "She does not even know the name of the man with whom her mother ran away."

"She is not going to be able to hide her head in the sand for much longer, though, is she?" Desmond was frowning. "It will not take the tabbies long to find out the details, Flave. If Uncle Quent remembers, other people will too. It could bode trouble for Lady Ponsonby. And for you."

"We are a big enough family, heaven knows," Uncle

James said. "And your family on your mother's side is almost as large."

"And families stand together," Uncle Quentin said.

"Heaven help us," Desmond murmured.

"What happened after the divorce?" Flavian asked.

"Eh?" Uncle James said.

"Havell did the decent thing and married the lady," Uncle Quentin said. "Apparently she was a beauty, even though she was no spring chicken, and older than he, if I remember rightly. They were given the cut direct by the whole of the beau monde, though."

"Is either of them still living?" Flavian asked. "And where did or do they live?"

Uncle Quentin tapped his teeth again, and Uncle James rubbed his chin with one hand.

"Damned if I know," Uncle James said. "You, Quent?"

Uncle Quentin shook his head. "But you might ask Jenkins," he said. "Peter Jenkins. He is related in some way to Havell—second cousin once removed or some such thing. He may know."

"First," Uncle James said. "First cousin twice removed."

Peter Jenkins happened to be dining at White's with friends. Flavian had to wait all of an hour and a half to catch him alone.

Agnes was exhausted. Not that the evening had been a busy one. It had been rather pleasant, in fact. She had donned one of the least fancy of her evening gowns and had dined with Flavian and his mother, then sat in the drawing room with them afterward. While she worked at some tatting and her mother-in-law drew up her embroidery frame, Flavian had read to them from Mr. Fielding's *Joseph Andrews*, an amusing spoof on Samuel Richardson's *Pamela*, which Agnes had read and not particularly enjoyed a few years ago.

He had read well and with very little stammering. And when he finally closed the book and set it on the table beside him, he had propped the side of his face on one hand and watched Agnes work, with an expression that might have been contentment or fondness or mere tiredness. He had not slept last night, after all, and she doubted he had slept this morning.

They were invited to Lord Shields's house the following evening for an impromptu party with family and friends. Flavian explained that some of his relatives had arrived in town and were eager to meet her. Agnes was a little wary of the word *party* that appeared in Marianne's invitation, but the dowager reminded her that town was still really rather sparse of company this early in the year. Anyway, if she was to stay with Flavian—and she *was going* to stay—she must meet the *ton* sooner or later.

She would allow Madeline to choose the most suitable of her evening gowns.

She was dressed now in a new nightgown. It was not nearly as daring and revealing as some she might have chosen. It covered her shoulders and upper arms and all but a modest expanse of bosom, and, despite the fineness of the linen, it was opaque. It did tend to cling a bit, though, according to Madeline, that was what it was supposed to do in order to show off her lovely figure.

She was not at all sure anyone but Madeline would see her in the nightgown. When Agnes had agreed this morning to give their marriage a week, they had not discussed what the nature of the marriage would be during that week. She did not know whether Flavian would come to her, and she did not know whether she would go and seek him out tonight as she had done last night—if he did not come, that was.

She ought not to want him to come. She had been

very angry indeed with him. Not angry in the way that a good quarrel might solve, but angry in a way that could not be mended, angry from the feeling she had been cruelly *used* and that sheer lust had made her into a willing victim. The fact that she was in love with him had been quite irrelevant. Indeed, that very fact had only made her more determined to exert some control over her life, to act with her head instead of her heart—or the cravings of her body.

But she had done a lot of thinking in the course of the day. And a lot of remembering.

She was sitting on the side of the bed when he came. He tapped on the door, waited a moment—she did not call to him—and came inside. He stood there in his dressing gown, which was tightly belted about his waist, looking gorgeous with his blond hair slightly tousled. She felt a tightening in her breasts and hoped that in the dim candlelight he could not see the evidence of that fact through her nightgown.

"Are you about to throw a s-slipper at my head?" he asked.

"I would probably miss and feel foolish," she said.

He folded his arms and tipped his head slightly to one side.

"It is to be a *marriage* for seven days, then, is it?" he asked.

"Oh, you are not going to get off that lightly," she said. "It is to be a marriage *forever*, Flavian. You married me. It does not matter why you did it. You *married* me, and you will jolly well live up to that commitment. I will not allow you *not* to. And I married you. It does not matter why I did it. For better or worse, we are married. People marry for all sorts of reasons. It is not those that matter. It is what they *do* with their marriages that counts. We are going to make this a *good* marriage. *Both* of us."

Good heavens, where had *that* all come from? Her heart was thumping so loudly that she was half-deafened.

He had not moved or changed posture. But his eyelids had drooped half over his eyes, and his mouth had curved upward slightly at the corners, and he was watching her keenly.

"Yes, *ma'am*," he said softly—and advanced on her.

And so they made love—tentatively, sweetly, slowly, and finally with fierce urgency. When they were done, she lay on her back half across the bed, minus her lovely new nightgown, Flavian heavy on top of her. They were both hot and sweaty and relaxed. Her legs were stretched on either side of his. He was still inside her. He was breathing deeply and evenly. She was about to follow him into sleep. He would wake up soon and move off her with a murmured apology, but she did not mind the slight discomfort of his weight. She would not mind if he slept on her all night.

Some things could never be stopped once they had been allowed to start, she thought. Passion could not. She had married him very largely because she wanted him. But having him on her wedding night had not slaked her appetite except very temporarily. Quite the opposite, in fact. She wanted him more and more.

She was deeply wedded to him—a strange thought.

But passion was not to blame, she thought, for what people did with their lives. If she had met Flavian while she was still married to William, she would not have given in to her attraction to him. She *knew* she would not. Which was another strange thought to be having when she was on the verge of sleep and utterly sated with passion.

"Mmm," Flavian said against her ear, tickling it with his breath, "I am not exactly a feather cover, am I. S-Sorry."

And he disengaged from her and rolled to her side,

his arm beneath her bringing her with him to lie against him from head to toe. What a glorious creation the male body was, she thought as she relaxed against him again and drifted off. *This* male body, anyway.

Flavian awoke with a crashing headache and a panicked urge to lash out at all about him. He got up off the bed, groped around on the floor for his dressing gown, belted it about his waist, and staggered to the window. He pushed the curtains wide and gripped the window frame on either side of his head before touching his forehead to the glass.

He gazed into the near darkness of the outdoors and counted his breaths. His hands gripped harder. He dared not release his hold yet. He might start laying about him with his fists if he did. He felt as if someone were pounding a drum inside his head, though the pain was receding gradually.

What the devil . . . ?

He remembered that trouble loomed.

And that he had been almost happy when he fell asleep. She had decided to stay with him, to work on their marriage. They had made love, and he had been happy.

With trouble looming.

Caused, he was almost sure, by Velma. She had gone digging, and she had found gold. Yet it seemed so out of character for her. She was all sweetness and light.

The drum pounded at his head from the inside again.

"Flavian?" The voice came from just behind him. "What is it?"

He had woken her. But, dash it all, was it surprising? His grip on the window frame tightened again, and he closed his eyes.

"I could not sleep," he said. "Go b-back to bed. I'll be with you shortly."

He felt her hand come to rest against his back, between his shoulder blades, just below his neck. For a moment he tensed. And then a door opened in his mind, and he knew it was what had woken him. Memory had come bursting in upon him—a whole set of memories that had been closed to him for years to such a degree that he had not even realized there was anything missing.

"God!" he said.

"What is it?" Agnes asked again. "What woke you in such a panic? Tell me. I am your wife."

"She schemed and lied," he said, "and broke his heart."

There was a short silence.

"Lady Hazeltine?" she asked.

"Velma, yes," he said. "It s-started the year we were fifteen."

He lowered his arms and turned from the window. Agnes was wearing her nightgown again, a flimsy, pretty new one. The room was chilly. He strode over to her dressing room and in the near darkness found a woolen shawl. He brought it back, wrapped it about her shoulders, and led her back to the bed. He seated them side by side on the edge of it and took one of her hands in his. He closed his other hand into a fist and rubbed it over his forehead.

"I lost a whole chunk of memory," he said. "And then it came b-back and woke me, and shut down again. It is how it used to h-happen when I was still at Penderris. Not so much now, though. I always assume I have remembered everything."

"Have you recalled it again?" she asked, turning slightly so that she could hold his hand with both of hers.

Yes, it was there. In the open. It was not going to wink out again.

"Len—Leonard Burton, my school friend who later became Earl of Hazeltine—had not c-come to stay that summer, as he usually did," he said. "He had to go home to Northumberland for some family event. I can't recall what. Marianne had just made her come-out and was off at a house party with our m-mother. David stayed in the house or close to it most of the time. He did not have the energy for much else. So I wandered about the park alone—riding, swimming, fishing, doing whatever took my fancy. I was easy to p-please. I always enjoyed just being home."

"And you visited Farthings Hall?" she asked.

"I do not think so," he said. "Not to see Velma, if that is what you mean. We were never really f-friends, except perhaps when we were very young. She was a girl."

He frowned at his bare feet, which were stretched out before him.

"*She* came to Candlebury, though," he said. "To see David, she always claimed. They were to be officially betrothed when she was eighteen, and m-married when she was nineteen—that had been planned by both sets of parents when she was still in the c-cradle. No one ever questioned it. She ought not to have come. There were only the two of us—David and me—there apart from the servants, and she never brought either a groom or a maid with her. She came by all sorts of different routes too. She had an uncanny knack of coming across *me* on her way to the house."

"Was it just coincidence?" Agnes asked.

"I thought so," he said. "She was always so s-surprised to see me and so full of apologies for disturbing me. But she always stayed to stroll or sit with me. Sometimes she spent so long with me that she never did get to the house to see David. Whenever she *did*, though, he would send immediately for a m-maid to sit with them and then for a groom to accompany her back to Farthings. She told me she liked David, even l-loved him, that she l-longed to be old enough to m-marry him so that she could look after him."

He could remember being annoyed the first few times she had found him and not simply ridden on and left him to his own company. But he had been *fifteen*, for God's sake. It had not taken him long. . . .

"And then I started touching her," he said, "and kissing her, even though she used to cry afterward and tell me we absolutely must not do it ever again. Because of D-David. Then one afternoon we went farther than kisses. Considerably farther, though not . . . all the way. And that was the end of it. She cried and t-told me she loved me. I told her I loved her too but that it was over, that we m-must not meet like that again. And I m-meant it. I could not do such a thing to my brother. I knew he adored her. I d-don't think I set foot outside the house for a week, and then I went to stay with another school friend who had been p-pestering me to visit him. It meant l-leaving David alone, but I was having a hard time looking him in the eye anyway."

"And all this you have just remembered?" Agnes asked him.

He frowned. Velma had come to Candlebury that summer because his mother and Marianne were away, and David was more or less housebound, and Len was home in Northumberland. She had come to see *him*. David could have held little attraction for a fifteen-year-old girl, not when he had a more robust brother, and not when that brother would surely be Viscount Ponsonby of Candlebury Abbey in the not-too-distant future.

But could she be blamed for such conniving?

"No," he said. "This I remembered, and the apparently random meetings during the next three years, and the t-temptation. She was a lovely girl, and I was a l-lusty boy. But the date for their betrothal was coming c-closer, and D-David was happy, though he once confided in me that he thought p-perhaps it was selfish of him to hold her to a promise made by our parents and hers so many years ago. She was always so *f-fond* of him, though, whenever they were together."

"What *have* you remembered, then, Flavian?" she asked.

He swallowed once and then again. She was holding the back of his hand against her cheek, he realized.

"When Velma turned eighteen," he said, "and plans were being made for a betrothal party and an announcement to be sent to the London papers, David suddenly refused to marry her. He said it would be unfair when he was not w-well enough to give her the life she deserved. He set her free to find someone else. He hoped she would go to London for a Season and make a b-brilliant marriage. She was inconsolable, and he was heartbroken. And all this I remembered too."

She set her lips against the back of his hand.

"Our families immediately devised an alternate plan," he said. "It seemed almost as if they were r-relieved, as if they were far h-happier with the idea of Velma's marrying *me*. And then D-David s-spoke privately with m-me."

He shivered and got to his feet to go and stand close to the window again. His hands found the pockets of his dressing gown and shoved inside.

"He asked me if it was t-true," he said. "And he asked me if I l-loved her. And he t-told me that I had his blessing anyway, and that he would not stop loving me. Though he did add, as a sort of j-joke, that if he only had a bit more energy, he m-might challenge me to pistols at d-dawn."

He opened and closed his hands inside his pockets. Agnes said nothing.

"She had told him—and sworn him to secrecy," he

said. "She had told him that she and I had l-loved each other p-passionately for three years and were l-lovers, and that I had assured her we would s-still be lovers after she married David, but that she had decided she could not c-continue with the deceit. She had b-begged him to set her free to m-marry the man she loved."

He could hear Agnes draw an audible breath.

"He believed her?" she asked.

"She was sweet and without guile," he said. "Or so we both thought. And perhaps her motive was understandable. She was more or less l-locked into a marriage plan in which she had had no say. But what she did was . . . cruel. He would have set her free if she had but asked."

Her arms came about his waist from behind, and her cheek came to rest against his back.

"Did you *explain*?" she asked.

"I d-did," he said. "I told him everything, as I have told it to you. I t-told him I did not w-want to marry her. And *he* told *me* that I would have little choice, given the determination of our families to bring about the match. And she would surely see to it that she got her w-way. I b-begged him to purchase a commission for me, and he agreed, even though I was his heir and ought not to have put myself at risk as a soldier. Worse, my going away to war for an indefinite time made it l-likely that we would never see each other again."

"You did not love her, then?" Agnes asked.

"I was *eighteen*," he said. "I had barely tested my wings."

"Did she love you?"

"I cannot answer for her," he said. "She was always ambitious, though. She always talked quite openly about the time when she would be a *viscountess* and half the world would have to curtsy and bow to her and obey her every bidding. Her father is a baronet, but he is not particularly well off. She m-might not have done so well on the marriage mart. Though, as it happened, she married an earl."

"Your friend?"

"Len," he said. "Hazeltine. Yes."

He must have fallen in love with her, though, he thought, when he was home on leave the year David died, must he not? He had left his brother on his deathbed in order to dash off to London to celebrate at the lavish betrothal ball the Fromes gave in their honor. Unless . . .

It frightened him to realize that there might still be great holes in his memory in places he did not even suspect. And he was beginning to wonder about those weeks of his leave. He was quite aware of the fact that he could not remember the whys of his behavior.

He turned to Agnes and wrapped his arms about her and rested one cheek against the top of her head.

"I am sorry," he said. "I am s-sure the last thing any new wife needs to hear in the middle of the night is the story of her husband's dealings with another woman."

"*Part* of the story," she said softly. She tipped back her head and looked into his face, her own dimly lit by the light from the window. "This is not the whole of it, is it? You do not remember the whole?"

His stomach churned slightly.

"The trouble is," he said, flashing her a grin, "that I cannot always remember what I cannot remember—or *that* I cannot remember. Perhaps there are still all sorts of gaps in my mind. I am a m-mess, Agnes. You have married a mess."

"We are *all* a mess." He could see the flash of her teeth in the darkness, and he could hear the smile in her voice. "I think it must be part of being human."

"But not many of us are walking around free and unfettered with heads like those cheeses with g-great holes in them," he said. "You have married a man with cheese for a head."

She was laughing now. So, astonishingly, was he.

"What an adventure," she said.

"Speak for yourself." He lowered his head and brushed his nose across hers. Briefly, he thought about warning her of what had been buzzing about Lady Merton's party the night before last. But there had been enough drama for one night. "Cold nose."

"Warm heart," she retorted.

"I *am* sorry," he said. "I am so sorry."

"I am not," she told him. "Come back to bed and pull up the blankets. It is chilly."

"I have something better to offer than b-blankets," he said.

"Braggart."

"If I cannot w-warm you more effectively than blankets," he told her, "I will need to find a mouse hole somewhere and curl up inside it for the r-rest of my life."

"Come and warm me, then," she said, her voice a soft caress.

"Yes, *ma'am.*"

He felt a dizzying sort of happiness, as though some great load had been lifted from his shoulders. What a relief to know he had *not* loved Velma.

At least . . .

But for the moment he was safe and even happy with his wife.

20

One of Flavian's aunts and two of his female cousins came during the morning to meet Agnes, about whose existence they had learned late yesterday upon their arrival in town. They ended up bearing her off with Flavian's mother for a drive in Green Park. It was his aunt DeeDee—a corruption of Dorinda, he seemed to remember—his mother's younger sister, and his cousins Doris and Clementine, her third and fourth daughters. Or was it the fourth and fifth? Dash it, he should know. Clemmie was the youngest, anyway, and yet another cousin about to make her debut into society. She was a giggler, Flavian discovered during the few minutes he spent in her company, but then, most girls her age were.

He wondered whether Agnes had been a giggler at that age, but would bet his fortune she had not been. She had married her William when she was eighteen, and if there had ever existed a duller dog and one less romantically inclined, he would be surprised to hear it. Not that he had known the man, of course, and not that Agnes had said much about him. But much was to be deduced. . . .

If Flavian had the right of it, she had married Keeping because her father's remarriage had made her feel like a stranger in her own home. She had married him because he was safe. Strange, that. For now *he*, Flavian, had married *her* for the same reason.

He stood outside the front door of Arnott House after handing the ladies into the open carriage, all five crowded in together, and waving them on their way. He brooded for a few moments before going back inside.

A family was a good thing to have, even if it sometimes seemed that its numbers must extend into the hundreds and that it was made up almost entirely of the noisiest, most talkative members of the beau monde, both on his father's side and his mother's. Yes, it could be a *very* good thing to have, for his family had always been close-knit. Every member pulled for every other member, even if there were sometimes squabbles among individuals, especially siblings.

Every member of the family currently in London would surely have been invited to Marianne's party this evening. And every one of them would go. Flavian did not know who else had been invited. And he did not know whether the little flaring of gossip about his wife at Lady Merton's party had been fanned into flame, though he would wager it had been. He was going to be prepared anyway if any mention of it should be made tonight.

Whether he would warn Agnes and so make her more nervous than she would be anyway of her first *ton* party, he had not decided.

He turned and made his way back into the house.

He reappeared dressed for the outdoors a short while later, after a groom had brought his curricle and pair up to the door. He shook his head after he had climbed up to the seat and taken the ribbons in his hands, and the groom, looking somewhat surprised, refrained from scrambling up behind. Flavian would rather not have any witnesses among his own servants to the visit he was about to make. Servants, even loyal ones, were always the worst gossips in the world.

He drove himself out to Kensington, following vague directions to a house that Peter Jenkins had heard was quite invisible among an unruly forest of trees, though he had never seen it for himself. Jenkins also had no knowledge of whether the house was lived in or empty. He had had no dealings with his relative for as far back as he could remember. Havell might be in Kensington or in Timbuktu for as much as he knew—or cared, his tone had implied.

Flavian found the house. Or, rather, he found the unruly forest and followed a bumpy trail into its midst until he discovered the house—larger and in somewhat better condition than he had expected, and surrounded by a small, well-kept, colorful garden. There was a thin trail of smoke coming out of the chimney. There was *someone* here, at least.

An elderly retainer, his dark coat shiny with age, answered the knock on the door. He looked openly surprised to discover that Flavian was not simply a traveler who had got lost in the woods and needed directions to find his way back to civilization. He showed the visitor into a parlor that was clean and tidy, if a little on the shabby side. The servant went to see whether his master and mistress were at home. His right boot heel creaked as he walked, Flavian noticed.

They arrived together no longer than a few minutes later, both looking as surprised as their butler, as though they were not in the habit of receiving unexpected visitors—or perhaps any visitors at all.

Sir Everard Havell was a tall man with receding hair that still retained some brown mixed in with the predominant gray. His face and figure were fleshy, the former florid, the complexion of a man who perhaps indulged rather heavily in the bottle. His blue eyes were pale and somewhat watery. He had the remnants of good looks, but he was not well preserved.

Flavian could not see even the faintest resemblance to Agnes.

Time had been a little kinder to Lady Havell, even though she was apparently older than her husband. Her figure was still good, though she must be close to sixty. Her hair was still thick and a becoming shade of silver gray. She was a handsome woman, though her face was lined. There was some animation in her dark eyes. She was pleased, Flavian guessed, to have a visitor, though obviously curious too.

He could see nothing of Agnes in her either. On the other hand, she bore a more than passing resemblance to Miss Debbins.

"Good day . . . Viscount Ponsonby?" Havell rather unnecessarily consulted the card Flavian had handed to the butler.

Flavian inclined his head. "I have the p-pleasure," he said, "of being Lady Havell's son-in-law."

The lady's eyes widened, and she pressed the fingers of both hands over her mouth.

"I married Mrs. Keeping a little over a week ago," he said. "Mrs. Agnes Keeping."

"Agnes?" the lady said faintly. "She married one of the Keeping brothers? Not *William* Keeping, surely? He was *such* an unappealing young man and years too old for her."

"Mr. William Keeping, yes," Flavian said.

"But he *died*?" she said. "And now she has married you? A viscount? Oh, she has done well for herself."

"Rosamond," Sir Everard said, "you had better sit down."

She did so, and her husband gestured Flavian to another chair.

She had no knowledge, then, of what had happened to her family after she left?

"And Dora?" she asked. "Did she make a decent marriage after all?"

"She has made no marriage at all, ma'am," Flavian said.

She closed her eyes briefly. "Oh, poor Dora," she said. "She was very much looking forward to marriage and motherhood—as we all do at the age of seventeen. I suppose she felt obliged to stay home with Agnes. Or perhaps no one would have her after Walter decided to divorce me. That man has much to answer for."

It was a strange perspective on past events. Perhaps it was an understandable one, however. It was always easier to blame someone else than to assume blame oneself.

Havell had poured two glasses of wine. He handed one to Flavian and drank from the other himself. Flavian set his glass down on a small table beside his chair.

"And Oliver?" Lady Havell asked.

"He is a clergyman in Shropshire, ma'am," he told her. "He is married with three children."

She bit her lower lip. "Why have you come, Lord Ponsonby?" she asked him.

Flavian sat back in his chair and eyed his glass. But he did not pick it up.

"Agnes was told n-nothing, ma'am," he said. "She was five years old, and I s-suppose the assumption was made that she would forget if she was not constantly r-reminded. She still knows virtually n-nothing. She does not want to know. She does not want to know who you are or where you are or even *wh-whether* you are. But her life has been shaped by your s-sudden and complete disappearance from her life. She has lived on the f-fringes of her own life ever since, afraid to feel too deeply, not lest she be hurt again, it seems to me, but lest she be tempted to do to someone else what you d-did to her."

"What *I* did to her," she said softly. "Well, and so I did too, Lord Ponsonby, for heaven knows I fell deeply enough in love with Everard that summer and spent far too much time in his company. I had no business being so self-absorbed when I had a husband and three children."

She looked at her husband briefly and half smiled at him.

"Poor Everard," she said. "For very honor's sake he was obliged to take me away when Walter denounced me quite publicly at a local assembly and announced his intention of divorcing me. We fled that very night, and only later did it occur to me that Walter had been drinking freely that evening, and it was common knowledge that he could not hold his liquor without making a cake of himself. I might have brazened it out, and our neighbors would have pretended that the whole nasty scene had not happened. But it seemed he had forced my hand, and then I forced his. Poor Everard was caught in the middle."

"I have never regretted that fact, Rosamond," he said gallantly.

She smiled at him. It was a sad, fond expression, Flavian thought.

"I really did dislike Walter quite intensely," she said. "But I loved my girls—and Oliver too. I ought to have gone back for their sakes. Even after a few days had passed I ought to have gone back. Everyone would have turned a blind eye. And Walter would not have carried through on his threat—not when he was sober. After a few days, though, I could not bring myself to leave Everard. I chose my personal happiness over my children,

Lord Ponsonby. Agnes is perfectly justified in not wanting anything to do with me. You will keep this visit to yourself, will you?"

"Not n-necessarily, ma'am," he said. "I will possibly tell her. She ought to know. What she decides to do with the knowledge is up to her."

As much as anything, she needed to know that she was Debbins's daughter. And undoubtedly she was.

"Besides," he said, "someone has been trying to find out something about my wife—preferably something that can be turned to spite. Already someone knows of the divorce."

"Ah," she said.

Havell said nothing.

Flavian got to his feet, and Havell followed suit.

"Thank you for receiving me," Flavian said. He crossed the room and took Lady Havell's hand in his. After a moment's hesitation, he raised it to his lips. "G-good-bye, ma'am."

"Good-bye, Lord Ponsonby." Her eyes turned suspiciously bright.

Havell accompanied him to the door.

"Life is never a simple matter, Ponsonby," he said as he stood in the doorway watching Flavian climb back to the seat of his curricle and possess himself of the ribbons. "Decisions that we make in the blink of an eye, often both unexpected and impulsive, can affect the whole of the rest of our lives in a drastic, irreversible way."

It was hardly an earth-shatteringly original thought. It was nevertheless a true one, Flavian thought. Only consider what had happened to *him* recently.

"I came for the knowledge," he said, "because it is b-better to know than forever to w-wonder. I did not come to judge. Good day to you, Havell."

"She adored those girls," Havell said, "if it is any consolation to Lady Ponsonby when you tell her of this visit. Both of them, the older one and the little child. She *adored* them."

But not enough to sacrifice her own happiness for their sakes, Flavian thought as he drove back out into the world—as though for the past hour he had somehow stepped right out of it. But who was he to judge? A mother ought never to abandon her children. It seemed a fundamental truth. A woman, once owned by a man, ought never to seek her own freedom and happiness, if that man would not help her to achieve both. Yet it was unfair, unjust. Debbins, it seemed, had publicly humiliated his wife and threatened worse. What would her life have been like if she had defied him and stayed and renounced the one man who had seemed to offer her a bit of happiness? What would Dora Debbins's life have been if she had stayed? And Agnes's? One thing was for sure: he would not have met her if her mother had stayed with her husband all those years ago.

How strangely random a thing life was.

And now he had the problem of what to do with his knowledge. Tell Agnes, when she had specifically told him she did not want to know? Withhold it from her? He might have been tempted to do the latter if there was not the risk that someone else would unearth the details and spring them on her without any warning in some very public manner.

Anyway, he thought as he made his way closer to home, if this week of his marriage had taught him anything, it was that openness and truth between partners were necessary if the marriage was to have a chance of bringing them any sort of happiness.

Now that he knew, he must tell her, even if only the fact that he had found and visited her mother.

He did not look forward to telling her.

He wished suddenly that Lady Darleigh had not asked him last autumn to grant her the favor of dancing with her particular friend at the harvest ball, lest she be a wallflower. He wished he had not gone back without any coercion at all for the after-supper waltz and had not therefore allowed himself to be enchanted. And he *wished* Vince could have waited six months or so before proving to the world how fertile he was, so that the Survivors' Club gathering this year might have been at Penderris Hall, as usual.

And he might as well carry this line of thinking to its logical and absurd conclusion. He wished he had not been injured in the war. He wished he had not been born. He wished his parents had not . . .

Well.

Agnes was dressed in one of her new evening gowns—white lace over silk of a deep rose pink. She had been dubious about it until Madeline had given it the nod of approval, though she had directed Madame Martin to abandon the large pink silk bows that were to have caught up the lace skirt in deep scallops and to replace them with tiny rosebuds and far shallower scallops. Agnes thought the neckline was a little too revealing, but her maid laughed at her misgivings.

"That's not *revealing*, my lady," she said. "You just wait till you see some."

She had just finished pinning Agnes's hair up in a style of smooth elegance when Flavian appeared in the dressing room doorway. He was dressed as he had been for the autumn ball last year in black and white with a silver waistcoat. He paused in the doorway and raised his quizzing glass to his eye. He looked her over unhurriedly.

"Enchanting, I feel compelled to say," he said and lowered the glass.

Madeline smirked and bobbed a curtsy and slipped out of the room.

Agnes got to her feet and turned. She smiled at him. It seemed a little extravagant to her that they were both dressed with such formal magnificence for what was to be little more than a family gathering at Lord Shields's home, but she was looking forward to the evening with some pleasure and only a little nervousness. The dowager's sister, who had told Agnes to call her Aunt DeeDee, and her daughters had treated her with kindness earlier today, after an initial half hour or so of reserve. The rest of Flavian's family would have had time to learn of his marriage and to recover from any surprise and disapproval at its suddenness. They would be polite, at the very least.

Flavian had been rather quiet at the early dinner of which they had partaken a couple of hours ago. He looked a bit somber now too, despite calling her enchanting.

She was feeling far more cheerful than she had this time yesterday. He had not loved Lady Hazeltine—not before he went to the Peninsula, anyway, and she suspected there were other lost memories surrounding that leave of his, when his brother had died and he had celebrated his betrothal, though not quite in that order. She did not know exactly what had happened, apart from the bare, indisputable facts, but she hoped to find out. For his sake, she hoped to find out.

He had propped his shoulder against the doorframe and crossed his arms over his chest.

"I paid a call earlier today," he said. There was a longish pause, during which she raised her eyebrows. "On your mother."

She wished then that she had not stood up. She reached behind her with one hand to clutch the edge of the dressing table.

"My mother." She fixed her eyes on his.

"She was remarkably easy to f-find, actually," he said. "Divorces are rare and always a bit scandalous, and people remember them. I did not expect, however, to discover her whereabouts so easily. She lives not too f-far from here."

Agnes took a step back until she felt the dressing table bench with the backs of her knees. She sat down heavily.

"You went looking for my mother," she said. "You *went looking* for her against my express wishes."

"I did." He was regarding her with hooded eyes.

"How dare you," she said. "*Oh, how dare you!* You *know* that she has been dead to me for twenty years. You *know* that I do not want to hear *of* her or *from* her. Ever. I do not want to know her name or her whereabouts or her circumstances. I *do not want to know*. Oh, how dare you go asking about her and finding out who she is and where she is. And how *dare* you call upon her."

She was alarmed to realize that she had raised her voice and was shouting at him. If she was not careful, she would be attracting the attention of her mother-in-law and the servants. She got to her feet and hurried toward him.

"How dare you!" she said more softly, thrusting her face close to his.

He did not move, even though she had come too close for comfort.

"Do you not *think*," she said, "that if I had wanted to know more about her or to find her anytime in the years since I grew up, I could have done it? Do you not think *Dora* could have done it if *she* had wanted? What my mother did to Dora was ten times worse than what she did to me. She destroyed Dora's whole *life*. And she must have caused our father unbearable pain and embarrassment. She must have hurt Oliver dreadfully. Do you think we could not have found her if we had wished? Any of us? We did not wish. *I* did not wish. I *do* not wish. She *abandoned* us, Flavian. For a *lover*. I hate her. *Hate*, do you hear me? But I do not enjoy hating. I choose rather not to remember her at all, not to think of her, not to be curious about her. I will never forgive you for finding her and *going to see her*."

She was gasping out her words, trying not to let her voice rise again. She stopped talking and glared at him.

"I am sorry," he said.

"How *could* you?" She brushed past him and went into her bedchamber. She stood at the foot of the bed, clutching the bedpost.

"Blocked memories, s-suppressed memories, memories we do not even know we are supposed to have—they all damage our lives, Agnes," he said. "And our relationships."

"This is about you, then, is it?" she asked him, whipping her head about to glare at him.

He had turned, though he still stood in the doorway. He looked broodingly at her.

"I think, rather, it is about *us*," he said.

"Us?"

"You were the one who s-said more than once that we did not know each other," he reminded her, "and that if we w-were to marry, we needed that knowledge. We married anyway, b-but you were right. We *need* to know each other."

"And that gives you the right to pry into my past and seek out my mother?" she asked him.

"And we n-need to know ourselves," he added.

"I know myself very well," she retorted.

He did not say anything. But he shook his head.

His words repeated themselves in her head and left

her feeling shaken. His knowledge of his own past, and therefore of himself, was marred by an uncertain memory. But that was not the same thing as a memory one had deliberately chosen to turn off for very good reason, was it?

"I will help you remember, if I can," she said. "And we will work on our marriage. I am determined that we will."

"*You* are determined," he said. "*You* will help *me* r-remember. So that I will be all better, and everything will be well with our marriage. By all give on your part, all take on mine. Because you need nothing. Because you have never needed anything but a little quiet c-control over your world. You gave in b-briefly to the wonderful chaos of life by marrying me against all your better instincts, but now you can control your m-marriage by helping me remember—if there *is* more to remember."

She turned suddenly to sit on the side of the bed, though she kept one hand on the bedpost.

"Is that why you went?" She was almost whispering. "To *do* something for me?"

"I thought perhaps you n-needed to know," he said. "Even if what I discovered was no more savory than you expected. Even if the knowing did not change anything. Even if you never w-wanted to see her for yourself. I just thought you needed to *know*. So that your mind would no longer keep touching upon the wound that has been festering deep inside since you were a child."

"Is that what has been happening?" she asked.

He shrugged. "I just thought it was something I could do for you."

She gazed at him, and their eyes locked on each other's.

"By the time I w-went, though," he said, "there was another, more urgent reason."

She continued to gaze.

"Divorces applied for by petition to Parliament are rare enough and p-public enough to be remembered," he said. "Someone wanting to know more about a Mr. D-Debbins of Lancashire and asking a few questions would almost inevitably discover that *he* had once m-made such a petition and had b-been granted his divorce."

Her eyes widened.

"I do not know to how many p-people you have mentioned your father's name," he said. "I m-mentioned it the afternoon I called upon Frome and his lady and Velma. I am sorry. It did not occur to m-me that— "

Agnes had jumped to her feet. "My father's identity is no secret," she said. "I am not ashamed of my father."

"If the search for information was m-malicious," he said, "then more will be discovered. It was easy enough for *me* to discover, Lord knows. There could be gossip, Agnes."

Lady Hazeltine had done this, she realized. And, oh, her motives would be malicious. Agnes felt no doubt about that.

"Tonight?" she asked.

"Unlikely," he said, "though even the fact that your father was d-divorced from your mother will cause talk, even among my family. I am sorry, but I had to w-warn you. If you would rather not go tonight but stay at home— "

"Stay at home?" She glared at him. "*Cower* at home, you mean? Never. And we are in danger of being late, which I understand is fashionable in town. I am *not* of London, however, or of the *ton*. I prefer to do my hosts the courtesy of being on time when I am expected or even early. Where are my shawl and my reticule?"

She brushed past him back into the dressing room, but he caught her by the arm as she passed. He was, amazingly, grinning.

"That's my girl," he said softly. "That's my Agnes."

And he kissed her hard and openmouthed on the lips before letting her go.

"Who *is* she?" she asked briskly as she picked up her things. "Just in case I should need the knowledge tonight. And where does she live?"

"Lady Havell," he said, "wife of Sir Everard Havell. They live in Kensington. And he is *not* your father."

She felt a little dizzy. Lady Havell. Sir Everard Havell. They were strangers to her. And she wished they might remain so. Kensington was very close.

She nodded and looked at him.

"Thank you," she said. "Thank you, Flavian."

He offered his arm and she took it.

. . . *He is* not *your father.*

Flavian would not have added that if he was not sure.

. . . *He is* not *your father.*

21

It had always amused Flavian that any *ton* party described in advance as "small" and "intimate," even one given before the spring Season proper began, almost invariably filled several rooms with guests. Anything larger was a "squeeze" and was the very ultimate in success for any hostess.

Marianne's small evening party looked to be just that when he arrived with his wife and mother, for of course they were early despite the delay his confession in Agnes's dressing room had caused. Flavian suspected, with an inward, half-amused grimace, that he was fated to become notorious for always arriving early to any social gathering. It hardly bore contemplating.

It did not take long for Shields's drawing room to fill, however, and for the guests to spill over into the adjoining music room. The dedicated cardplayers among them soon discovered the salon across the hallway, where tables had been set up for their convenience, and the refreshment room next to it did not go long undiscovered.

Of course, any house except perhaps the largest mansion could be filled quite respectably just with his family members. Not that all of them had come to town yet, but there were enough, by Jove. And all of them wanted to pump Flavian by the hand, even if they had seen him during the past few days and already done so. They also wanted to kiss Agnes's cheek, and say all that was proper to the occasion, and—in the case of a few of the younger male cousins—a few things that were improper, for Flavian's ears alone, to the accompaniment of bawdy guffaws that brought frowns from the uncles, reproachful glances from the aunts, and the fluttering of fans from the female cousins, who suspected they were missing something interesting.

There were other guests who were not family, of course. Marianne took it upon herself to introduce Agnes, who looked lovely enough and dignified enough to be a duchess, Flavian thought with considerable pride, though this evening must be a severe trial to her. And this was only the beginning.

Perhaps, he thought after a while, his warning to her had been unnecessary. Even if word had spread about her father and his divorce, no one seemed inclined either to remark upon it or to shun the man's daughter.

Even as he thought it, he heard Sir Winston and Lady Frome and the Countess of Hazeltine being announced. He was halfway between the drawing room and the music room, talking with a group of relatives and other acquaintances. Agnes was on the other side of the drawing room with Marianne, who was leaving her side to hurry toward the door, her right hand extended, a smile of welcome on her face.

Well, of course they had been invited. They were not even mere acquaintances, after all. They were neighbors in the country.

And was it his imagination, Flavian wondered, or had the buzz of conversation faltered slightly while people glanced from the new arrivals to him and to Agnes? But it was over in a moment, and the Fromes and Velma proceeded farther into the room to mingle with the other guests.

Though it had *not* been his imagination. Mrs. Dressler had set one gloved hand on his sleeve.

"I daresay your mama was disappointed, Lord Ponsonby," she said, "when you married before you could meet Lady Hazeltine again this spring. It was a very sad thing when your betrothal to her came to an end all those years ago. You were *such* a handsome couple. Were they not, Hester?"

The lady applied to—Flavian could not at the moment recall her last name—looked a trifle embarrassed.

"Indeed they were, Beryl," she said, "but Lady Ponsonby is really quite lovely, my lord."

His mother and Marianne and Shields, as well as the Fromes and Velma, had been in London for a few days before he arrived with Agnes, Flavian recalled. He wondered, belatedly, whether during those days they had kept their matchmaking plans to themselves, all of them, or whether they had divulged their hopes to a select few of their acquaintances.

He would wager upon the latter.

Velma caught his eye across the room, smiled warmly, and raised one hand in greeting. But she did not approach him. She mingled with the groups around her, looking poised and lovely.

He forgot about her. He did what one did at such parties. He mingled and talked and listened and laughed. He kept an eye upon Agnes, but she did not appear to need his support. She was always occupied when he glanced her way and always smiling graciously, a becoming flush in her cheeks.

Dash it all, he thought at one point in the evening, as if he had been struck by some earth-shattering revelation, he was *glad* he had married her. He would not be married to anyone else in the world. Not for any consideration. Inevitably, he wanted her. But that thought, in the middle of a party while they were surrounded by at least a few dozen of his family members, was unworthy of him. His feelings for her went beyond the sexual. He was deucedly *fond* of her. He was beginning to understand Hugo and Ben and Vincent and how they must feel about thcir wives.

There was to be no formal supper, but the refreshment room positively groaned with delicacies both savory and sweet, and even offered a few tables at which guests might sit while they ate, if they so chose.

Flavian was sitting at one of the tables, eating more than his fair share of lobster patties, while Miss Moffatt was giving a brief recital on the pianoforte in the music room. He was with his cousins Doris and Ginny, and young Lord Catlin, who appeared to consider himself the latter's beau, though Ginny was giving him no noticeable encouragement. Flavian was relaxed and enjoying himself.

Yes, the warning had been unnecessary, but he was glad he had given it, glad he had told her. It was over with, and tonight he would make amends.

That was when Cousin Desmond strolled up to join in the conversation for a minute or two. He would not pull up a chair, though, and he plucked at Flavian's sleeve and gave him a significant look, coupled with a slight jerk of the head. Flavian put the rest of his patty into his mouth, excused himself, and got to his feet.

"What is it, Des?" he asked when they were out of earshot of the others.

"I am as sure as I can be, Flave," Desmond said, "that neither m' father nor Uncle Quent have uttered a word to anyone. Jenkins would not have done so either. And *I* certainly have not said anything."

"About the d-divorce?" Flavian asked.

"About Lady Havell," Desmond said, gripping his shoulder and squeezing.

"Ah," Flavian said. "Well. We could not have expected the g-gossips to be content with half a s-story, could we? It was bound to come out."

"I just heard the word *whore*," Desmond said. "And the words *whore's spawn*. Sorry, Flave. Not in the hearing of any lady, of course, though they are starting to buzz too. I thought you ought to know."

"Indeed." Flavian straightened the cuffs of his coat, ran a light hand over his neck cloth, grasped the handle of his quizzing glass, and strolled into the drawing room. He gazed about him with lazy eyes and curled lip in an expression he knew held people at bay.

It was instantly apparent that something had shifted in the atmosphere of the party, even apart from the slight hush his appearance caused. His relatives, almost to a man—and woman—were smiling more brightly and chatting more animatedly than was necessary. Marianne was looking more ostentatiously gracious than a hostess needed to look at this late stage of her party. Shields looked a bit tight about the lips. Flavian's mother was seated in one corner, with Aunt DeeDee beside her and patting one of her hands. Velma was at one side of the room, fanning her cheeks and looking sweetly sad. Agnes was in the middle of the room, a bit of a space all around her except for that occupied by one lady with tall hair plumes—Lady March, whom he had encountered at Middlebury Park last autumn, he believed.

Flavian took in the whole scene in the blink of an eye, as well as the fact that the room was surely fuller than it had been earlier, despite that bit of an empty space at the center. Had the music room and the card room completely emptied out? But, no, someone was still trilling away on the pianoforte.

He strolled unhurriedly toward the center of the room, and a path opened for him as if by magic.

"Oh, yes, Lady March," Agnes was saying, and it seemed to Flavian that she had deliberately raised her voice so that more people than just the March lady could hear her. "You are quite right about one thing. Lady Havell is indeed my mother, though Sir Everard Havell is not my father. My father is Mr. Walter Debbins from Lancashire. Had you not heard? I thought it was common knowledge. He and my mother were divorced twenty years ago when they discovered themselves sufficiently unhappy with each other. Not many married couples have that sort of courage, do they?"

She was smiling, though not with artificial brightness. The color was higher in her cheeks, though not unbecomingly so. She looked perfectly poised as she faced scandal and possible ostracism even before the Season began in earnest.

"Indeed," Lady March said faintly. "And I wonder if Viscountess Darleigh of Middlebury Park, my niece, is aware of exactly who you are, *Lady* Ponsonby. I understand she befriended you when you were plain Mrs. Keeping."

"And I befriended her," Agnes said, her smile softening, "when she was new to her title and position and had been abandoned, even if only temporarily, by her own family. My father made a happy remarriage to my stepmother nine years ago, as my mother did to Sir Everard eighteen or nineteen years ago. They have lived a retired life together in Kensington ever since. Sometimes all really *is* well that ends well, ma'am, would you not agree?"

She smiled warmly at Flavian as he approached, his quizzing glass to his eye and trained upon Lady March's plumes. They were of an extraordinary height. She must have them specially made, though Lord knew how she managed to get into a carriage with them. Had March had a hole sawn in the roof? He lowered his glass, smiled languidly, took his wife's hand in his, and raised it to his lips.

"I called upon them there this afternoon," he said on a sigh. "My mother-in-law and all that. Have you m-met them, ma'am?"

Lady March appeared to crumple slightly under the full onslaught of his most sleepy gaze, though her plumes, made of sterner stuff, still stood stiffly at attention. He had left her with only one thing to say, and she said it.

"I have not had that pleasure, Lord Ponsonby," she said, her voice almost vibrating with outrage.

"Ah," he said, "a pity. Charming couple."

But she had been bested. So had everyone else who had shared her desire to be spiteful, to embarrass the new Lady Ponsonby, to cut her down to size, perhaps to ensure that she was given the cut direct by the *ton* as her mother had, merely because she was the daughter of that mother.

And because she had dared come between him and Velma, Countess of Hazeltine?

He looked toward where Velma had been standing when he came into the room. She was still there, slowly fanning her face, smiling sweetly. Their eyes met, and he inclined his head in acknowledgment of the fact that he understood.

She had lied to his brother most cruelly because she had decided to marry *him* instead, to be Viscountess Ponsonby for longer than just a few months or years until consumption killed David. She had *lied* when she might simply have explained to David that she wished to be set free and then have waited until after his death to set her cap at *him*.

What Velma had wanted, she had almost always got.

He could remember that now. She had been blessed with parents who doted upon her and could deny her nothing.

How strange that memory could so have shut down until last night.

"Have you eaten, my love?" he asked Agnes, offering his arm for her hand.

"I have not," she said. "I have been too busy meeting all your family and acquaintances, Flavian. But I am famished."

He led her in the direction of the refreshment room, though it seemed that half his aunts and uncles then present, not to mention about a quarter of the cousins, wanted to talk to them, to touch them, to laugh with them. To show the family joining ranks, in other words.

There would be no scandal, Flavian guessed. Gossip, yes, for a while. The bulk of the *ton*, newly arriving in town over the next month, would be regaled with the story of the new Viscountess Ponsonby's lineage and would chew it over in drawing rooms and clubs for a week or so before turning its attention to more recent and more salacious gossip.

Agnes had rescued herself.

"I could not eat a *thing* if my life depended upon it," she said as he showed her to a table.

"Then I shall f-fetch you some tea or lemonade," he said, "and toast you for your brilliance, Agnes."

"Forewarned is forearmed," she said. "I have never known the truth of that before tonight. And I have you to thank."

She looked pointedly at him when he returned with two glasses.

"*My love*?" she said, raising her eyebrows.

He was baffled for a moment. But he *had* called her that in the drawing room, had he not?

"It seemed the right thing to say at the t-time," he

said, raising his glass to toast her and watching two cousins make their way toward them. "My love."

They did not talk privately again that night. They did not make love either. He came to her bed—it was very late, and she was already lying down. He snuffed the single candle, lay down beside her, drew the bedcovers warmly over them, and wrapped his arms about her, drawing her against him. He sighed once against the side of her face, and was asleep.

This was what she most needed, she realized. She needed to be held just like this. She needed the warmth of him.

She dreaded to think what would have happened this evening if he had not warned her, if he had not found out her mother's identity and whereabouts for himself and actually gone to Kensington to call upon her.

Even so . . .

Well, even so she was weary to the marrow of her bones. Too weary to sleep. As if meeting so many members of his family was not enough for one evening, some of them stern and pompous, some hearty and welcoming, most polite and willing enough to give her a chance. Of course, now there was not much they could do about it, bar snubbing and offending Flavian, who was, after all, the head of the family, at least his father's side of it. And as if meeting what seemed an endless stream of unrelated strangers was not enough for one evening. How *could* everyone keep claiming that London was still empty of company? What on earth was it going to be like after Easter?

And as if seeing the arrival of the Countess of Hazeltine with her parents was not enough for one evening, and watching the ease with which she moved about the drawing room, mingling with Marianne's guests, looking lovely and a bit fragile. And of course everyone present would remember that she had once been betrothed to Flavian—two beautiful people. And Agnes would wager that everyone knew that Velma and her parents and Flavian's mother and sister had hoped to see a renewal of their courtship and betrothal this year. Everyone would be watching now to see how the two of them behaved in company with each other—and how the new wife would behave. And *whether she knew*.

Oh, it had all been *quite* enough to deal with in one evening, well before Agnes had felt something change in the atmosphere of the room about her, rather as though an invisible hand were making its stealthy way up her spine in the direction of her neck. Just so the whispers of impending scandal crept about the *ton*, she realized. And she had known what was coming several minutes before it actually did come, first with a strange sort of space growing around her, even though the room seemed to be more crowded, and then with the arrival of Lady March at her side.

"Ah, *Lady Ponsonby*," she had said, the emphasis sounding faintly malicious, "I was never more surprised in my life than I was a few minutes ago. I understand you are the daughter of Sir Everard and Lady Havell."

Strangely, once it was all out in the open, Agnes had felt calm again. The invisible hand on her spine disappeared, was shrugged off for the ghost it was. She was also again and instantly aware of how much she owed to Flavian, furious though she had been with him earlier in the evening.

She curled against him now and felt herself sliding toward sleep after all. Part of her yearned to be back in her own peaceful life with Dora in the cottage at Inglebrook. Except that it was no longer her own life. *This* was. She had married Flavian.

Given the choice, would she go back? Would she undo everything that had happened?

She fell asleep before she had answered her own questions.

Flavian was gone when she awoke in the morning, and she realized she must have slept late, an unusual thing with her. There was a cup of chocolate on the small chest beside her bed, but its top was a film of gray, and she guessed the drink was cold. She felt a bit glum as she dressed, even though it was a bright, sunny morning. He would doubtless be gone by the time she went down to breakfast, and she would not see him again until goodness knew when. And what would she do with her day? Would her mother-in-law have something planned? Or would she advise remaining at home in the hope that whatever scandal had been brewing last night would blow over before she emerged again?

What *was* life going to be like after Easter?

Flavian had not gone out, however. He was at the breakfast table, reading the paper while his mother read a letter that must have come with the morning post. Flavian lowered the paper to bid Agnes a good morning and gestured with his head toward her place at the table.

"You have l-letters," he said. "Plural."

She fell upon them with what she suspected was undignified eagerness while he watched. She had had none since they arrived in London, and realized how very isolated she had felt. Now suddenly there were *three*, all of them in handwriting that was familiar to her. She set aside Sophia's and Dora's to read at leisure after she had read her father's.

It was very typical of him—brief and dry. He was pleased to hear of her marriage to a titled gentleman and trusted that her new husband also had the means with which to support her in some comfort. His health was tolerably good, and her stepmother, she would be pleased to hear, was enjoying her usual robust health, though unfortunately the same could not be said for either her sister or her mother, both of whom had taken a chill earlier in the spring and had not yet shaken off its full effects, though they were eating rather better than they had even just a week or so ago, and he entertained the cautious hope that another month would see them restored to full health. He was her affectionate father, etc. etc.

Affectionate. Had he ever been? Well, at least he had never been openly unkind or cruel, as many fathers were.

"Your f-father, I assume?" Flavian asked. "It was franked in Lancashire. Is he likely to turn up on my doorstep, horsewhip in hand?"

"Oh, surely not, Flavian," his mother said, looking up from her own letter. "Even gentlemen from *Lancashire* know how to be civil, I trust?"

"He simply hopes that you are able to provide for me," Agnes said, and his eyes laughed at her even as he tipped his head slightly to one side and looked more searchingly at her.

"He does not disapprove?" he asked. "Or wish he might have attended the w-wedding?"

"No." She shook her head and broke the seal on Sophia's letter.

"I heard someone say yesterday," Flavian said before she started reading it, "that we are b-bound to suffer for all this lovely spring weather we are having. One can always depend upon at least o-one person to say it. But on the chance that he may be right, shall we make the m-most of the sunshine before the suffering begins? Shall we walk in Hyde Park?"

"Today? This morning?" She gave him her full attention. "Alongside Rotten Row? To see and be seen?"

He lifted one eyebrow.

"Your new outfits are very fetching," he said, "and I can understand your d-desire to show them off. B-but I was hoping to be more selfish and have you to m-myself. There are other, more secluded paths to walk."

Her heart turned over.

"I would like nothing better," she assured him.

He closed his paper and got to his feet.

"Is half an hour long enough to r-read your letters and get ready?" he asked.

"Flavian!" his mother protested. "Agnes will need at least an hour just to get ready."

Agnes smiled. She could have been ready in ten minutes.

"Shall we say three-quarters of an hour?" she suggested.

An hour later they were strolling in an area of Hyde Park that felt more like the countryside than part of one of the largest metropolises in the world. The path was rough underfoot, the trees thick and green around them, the stretches of grass visible between their trunks slightly more overgrown than the lawns elsewhere. Best of all, there was no one else in sight, and the occasional sounds of voices and horses were distant and only served to emphasize their near seclusion.

Agnes inhaled the smell of greenery and felt a rush of contentment. If only every day could be like this.

"Do you miss the countryside, Agnes?" he asked her.

"Oh, I do," she said in a rush. "But how foolish I am. Any number of people would give a great deal to be in London as I am, to be looking forward to the social Season, to have a dressing room full of new clothes and the prospect of balls and parties and concerts at which to wear them."

They had stopped walking at the top of a slight rise in

the path as though by mutual consent, and they both tipped back their heads to gaze upward through the branches of a particularly large and elderly oak to the blue sky above. He turned about in a complete circle.

"Are you all right?" he asked her. "After last night?"

"Yes." She laughed slightly. "Is that what is known as a baptism by fire, do you suppose? But who would so diligently have sought out the skeletons in my closet? And why?"

"Velma," he said. "Because she d-did not get her way."

She had suspected it, *known* it, really. But what did the countess have to gain now? Flavian was not going to divorce *her*, after all, merely on the strength of who her mother was.

Because she did not get her way, he had just said. Was that sufficient motive? Simple spite?

She drew a deep breath and released it slowly.

"Tell me what you know about her," she said. "About Lady Havell, that is. My mother."

Neither of them was looking at the sky any longer. They moved off the path into the even-deeper seclusion of the ancient trees, and she stood with her back against the trunk of an oak, while he stood in front of her, one hand braced against the trunk on one side of her head.

"They have been shunned by society ever since their m-marriage, I would guess," he said. "I believe they are fond of each other but not particularly h-happy."

"He is definitely *not* my father?" she asked him.

He shook his head. "I am as sure as I can be that she was faithful to your father until after she left him. You were five years old by then."

She closed her eyes and lifted one gloved hand to set against his chest. At the same moment they both heard a group of people approaching along the path, talking and laughing until they must have spotted the two of them. There was a self-conscious silence then as the footsteps went past, and some stifled giggling after that until the group had passed out of earshot.

"One can only h-hope," Flavian said on a sigh, "that we were not r-recognized, Agnes. There is nothing more damaging to a man's reputation than to be seen in close and clandestine embrace with his own *w-wife*."

"What a pity," she said, "that they misinterpreted what they saw."

"And *that*," he said, "is even more lowering."

He took a firm step closer, pressing her to the tree along her full length before kissing her openmouthed. She laughed in delighted surprise when he lifted his head a moment later and regarded her lazily. And she wrapped her arms about him as his came about her, and they kissed at far greater length and with warm enthusiasm.

"Mmm," he said.

"Mmm," she agreed.

He took a step back and clasped his hands behind his back.

"She admits," he said, "that you have every right to hate her. She admits that she abandoned you and your s-sister—and your brother too—when she might have stayed. She r-ran away, she told me, after your father had denounced her at an assembly and told her for all to hear he would divorce her for adultery. She had f-flirted rather too incautiously with Havell, she said, but had done nothing more indiscreet than that until she ran away. She might have returned. Apparently your f-father had had too much to d-drink, and everything might have been patched up if she had gone home a few days later. But she d-did not go."

Agnes closed her eyes again, and there was a long silence, during which he stood where he was, not touching her. It was all so believable. Her father did not drink to excess very often. It was very rare, in fact. But when he did, he could say and do foolish, embarrassing things. Everyone knew it. Everyone made allowances and conveniently forgot his lapses.

And her mother, it seemed, had acted upon the sudden impulse not to return home when she might have done so and had chosen to remain with the man who then became her lover and, later, her husband. A sudden, impulsive decision. She might just as easily have decided the other way. Just as she, Agnes, might just as easily have said no to Flavian the night he returned from London with a special license.

The course of one's whole life—and the lives of those intertwined with one's own—could be changed forever on the strength of such abrupt and unconsidered decisions.

"You did not say I would call on her?" she asked him.

"I did not," he said.

"Maybe one day I will go," she said. "But not yet. Maybe never. But you are right. It is as well to know. And to know that Dora and Oliver are my full sister and brother. Thank you for going, and for rescuing me from shock and embarrassment last evening. Thank you."

She opened her eyes and smiled at him.

From a distance they could hear the sound of other people drawing closer.

"Shall we move on?" He offered his arm, and she took it.

They walked in silence until they had passed an older couple, exchanging smiles and nods as they did so. The day was growing warmer.

"Would you like to go to Candlebury, Agnes?" he asked her.

"Now?" she asked in surprise. "But there is the Season, my presentation at court, the ball to introduce me to the *ton*. Everything else."

"If you want them," he said, "we will stay. But everything can wait if we choose—if *you* choose. It can all wait a month or two months or a year or ten. Or f-forever. Shall we go to Candlebury? Shall we go h-home?"

She stopped walking again and drew him to a halt. She could see the Serpentine in the near distance. Soon they would be among other people walking beside the water.

"But you have been avoiding Candlebury Abbey for years," she said. "Are you sure you want to go there now? Are you doing this for me?"

"For us," he said.

She searched his eyes, longing welling up inside her. *Shall we go home?* he had said. There were memories there for him. Conscious, painful ones of his brother's last days. And unconscious ones, she suspected. She suspected too that it was both facts that had made him reluctant for so long to return there. Now he wanted to go—for her sake and for theirs.

She smiled slowly at him.

"Let's go home, then," she said.

22

My love, he had called her at Marianne's party, entirely for the ears of all the guests there. *My love,* he had called her a short time later in the refreshment room, in order to tease away the stress of the past half hour or so.

My love, he thought now, sitting beside her in his carriage, watching her profile as they approached the top of the rise above Candlebury after turning through the gates a short while ago. He wanted to see her expression when she saw the house. It almost always took the breath away, even when one had a lifetime of familiarity with it.

My love. The words sounded silly when spoken in the silence of his own thoughts. Would he ever speak them aloud so that she knew he meant them? And *did* he mean them? He was a bit afraid of love. Love was painful.

He watched her, he realized, because he did not want to have that first glimpse of Candlebury himself. He really did not want to be where he was, moving ever nearer to it. Yet he would not be anywhere else on earth for all the money in the world. Was there anyone more muddleheaded than he?

She was looking prim and trim and beautiful beside

him, clad in a dark blue carriage dress, which was expertly and elegantly cut to hug her figure in all the right places and to fall in soft folds elsewhere. Her chip straw bonnet trimmed with tiny cornflowers had a small enough brim that he could see around it. Her gloved hands were folded neatly in her lap. Her head was half-turned from him, and he knew she was gazing at the half-wild meadowland beyond her window and seeing all the wildflowers growing there and imagining herself tramping among them, an easel under one arm, a bag of painting supplies in the other hand.

And then the carriage topped the rise, and her head turned to look into the great bowl-like depression below. Her hands tightened in her lap, her eyes grew larger, and her mouth formed a silent O.

"Flavian," she said. "Oh, it is *beautiful*."

She turned to smile at him and reached out a hand to squeeze one of his, and if he had been in any doubt before this moment, he doubted no longer. He loved her. Idiot that he was, he could not be content with safety. He had had to go and fall in love with her.

"It is, is it not?" he said, and he looked beyond her shoulder and felt somehow as if the bottom had fallen out of his stomach.

There it was.

The house was built on the far slope of the bowl, a horseshoe-shaped mansion of gray stone that often gleamed almost white when the sun shone on it at a certain angle in the evenings. To one side of it and connected with it were the remains of the old abbey, most of them virtually unrecognizable moss-covered ruins, though the cloisters were still almost intact, and usable with their walkway and pillars and central garden, which his grandmother had made into a rose arbor.

It was the only really cultivated part of the whole

park, apart from the kitchen gardens at the back. The rest was rolling, tree-dotted grassland and wooded copses and graveled walking paths and rides, in the style of Capability Brown, though not designed by him. This inner bowl had been planned to look secluded and rural and peaceful, and it succeeded admirably, Flavian had always thought. There was a river and a deep natural lake and a waterfall out of sight over the rise to the left of the house. And a genuine stone hermitage. Follies had always been unnecessary at Candlebury.

"It is very d-different from Middlebury Park," he said.

Middlebury was actually rather old-fashioned, with its carefully tended topiary garden and formal floral parterres forming the approach to the house. But it was grand and lovely, nevertheless.

"Yes." She looked back out through the window, but her hand remained covering his. "I *love* this."

And he felt like weeping. Home. *His* home. But the latter thought served only to remind him of how he had always been quite adamant about thinking of it as *David's* home, even though he had known from a relatively young age that it would be his before he had grown far into adulthood. But David had loved it with all the passion of his soul.

"We will p-probably be called upon to inspect the servants," Flavian said.

They had remained in London for two days after deciding to come here. He had felt obliged to give the servants some notice of his coming. And there was a tea at his aunt Sadie's that Agnes had promised to attend. Delivery of the rest of her new clothes, as well as a pair of new riding boots for which he had been fitted at Hoby's, was expected within a day or two. And Agnes wanted to call upon her cousin, who lived in London—or rather the late William Keeping's cousin, Dennis Fitzharris. He was the man who published Vincent and Lady Darleigh's children's stories, so Flavian gladly accompanied her and enjoyed himself greatly.

His mother had been less upset than he had expected by their decision to come to Candlebury. Perhaps it would be as well, she had said, for them to leave town over Easter and even for a few weeks after. By that time the new Lady Ponsonby and her story would be old news and only sufficiently interesting to bring everyone out in force to meet her at the ball they would give at Arnott House. Flavian had let his mother believe they would return in a month or so. And who knew? Perhaps they would.

At least she had not suggested accompanying them.

"Will that be a formidable experience?" Agnes asked, referring to the parade of servants that probably awaited them at the house.

"One must remember that they will be agog with eagerness to see us," he said. "Both of us. They have not seen me since I inherited the title. And I am returning with a b-bride. This will be a h-happy day of celebration for them, I daresay."

"And for us too?" she asked him, turning her face back to his.

He raised their hands and kissed the backs of hers.

"I understand," she said, though he had said nothing, and he believed she probably did.

Magwitch, the butler, and Mrs. Hoffer, the housekeeper, were standing side by side outside the open front doors. Within, Flavian could see a row of starched white aprons on one side and a row of white Vs—shirtfronts, he guessed—on the other. The servants were lined up to receive them.

He was home. As Viscount Ponsonby.

David was gone, a part of family history.

* * *

Agnes really did think the house and park beautiful. Indeed, she thought Candlebury Abbey must be one of the loveliest places on earth. She would be happy if she never had to leave it.

They spent three days together, she and Flavian, wandering about the park together, hand in hand—yes, indeed. She made no remark upon it when he first took her hand in his as they walked, and laced their fingers. She almost held her breath, in fact. It seemed so much more . . . tender than walking with her arm drawn through his. But it was no momentary thing. It seemed to be his preferred way of walking with her when they were alone.

The park was larger than she had thought at first. It extended beyond the bowl-like depression in which the house was situated. But all of it—lawns and meadows and wooded hills, paths and rides, all of it—was designed to look natural rather than artificially picturesque. The lake and the waterfall too were natural, and the stone hermitage to one side of the falls was not a folly but had at one time been inhabited by monks for whom the abbey was too crowded and busy a place.

"I always l-liked to think," Flavian said, "that they all left behind them something of the p-peace they must have found as they meditated here."

She knew what he meant. It seemed to her that they found peace together at Candlebury during those days—almost. Except that there was a depth of brooding in him just beyond where she could penetrate with her companionship. It was understandable, of course. She had expected it.

He had shown her about the house and about the ruins of the old abbey. But there was one set of rooms he avoided, and he pretended not to notice when she stopped outside the door, waiting expectantly for him to open it. He walked on past, and she had to hurry to catch up to him.

They had a few callers, among them the rector of the village church. But although the rector expressed the hope that he would see them at church on Sunday, Flavian returned a vague answer that sounded like a resounding no to Agnes.

"We will not go to church on Sunday?" she asked after the rector had left.

"No," he said curtly. "You may go if you wish."

She looked closely at him and understood in a flash. The churchyard must be where the family graves were. And his brother's grave. The set of rooms they had not entered while exploring the rest of the house must have been his brother's.

The loss of parents, siblings, spouses, even children was something all too many people experienced. The death of loved ones was all too common an occurrence. It was almost always sad, painful, difficult to recover from, especially when the deceased had been young. But it was not rare. She had lost a husband. His brother had been dead for eight or nine years. But Flavian had never let him go. He had come home from the Peninsula because his brother was dying, but he had left before David actually died. Flavian had been on his way to rejoin his regiment when it happened and had not returned until after he was wounded.

Those details at least were not among his missing memories. She knew he felt deep shame and unresolved grief.

"I will not go to church without you," she said. "Is there a way to get to the top of the waterfall?"

"It is a b-bit of a scramble," he said. "We used to make d-dens up there as boys and hold them against trolls and pirates and Vikings."

"I can scramble," she told him.

"Now?"

"Is there a better time?" she asked.

And off they went, hand in hand again, and she might almost imagine that he was happy and relaxed and at peace.

They shared a bedchamber, the one that had been his as a boy, without any pretense of having a room each. A small room next door had been made into her dressing room. They slept together each night, always touching, usually with their arms about each other. They made love, often multiple times in the course of the night.

Life seemed idyllic.

And then, one night, Agnes awoke to find herself alone in bed. She listened, but there was no sound of him in his dressing room. His dressing gown was gone from the floor beside the bed. She donned her nightgown and fetched a shawl from next door. And she lit a single candle.

She looked in the drawing room, in the morning room, in the study. She even looked in the dining room. But there was no sign of him. And when she peered out of the drawing room window, she realized that she would not see him even if he was out there. It must be a cloudy night. All was pitch-dark.

And then she thought of somewhere else to look.

She picked up her candle, went back upstairs, and made her way to the door she had never seen open. There was no light beneath it. Perhaps she was wrong. But part of her knew she was not.

She rested a hand on the doorknob for a long time before turning it slowly and silently. She pushed the door a little way open.

The room was in darkness. But her candle, even though she held it behind her, gave sufficient light that she could see an empty bed in the middle of the room, with a still figure seated on a chair beside it, one hand resting on the bedspread.

He must surely have seen the light, even if he had not heard the door opening. But he did not turn.

She stepped inside and set the candle down upon a small table beside the door.

It had felt amazingly good to be back, to be home. It always had. Even though he had quite enjoyed school, he had always longed for the holidays, and on the few occasions when Len had tried to persuade Flavian to go with him to Northumberland for the long summer holiday, he had always found an excuse not to go. This was where he had belonged, where he had wanted always to belong.

His very love for Candlebury had been his pain too. Why did that pair always go hand in hand? The eternal pull of opposites? For the only way Candlebury could belong to him for the rest of his life was through the death of David without male issue. And though he had known it would happen, he had not *wanted* it to happen. His love of home had made him feel guilty, as though he resented the fact that his brother stood in the way of his happiness. It was not *like* that.

Ah, it was never like that, he was telling his brother when he awoke with a start. *It never was, David.*

Fortunately he had not been speaking aloud. But he was fully awake and rattled. And feeling guilty again. He had not been to see his brother. Idiot thought, of course. But he had been avoiding David since his return, avoiding his rooms, avoiding the churchyard, avoiding all mention of him or thought of him.

Why had he never felt this way about his father, much as he had loved him?

It was clear he was not going to go back to sleep, even

though Agnes felt warm and comfortable against him and he was tired. Briefly he thought of waking her, of making love to her. But there was a strange blackness in his head. It was not exactly depression. Or a headache. Just . . . blackness.

He eased himself out of the bed, found his dressing gown on the floor and drew it on, and let himself quietly out of the room. It was an unusually dark night, but he did not light a candle. He knew his way without needing any light. He let himself into David's bedchamber and felt his way to the window. He pushed back the curtains, though there was not a great deal of light to let in. He could make out the shape of the bed, though, and of a chair against one wall. He drew up the chair to the side of the bed and sat on it. He set one hand flat on the bedspread.

It was where he had always sat when his brother was too unwell to get up. It was where he had sat for many hours both day and night during those final weeks. And he had always set his hand on the bed so that David could touch it whenever he wanted and so that *he* could touch *David*.

Why had they always been so much closer than any other brothers he had known? They were as different as night and day. Perhaps that was why. The balance of opposites again.

The balance was no longer there.

The bed was empty.

What had he been expecting? That a ghost or spirit would have lingered? That there would be some sense of his brother here? Some comfort? Some absolution?

Why did I leave you to die alone?

He knew why. He had been head over ears in love, and he had wanted to celebrate his betrothal before returning to the Peninsula.

But why was I going back there?

He had known David was dying when he came home on leave. He had not really expected that he would go back, although he had set a date for doing so. He would inherit the title and properties and have all sorts of responsibilities to keep him at home. He certainly had not intended going back while his brother was still dying.

Why did I leave you?

Flavian did not hear the door open behind him, but he was aware of dim light and then of a slightly brighter light, of the door closing softly. He had woken her. He was sorry about that. And strangely glad. He was not alone any longer. He did not have to do his living alone.

He did not turn, but he waited for her to come close, as he knew she would. Then he could smell her familiar fragrance, and one of her hands came to rest lightly on his shoulder. He raised his own hand to cover it and tipped back his head until it came to rest against her bosom. He closed his eyes.

"Why did I leave him?" he asked.

It did not occur to him to offer her his chair or to draw up another for her.

"You were here for a few weeks after coming home on leave?" she asked him.

"Yes," he said.

"Did you sit with him all that time?" she asked.

"Yes."

"You joined the military three years before that," she said, "because you did not want to be trapped into marrying Lady Hazeltine—or Velma Frome, as she must have been then. Yet after being home for a few weeks, all the time sitting here with your brother, you were so eager to marry her that you left him and went to London to your betrothal ball and then dashed off back to the Peninsula. How did that come about, Flavian? What else happened during those weeks?"

"I went out for w-walks and rides," he said. "It was emotionally d-draining to be here in this room all the time, even though he was p-peaceful. He was just s-slipping away, and there was nothing I could do. . . ."

He closed his hand around hers and drew her forward to take her on his lap. He set one arm about her waist, and she twined one about his neck.

Ah, God, he loved her. He loved her.

"And did you meet Velma outside, as you had used to do?" she asked.

And suddenly that great yawning core of blackness exploded into the searing light of a crashing headache, and he gasped for air. He pushed her off his lap, staggered to the window, fumbled with the catch, and raised the sash until he could feel cold air blowing in. He rested his balled fists on the windowsill and bowed his head. He waited for the worst of the pain to go away. Everything was wide-open. He could remember . . .

. . . everything.

"They were in London for the Season," he said. "But they came h-home. I think my mother m-must have written to Lady Frome. Velma had not taken well with the *ton* after a few years of trying. Frome is not well-off or particularly well connected. She could have found a husband even so, but she aimed too h-high. She wanted a title, the grander the better. None of this was ever said in so m-many words, of course, but it was not d-difficult to piece together the truth. But I was home, and David was d-dying, and . . ."

And they had come. He was not sure Sir Winston and Lady Frome had come from any other motive than concern for their neighbor. And he was not sure his mother had written to Lady Frome for any other purpose than to inform her of the imminent demise of her son. He *hoped* none of them had had any other motive.

Velma had come almost daily to inquire about David, though she never came up to the sickroom. Sometimes she came with one or the other of her parents, but often she came alone, without either maid or groom, and on those occasions his mother had directed him to escort her home. And whenever he went outside for a breath of air, whether on foot or on horseback, almost invariably he came upon her—or, rather, she came upon him. It was *just* like old times. And always there were tears and sweet sympathy and tender memories of when they had been younger.

He had been soothed by her sympathy. He had begun almost to look forward to seeing her. Watching life ebb away from a loved one must be one of the most excruciatingly wretched experiences anyone could be called upon to endure. Even though he had seen more than his fair share of death in the wars, none of it had prepared him for what he was going through now.

One afternoon, while they were sitting in a little clearing above the waterfall, looking down at the lake, listening to birdsong and the sound of water, he had kissed her. Quite voluntarily. He could not blame her for it.

And she had told him that she loved him, that she adored him and always had. She had told him she would make the best viscountess he could possibly dream of. She had told him they must marry as soon as possible, by special license, so that they would not be delayed by the year of mourning that lay ahead when David died. And she would be by his side to support him through that year. She looked good in black, she had told him. He must not be afraid that she would look dowdy and let him down. Oh, she adored him.

And she had thrown her arms about his neck and kissed him.

He had apologized stiffly for *his* kiss, begged her forgiveness, told her that he could think of nothing at that moment beyond the fact that David was alive but desperately ill, that his brother needed him, and he needed his brother. That all else in his life was on hold. He had apologized again as he scrambled to his feet and offered a hand to help her up.

She had been in tears, and he had felt like a monster.

The following afternoon Flavian had been called down to the drawing room from the sickroom and had found his mother there with a pale, marblelike face. With her were a weepy-eyed Lady Frome and a stiffly formal and clearly furious Sir Winston Frome.

Apparently Flavian had declared his love for Velma the previous afternoon before debauching her, but he had then informed her that there could be no question of their marrying for some time to come, what with all the uncertainty surrounding the illness of his brother.

All of which, Frome had declared, was monstrously unacceptable, to put the matter mildly. What if Major Arnott's *merrymaking* of the previous day had consequences? Lady Frome had sniffled against her handkerchief, and Flavian's mother had flinched. Major Arnott's honor as an officer and a gentleman dictated that he make restitution and make it without delay.

The death of David might cause that delay. Frome had not said as much. None of them had, but his meaning had been clear. He had not demanded marriage by special license. That must have appeared unseemly to him, as it had not to his daughter. But he *had* demanded an instant and public betrothal. There was to be nothing havey-cavey about it. In fact . . .

They had leased a house in London for the Season and had not let it go when they returned home. They would go back immediately, have the announcement put in all the society papers, and invite the *ton* to a grand betrothal ball, after which they would have the banns called at St. George's on Hanover Square.

Flavian had found himself unable to protest as vociferously as he would have liked, though he had denied ruining Velma. He had kissed her, though, and it could be said with some justification that he had compromised her. Her mother had wept. Her father had blustered and chosen to believe his daughter's more extreme version of what had happened between them. How could he, Flavian, have continued to call Velma a liar in the hearing of her parents—his neighbors and friends? But it was *so* much like what she had done once before, three years ago, except then she had made her accusations only to David, in order to get him to cancel their betrothal plans. This time she had left nothing to chance.

"And so you went to London," Agnes said, and Flavian awoke to the realization that he had poured out the whole story to her. "And then went back to your regiment."

"David could see no honorable way out of my going," he said. "But when I assured him I would rush b-back the morning after the ball, he m-made me p-promise not to come back at all. He could not be sure, he told me, that he would die within a month." He paused and took a great gulp of the cold outdoor air. "If he did *not* die, and I could n-not be saved by the necessity to mourn, then I would be forced to marry and would be trapped for life. He m-made me promise to return to the Peninsula as I was scheduled to do. Perhaps, he s-said, Velma would find someone else to marry while I was gone. Or perhaps something else would crop up to save me. He made me promise, and I went."

He swallowed against a lump in his throat, fought tears, and lost the battle. He tried desperately at least to weep silently until he could get himself under control.

And then her arms came about him from behind, and the side of her face came to rest between his shoulder blades. He turned and gathered her up into a tight hug and sobbed ignominiously against her shoulder.

"He died alone," he gasped out. "Mother was in town with m-me. So was Marianne. There were only his v-valet here and the other s-servants. I was on the ship back to Portugal."

She kissed him on the tip of one ear.

"I am so sorry," he said. "I have soaked your shawl."

"It will dry," she told him. "Did you forget all this when you were brought back home later?"

He lifted his head, frowning.

"She had met Len a number of times," he said, "when he came here to stay with me as a boy. But at that time he was not expecting to succeed his uncle to the earl's title. He had it by the time I was brought home, though. She w-wanted it. I think I knew that, even though I did not know much of anything at all. And I knew she would get it if she c-could. I tried to warn him. I think I t-tried. And then she c-came to tell me she was ending our engagement and was going to m-marry him. And I tried to stop it—but all I could d-do was destroy the drawing room at Arnott House. I— He did not come. Len never came. George came instead and took me off to Penderris."

Agnes moved her head so that her lips were almost touching his.

"Come back to bed," she said. "Come and sleep."

He had kept her up for what felt like half the night.

"Agnes," he said, "were you waiting for me there? At Middlebury? Were you always waiting for me? And was I always waiting to meet you?"

She was smiling, he could see in the flickering light of the candle.

"All my life," she said. "And all your life."

"Does life happen that way?" he asked her.

"I think it does sometimes," she said, "incredible as it sounds. And do you realize you have stopped stammering?"

"I h-have?" He raised his eyebrows in surprise. "You must be freezing, Agnes. Let's go back to bed."

"Yes," she said.

He glanced toward the empty bed as he led her to the door. It *was* empty. David was gone. He was at rest. They had said good-bye to each other, and David had smiled at him. He remembered now. His brother had sent Flavian away to save him, and he had given him his blessing.

"Live happily, Flave," he had said. "Mourn a little for me if you will, and then let me go. I will be in good hands."

23

It was Easter Sunday morning, and the sun shone from a clear blue sky. There was warmth in the air. The church bells pealed out the glad tidings of renewed life, and the inhabitants of the village of Candlebury stood about on the churchyard path greeting one another, wishing one another a happy Easter while their children darted about among the nearer gravestones as though they were a playground constructed specifically for their amusement.

The rector stood outside the church doors, smiling genially and shaking hands with his parishioners as they came out of the church, his vestments lifted by the slight breeze.

There was a heightened buzz of excitement this morning, even apart from the joy that Easter always brought. For Viscount Ponsonby—Mr. Flavian, that was—had come home at long last, apparently none the worse for his long and dreadful ordeal, but actually looking more handsome than ever. And he had brought a *bride* with him, and she was not that Miss Frome, who had abandoned him, poor gentleman, all those years ago at just the time he had most needed loved ones about him, and had gone off and married an earl.

Mr. Thompson would lose his wager with Mr. Radley,

though he did not look particularly upset about it this morning. He had wagered that, now the countess was widowed and back living with her mama and papa at Farthings Hall, she would maneuver matters so that she would marry the viscount after all, and before summer was out too.

The new viscountess was not the sort of dazzling beauty Lord Ponsonby might have got for himself, handsome and rich as he was, not to mention the title. But everyone was glad of that fact. He had not chosen on looks alone. Not that the viscountess was not a beauty in her own way. She was nicely dressed and elegant, without being ostentatious about it and making all the rest of them feel rustic and shabby. She had a neat figure and a pleasant face, and she smiled a lot with what appeared to be genuine good humor. She looked them all directly in the eye as she smiled. She had done it when she went into the church on the viscount's arm, and she had done it again when she came out. And she lingered on the path with her husband, exchanging a few words with some of their number.

Most of the conversations beyond the earshot of Lord and Lady Ponsonby centered upon them, as was only natural. The previous viscount had suffered ill health for years before his death, poor gentleman, and they had scarcely seen him. And this one had been gone since even before his brother's demise. Now he was back, looking fit and healthy and handsome and . . . happy.

Any new bridegroom ought to look happy, of course, but it did not always happen, especially among the rich and titled, who married for all sorts of reasons, most of which had nothing to do with love or happiness.

The bride looked happy too.

And was it true that they had promised a *garden party* for everyone at some time during the summer? Yes, it most certainly *was* true. They had said so to Mrs. Turner, head of the altar committee, when she had called upon them two days ago, and Mrs. Turner had told Miss Hill in strictest confidence, and, well, they all knew what Miss Hill was like.

Agnes did her best to memorize a few names and faces and occupations. It would take a while, as she confessed candidly to some of the people to whom she was introduced. She begged the indulgence of a little time while she became acquainted with the neighborhood and everyone in it. Everyone seemed perfectly happy to grant her as much time as she needed.

It must be the weather, she thought, that made this setting seem so idyllic and these people so amiable. She had never felt such a sense of home as she felt here. And she had never felt so happy. She had done the right thing. She *had.*

Were you always waiting for me? And was I always waiting to meet you? he had asked a few nights ago.

All my life, she had replied. *And all your life.*

And, foolishly extravagant though the words sounded, they felt true. They surely *were* true.

"Agnes," he said now, bending his head closer to her ear so that she would hear clearly above the babble of voices and the lovely pealing of the bells, "will you come with me?"

She knew where without having to ask. And she was glad of it. He had one more thing to do. She nodded and took his arm.

There was no vault for the family Arnott, Viscounts of Ponsonby, and their families for more than two centuries back. But there was a separate area of the churchyard, well tended and set off from the rest by low and neatly clipped box hedges. The newest grave with its white marble headstone stood just a few feet inside the gate.

David Arnott, Viscount Ponsonby, it read, together

with the dates of his birth and death and a rather flowery inscription informing the world of his blameless existence and instructing angels to carry him up to the throne of heaven, where he would be welcomed with open arms. A marble angel, wings spread and trumpet held to its lips, stood atop the headstone.

"He wanted something simple and to the point," Flavian said. "Poor David. He used to shudder and laugh at the sorts of things people put on gravestones. Our grandfather, whom we remembered as a foul-tempered old tyrant, is written of as though he had been a saint."

But he spoke fondly and with a slight smile on his face, Agnes noticed—and without a trace of a stammer.

"A graveyard ought to be a place of horrors," he said. "It is not, though, is it? It is peaceful here. I am glad he is here."

His grip on her hand had tightened, and she saw, when she stole another glance at him, that his eyes were bright with unshed tears.

"I did love him," he said.

"Of course you did," she said. "And of course he knew it. And he loved you in return."

He leaned down and set a palm flat on the grave before straightening up.

"Yes," he said. "Yes. Do you believe in an afterlife, Agnes?"

"I do," she told him.

"Then be happy, David," he said.

They had walked to church, even though it was all of two miles. They began the walk home after waving farewell to a few villagers who lingered. Agnes raised her parasol to shelter her face from the brightness of the sun.

"I am so glad we came here," she said. "Will we go back to town now that Easter is over and the Season will begin?"

"Maybe later," he said. "Maybe not. Do we have to decide now?"

"No," she said.

"Those were very civil letters I had from your father and your brother yesterday," he said. "Shall we invite them to visit us during the summer? And your sister too? Perhaps we can have the garden party while they are all here."

"I would like that," she said. "And I think I will *write* to my mother. I may never go to see her. Indeed, I doubt I ever will. But I think I will write. Ought I, do you think?"

"There is nothing you *ought* to do," he said. "But write to her if it is what you wish to do. She will be pleased. So, I think, will you."

He stopped walking when they came to the top of the rise before the descent into the bowl of the inner park about the house. She heard him inhale deeply and exhale on a sigh.

"This is *not* happily-ever-after, is it?" he asked her.

"No," she said, "but there are moments that feel like it."

"This moment?" he said.

"Yes."

"Have I told you that I love you?" he asked her. "Deuce take it, Agnes, but they are the hardest words in the English language for a man to say. I have *not* said them. I would have noticed if I had."

"No," she agreed, laughing, "you have not."

And her heart yearned to hear just those three simple words strung together into the loveliest phrase ever uttered. *If*, that was, the speaker was the right man.

He turned to her, took her parasol and tossed it unceremoniously to the grass beside the path, grasped both her hands, and brought them to his chest, where he held them with his own. His green eyes, unprotected by any hooding of eyelids, gazed into hers.

"Agnes Arnott," he said, "I l-l-l— "

"I love you," she said softly.

"That is what I am t-trying to say," he told her.

"No," she said, smiling. "*I* love *you*."

"Do you?" He raised their clasped hands to his lips. "Do you, Agnes? It is not just my title and my money and my irresistible good looks and charm?"

She laughed. "Oh, well, and those too."

He grinned at her and looked like the blond, handsome, carefree boy he must once have been.

"I love you," he said.

"I know."

He wrapped his arms about her waist, lifted her from the ground, and spun her twice about, at the same time tipping back his head and howling out his happiness.

And he *was* happy. So was she.

Agnes braced her hands on his shoulders, looked down into his face, and laughed.

Read on for a look at the next book in the Survivors' Club series by Mary Balogh,

ONLY A PROMISE

Available from Signet in May 2015.

There could surely be nothing worse than having been born a woman, Chloe Muirhead thought with unabashed self-pity as she sucked a globule of blood off her left forefinger and looked to see if any more was about to bubble up and threaten to ruin the strip of delicate lace she was sewing back onto one of the Duchess of Worthingham's best afternoon caps. Unless, perhaps, one had the good fortune to be a duchess. Or else a single lady in possession of forty thousand pounds a year and the freedom to set up one's own independent establishment.

She, alas, was not a duchess. Or in sole possession of even forty *pence* a year apart from her allowance from her father. Besides, she did not *want* to set up somewhere independently. It sounded suspiciously lonely. She could not really claim to be lonely now. The duchess was kind to her. So was the duke, in his gruff way. And whenever Her Grace entertained afternoon visitors or went visiting herself, she always invited Chloe to join her.

It was not the duchess's fault that she was eighty-two years old to Chloe's twenty-seven. Or that the neighbors with whom she consorted most frequently must all have been upward of sixty. In some cases they were very much upward. Mrs. Booth, for example, who always carried a large ear trumpet and let out a loud, querulous "Eh?" every time someone so much as opened her mouth to speak, was ninety-three.

If she had been born male, Chloe thought, rubbing her thumb briskly over her forefinger to make sure the bleeding had stopped and it was safe to pick up her needle again, she might have done all sorts of interesting, adventurous things when she had felt it imperative to leave home. As it was, all *she* had been able to think of to do was write to the Duchess of Worthingham, who was her mother's godmother and had been her late grandmother's dearest friend, and offer her services as a companion. An *unpaid* companion, she had been careful to explain.

A kind and gracious letter had come back within days, as well as a sealed note for Chloe's father. The duchess would be delighted to welcome dear Chloe to Manville Court, but as a guest, *NOT* as an employee—the *not* had been capitalized and heavily underlined. And Chloe might stay as long as she wished—forever, if the duchess had her way. She could not think of anything more delightful than to have someone young to brighten her days and make her feel young again. She only hoped Sir Kevin Muirhead could spare his daughter for a prolonged visit. She showed wonderful tact in adding that, of course, as she had in writing separately to him, for Chloe had explained in her own letter just why living at home had become intolerable to her, at least for a while, much as she loved her father and hated to upset him.

So she had come. She would be forever grateful to the duchess, who treated her more like a favored granddaughter than a virtual stranger and basically self-invited guest. But oh, she *was* lonely too. One could be lonely and unhappy while being grateful at the same time, could one not?

And, ah, yes. She was unhappy too.

Her world had been turned completely upside down *twice* within the past six years, which ought to have meant if life proceeded along logical lines, as it most certainly did not, that the second time it was turned right side up again. She had lost everything any young woman could ever ask for the first time—hopes and dreams, the promise of love and marriage and happily-ever-after, the prospect of security and her own place in society. Hope had revived last year, though in a more muted and modest form. But that had been dashed too, and her very identity had hung in the balance. In the four years between the two disasters, her mother had died. Was it any wonder she was unhappy?

She gave the delicate needlework her full attention again. If she allowed herself to wallow in self-pity, she would be in danger of becoming one of those habitual moaners and complainers everyone avoided.

It was still only very early in May. A largish mass of clouds covered the sun and did not look as if it planned to move off anytime soon, and a brisk breeze was gusting along the east side of the house, directly across the terrace outside the morning room, where Chloe sat sewing. It had not been a sensible idea to come outside, but it had rained quite unrelentingly for the past three days, and she had been desperate to escape the confines of the house and breathe in some fresh air.

She ought to have brought her shawl out with her, even her cloak and gloves, she thought, though then of course she would not have been able to sew, and she had promised to have the cap ready before the duchess awoke from her afternoon sleep. Dratted cap and dratted lace. But that was quite unfair, for she had volunteered to do it even when the duchess had made a mild protest.

"Are you quite sure it will be no trouble, my dear?" she had asked. "Bunker is perfectly competent with a needle."

Miss Bunker was her personal maid.

"Of course I am," Chloe had assured her. "It will be my pleasure."

The duchess always had that effect upon her. For all the obvious sincerity of her welcome and kindness of her manner, Chloe felt the obligation, if not to earn her living, then at least to make herself useful whenever she was able.

She was shivering by the time she had completed her task and cut the thread with fingers that felt stiff from the cold. She held out the cap, draped over her right fist. The stitches were invisible. No one would be able to tell that a repair had been made.

She did not want to go back inside, despite the cold. The duchess would probably be up from her sleep and would be in the drawing room bright with happy anticipation of the expected arrival of her grandson. She would be eager to extol his many virtues yet again though he had not been to Manville since Christmas. Chloe was tired of hearing of his virtues. She doubted he had any.

Not that she had ever met him in person to judge for herself, it was true. But she did know him by reputation. He and her brother, Graham, had been at school together. Ralph Stockwood, who had since assumed his father's courtesy title of Earl of Berwick, had been a charismatic leader there. He had been liked and admired and emulated by almost all the other boys, even though he had also been one of a close-knit group of four handsome, athletic, clever boys. Graham had spoken critically and disapprovingly of Ralph Stockwood, though Chloe had always suspected that he envied that favored inner circle.

After school, the four friends all took up commissions in the same prestigious cavalry regiment and went off to the Peninsula to fight the forces of Napoleon Bonaparte while Graham went to Oxford to study theology and become a clergyman. He had arrived home from the final term at school upset because Ralph Stockwood had called him a sniveling prig and lily-livered coward. Chloe did not know the context in which the insult had been hurled, but she had not felt kindly disposed toward Graham's erstwhile schoolmate ever since. And she never had liked the sound of him. She did not like boys, or men, who lorded it arrogantly over others and accepted their homage as a right.

Not many months after they had embarked for the Peninsula, Lieutenant Stockwood's three friends had been killed in the same battle, and he had been carried off the field and then home to England so severely wounded that he had not been expected to survive.

Chloe had felt sorry for him at the time, but her sympathies had soon been alienated again. Graham, in his capacity as a clergyman, had called upon him in London a day or two after he had been brought home from Portugal. Graham had been admitted to the sickroom, but the wounded man had sworn foully at him and ordered him to get out and never come back.

Chloe did not expect to like the Earl of Berwick, then, even if he *was* the Duke of Worthingham's heir and the duchess's beloved only grandson. She had not forgiven his description of her brother as a lily-livered coward. Graham was a *pacifist*. That did not make him a coward. Indeed, it took a great deal of courage to stand up for peace against men who were in love with war. And she had not forgiven the earl for cursing Graham after he had been injured without even listening to what he had come to say. The fact that he had undoubtedly been in great pain at the time did not excuse such rudeness to an old school friend. She had decided long ago that the earl was brash, arrogant, self-centered, even heartless.

And he was on his way to Manville Court. He was coming at the duchess's behest, it must be added, not because he had chosen of his own free will to visit the grandparents who doted on him. Chloe suspected that the summons had something to do with the duke's health, which had been causing Her Grace some concern for the past couple of months. She fancied that he was coughing more than usual and that his habit of covering his heart with one hand when he did so was a bad sign. He did not complain of feeling unwell—not, at least, in Chloe's hearing—and he saw his physician only when the duchess insisted. Afterward, he had called the doctor an old quack who knew no better than to prescribe pills and potions that served only to make the duke feel ill.

Chloe did not know what the true state of his health was, but she did know that he had celebrated his eighty-fifth birthday last autumn, and eighty-five was an awfully advanced age to be.

However it was, the Earl of Berwick had been summoned and he was expected today. Chloe did not want to meet him. She knew she would not like him. More important, perhaps, she admitted reluctantly to herself, she did not want him to meet *her*, a sort of charity guest of his grandmother's, an aging twenty-seven-year-old spinster with a doubtful reputation and no prospects. A pathetic creature, in fact.

But the thought finally triggered laughter—at her own expense. She had whipped herself into a thoroughly cross and disagreeable mood, and it just would not do. She got determinedly to her feet. She must go up to her room without delay and change her dress and make sure her hair was tidy. She might be a poor aging spinster with no prospects, but there was no point in being an abject one who was worthy only of pity or scorn. That would be too excruciatingly humiliating.

She hurried on her way upstairs, shaking herself free of the self-pity in which she had languished for too long. Goodness, if she hated her life so much, then it was high time she *did* something about it. The only question was *what*? Was there anything she *could* do? A woman had so few options. Sometimes, indeed, it seemed she had none at all, especially when she had a *past*, even if she was in no way to blame for any of it.

Read on for a look at one of
Mary Balogh's most beloved titles

BEYOND THE SUNRISE

Available from New American Library
for the first time
in trade paperback in February 2015.

The entertainment in progress at Haddington Hall in Sussex, country seat of the Marquess of Quesnay, could not exactly be dignified by the name of *ball*, though there was dancing, and the sounds of music and gaiety were wafting from the open windows of the main drawing room. It was a country entertainment and the numbers not large, there being only two guests staying at the house at that particular time to swell the ranks of the local gentry.

It was not a ball, but the boy sitting out of sight of the house on the seat surrounding the great marble fountain below the terrace wished that he was inside and a part of it all. He wished that reality could be suspended and that he could be there dancing with *her*, the dark-haired, dark-eyed young daughter of his father's guest. Or at least looking at her and perhaps talking with her. Perhaps fetching her a glass of lemonade. He wished . . . oh, he wished for the moon, as he always did. A dreamer—that was what his mother had often called him.

But there were two insurmountable reasons for his exclusion from the assembly: he was only seventeen years old, and he was the marquess's *illegitimate* son. That last fact had had particular meaning to him only during the past year and a half, since the sudden death of his mother. Through his childhood and much of his boyhood, it had seemed a normal way of life to have a father who visited him and his mother frequently but did not live with them, and a father who had a wife in the big house though no other children but him.

It was only in the year and a half since his mother's death that the reality of his situation had become fully apparent to him. He had been a fifteen-year-old boy without a home and with a father who had financed his mother's home but had never been a permanent part of it. His father had taken him to live in the big house. But he had felt all the awkwardness of his situation since moving there. He was not a member of the family—his father's wife, the marchioness, hated him and ignored his presence whenever she was forced to be in it. But he was not one of the servants either, of course.

It was only in the past year and a half that his father had begun to talk about his future and that the boy had realized that his illegitimacy made of that future a tricky business. The marquess would buy him a commission in the army when he was eighteen, he had decided, but it would have to be with a line regiment and not with the cavalry—certainly not with the Guards. That would never do when the ranks of the Guards were filled with the sons of the nobility and upper gentry. The legitimate sons, that was.

He was his father's only son, but illegitimate.

"You are not at the ball?" a soft little voice asked him suddenly, and he looked up to see the very reason why he had so wished to be in the drawing room—Jeanne Morisette, daughter of the Comte de Levisse, a royalist émigré who had fled from France during the Reign of Terror and lived in England ever since.

He felt his heart thump. He had never been close to her before, had never exchanged a word with her. He shrugged. "I don't want to be," he said. "It is not a ball anyway."

She sat down beside him, slender in a light-colored flimsy gown—he could not see the exact color in the darkness—her hair in myriad ringlets about her head, her eyes large and luminous in the moonlight. "But I wish I could be there even so," she said. "I thought I might be allowed to attend since it is just a country entertainment. But Papa said no. He said that fifteen is too young to be dancing with gentlemen. It is tiresome being young, is it not?"

Ah. So she had not been with the company after all. He had tortured himself for nothing. He shrugged again. "I am not so young," he said. "I am seventeen."

She sighed. "When I am seventeen," she said, "I shall dance every night and go to the theater and on picnics. I shall do just whatever I please when I am grown-up."

Her face was bright and eager and she was prettier than any other girl he had seen. He had taken every opportunity during the past week to catch glimpses of her. She was like a bright little jewel, quite beyond his reach, of course, but lovely to look at and to dream of.

"Papa is going to take me back to France as soon as it is safe to go," she said with a sigh. "Everything seems to be settling down under the leadership of Napoleon Bonaparte. If it continues so, perhaps we will be able to return, Papa says. He says there is no point in continuing to dream of the return of a king."

"So you may do your dancing in Paris," he said.

"Yes." Her eyes were dreamy. "But I would just as soon stay in London. I know England better than I know France. I even speak English better than I speak French. I would prefer to belong here."

But there was a trace of a French accent in her voice. It was one more attractive feature about her. He liked to listen to her talk.

"You are the marquess's son, are you not?" she asked him. "But you do not have his name?"

"I have my mother's name," he said. "She died the winter before last."

"Ah," she said, "that is sad. My mother is dead too, but I do not remember her. I have always been with Papa for as long as I recall. What is your name?"

"Robert," he said.

"Robert." She gave his name its French intonation and then smiled and said it again with its English pronunciation. "Robert, dance with me. Do you dance?"

"My mother taught me," he said. "Out here? How can we dance out here?"

"Easily," she said, jumping lightly to her feet and stretching out a slim hand to him. "The music is quite loud enough."

"But you will hurt your feet on the stones," he said, looking down at her thin silk slippers as she led the way up onto the terrace.

She laughed. "I think, Robert, that you are looking for excuses," she said. "I think that your mother did not teach you at all, or that if she did, you were unteachable. I think perhaps you have two left feet." She laughed again.

"That is not so," he said indignantly. "If you wish to dance, then dance we will."

"That is a very grudging acceptance," she said. "You are supposed to be thrilled to dance with me. You are supposed to make me feel that there is nothing you wish for more in life than to dance with me. But no matter. Let us dance."

He knew very little about women's teasing. It was true

that Mollie Lumsden, one of his father's undermaids, frequently put herself in his way and showed herself to him in provocative poses, most frequently bent over his bed as she made it up in the mornings. It was true too that on the one occasion when he had tried to steal a kiss she had whisked herself off with a toss of the head and an assurance that her favors did not come free. But there was a world of difference between the buxom Mollie and Jeanne Morisette.

They danced a minuet, the moon bathing the cobbles of the terrace in a mellow light, both of them silent and concentrating on the distant music and their steps—although his attention was not entirely on just those two things either. His eyes were on the slender moonlit form of the girl with whom he danced. Her hand in his was warm and slim and soft. He thought that life might never have a finer moment to offer him.

"You are very tall," she said as the music drew to an end.

He was close to six feet in height. Unfortunately his growing had all been done upward. To say that he was thin would be to understate the case. He hated to look at himself in a looking glass. He longed to be a handsome, muscular man and wondered if he ever would be anything more than gangly and ugly.

"And you have lovely blond hair," she said. "I have noticed you all week and wished that I had hair that waved like yours." She laughed lightly. "I am glad you do not wear it short. It would be such a waste."

He was dazzled. He was still holding her soft little hand in his.

"I am supposed to be in my room," she said. "Papa would have forty fits if he knew I was out here."

"You are quite safe," he said. "I shall see that no harm comes to you."

She looked up at him from beneath her lashes, an imp of mischief in her eyes. "You may kiss me if you wish," she said.

His eyes widened. What Mollie had denied, Jeanne Morisette would grant? But how could he kiss her? He knew nothing about kissing.

"Of course," she said, "if you do not wish to, I shall return to the house. Perhaps you are afraid."

He was. Mortally afraid. "Of course I am not afraid," he said scornfully. And he set his hands at her waist—they almost met about it—and lowered his head and kissed her. He kissed her as he had always kissed his mother on the cheek—though he kissed Jeanne on the lips—briefly and with a smacking sound.

She was all softness and subtle fragrance. And her hands were on his shoulders, her thumbs against the skin of his neck. Her dark eyes looked inquiringly into his. He swallowed and knew that his bobbing Adam's apple would reveal his nervousness.

"And of course I wish to," he said, and he lowered his head and laid his lips against hers again, keeping them there for a few self-indulgent moments and noting with shock the unfamiliar effects of the embrace on his body—the breathlessness, the rush of heat, the tightening in his groin. He lifted his head.

"Oh, Robert," she said with a sigh, "you can have no idea how tiresome it is to be fifteen. Or can you? Do you remember what it was like? Though it is entirely different for a boy, of course. I am still expected to behave like a child, when I am not a child. I must be quiet and prim, and welcome the company of your father and mother—no, the marchioness is not your mother, is she?—and of my own papa. And I am to be denied the company of the young people who are at present dancing and enjoying themselves in the drawing room. How will I endure it here for another whole week?"

He wished he could pluck some stars from the sky and lay them at her feet. He wished that the music would continue for a week so that he could dance with her and kiss her and help see her to the end of the boredom of an unwelcome visit to the country.

"I will be here too," he said with a shrug.

She looked up at him eagerly—the top of her head reached barely to his shoulder. "Yes," she said. "I shall steal away and spend time with you, Robert. It will be fun and my maid is very easy to escape. She is lazy, but I never complain to Papa because sometimes it is an advantage to have a lazy maid." She laughed her light, infectious laugh. "You are very handsome. Will you take me to the ruins tomorrow? We went there two days ago, but the marchioness would not let me explore them lest I hurt myself. All I could do was look and listen to your father tell the history of the old castle."

"I will take you," he said. But he noted the fact that she had spoken of *stealing* away to be with him. And of course she was right. It was not at all the thing for the two of them even to have met. They certainly should never have talked or danced. Or kissed. There would be all hell to pay if he were caught taking her to the ruins. He should explain that to her more clearly. But he was seventeen years old, and the realities of life were new to him. He still thought it possible to fight against them, or at least to ignore them.

"Will you?" she asked eagerly, clasping her hands to her slender, budding bosom. "After luncheon? I shall go to my room for a rest, as the marchioness is always urging me to do. Where shall I meet you?"

"The other side of the stables," he said, pointing. "It is

almost a mile to the ruins. Will you be able to walk that far?"

"Of course I can walk there," she said scornfully. "And climb. I want to climb up the tower."

"It is dangerous," he said. "Some of the stairs have crumbled away."

"But you have climbed it, have you not?" she said.

"Of course."

"Then I shall climb it too," she said. "Is there a good view from the top?"

"You can see to the village and beyond," he said.

The music was playing a quadrille in the drawing room.

"Tomorrow," she said. "After luncheon. At last there will be a day to look forward to. Good night, Robert."

She held out one slim hand to him. He took it and realized in some confusion that she meant him to kiss it. He raised it to his lips and felt foolish and flattered and wonderful.

"Good night, Miss Morisette," he said.

She laughed up at him. "You are a courtier after all," she said. "You have just made me feel at least eighteen years old. It is Jeanne, Robert. Jeanne the French way and Robert the English way."

"Good night, Jeanne," he said, and he was glad of the darkness, which hid his blushes.

She turned and tripped lightly over the cobbles of the terrace and around to the side of the house. She had, he realized, come out through the servants' entrance and was returning the same way. He wondered if she had come out merely for the fresh air or if she had seen him from an upstairs window. The window of her bedchamber overlooked the terrace and the fountain.

He liked to believe that it was his presence out there that had drawn her. She had called him tall. She had not commented on his thinness, only on his height. And she had called the blondness of his hair lovely and had approved of the fact that he liked to wear it overlong. She had called him handsome—very handsome. And she had asked him to kiss her. She had asked him to take her to the ruins the next day. She had said that at last there would be a day to look forward to.

He was no longer merely attracted to her slim dark beauty, he realized, the sounds of music and gaiety from the drawing room forgotten. He was deeply, irrevocably in love with Jeanne Morisette.

Read on for an excerpt from another of Mary Balogh's most beloved titles

LONGING

Available from New American Library
for the first time
in trade paperback in March 2015.

It was rather late in the day to go walking, especially in a strange place. But the night was warm and moonlit, and the hills beckoned invitingly. Besides, a day and a half of traveling had made him stiff and restless, and since his arrival soon after noon he had been busy with his housekeeper and his butler. His agent had called to pay his respects and make arrangements for the coming days. And there had been Verity to amuse. If the journey had made him irritable, it had made her positively petulant. It was harder for a six-year-old to sit still and idle for hours on end than it was for an adult.

Now she was in bed, coaxed there by an elderly and indulgent nurse, and put to sleep by the stories he had read to her.

He was unable to give in to his own tiredness. Everything was so strange. He had been the owner of this property for longer than two years—ever since the death of his uncle, his mother's brother—but he had never been here before. He did not even know much about it except that the quarterly reports sent by his agent showed it to be extremely prosperous. But then, aristocrats, whose names and titles and wealth had grown out of large landed estates over several centuries, still frowned upon the idea of making money out of industry. It seemed very middle-class and not quite the thing at all. Times were changing, but very often times changed faster than people.

Alexander Hyatt, Marquess of Craille, was the owner of a large area of land in one of the valleys of South Wales and the ironworks and coal mine on that land. The back of beyond, as his mother-in-law liked to describe it. It was not a compliment. She had been aghast when he had told her that he was going to take her granddaughter there for an indefinite period of time. It was in vain that he had reminded her that he also owned a castle there—Glanrhyd Castle—that had been built by his uncle's predecessor.

Alex, standing at his bedroom window, still fully clothed, decided that late or not, strange or not, he was going to go out for a walk after all. The little he had seen of the surrounding area during the day had fascinated him—the narrow valley with steep, heather-covered hills to either side, the river at the bottom with rows of terraced houses beside it and on the lower slopes, the ironworks below the castle, largely hidden by the trees of the park. Glanrhyd Castle itself was built above the valley floor, a little removed from both the works and the houses.

The hills fascinated him. Steep, and yet not sheer, they closed in the valley, making it like a little world cut off from the outside. He felt almost as if he were in a foreign country. In a way, he supposed, he was.

He took a cloak with him in case the night was chillier than it had felt through his open window. But it was still almost warm outside. He strolled the gravel walks bordering the sloping lawns of the park and stood still to breathe in the fresh air and to listen to the sounds of insects. But he was not satisfied with such a sedate walk. The hills called to him. If he walked a little way across and up the slope beyond the park gates, he would be able to look down on the valley and have a more panoramic view of it than he had had from the house. It would probably look lovely in the moonlight.

He did not intend to walk far as he soon realized that the hills did not ascend smoothly from the valley to the top. Rather they were rolling hills with peaks and hollows and even some sharp, unexpected drops. But there was no real danger as long as he was in no hurry. There was light enough to see by. And his guess had been correct. From above, and without the obstruction of the trees, he could see that the town was picturesque despite the smoking chimneys of the ironworks and despite the black coal tips he could see farther down the valley. Moonlight gleamed off the water of the river, which was broader than it had seemed from below. The houses, in long, snaking lines, looked sleepy and hugged the side of the hill as if for protection. There were very few lights. Obviously his workers went to bed early. Not that it was really early. He supposed it was close to midnight.

He should turn back. But there was a pleasant coolness in the air now, and he was reluctant to give up this only part of the day he had to himself. If he strolled a little farther on, he thought, he would be able to look back up the valley from the other end of the town. Perhaps he would be able to see the castle above the works. It had been fancifully built, with numerous towers and turrets and long windows. He had been rather amused when he first set eyes on it. And rather pleased too. Somehow it escaped vulgarity, ornate as it was. Somehow it seemed to suit its setting.

He was not sure when he first became aware of a sound that was neither water nor wind nor insects. At first it was a feeling that seemed not quite associated with the ears. But it became more marked as he strolled on. It was the sound of voices. The murmured sound of many voices.

Alex stood still and concentrated. Where was it coming from? From below? But almost all the lights were out in the houses, and the works were too far away, although some men would be on shift there. From the mine, then? No, the sound was coming from the hills.

He walked on more warily, more alertly, until the sound was unmistakably that of voices—men's voices. And then there was one voice, speaking above the rest until they all fell silent, and speaking on. In a strange language, doubtless Welsh.

As he drew closer, Alex realized that he was approaching another of those unexpected peaks, behind which there was presumably another dip and a hollow. He could tell that he was close now. The voice was distinct. Whoever it was was in that hollow. He climbed carefully, ducking down as he approached the top so that his head would not be seen against the skyline. He inched up the last few feet so that he could look down.

His jaw almost dropped. Certainly his eyes widened. It was a large hollow, far larger than he had expected, and it was packed tight with men, now silent. Hundreds of them. Every single man from the valley below must be there.

The man who was addressing them was standing on a slight rise at one end of the hollow, so that all would be able to see him. He was a big man, not particularly tall, but broad and strong-looking. He had a commanding presence, as he would have to have, Alex thought, to have called such a large gathering to order.

A meeting? On the mountain at midnight? He noticed suddenly that not one of the men held a lantern or any other light. It was true that the moonlight was bright enough, but it was surprising nonetheless that there were no lights. It was a clandestine meeting, then?

At first he thought he must be wrong. The broad, dark-haired speaker stepped down to give his place to a tall, thin man dressed all in black. He too spoke in Welsh, but it was clear from the way he spread his arms and from the tone of his voice when he began to speak that he was a preacher. And that he was praying. The men all bowed their heads reverently and remained silent throughout the lengthy prayer, only the occasional "Amen" interrupting the preacher's voice.

A prayer meeting? Alex frowned and then felt amusement. He had been told that the Welsh were a devout people and that they were nonconformist almost to a man. But a mass prayer meeting at midnight when they should be at home asleep? He felt again the foreignness of this new home of his.

He probably would have retreated and left them to it if he had not spotted the woman. Like him, she was not part of the meeting. As far as he could see, its members were exclusively male. Like him, she was silently spying on it. She was hiding behind some large rocks a little lower than his hill and some distance away. She would not be able to see him. He edged over a little to his left to make sure.

He wondered what she was doing there and why she could not join the prayer meeting openly. Unless women were forbidden to do so. It looked as if that might be the case. It was impossible to tell if she was young or old. She wore a dark dress, which blended well with the rocks, and a lighter shawl, which was drawn up over her head. But she looked slim. She looked young. He watched her, intrigued, and ignored the feeling that he was spying on something that was none of his business.

Actually it was his business. This was his land. These were his people.

And then the prayer was finally at an end and the

preacher stepped down to be replaced by the first speaker. Alex wished he could understand what was being said but realized that he must become accustomed to hearing Welsh spoken all around him. He was the intruder, after all. It was their country, not his.

And then suddenly he did understand. The language had switched to English—heavily accented but nevertheless quite understandable. The Welshman was introducing a speaker who was English. His fame had spread throughout the land and they were honored and privileged to have him bring his oratory to Wales. Would they all welcome Robert Mitchell?

They did so as a small, bespectacled, insignificant-looking young man took his place on the rise and lifted his arms for silence. He did not get it for some time. The men were applauding and whistling.

Robert Mitchell? Hell!

Robert Mitchell was one of the more famous of the Chartist orators who were traveling endlessly and tirelessly throughout the industrial districts of England and Wales these days, trying to persuade the people to put their signatures to the great Charter that was to have been presented to Parliament a few months ago but which still had not appeared there. The most famous orator of all, Henry Vincent, was in jail in Monmouth.

This was a Chartist meeting? Alex flattened himself against the hill suddenly and grew cold. He had not realized that Chartism had taken a hold at Cwmbran. Barnes, his agent, had never made mention of it. But Alex might have guessed, he supposed.

Robert Mitchell was speaking in a voice whose volume and resonant power belied his appearance. He was explaining simply and clearly what the object of the Charter was, what six basic demands it was to make of the government—the vote for every British male, annual

Parliaments, secret ballots, and so on. Alex was quite familiar with the Charter's demands. He was even sympathetic to them. But Chartism had somehow become the movement of the industrial working classes and it had become a movement of protest. Many feared that it had become revolutionary in its aims and methods.

This secret midnight meeting made him feel suddenly uneasy about Chartism. Why the secrecy if the aims were open and honest ones? He had never had to think too much about it before. It had never touched him closely. Now suddenly it was very close indeed.

The woman was still there, he noticed as Robert Mitchell harangued the crowd with the necessity of adding their signatures to the Charter and of paying their pennies to join the Chartist Association.

"There is power in numbers, my friends," he shouted, stabbing the air with one fist and causing Alex to break out in a sweat. There was danger in the idea even if it might seem a reasonable one. Such was the power of the man's oratory that his audience was responding to it with raised fists of their own and with shouts of assent. There were even some fervent amens.

"Everyone will sign the Charter." The speech had ended and the stocky Welshman was back on the rise, though he still spoke in English out of deference to the guest speaker. "Unanimity is essential, men. Those who do not sign tonight or pay their pennies tonight will be asked why tomorrow."

There seemed to be a definite threat in the words. But there were no dissenting voices, only universal enthusiasm as far as Alex could see. He would have a few questions to ask of Barnes tomorrow. But first, he would dearly like to know who the leader was, the strong fiery Welshman who seemed to hold the men in the palm of his hand as well as Mitchell had. And who the preacher was.

The woman was moving away, cautiously leaving the protection of the rocks behind which she had been hiding and circling behind the rise that stood between her and the gathered men. The meeting would be breaking up soon. She was making her escape in good time. She was making her way in his direction, Alex could see.

He waited until she had passed the slope on which he lay, without looking up and seeing him, and then he followed her as she quickened her pace, her shawl held close about her head and shoulders. She had a long, lithe stride. She was undoubtedly a young woman. And a shapely one. His eyes moved over her from behind. Long legs. Shapely hips.

He waited until she hurried down into another hollow. Once out of it, he could see, she would be able to turn directly downward and would be in the town within a few minutes. He came up behind her, reaching a hand around to cover her mouth even as she sensed his presence and turned her head sharply. Large, frightened eyes looked into his while he hurried her behind some rocks so that they would be out of sight of anyone leaving the meeting early.

"You were not invited to the party?" he asked her, turning her so that her back was against the rocks. He removed his hand from her mouth but stood very close to her, his body almost against hers. Oh, yes, she was young. And beautiful. Her shawl had slipped from her head to reveal long hair worn loose. It looked almost black in the shadows. So did her eyes.

"Who are you?" She spoke to him in English, with a strongly lilting Welsh accent.

"It is a pity women are not invited to sign the Charter," he said. "Would you have signed it and given them one more signature?"

She leaned her head back against the rock. Some of

the terror had gone from her eyes, but she was breathing raggedly. "I don't know who you are," she said. "You are English. A spy? Did Mr. Barnes bring you in?"

"Who was the man leading the meeting?" he asked. "The dark, well-built Welshman?"

Her lips clamped together.

"He is from Cwmbran?" he asked. "He works there, perhaps?"

"I didn't know him," she said. "I don't know who he is. There are men from other valleys at the meeting. They are not all from Cwmbran."

He nodded. He did not believe her for a moment. "And the preacher?" he asked. "The one who opened the meeting with a long prayer? Who is he?"

Again the clamped lips. "I don't know him either," she said when he waited for an answer.

"And I suppose," he said, "you did not recognize any of the men at the meeting either. They were all from other valleys. They just happened to choose this site for their meeting."

"I suppose so," she said lamely after a while. But she lifted her chin. "Who are you? Have you come to make trouble? It was a peaceful meeting. There was no harm in it. It is merely a petition to be presented to Parliament."

" 'There is power in numbers, my friend,' " he quoted softly. "The words can be made to sound almost seditious, can't they?"

"There is power," she said, "in a number of signatures. That was what he meant. Who are you?" The fright was back in her eyes and in her voice suddenly. "What do you want with me?"

It must have been sudden fright over her realization of the fact that she was alone on the mountain with a stranger, he thought. She tried to step forward and around him, but he stood his ground so that for a moment, before she flattened herself against the rock again, her body pressed against his. Firm, generous breasts, warm thighs. He set one hand against the rock beside her head.

"And who are you?" he asked. "Are you from another valley too and don't know yourself?"

Her chin came up but she said nothing for a while. "I shall scream," she said.

"Then I shall do this." He leaned forward and set his mouth over hers. But it was not a wise move. Her mouth was warm and soft. And he too was suddenly aware of how very alone they were, surrounded by shadows and cool night air and the droning of insects. Seduction had not been on his mind when he had pursued her and was definitely unwise under the circumstances. He drew his head back a few inches.

Her eyes were wide with terror and indignation. But she was a woman of some courage, he realized. Her chin stayed up and her eyes remained steady on his and she got herself silently under control.

"My guess is that you would not be overeager, anyway, to make your presence on the mountain known to any of the men back there," he said. "I have the feeling that they would be a trifle annoyed. Who are you?"

"Let me go," she said. "Any one of them would pound you into the ground for touching me. But I'll not betray you if you will not betray me."

"Ah," he said, "an amicable bargain." He took one step back from her. "So all those men would punish me for frightening you and stealing a kiss from you, would they? All those men you do not know."

She ignored his last words. "I was not frightened," she said.

He grinned at her and wished that circumstances

were such that he could attempt seduction. It would be very sweet. He thought ruefully of how long it had been since he had had a woman. Too long. But now was not the time.

He stepped to one side so that she could make her escape. "If I were you," he said, "I would stay off the mountains this late at night. There are too many dangers for a woman alone."

"Thank you." Her voice was heavy with sarcasm. "I shall remember that."

"And I shall remember this night," he said, "and some of the faces of the men at the Chartist meeting. Perhaps I will see those faces again one day—in the other valleys. I believe I may see yours a little closer than that."

"Not if I can help it," she said.

He grinned and gestured to the downward slope just beyond the shadows in which they stood. "Go," he said, "before anyone else comes down and sees that you are out of your bed at this hour and in a place that no woman has any business being."

He watched her make the effort not to bolt like a frightened rabbit. She lifted her shawl over her head again, her eyes on his, and then walked past him and out into the open, her back straight.

"Good night, maiden of Cwmbran," he said softly.

From *New York Times* bestselling author

Mary Balogh

Beyond the Sunrise

At fifteen, Jeanne, the privileged daughter of a royalist émigré, fell for Englishman Robert Blake, bastard son of a marquess, but his questionable birth rendered him forbidden. Forced to part, they were still young enough to believe in tomorrow.

Eleven years later, during the Peninsular Wars, they meet again, both of them spies, and destined to be on opposing sides. Passion flares between them once again, but for Joana and Robert, falling in love could be the most dangerous risk of all.

FEBRUARY 2015

"Mary Balogh sets the gold standard in historical romance."
—*New York Times* bestselling author
Jayne Ann Krentz

Available wherever books are sold or at
penguin.com

facebook.com/LoveAlwaysBooks

S0551

From *New York Times* bestselling author

Mary Balogh

Longing

The illegitimate daughter of an English lord, Sian Jones abandoned her heritage to live in a stalwart coal mining community. But Sian's principles are shaken when she accepts a job as governess under Alexander Hyatt, Marquess of Craille—an oppressive symbol of everything she has come to resist.

But she never expected Alexander to upend all her expectations—as he's sympathetic to her cause. Now, caught between two worlds, Sian must make a choice that will define her future—one that can only be made in the name of love.....

MARCH 2015

"When it comes to historical romance, Mary Balogh is one of my favorites!"
—*New York Times* bestselling author Eloisa James

Available wherever books are sold or at penguin.com

facebook.com/LoveAlwaysBooks

S0552

LOVE
ROMANCE
NOVELS?

For news on all your favorite romance authors, sneak peeks into the newest releases, book giveaways, and much more—

"Like" Love Always on Facebook!

LoveAlwaysBooks

N A L

Penguin Group (USA) Online

What will you be reading tomorrow?

Tom Clancy, W.E.B. Griffin, Nora Roberts,
Catherine Coulter, Sylvia Day, Ken Follett,
Kathryn Stockett, John Green, Harlan Coben,
Elizabeth Gilbert, J. R. Ward, Nick Hornby,
Khaled Hosseini, Sue Monk Kidd, John Sandford,
Clive Cussler, Laurell K. Hamilton, Maya Banks,
Charlaine Harris, Christine Feehan, James McBride,
Sue Grafton, Liane Moriarty, Jojo Moyes, Jim Butcher...

You'll find them all at
penguin.com
facebook.com/PenguinGroupUSA
twitter.com/PenguinUSA

Read excerpts and newsletters, find tour schedules and reading group guides, and enter contests.

Subscribe to Penguin newsletters and get an exclusive inside look at exciting new titles and the authors you love long before everyone else.

PENGUIN GROUP (USA)
penguin.com

s0151